THE BROTHERS BOSWELL

'Satisfyingly riddled with murky emotions, complex characters and shady scenarios, and combining scholarly research with a thriller-like trajectory, it's a fascinating tale not only of jealousy, obsession and the grip of delusional logic but of 18th-century London and Edinburgh.'
Metro

'Fascinating… expect zestful writing and brilliant sketches of Georgian London and its grandees, writers, servants, whores, innkeepers, theatre folk and watermen.'
Sunday Times

'So richly drawn you can feel the lice crawl… The mood is dark, the characters flawed to the point of unpleasantness – but this grimy world, partly seen in flashback, has you gripped… Baruth's picture of 18th-century society was the real, if hellish, thrill of this book.'
Scotsman

'18th-century London is grittily evoked in this highly rewarding book.'
Daily Mail

'An exciting, suspenseful story of two literary men menaced by a madman… One of the novel's several wonders is that the mad brother is just as compelling a character as his soon-to-be-immortal sibling. If you're interested in Boswell and Johnson, or in 18th-century England, or in brilliant storytelling, *The Brothers Boswell* is not to be missed.'
Washington Post

'A chilling literary thriller… the subtle way the author examines his character's twisted mind draws the reader in, as does the evocative prose.'
Publishers Weekly

THE BROTHERS BOSWELL

PHILIP BARUTH

CORVUS

First published in the United States of America in 2009 by Soho Press.

This paperback edition first published in Great Britain in 2011 by
Corvus, an imprint of Atlantic Books Ltd.

9 8 7 6 5 4 3 2 1

A CIP catalogue record for this book is available from
the British Library.

ISBN: 978-1-84887-446-6

Printed in Great Britain by Clays Ltd, St Ives plc

Corvus
An imprint of Atlantic Books Ltd
Ormond House
26-27 Boswell Street
London WC1N 3JZ

www.corvus-books.co.uk

TO JOE CHANEY,

the sort of friend you call when it becomes
necessary to go to Scotland.

PART ONE

The Riverine Excursion

Saturday 30 July

Mr. Johnson and I took a boat and sailed down the silver Thames. I asked him if a knowledge of the Greek and Roman languages was necessary. He said, "By all means; for they who know them have a very great advantage over those who do not. Nay, it is surprising what a difference it makes upon people in the intercourse of life which does not appear to be much connected with it." "And yet," said I, "people will go through the world very well and do their business very well without them." "Why," said he, "that may be true where they could not possibly be of any use; for instance, this boy rows us as well without literature as if he could sing the song which Orpheus sung to the Argonauts, who were the first sailors in the world."

He then said to the boy, "What would you give, Sir, to know about the Argonauts?" "Sir," said he, "I would give what I have." The reply pleased Mr. Johnson much, and we gave him a double fare. "Sir," said Mr. Johnson, "a desire of knowledge is the natural feeling of mankind; and every man who is not debauched would give all that he has to get knowledge."

We landed at the Old Swan and walked to Billingsgate, where we took oars and moved smoothly along the river. We were entertained with the immense number and variety of ships that were lying at anchor. It was a pleasant day, and when we got clear out into the country, we were charmed with the beautiful fields on each side of the river.

—From *Boswell's London Journal, 1762–1763*

London, England
Saturday, the 30th of July, 1763
11:42 A.M.

* * * * * *

1

IN THE RARE event that one man must follow two others without being observed, follow them closely from first light to summer dusk, certain conditions are best met. Those being followed should stand out vividly from the world passing around them; he who follows, of course, should not. And the following itself should occur in the thick of a crowd as alien and uncaring as is practicable.

All of which is to say that conditions today are very near the ideal.

Having shaken off its morning torpor, Fleet Street has moved without interval into the irritability of early afternoon. Carters jostle peddlers, and servants swarm the lane between shop windows and the row of posts protecting them from the street. Everyone seems to be wrestling some greasy package home, or if not, then envying his neighbor's. A coach comes rocking out of Hen-and-Chicken Court and drives straight at the crowd, only to have the ranks suddenly part and reform, swallowing it whole. Sullen chairmen jog by bearing their sedans, beggars sprawled against the wall pull in their ankles only at the last instant, and neither party seems aware of the interaction, or lack thereof. All is one general fabric of gray and brown discontent, no particle detachable from the whole.

Until I spot the two of them, coming along in the distance.

They are framed momentarily by the thick stone arch of Temple Bar, and the effect is uncanny, like the first seconds of a magic lantern show, when the pretty pictures suddenly begin to crawl in the candlelight. It is not just the movement that strikes one, but the *meaning*. For once the painted emblems have started into motion, there is a palpable significance, a meaning, an inevitability to their progress. One understands intuitively that the images will not stop until the catastrophe. And therein lies the viewer's chief satisfaction.

Of course in this case, given that the plot and the catastrophe are of my own composition, my satisfaction in watching the pair advance is at least doubled.

Once the two of them make their way beneath the Temple arch, though, once their movements are no longer properly framed, they are simply two gentlemen again, picking their way along down Fleet. But two gentlemen such as the City has never seen before and will never see again. There is no mistaking them for anyone else, you may take my word. Especially with the larger, older, and testier of the two so very much larger and older and testier. Even plagued as he is by phantom pains in his back and his legs, Samuel Johnson bulls forward through the Saturday morning crowd, not walking his oaken stick but brandishing it.

He is fifty-four years of age, a large-boned, large-nosed, large-eyed, big-bellied man, and the smaller and less determined catch sight of him at the last second and scatter as he comes. Here is what they see bearing down on them just before they jump: the vast body is packed into a rusty brown suit of clothes, waistcoat creaking at the buttons, flashing the dull white shirt beneath. Black worsted stockings and old black shoes, shoes rarely wiped and currently spattered, silver buckles half the size of the prevailing fashion because small buckles are at once conservative and cheap. A small unpowdered wig, brown and shriveled, rides the head like a *mahout*.

Johnson's mood seems cheerful enough this morning, for Johnson, and he carries this good humor truculently along with him as he comes.

The younger man striding brilliantly alongside seems small only by way of comparison. In his own right he is brutishly healthy, leaning but never quite toppling to fat. Of just under middling height, maybe five feet six inches all told. The complexion is dark by City standards, but tinged with rose at his neck and plump cheeks. And he is radiantly happy, anyone can perceive this, no matter the distance.

The importance of the day's outing to the younger man shows in every considered detail of his appearance: he is wearing his own hair, but meticulously dressed, powdered, and tied back with sober black silk; snowy stockings; a military cock to his hat that he has affected rather than earned; and a smart, silver-hilted, five-guinea blade got by hoaxing Mr. Jefferys, sword-cutter to His Majesty. He wears his genteel new violet frock suit, with its matching violet button, as though it were a coronation outfit. And his shoes have been wiped to within an inch of their lives. This is James Boswell, age twenty-two.

And what makes you simply want to murder the pair of them, more than anything else, is the perfectly ludicrous way they seem to complete one another. Not quite opposites, but different in a thousand complementary ways. Two odd human fractions who have stumbled somehow onto the secret of the whole number.

It is this sense of *completion* that draws heads around as they saunter down Fleet, not the barking volume of their talk, which is high enough, of course. And it is this wholeness that brings the occasional snicker, from the coal-heavers and the milk-women and the bankers. Those doing the snickering tell themselves and one another that they've never seen such a mismatched pair in all their lives, *sweet Jesus,* but this is a thin attempt at self-comfort. If, rather than matched, these two men are mismatched, then north is south, hot cold, and our own lots in life momentarily less meager.

The truth is easier to see, but a great deal harder to recognize, and to accept: these two men have one another suddenly, and don't seem much to need anybody else. Their friendship of two months could not be any more clearly destined to last two lifetimes.

The sight of them suggests a completion we all seek in our friendships, our whole lives long, and do not find; at a deeper, blacker level, it is what we seek from the cradle each inside ourselves, and never discover. We are fragments scattered about loose in the world, yet in some way now these two men are not, not any longer.

What can all the rest of us do, then, but point them out on the street and laugh?

JAMES'S DELIGHT AT walking down Fleet Street with his hero lends him an almost visible shimmer. Just as evident, though, is his anxiety that some small thing may unexpectedly cloud the skies of Johnson's amiability. Even in his joy he is continually scanning the older man's face for weather signs.

Oh, this James is solicitous, and for this too you could murder him.

But after all, currying favor is James's explicit purpose for coming up to London in the first place. Somehow he has secured permission to spend the bulk of this year begging a commission in the King's Guard from those who would vastly prefer not to give it him. And to that official errand James has added another entirely his own: to worm his way into the hearts and affections and appointment books of as many full-scale London authors and notables as he can manage in the space of nine months.

It took six of those months merely to make the acquaintance of Johnson, author of the *Dictionary* itself, England's undisputed and ill-tempered literary lion. But having done so, James has wasted no time parlaying the acquaintance into a friendship, and that friendship into something now just shy of actual foster-fatherhood.

This morning, he showed up on Johnson's Inner Temple doorstep at just a touch past nine-thirty for their ten o'clock meeting, so afraid was he of being thought less than punctual. He stood for a moment, pondering. Lifted his fist to knock, dropped it without knocking. Then, lest he seem overeager and boyish, James strolled around the corner, looking to kill time, looking for amusement.

I stood and watched him all the while he stood and watched Fleet Street.

He settled his attention on the Temple Bar, as well he might: set into cornices of the stone arch are statues of Charles I, the Stuart martyr, and Charles II, whose itch for actresses brought women to the English stage. And something else: on iron pikes atop the stone pediment sit two now-desiccated heads. For reasons that no one including James knows, James is all but addicted to the terrifying jolt of a good hanging or dismemberment; these two skulls, circled by flies and touched with the gore of history, seize and hold his attention.

He is predictable, is James.

A sharp little shopkeeper hard by the Bar sized up the situation and trotted out with a cheap pair of spyglasses, half-penny the look, and James delightedly fished in his pocket for change. Then, after having his sleeve pulled twice, and paying cheerfully for two more long looks, James simply struck a bargain to buy the glasses outright.

After another ten minutes, when he had finished searching the desiccated heads for meaning, for sensations, he dropped the glasses into his deep coat pocket and retraced his steps to #1 Inner Temple Lane.

I followed after a moment, marveling at the endless seepage of unforeseeable detail into even the tightest plans, the capillary action of disaster. Who but the Lord Himself could have foreseen that James would suddenly acquire the ability to see great distances? The ability to search the boats before and behind him on the river every bit as casually as he might search his own waistcoat pockets?

Not for the first time, I wondered if the Lord might be plotting against me, somehow, and I added the spyglasses to Johnson's stick and James's sword, the small running mental list of objects to which I must pay particularly close attention this day.

So HERE IT is now, just before noon, and they have had their late-late-morning coffee at Child's, and a separate dish of chocolate for James. They have sauntered for a good twenty minutes under the leafy trees of Hare Court, tuning up their voices and their respective pomposities. And now they're off for their true lark of the day—a float down the eastern stretch of the Thames.

But of course this is Dictionary Johnson, who birthed the entire sanctioned English lexicon from his own singularly overstuffed vocabulary, and so a float down the river cannot remain merely a float. God forbid.

A *riverine excursion,* they're calling it. And it sounds so altogether grand that I have decided to take a riverine excursion of my own.

They come down Middle-Temple Lane, a moist wind filling their noses, and there, in the dark frame created by the Harcourt Buildings, lies the silver water of the Thames. They lift their well-fed faces at the pleasant shock of the river: the glittering length of it just behind a line of unremarkable city roofs, coiling through the city with all the drowsy power of a boa constrictor. And on it, every device for flotation known to mankind, moving everywhere and at every speed at once: wherries and barges, sloops and fish-smacks, skiffs and cheap wooden bottoms and the occasional grand racing yacht, twelve oarsmen pulling all at once. Gulls crash and tilt and screech overhead, and the stink of fish and water rot comes up sharp with the wind.

As the two men approach the Temple Stairs, and the loafing watermen sense the approach of custom, a predictable form of hell breaks loose. Everyone shouts at once, addressing their shouts to Johnson alone because they all have the menial's highly developed nose for power.

Westward or Eastward, Sir! Row you straight, row you quiet!
Sculler! Sculler, maybe, gents? Sculler!
He'll drown you, that one! Don't be daft, Sir. Oars here now!

For all their crowding and jostling, the watermen observe a thin protective bubble around their marks, pawing the air but never once putting a hand to Johnson's coat. And he points without hesitation to a young man about fifteen years old, standing off to one side, and barks, "Take us out then, boy," and the crowd of rivermen explodes in curses and righteous indignation.

The boy leads them quickly down the center stair to the river. He is wearing the arms of the King on his uniform, and no doubt this is part of the reason Johnson chose him. Johnson has a pension of 300£ a year from the King, and I imagine that in some secret way the King's arms signify to Johnson not only the great and benevolent power of the Crown, but the great and benevolent power of Sam Johnson. And, too, the King's men are watched more carefully by the Crown, and so they are less likely to cheat you, more likely to get you there clean and dry. Not much less, and not much more, but a bit.

After some fiddling, the boy draws his narrow red sculler up flush to the step, and Johnson climbs ponderously aboard. The long craft bobbles and then steadies. When Johnson is seated in the center, James steps relatively lightly into the rear, checks his seat for water, finds none, and sits.

And as they draw away, holding their hats—James's violet suit shrinking slowly to the size of an orchid—one of the bigger watermen on the stair breaks off shouting curses at the boy piloting the sculler, turns abruptly toward the spot where I'm standing, and crooks his finger at me.

THE BIG WATERMAN has his head shorn down to the scalp. Sweat stands from the tough brown skin as he hauls his oars. He is forty-five maybe, or fifty. He wears the arms of the Lord Mayor, a looser and less appetizing outfit than the King's. A pile of smooth river rocks stands in the bilge wash beside his own seat, just to one side of his boot, within easy reach. He is a very strong man, outfitted with the several weapons natural to his trade, and he pulls the oars with just this awareness in his air.

It's the Lord Mayor's men that dominate the movement of stolen merchandise on the river, and in the back of the sculler, behind my seat, I can see a nasty set of long gaffs and hooks, these for retrieving goods thrown from ships, these for cadging fish from passing smacks when traffic is tight. And, no doubt, for the occasional pitched battle between boats, battles for which guns are too loud and knives too short. Lord Mayor's men view the river as the sea, and the sea as a sovereign entity unto itself.

Johnson and James are a short ways ahead of us, gliding along near the center of the river. Traffic moves quicker there, and the view is more pleasant. The wind is a caress, not the cuff you get peering south from the Temple. The ride is smoother as well; no need to row around wharves and stagnant debris and docks and moored vessels, as you do continually nearer the banks. As my sculler is doing at the moment.

"What do you want with 'em?" the waterman says suddenly.

"I beg your pardon?"

"What d'you want with the folk we're pacin' is what I mean, sir."

I say nothing.

He keeps his head down, eyes on the mucky bit of bilge rolling back and forth across the little hull. He could look back into the shade under the thin green woolen canopy, but he does not. He does not want to push too hard, does not want to risk the shilling I have promised him. When I offered him three times the standard fare, as long as he would shadow another boat, keep mum, and take my lead on the water, the waterman didn't bat an eye. "Glad to be of service, sir," he had said, pumped full of sudden courtesy.

But now he cannot leave it alone.

"Nothing but curious, sir," he drawls. "A man likes to know why he goes where, don't he?" He scratches at his leg, then the slick crown of his scalp. A pair of rowers passing the other way yell a sudden, friendly volley of obscenities at him, but he shows no sign of hearing or recognition. He continues to pull the oars and to watch the roll of bilge water. "For a jest or to come at a shilling, is why people usually follow people," he continues. "Or to catch a girl's sneakin' about. Always struck me there's the couple ways of it."

I have my eyes on the river.

The waterman is jovial now, enjoying the sound of his own voice in the open air, and the anger gathers slowly in my chest, not for the first time this morning. I can feel it stirring abruptly inside me, the anger, a large dog awakened by a small noise.

He clucks his tongue. "Your clothes are too swell for a footpad, my fine friend. There ain't no lady in the sculler there to follow. And you don't strike me as bein' in a joking mood, you don't mind me saying." He spits over the gunwale. "And so I'm curious, now, nothing but that. A hint of why we're running behind these two? I'll be close as the grave, trust me, sir."

Again, I say nothing for a moment, and then reach into my pocket and bring up a pair of coppers, holding them out on my palm for an instant. And then I pitch them over the side and into the water. Almost immediately, a young mudlark near the boat dives to catch the coins before they can touch silt. "Your fare is tuppence lighter, man," I say. "The full shilling was for quiet, and following my instructions."

He holds up a hand to signal enough, attends to his oars, swinging his head up and about to avoid other boats, and to keep James and Johnson's red sculler in sight. Although the woolen canopy keeps off the sun, it blocks the wind, and without that breath of air the day is hottish, a creeping late July heat. And the wool traps the light stench of the waterman's little boat itself, fish and sweat and damp wood and river slime. But it is the sight of the two of them on their excursion, the bigger and the slightly less big, sitting in their merry little boat out there in the very center of the Thames, never quiet but always talking, talking, talking that saps the pleasure from the ride.

After only five minutes or so on the river, I see their red skiff abruptly angle through the cluttered forest of masts toward the Old Swan Stairs. I have already told the waterman to expect as much, and he draws quickly across the flow of traffic to allow me to watch them come in for their landing. Predictable, to a fault. Greenwich is another long pull down the river, so why are they rowing in at the Swan, disembarking, walking the seven crowded blocks around London Bridge to the rank fish-market at Billingsgate and then re-embarking for Greenwich?

Because, my friends, James is nobody's hero: he has not got the heart for the bit of white water under the spans, or the way the boat drops away from you suddenly when you shoot the bridge. And why else? Because they are both of them cheap. They'll both squeeze a crown until King George weeps, and the fare doubles at the bridge.

But as I watch them re-bobble their way heavily back out of the sculler, I have a thought. A mudlark is treading water not so far from us, and I wave him over.

"Hey there you, lark," I call, as softly as one can.

He swims to me at a leisurely pace, his strong arms dipping and flashing in the water. Once beside the boat, he keeps himself suspended in the water with slow, easy movements of his thick legs and cupped hands. Mudlarks spend hours a day in the current, carrying and finding and ferreting out things that are awkward for men on a boat or on shore to come at. No doubt this waterman and this mudlark have worked together at some point in the past, to move some package of something off the river before it could be stamped and taxed, but they ignore one another now.

"See that red sculler there," I say, "putting off passengers at the Stair now?"

The mudlark looks, turns back. He has sharp features, good teeth, and the articulate shoulders of a man who swims for his living. A penny pouch hangs dripping from his neck, a rusted knife from his belt. He narrows an eye at me, trying to figure out what my game might be. "Aye. I see 'em right enough."

"There's a half-penny for you if you pull the coat of that boy rowing them, and ask him what the two gentlemen talked about. There's a penny, though, if you remember it when you get back here to me, remember it all exactly."

"Penny, eh? There's a generous man."

"A penny if you have the details exact."

The mudlark nods his head slowly, and then gives a wink and rolls over in the water. His milky outline glimmers, darkens, and then vanishes, before he sounds, like a dolphin, a good thirty feet from the boat. In a moment his hand reaches out of the water near the Stair, and halts the boy's sculler.

They talk for a moment, and then the mudlark slips back into the water and makes his way back to where the waterman holds us still in the river.

Instead of treading water this time, the mudlark hauls himself directly up onto the small gunwale of the boat and perches there, bringing his feet over the edge and sliding them into the warm bilge at the boat's bottom. His body has long ago become a thing of the river, sleek and beach-white, nipples dark wet sand-dollars. His hair is slick and brown as an otter's coat. He clucks his tongue at the waterman, who continues to ignore him, continues to fail to recognize him.

"Well, then," I say. "What said he?"

The lark seems to have all the time in the world, and he examines his water-wrinkled hands and dirty fingernails before speaking. Then he rubs the muscles of his left arm, as though it is sore, before meeting my eye. The look is direct, a bit defiant, a bit provoking.

And then he says, "It's to be like that, is it?"

By definition, to traffic with the mudlarks is to traffic in nonsense, but I have no time for it this morning. I rest my hand on the hilt of my sword and lean out of the canopy's shade. "If you have anything to report, friend, I have what I promised. Good as my word."

The waterman clears his throat loudly, nudging it along, and the lark finally purses his lips and nods. He rubs his hands together briskly. "Good as your word, then. Well, sir, the boy says the two men talked about speakin' in old languages. All the way from Temple Stair."

I wait, but nothing more is forthcoming. "Old languages, you say?"

"That's it. Like Greek or Roman. What a man should learn o' that, and how much, and if, and so on. Like that."

I reach into my pocket, letting the music of the coins work. "Anything else the boy said?"

He thinks for a second, eyes on the small change now sifting in my hand. Then he's got it. "The big one asked the boy what he'd give to know about the Argo Knights. The first sailors in the world, the big one said."

"The Argonauts, you mean."

"That's it, sir."

"And the boy replied?"

"The boy replied he'd give whatever he had."

I'm amazed again at the ability of the river to teach every man on it, no matter how young, to cant so flawlessly. "My, what a simple, artless thing to have said. And the big one liked that, I imagine."

The lark gives a canny look, nods, blows water from his nose out over the gunwale. He turns back, smirking at his own crassness. "Boy said the big one give him a double fare for that." There's a silence, and then the mudlark brushes his wet hair from his brow. He is searching my face again, scrutinizing it. I realize he's waiting for his coin, and I fish it out of my pocket. He takes the penny, works it into the small leather bag about his neck, gives the cord a tug to seal it up.

And then, as though lost in an afterthought, he looks up at me solemnly and says, "I'd give all I've got to know them Argonauts as well, sir."

"Fine, then. Give me the penny pouch there on your neck, and I'll teach you."

He snorts at that and slides back into the water, leaving the damp mark of his arms on the gunwale. As his churning legs take him away from us, he says, very distinctly, "Well, and if you'll kiss my arse, sir, I'll teach you somethin' as well."

With that, the waterman is up from his seat, a rock in his hand. He cocks his arm, but the mudlark has already darted beneath the water, so there is no way to tell whether the rock finds its mark when the waterman fires it into the Thames. In a moment the swimmer's head surfaces several boats away, bobbing in the center of a ragged wedge of swans. And there is something ancient and timeless, something Grecian about the sight of him there in the current, the fine wet brow crowned with swans

He blows me a kiss.

The waterman heaves another rock, and the lark's head vanishes in the chaos of white wings.

It is good to know the snippet of talk about the Argonauts. No doubt James is already thinking about how to frame this bit of classical chat in his journal. He is keeping a journal of his year in London, oh yes, he certainly is, with entries for every day down to the most insipid. He has become really quite fanatical about keeping it up, and he has read me some of the entries of which he was particularly proud. Once or twice he has given me a handful of pages to read for myself, just a snippet he cannot resist sharing.

He has never let me read through the thick packet on my own, although I know he has friends who have seen the lot. Friends who receive regular installments through the post, like a serial novel written at a penny a word.

And I will admit, I envy him that bundle, because this journal of his gives him the chance to take the stuff of his life and spread it all out carefully in his mind and then cherry-pick it, rearrange it, and lay it all calmly together again. What is fine, what is extraordinary, what is brilliant becomes more so; what is ugly and unwanted is cast aside.

He can make of himself just such a character as he pleases in the romance of his own life. And he can pick his readers as he might his servants.

This scene today, though, needs no touching up after the fact: the two of them sailing down the Thames, as Johnson instructs his young prodigy in the shape of human history and knowledge—this is just as James would have it, but exactly, to a tittle. Which is to say that James has done all of the important scene-shaping in his own mind, long before he proposed the jaunt to Johnson, long before he prompted the conversation about the usefulness of ancient languages. All so that tonight or tomorrow he may tell his journal an entirely true story about playing Plato to Johnson's Socrates. He has found a way not merely to write a true romance but to live it as well, and I do envy that.

And so I imagine him stepping off the sculler now, relentlessly searching the Old Swan Stairs for choice bits with which to flesh out tonight's entry. He is repeating Johnson's phrases over and over to himself, no doubt, rehearsing them so he cannot forget, God forbid.

Above all, he is avidly watching himself live out the most perfect day of his life, which means that the most perfect day of his life has only half his attention in the doing of it, something that strikes me as ironic and sad.

But the ironies do not end there, of course. Although there is no way for James to know it, the fact is that he may not himself be the one to record today's outing in his London journal. I may be doing so in his stead, depending on the directions the day's events take. And so today I am on the lookout for choice bits as well. Everything rests on the outcome of today's excursion.

If matters work out favorably, Johnson and James and I may share a pleasant ride together back to London this evening. If not, I may return by water alone, certainly not an outcome to be wished, but a real and unpleasant possibility. In which case, I will use my copy of James's key to let myself into his Downing Street lodgings. The bundle of manuscript I will pull from the little mahogany tea-chest that James purchased last November to hold it, then unknot the twine binding it. Then I will take a glass of negus and record this day, down to the wash of insignificant details that have given the morning its savor: the extra dish of chocolate, the bit of mercenary chat with the boy rowing the sculler, not excepting the Argo Knights themselves. And in addition I will include even those snippets that James—who includes everything, no matter how seamy or silly—would decline to include.

The manuscript journal of James's year in London will never see print, as he now hopes, but it will be complete in every important sense: an artistic whole. And it will be treasured in the archives at Auchinleck for as long as I live, and after. Before I leave London, I will do for James what he will no longer have the power to do for himself: fashion an end to the romance he has woven of his own ephemeral existence.

And if you knew James as I know him—as only a younger brother can know an older—you would understand that all of this will constitute an act of the utmost kindness.

2

One of those piddling details even James would decline to include about the most perfect day of his life: what he did prior to showing up on Johnson's doorstep this morning.

He left Downing Street an hour before daybreak, whistling a silky air in the quiet street. It is difficult to shadow a man at that hour; there are few enough about to make any single shape stand out after a block or more. And I cannot risk even a single close glance, as there is not a man alive who knows my clothing, my walk, my air so well as James. But the difficulty was more apparent than real: in turn, I know James well enough to predict where he was most likely headed.

And so I waited for him a block and a half away, in St. James's Park. During the day the Park is drill-ground for the Footguard, and playground for ladies and gentlemen of the Court, and of course at ten o'clock in the evening, the Park's many doors are all closed and locked with a great show of punctuality. And it all means absolutely nothing: there are seven thousand official keys scattered about the city, and ten thousand counterfeits taken in wax from these original seven.

As a result, the Park is a very different place after dark and before the dawn. This difference is what James continually craves and must have.

At that hour, with the moon down and the sun still skulking below the horizon, the forest in the center of the Ring remains an impenetrable black. The endless winding brick wall surrounding the Park is likewise invisible in the darkness. But within this gloom, the vast empty dirt-packed space of the Ring itself takes on a dull luminosity, picks up the leavings of the moon and gives back a quarter-light, just enough to perceive the outline of figures moving at one slowly from the trees.

And they come, these figures, these women, at the first hint of movement. Stepping out from the oaks, rising from dark prone humps on the dirt. Country girls in chip hats and red cloaks, middle-aged jades simulating country girls in chip hats and red cloaks. Faces pallid with ceruse. And in snagged yarn stockings and leather shoes. Home-spun gowns and gypsy hats. Greasy cotton dresses topped by small natty capes, these *coqueluchons* thrown open with a butcher's matter-of-factness, should you rest your gaze at the bodice, even for a moment.

These women are gifted, more than most, with the predatory intuitions of the city. They came toward me when I entered the park, but after three or four steps they stopped, rested on their scraped leather heels, sensing. They marked the value of my suit, the angle of my hat, the drop of my lace. But even in the quarter-light there was something off-putting in my air, and they slowly moved off again. They saw in my stride that my purpose here in the Park was not complementary to their own. That I was somehow, just perceptibly, working at cross-purposes.

There is a large stair that drops down in stages from a set of townhouses in the southeast corner of the Park wall, and they allowed me to step unmolested into the shadow of that stair and lean against the damp brick.

But when James sauntered through a small archway away off to my left, the woman nearest him picked up his trajectory immediately, because there was nothing at all in his air that bespoke caution, or prudence. Far from it, in fact. The violet suit managed to pierce even the dark at the wall, and when he moved to the Ring, it was nothing like the furtive movements these women must see so often. No, he approached them with a clear relish, like a fond country squire come to rough-house with his pack of hunting dogs.

James knows very well the codes and the jealousies of these women, and he played with their need. The small young tart who picked him up as he entered wore a long blue hooded cloak, and James received her with a delicate bow. They began to walk the Ring together. No doubt he was asking price, name, any fictitious scrap of personal history—born in Shropshire, married young, widowed, new to the trade this night—because he collects these mendacious little wisps for his journal, the way other men collect porcelain or statuary.

In his turn, James is always a highwayman, or a black-listed actor, or a half-pay officer, a bit deaf from cannon fire. His assumed characters are always plucky but impoverished, and nearly always will James try to wheedle his way out of paying for what crude pleasures he takes. Very occasionally he saves a shilling or two this way, but it is the pretense itself that always delights James. As much as they are about having sex, these expeditions into the park are always also about having other selves, silly childish romanticized selves, and it is impossible to say which particle of his need I find the more pitiable.

This morning he was careful not to take the first woman's hand, nor did he allow his own arm to be taken. Instead, he strolled along, with the nymph strolling beside him, until—at some line invisible to him and to me—the nymph grew a bit more frantic and tried to halt his progress, tried to jolly him and pull at his coat, hook it with her nails. But James did not halt. He ambled just past the invisible line, saying what would amount to his good-byes, until the next woman drifted out from the trees, to cover her own sixteenth of the Ring. He repeated this process again and again, with drab after disposable drab.

In this way, James had what he most desired: their need for his money, expressed as need for James himself, and brought to its most powerful expression again and again at each invisible boundary.

When he eventually selected, he selected not one but two, a tall and a short, black hair and blonde, and he took them to a segment of the wall past the Old Horse Guards building. I could smell the metallic tang of the ceruse, they passed so close to my own blind. He took them to a kind of shallow brick alcove where the women unhooked and unlaced and set ajar the fronts of their gowns, and slouched casually against him as he moved his hands over them. He dropped his face into the common mass of their hair, inundating himself with their smell, their reality. The taller woman used the flat of her hand to burnish the front of his breeches, with as much care and passion as she might use to whitewash spit from a tavern wall.

He stood and fondled them and bartered lies with them, those two Shropshire innocents new to the trade. *A veteran of the wars in the Havana,* he whispered, *a peer of the Realm cruelly cheated of my inheritance.* But it went no further, no further than what James innocently calls toying. It went no further because James did not come to the Park in search of consummation, but merely to have his passion tuned for his real tryst of the morning. A young Edinburgh girl, actually, come up to Town just two days ago. A girl James knows quite well.

One Peggy Doig. A housemaid, and mother of his eight-month-old natural son.

Fortunately, dear Peggy's lodgings lay up the Strand, on a perfect bee-line between the Park and Johnson's rooms in the Temple, and so once James had settled his double reckoning, and then fastidiously splashed his hands at a street well near Charing Cross, there was no need for him to take even a step out of his way.

From her family's dingy tenement on the south back of the Canongate in Edinburgh, Peggy Doig has traveled to London and landed finally in a flat above a disheveled chandler's shop up the Strand. Still, it must seem awfully grand to her. The building rubs shoulders uncomfortably with an iron-monger on one side and a coffin-maker on the other. From her bitty garret window, she can no doubt take in both the stench of the smelting fire and the sweet pine-shavings smell of new death. The shop is owned by her brother-in-law, the candle-maker.

Her older sister keeps house here and works on-again-off-again as a parish midwife. Twice has the parish sent a different young girl to clean house for the couple, to allow Peggy's sister to devote herself entirely to wrestling infants from the growing number of parishioners out of whom they must be wrestled. Twice has the couple found fault with the young mop-squeezers in question and sent them away. One was beaten—badly, I take it—and then sent packing, though she is agreed to have been so provoking as to have asked for it.

Eventually it was decided within the larger Doig family that rather than clean house for an aging widow in Edinburgh, at poor wages, Peggy might just as well serve her sister in London for none. If the family knew that the father of her bastard had also been in London for a year, they seem not to have cared a whit.

The girl wrote James a short, inarticulate note two days ago, explaining and all but apologizing for her sudden presence in London, and finally offering—should he have a moment free some afternoon—to meet and pass on tidings of his child.

This letter of Peggy's I have now, this moment, in my coat pocket.

I found it nestled in the lining of James's tea-chest last night, alongside a small packet of letters to John Johnston, a childhood friend who has managed the whole awkward affair of the birth this year that James has been in England. It was Johnston who attended the mother following the birth, held the infant, and saw to it that the boy was named Charles, in accordance with the wishes of the father, who happened that night to be attending a rout thrown by the Countess of Northumberland, some four hundred miles away. It was Johnston who passed on the money to set the child up with a wet-nurse, and to keep the Doigs from noising the business about.

This whole packet of letters I have in my pocket, in fact, the stiff paper rasping against the cloth. It rides there like a hornets' nest, fragile, intricate, almost entirely defined by its potential for pain.

James wrote back that he'd love to see her, and see her for more than a moment, but that she must arrange something private for them.

And so yesterday Peggy wrote James a second letter, much more to the point. It told him the number of the house, how to enter by the doorway of the coffin-maker next door, which served her staircase just as well, how to reach the room she now had of her own, the garret four flights up. The garret itself had no lock—this by design, one must imagine, to make the watching and the beating of housemaids that little bit easier on the chandler's wife. The letter hinted that the chandler would be occupied by his early customers—it was all but unheard of for him to leave his shop before the noon meal—and that the midwife would be sitting with a woman in the last hours of her confinement. Peggy might steal an hour or more before she began her work for the day, she said, by working twice as fast in the afternoon. James was to rap thrice at the garret door.

She said that it would be sweet to see him again, after such an absence. *Sweet,* that was the very word she used.

I could have told her that James would not be content with an hour. But she didn't need anyone to tell her about James and his particular appetites, after all.

For the record, I was right: it was more than two and a half hours from the time he entered to the time James exited the coffin-maker's door and stood again on the street. He couldn't have looked any more self-satisfied. Rather than attract attention by dashing away, he made a point of pausing and seeming to examine a small dark mahogany coffin standing erect in the window. He studied it from several angles, playing the grieving father. Then, to complete the effect, he called the carpenter over and dickered with him over the child's box for a moment or two, before cheerfully giving it up and heading on up the Strand.

I stayed with him until he finally rang for Johnson, and I watched the two of them walk arm in arm to Child's, where they took their seats and called for their coffee. And then I turned back to the coffin-maker's shop, and Peggy's garret.

I had about forty-five minutes, as near as I could reckon it. The coffee would take them at least half an hour, and you could bet your soul the two wouldn't be leaving before James had had his dish of chocolate as well.

BEFORE SHE MET James, Peggy was housemaid to Mrs. MacKenna, who still owns the floor above the Boswell flat in Parliament Square. By chance James saw the girl one morning, sprawled in the staircase, scrubbing the steps with a pail of damp sand.

Her hands were brown from rottenstoning the widow's risp and doorknob. But her small feet were bare and white, and James was immediately entranced by them.

He wrote later to Johnston that they were more temptation than any man could stand, these two dainty lumps of muscle and toenail. "My father," he wrote, "had always insisted that stockings and shoes be worn in the tenement's common staircase, and given that this was the express wish not simply of a fellow tenant, but of a High Court Justice, it was obeyed by all the building's inhabitants as a very commandment. And yet here was this girl, and here were her pretty naked feet, lying like opals cast among the sand."

I thought of these words because the feet were the first part of her I saw when I rapped thrice, then turned the handle very quietly, and opened the door an inch or two. They lay there on the counterpane before me, the very feet themselves. And to me they seemed like the feet of a young housemaid, just as much as would support her in wielding a broom, nothing more nor less. A bit dustier at the sole than one might wish them. Nothing to covet. Nothing to make a man risk an inheritance.

She'd obviously decided to have a well-deserved catnap before setting about the cleaning her sister had assigned her for the day. The morning light was falling on her from the garret window, and she was curled in it, a drowsy dark-haired creature, with her back to me.

But she was not yet asleep. "Mr. Boswell," she murmured, without raising her tousled head. Instead, she moved a strand of hair from her face, clearing her pretty profile, and then lay the arm down again, quiescent.

I made a humming noise in my throat that might be taken for assent. Not an intelligible word, hence not a lie, but a sound.

And in this case, of course, even a *yes* would not have been entirely amiss.

At the sound, a hint of mischief touched up the corner of her mouth. She was enjoying London, it seems. I stepped into the room and closed the door behind me. My boots on the floorboards, I imagine, sounded no different than the oh-so-careful step of her child's sire.

"You said I shouldn't see you for many months," she murmured, her voice thick with half-sleep. The voice was also playful and pleased, pleased that Mr. Boswell had not refused to see her altogether in London but had in fact come all the way to her room and broken his passion to her again, after so many months of silence; pleased that he had deigned to speak with her about their child, almost as though they were parents, man and wife even, they two together, rather than merely two dumb creatures who had come together in a rut to multiply; pleased that he could not resist returning this morning for more of her; pleased with the world, suddenly; pleased as punch with herself.

She stretched on the bed, in nothing but a rumpled white smicket, unbending the white leg with its tracery of black down, languidly flexing the foot, no doubt bracing for the grip of James's hands on her thigh, her shoulders, her hip. As I say, she needed no one to tell her of his appetites.

It was a quiet, warm little room, although I could hear horses' hooves and ostlers' curses drifting up from the Strand. Other than the small bed, the garret was devoid of furnishings. Almost entirely devoid: her battered travel trunk she had covered with a strip of cheap lace, and on this strip she had placed her pins, a brush, her mob cap. A tiny, pretend dressing table.

I went to the bed and sat at the bottom of it. My weight caused her body to dip toward me slightly on the straw-filled matt. She did nothing to counter the movement, but rested almost coyly in mid-motion, so that a simple nudge at her hip would have brought her rolling over to me. This is how ready to hand she was for him. I took one of the dags from its holster in the lining of my coat, and I laid it across my knee.

"Good Mr. Boswell," she cooed, eyes still closed, still facing the wall, still waiting. So passive was she in this foolery with James that she could not initiate even a look. She must wait to be rolled to her back, she must wait to be gazed upon.

I reached out a hand and took the hem of the smicket in my fingers, tugged it down sharply where it had ridden up on her leg.

"Cover yourself and be a woman, Peggy Doig," I whispered back at her.

Her head jerked around, and in that instant I had my left hand over her mouth, and her head pushed back into the tan sack she'd been allowed as a pillow. Before she could struggle more than a bit, I brought the pistol up from my knee and touched the fat gold heart-shaped butt to her flushed cheek, held it there, the snubbed barrel an inch from her eye.

The kiss of the gold had its effect: she slumped back, limp as milktoast, breath coming in strained little hitches, but the eyes as open and seeing, no doubt, as they had ever been during her eighteen dun years of life.

Even before I could speak, the eyes began to swim.

I held her mouth, but I tipped the dag back from her face. "Peggy Doig, I want you to know that everything James knows, I know as well. I know that the chandler is below-stairs, and that you fear him only slightly less than you fear death itself. And so I know what will happen in the next ten minutes."

She watched me, and there was recognition in that gaze, as I knew there would be. I went on, softening my tone.

"I will put away my pistol, you will lie still. And we will talk together. And then I shall leave, good as my word. But should you scream, I will scream louder, I will absolutely raise the house, and I will inform your brother-in-law of the details of your morning, or at least the last two and a half hours of it. I will show him your letters to James, and James's by way of return. And he will need to leave off peddling his candles and bad beer and soap. You are not kind to him, or to your sister, in these little missives, you know. And so when he's read them, you will suffer the fate of the previous mop-squeezers in this house, that is, to be beaten until you cannot walk, and then to be pitched out into the gutter like so much dirty tallow."

I slowly pulled my hand from her mouth, and drew back.

"It's you," she managed to whisper. There was bewilderment in the word, and some faint whiff of something like betrayal.

"Me," I said. She has seen me with James, seen me loafing at the Cross in Edinburgh, something half-glimpsed a hundred times but never brought into focus.

From my pocket, I drew the packet of letters, her last of yesterday on top and visible beneath the green silk ribbon. The swimming eyes closed tightly, and her face was suddenly wet, shining in the stray rays from the window.

"Open your eyes, Peggy Doig."

She did so, managing a few strained, miserable words as well. I saw that her hands were clenching and unclenching mindlessly on the counterpane. "But what is it ye want, sir? I've not done anything to—"

I brought out the second dag from its pocket beneath my right arm, and she was immediately silent. I held the two of them in front of her, and we looked at them together. They were lovely things, the pair of them, Doune locks so that they might be half-cocked, ready to fire as they were drawn. Shortened barrels for riding snug in a fitted inside pocket, each no longer than the tip of my finger to the heel of my hand. Balanced in the way that only a brace of Highland flintlocks will balance.

And of gold. Not merely inlaid with gold, not merely gold-mounted, but entirely of gold, though not polished up: the deeper luster of gold gentled into everyday use, like a wedding band or a dark golden comb. They were like something royalty might wear or wield, that massy and that enchanting, without hollow or alloy. Only the shot and the powder itself were black, deep in their chambered hearts. And even those bullets the smith dusted with gold, so intent was he upon completely transforming the brutal into the lovely.

"Bonnie things, aren't they, Peggy Doig?"

She knew better than to say no. "If ye say so, sir."

Peggy had never before seen such things, clearly. And neither had I before these came into my possession. Only blue steel is strong enough to bear repeated firing without melting or exploding, everyone knows it. But the maker of these cared nothing for constant use. These were designed to be used once or, in great necessity, twice each. The goldsmith who had them before me told me they were poured for an assassin in King George's pay: each dag designed to fire one bullet into the head of one target, and then the pair to be melted down and converted into the killer's reward. George had ordered one bullet for Bonnie Prince Charlie, and the other for Flora Macdonald, the Prince's ally on the island of Skye, she who dressed him as a waiting maid and spirited him to France.

At least this was the goldsmith's cant. But whatever the truth of their history, the dags have spoken to my heart these last weeks in London, the wonder and the rage, and for that reason I can sit sometimes in my small room near the Bridge and stare down at the pair of them in my hands for an hour or even two together, and never note the ticking of the clock. If envy truly has a color, that color is not green, but gold.

I clinked the barrels one against another, and she flinched.

"Shall I ask my questions, then?"

She drew in a little shudder of breath, laid her head back on the pillow, eyes on the window. Then she nodded. Her hand went to the linen at her thigh, and she drew the garment down further, held it down, hand knotted in the thin material. She didn't want me to see the move, because she was thinking about how to guard what lay beneath, despite what I'd said. But I looked at the hand, then back into her eyes.

"You needn't worry about your woman's honor. I could not be less interested, I assure you. And I think it only fair to point out that your excessive concern comes a bit late in the game. But I am here to do two things, and the first is to satisfy my own curiosity. I must ask you those few things I have no way of knowing for myself. First off, what did James have to say about your own situation today? What said he on that score?"

"My situation, sir?"

"Don't play the fool. That situation in which you and James searched diligently beneath one another's clothing and discovered a baby."

A short pause. "He said I mustn't ever fall into such a scrape again."

I laughed, quietly but from deep down. I could not help myself, for the life of me. "I thought as much. That was merely a question to confirm what I knew had to be so. Now my real question, Peggy Doig, that which only you can answer for me."

She braced for it, and I could see authentic curiosity kindling.

"It is this." I took in the young, spotless skin, the artless cascade of her hair. Her nose was long and very thin, turned down at the tip, a single element of elegance in an otherwise freckled, rustic face.

"Why do you let him make a nothing of you?"

She brought her gaze back to me, but there was perplexity there. "Sir?"

"A *nothing*," I whispered at her. "He pushed you or he wheedled you into giving yourself up to him in Edinburgh, and he treated you like a rag doll he kept in a closet above the flat, to play with at his leisure. And when he'd played with you and got you with child, he threw you back into the closet where he found you, with ten pounds for your trouble."

Someone yelled in the street, and she waited before answering me, as though the voice might belong to someone coming to her aid. But then she spoke. Her own voice was gravelly with swallowed tears, but she defended him—and, I suppose, the child. "He's taken notice of the lad, sir. He's said the boy's to be called Boswell. He's said he ain't ashamed if 'tis known."

"Of *course* it is to be called Boswell. Do you not see? Everything must bear his name, like a knock-off pamphlet. This is hack publication, not fatherhood."

"He's set us up a nurse for him. The boy's to be schooled when he's of an age."

"It means *nothing,* you silly *hamely* Scots fool. Nothing in kindness, nothing in law. The boy will inherit nothing, and James will do little for him but encourage his dissatisfactions. But that is beside the point. My question pertains to you. Why do you allow James *yourself,* here, now, after what has passed? Why do you seek him out, when he has cast you off and left you to litter on your own down some cold little Edinburgh wynd?"

It was a question she couldn't answer, for modesty, or shame, or self-loathing.

"Is it that he's had you, and you think yourself without value to anyone else? God grant it is not that you *love* him, Peggy Doig, or that you believe that you've taken over some small portion of James's heart. Because there is only room for one in that desiccated heart of his, and he is himself already lodged there."

I held the golden pistol-butt to her cheek again. She twisted away from it. "Why, Peggy Doig? Enlighten me. Why do you suffer him? Why do you defend his smutty hands on you? What could there possibly be to draw you back to him? It can't be money, because he offered money only when you'd agreed to take the child and leave him in peace."

She said nothing, moved not a muscle.

"God's plague on you, girl! Answer me! Why?" I spat the question at her, bringing my face down much closer to hers. But she closed her eyes tightly again, rolled to her side.

We stayed that way for a few seconds. I could see in her breathing that she'd mastered the tears. She was still shocked, but now looking to live through this strangeness. Beneath the new London linen and the tears, she was a hardened little Canongate *deemie*, and, when all was said and done, she trusted my country and the cut of my coat. Edinburgh gentlemen don't murder girls in garrets. They may beat them, they may starve them, or both, over and over again, but the girls live to tell the tale.

And then she answered. "I'm sorry—I can't say, sir. I don't *know* why, sir, truly I don't. I don't know, I don't."

"You know why. You sent him a letter telling him how to find you, and when the way would be clear, you waited here for him like a little pussy in the sun. Don't tell me you don't know why, Peggy Doig. Don't insult me that way. I won't have it."

"You think me a hizzie, but it ain't so." Her voice was pleading, as much with herself as with me. "I don't know why, but still he's father to my boy, sir. It's wrong what we done today, I know't. But he's my lad's only hope in the world."

"Then in fact the lad is hopeless. You must see that. You must *sense* that, if you have any sense or any heart at all."

And then she brought out some small part of the whole, before she could stop herself, something I might have expected and that I'm sure she believed. Whether or not she thought saying it would help her leave the garret alive, or whether she thought it was her last word before dying, she blurted it out and it was as sincere as a child's prayer in a hurricane: "Mr. Boswell's a lovely man. He's a lovely happy man to be with, whatever else. You know it yourself, sir."

I held my breath, and I uncocked the dags, because I could not trust myself not to shoot her by impulse alone. The anger was awake now, entirely awake and livid, pouring through my chest, down my arms. I could feel it heating my cheeks. But it wasn't her, I realized that even in the midst of it, so much as it was him and what he'd done to the inside of her little black head. A thing that only James could manage: he'd made her genuinely grateful for his whoring her out to himself.

But I'd expected something similar before I entered the room. And I had laid my own plans as well. So I told her the very least of what she should know. "Listen well, fool. I followed your lovely happy man this morning, you know, every step of the way before he came to you, and I can tell you that you weren't the first he had before his cup of tea."

She threw her arm over her face, twisted on the bed.

"He was with the nymphs in St. James's Park, Peggy Doig, and by my count you were number three this day. Three as in one more than two, and one less than four. And you may very well not be the last. And don't think for an instant that your Charles will be the last of his kind either. He likes his housemaids, James does, and waiting maids and laundry maids and charwomen, and if you're wondering why he's a happy man it's because the Kingdom's packed to the rafters with them."

A whisper, barely audible: "Don't say sich things. Please, sir. Just leave me be."

"But I said there were two things I've come to do. The second is to give you this." From my coat I took a small heavy leather purse, and I threw it onto the mat next to her. It bounced and clinked and settled, and she knew it was full of guineas without once touching it. Her hands stayed where they were, but she looked at it, and the hand went back to her smicket, holding it down against her leg.

"There are fifteen guineas there. As much, I should imagine, as you would make in two years of trundling your mop. With the ten James has given you, you have now twenty-five in total, a small fortune for a girl such as yourself. It is yours upon one condition only, and that is that you never see James again. Never for a moment, even."

She was still covering her face, but she was listening, searching the sky beyond the window, breath coming in small slow gasps. A part of her had begun to hope against hope, even amid the horrors of the morning, that she might somehow be bailed from the confinement of her own life. She had no way of knowing that the guineas, like the letters, had been taken from James's rooms last night, while he was sitting up late with Johnson and his stone-blind charity-case Miss Williams.

I went on, letting her mind work. "Now that he knows where to find you, now that he knows this room, and the trick of the coffin-maker's stair, he will be back, and soon. His talk about many months was a fit of post-coital responsibility. And when he comes back it won't be for anything but finally to consume you, like a left-over pudding, for which he has a half-hearted late-night craving. That is the long and short of it. And in so doing he'll ensure that you destroy even what little security you have here, which is little indeed, and it will all be lovely and happy until you are cast out onto the street, and in the end he will be not a particle the worse for wear.

"And that is why I insist that you leave London, and take up Charles again from whatever Edinburgh foster-mother you've found for him, and make yourself a new nest somewhere far from James Boswell and his grimy doings."

She rolled over, lifted herself on an arm, swiped at her damp, blotchy cheek. Her tone was tinged with an unmistakable outrage, something of which I wouldn't have imagined her capable, in her position.

"How can you say these things of him? How *can* ye? You of all people, who know the man *best,* sir? He is your brother, after all, i'nt he? *In't* he now?"

I cocked the dag audibly in my right hand, and I shuffled closer to her on the bed, so that the barrel came to rest against the skin of her throat. And then, because I truly could not prevent myself, I felt myself surge forward and the barrel sank deeper still into the sinews of her neck. Panic flooded back into her eyes, and she gave a little involuntary cry, face crushed down into the pillow.

I held it there for a long instant, my hand actually shaking with rage, until I had my voice again. "Here it is, girl. If I catch you with James again, I will kill you, and I will kill your son Charles. I'll slaughter you both—listen well to me, now—and no one will protect you, no one will keep you safe. Not the watch, not James, not an army of brothers-in-law. Better that you should both be dead, and pennies rusting on both your eyes, than that he should unravel the stuff of your lives like a nasty child savaging a rag doll. Believe me, Peggy Doig, when I say this, for I am genuinely mad. The fact has been proven, and the best doctors at Plymouth have washed their hands of me. So you will take this money, and you will make a life for yourself in which James has no part, because whatever part he makes up will go rotten sooner rather than later, and no one knows it better, as you say, than I myself."

I drew back the pistol, and her breath came in a coughing rush, as did fresh tears. But I had no more time to argue, and without another word I withdrew from the bed and stepped to the door.

Before opening it, I said, "Your letters are in my pocket now, and I shall keep them. Think of that when you think about telling your sister or anyone else of what's happened between us this morning. I can find you anywhere in the Kingdom, should you and James see one another again, because I know everything that James knows, and always will. If I were you, I'd let it be said that your boy died of the smallpox, or by pitching off the back of a fishing boat, and I'd smuggle him off somewhere else, somewhere fresh. But whatever I did, I would separate my life and my line from the Boswells, for once and for good. If I loved my little bairn. If I wanted what was indeed best."

She had curled into a small ball on the bed, head in her arms, hairy white legs doubled up beneath the chemise. The irresistible feet were buried miserably beneath the counterpane. She was crying, but so softly and forlornly that I lost the sound when I closed the garret door behind me. Whatever she might think of me, she thought nothing good of her brother-in-law the chandler. She didn't want to call him out of his little hole full of candles and knick-knacks, even now.

I felt for her, truly I did. Her world was hemmed round by men for whom nothing good might be said, or so it must have seemed to her. She had no way of knowing that I had done her the single greatest kindness of her life.

I remain convinced of it, even today. For in February of 1764, only some six months after our morning's discussion, James will be desultorily studying law in Utrecht, and he will receive a letter informing him that his illegitimate infant son has died. Without his ever having laid eyes on the boy, the boy will be no more. James will write pained letters to Johnston and a few other of his confidants, and he will actually shed a tear or two—he has that capacity—but in a week the subject will pass forever from his mind.

James will never bestir himself to attend a funeral, he will never see a body, and of course he will never lay eyes on pretty Peggy Doig again. And it sustains me, during these harsher, colder winters at the far end of my life, to imagine little Charles alive somewhere in the Hebrides or deep in the fields of the English countryside, a carpenter or a master printer by now, with no knowledge of his father and with no true understanding of his bliss.

3

As THE RIVER uncoils to the south, London goes to ground. Over the space of fifteen waterborne minutes, it melts unceremoniously from sight. Clusters of docks and wharves no longer clutch at the current. One outpaces the smoking kilns and the mountains of coal rising from the side of the water, tiny colliers attacking them madly with tiny shovels. Watermen suddenly leave off shouting obscenities, as though the increasingly open countryside were a chapel.

The air cleanses itself of burnt lime-stench and the smoke of brewers and soap-boilers, while the river itself outruns the slag and runoff and sewage. Broad fields of green and tan elbow out the warehouses, then begin to link and stretch away in patchwork as far as the eye can see, gorgeous, tended, verdant. The banks of the river are suddenly lush with grass and reeds, beds of marsh willows, rather than brick and waterlogged lumber. The wind is tamed. Sunshine pours down now on my little green canopy, sweet and heavy as honey. I am sweating through the arms of my coat, but in the relative quiet I welcome the heat. I catch myself dreaming over the water.

Insects are suddenly at play in the canopy with me, but the indolence of the open fields is such that I cannot bring myself to swat them. For long moments, I have the pleasant, forgetful sense that I am on holiday, with a friend.

I recognize the sensation, this sudden extra-London calm, because today's excursion is my second by river to Greenwich this week. Once I learned that James and Johnson were to take a Saturday afternoon excursion to Greenwich together—and once I had decided to make myself a *de facto* member of their party—it seemed prudent to reconnoiter so the day could not fail to run smoothly. And so I made this same trip this past Wednesday, three days ago, by way of a dry run. That simulation, along with a memorandum James wrote to himself Tuesday night, laying out a number of things the two hoped to see and do come Saturday—these things have made my planning for today a great deal easier.

Rather than following James and Johnson in their second, longer boat all the way to Greenwich, rather than hiding in the river traffic like a thief, I have told the waterman to move out ahead and to take a long comfortable lead. My thought is, let them follow me for a bit. They are content to let their own oarsman dawdle. They have nothing to accomplish today. I have a good, long list.

As we pass, near enough in the water that I might reach out and notch their boat with my sword, Johnson is braying about the canny vulgarity of Methodist preachers. I watch the two of them through a tear in the wool shrouding me. Seeing them that way is a strange thing, a feeling not merely of alienation but of inhabiting different realms altogether, with different relation to the earth and the men and things on it. The dead spying on the quick.

Johnson and James have oranges torn open on their laps, and they are pulling the flesh from the rinds and casting them into the flood. I see trout and shad rising to their leavings, and silver minnow cloudbursts.

In the long, thin craft, Johnson's size is magnified: he seems vaguely inhuman, a river-troll, a great hunched mass at the center of the boat, hoarding his powers, sucking his fruit. The heavy-lidded, amphibian eyes and the thick lips are in constant terrible motion as he speaks. He is correcting James, something I expect I might have heard no matter the moment I happened to pass them by.

"*No,* sir, no, no, no," Johnson is loudly insisting, "preaching of drunkenness as a crime, as something that debases reason—the noblest faculty of man—this sort of preaching will do nothing with the vulgar. They care not a *farthing* for reason. They will spit in your eye. The Methodists know this well. But tell the poor that they might have died dead drunk, and been roasted everlastingly for their sins, roasted until their blackened flesh fell from their bones," he spits out a seed and thrusts a thick finger at the sky, again and again, "and *then,* sir, you will affect them as you ought. This is the key, and the only key, to the success of an English Methodist."

And then our boat is past, and off and away. Johnson's voice becomes only a faint vibration at the margin of my consciousness, and then nothing at all.

The waterman has understood by this point that he is to remain silent, and he does so, staring back toward the city we have left, pulling both sullenly and mightily, the quicker to unload his odd cargo and be off home. Once or twice, children gathered on the banks call out gaily for silver, and when they do, I pitch a bit of change into the reeds. They wade out into the shallows after it like long-limbed monkeys, racing, diving, delirious with joy at the prospect of a copper.

But mostly there is silence, only the sound of water curling about the oars. And there is nothing left but to warm my face in the sun, huddle up in my own mind, and consider—as I am especially wont to do these last several weeks—of the promise James once made me.

ONE NOVEMBER NIGHT when James was fifteen and I was twelve, two men visited our family flat in Edinburgh's Parliament Close. This would be the tail end of 1755. These men had climbed the four stories to speak with my father, and when they'd stripped off their coats, he took them down the narrow hallway to the room where he had always received clients before clawing his way onto the bench of the High Court the year before.

As they passed the room James and I shared, I recognized the taller of the men to be Lord Kames, one of my father's most powerful colleagues on the Court.

The other man wore the upturned silk nightcap of an artist or a scholar, a particular oddity in our flat. My father had few acquaintances outside the legal universe, very much by choice. He'd once told James, who had smuggled a small book of poems to the table with him, "A gentleman does not come to the table, Jemmie, with *shite* on his boots or rhymes in his hands."

But this little man was no lawyer. He carried a folio under his arm, and he carried it not as though it contained watercolors or poems but as though it contained preliminary designs for the Afterlife itself. And so I guessed, *architect*.

I was right, as it turned out. After the men had been shut up in the consultation room for upwards of an hour, my father knocked on our door. "James," he said to my older brother, and the two of them left the room without another word, according to some previous understanding. I realized once they were gone that James hadn't changed into his robe and slippers after supper; he'd remained fully dressed in one of his best dark velvet suits, cravat tied, propped in a chair, reading his Longinus. I saw then that he'd simply been prepping his role: classical son, learning his Latin, getting his Greek.

Another twenty minutes or so went by, and then the four of them emerged. In the hallway, the two men shook my brother's hand, and then they and my father put on their greatcoats and hats and left the flat.

James came back into our room, and we worked in silence for a moment, and then he cocked his head to listen. My mother was in her room with Davie, my little brother, who had a croup. There was no sound but the distant sound of singing from the street. Satisfied, James put down his text and walked over to the chair where I sat.

"They've gone for gin and oysters," he said and crooked a finger. "Come, Johnny."

And without another word, we walked down the hall to my father's consultation room, and James opened the door and walked me over to my father's desk. On the desk lay the folio.

James drew it closer to us, fingered the unmarked leather cover without opening it. He toyed with the raised edges.

"Did you know the man with Lord Kames?" he whispered.

I said I didn't, but that I'd guessed he was an architect.

James looked at me with surprise, and a complimentary nod of his head. "He is Mr. James Craig," James went on, "and he is in fact an architect. Can you guess what plans he brought to show father?"

"The new house at Auchinleck," I whispered. My father had been talking about a new house on the family estate for years, but recently his talk had been edged with decision.

James tapped the cover with his finger, and his smile blossomed into genuine self-satisfaction. His fifteen-year-old face was all but illuminated with the sense of *knowing*.

"He has another architect for the new house. This plan," he lifted the cover, "is for Edinburgh, another Edinburgh. A new companion city, to the north. To be built from scratch."

It was an architect's early outline, but sharp enough in detail. At the bottom of the parchment was the North Loch, the present boundary of the city. Clearly the Loch was to be drained, dredged, and regularized and landscaped. And beyond that vast, hypothetical feat of engineering lay a perfect theoretical grid of streets, these linking and enclosing two large imaginary public squares. The streets were already labeled, grand names like Queen's and Castle. Tiny but discernible rows of trees lined the pavements. It was mathematically precise and yet fantastic, otherworldly.

James watched my face as I puzzled over the details. "There is to be a proposal floated next year for the building of a bridge here," he touched the paper carefully, experimentally, "coupled with some general discussion of extending the city's Royalty to here," he stroked an area far to the north, an area of farms and meadows and swampland. "In a few years, when public discussion allows, there will be a contest announced for designs for the New Town. And this design, with some alterations, will be selected. Mr. Craig, the man you saw tonight, will be given a gold medal and the freedom of the city."

James turned full to me, again with the air of a schoolmaster. It was the air I could ever least forgive him. "And why, would you suppose, does father show me this? Introduce me to the men who will build it? Let me in on the secret of the rigged competition, a secret that even most of his friends don't know he has broken?"

I remember wondering if he were goading me, forcing me to say it so that he could revel in the obvious.

"Why would you suppose?" he urged.

I brought it out then, the pebble of resentment in the dress shoe of our relationship: "Because you are eldest."

Now his look of self-satisfaction ripened into delight. "Yes, I am eldest. And Father would like me to join with Lord Kames and the rest of the eldest sons of the oldest families in Scotland in a longstanding war they have running. It is a war against the second- and third- and fourth-eldest sons of the oldest families in Scotland. It is a club, and he admits me tonight. He shows me that he trusts me never to reveal these plans, plans that will undoubtedly make the Lords and the magistrates rich. Filthy rich. Far, far filthier richer than any of them are today."

"And you break his trust."

James nodded, his well-fed cheeks dimpling. He seemed about to giggle. "Exactly. Without even half an hour intervening, I break his trust."

"Why, though? For what reason?"

"You do me the credit of assuming I have a reason. It is much appreciated."

"Seriously, now. Why are you so throng about telling what you've promised not to tell?"

"Mind your English. Say 'why are you so very concerned with'."

"Why are you so very concerned with telling, then?"

"To show my trust in you."

This stopped me. "Thanks, then, Jemmie."

"And why else?" he prodded.

I looked back down at the plans, shrugged my shoulders.

He prodded again. "Guess."

"I can't. There's nothing to be guessed."

Here was the thing he had risked my father's strap to say. And these are the exact words he used to say it. I remember them with an unnatural clarity, in the way that a childhood prayer unspools from memory, every word of equal gravity and every word somehow palpably in its place.

"Because if there are to be new cities," James said to me, "even secret new cities, then eldest and second-eldest brothers must always enter together. One can't be shut up in the reek of the close, while the other crosses over into fresh air and new-built homes. I despise the idea. It is an offense against one's own blood, for the sake of other firstborn of other families.

"Our father's sons should be united. And that shall always be the case with the Boswells, Johnny, you have my word on it."

I cannot express the profundity of the effect these words had on me at that moment. I was transported. It was the sort of magic my brother James has always been able to work, all the years of his life, the iridescence of unexpected sincerity, the audacity of emotional revelation, the ability to transmute the maudlin into the genuine. You may begin listening to him in skepticism but more often than not you finish in sympathy, more genuine even than you will allow yourself to admit.

You tell yourself that all of this is by way of humoring him, but it is not. It is the authentic force of his personality, working on you.

He actually took my hand then. "Father will imagine and construct distinctions between us, distinctions of a million kinds. And he will expect that they will endure after his own life is over, but you and I will never honor them, never once. We shall be better and closer than that."

For that, I forgave him even his schoolmaster's air.

For that, I forgave him everything: the self-blindness and the lust for attention and the unbridled egocentrism and the later buffoonery. For that, I loved him without reserve, as his younger brother and unashamed of it. From the age of twelve, I defended him and protected him, from himself quite as much as from others. It wasn't so much that he earned my devotion on that night but that he conjured it and then took it, with his shocking promise of common cause.

And I loved James in that way, unreservedly, until such time as his explicit promise was explicitly broken, and he did what he said he would never do: he kept a city secret and hidden from me. Not merely a city, but a city poised at the archway of an entire universe. And I saw that for all of his talk, the ancient war between brothers was very much under way.

From which time I loved him reservedly.

And in those newly scoured spaces of my heart, I began to resent him—just a bit at first, then later with great energy and imagination. I am every bit his brother in power of imagination, I assure you.

Finally, in the very blindest corners of the closes and wynds of this heart I have been describing to you, I came to something not unlike hate. It was unfamiliar to me at first, but eventually I began to excel at it, this something not unlike hate. And as with any unexpected talent—like painting landscapes on the blanched shell of an egg or shooting hummingbirds with a pistol—I came to cultivate it for its own sake.

PART TWO

This Play with No Name

Sunday 9 January

I dined at home and drank tea with my brother. We were very merry talking over the days when we were boys, the characters of Mr. Dun, Mr. Fergusson, Mr. McQuhae, and Mr. Gordon and the servants who were then in the family. In short, an infinite number of little circumstances which to ourselves were vastly entertaining.

—From *Boswell's London Journal, 1762–1763*

Edinburgh, Scotland
July 1759

* * * * * *

4

IT IS DIFFICULT to conceive how pathetic and naïve I am in middle July of 1759, at just sixteen years of age, but here is a bright case in point: I am race-walking down the High Street to the Cross, occasionally even breaking into a dogtrot, dodging caddies and chairmen and slow-moving carts because I am to meet James there at half past noon, and I am afraid to be late. The sun is bright, opulently so, but I am all but unaware of it, this pleasant day of only a handful or so a year we have in this wretchedly dark country.

The music bells are playing from the tower of St. Giles, some careless popular air that I half-recognize but cannot name, but in my hurry they sound like warning bells, fire in the city, approaching armies.

Why am I afraid to be late?

True, it is not often that James takes me to the theater, and I don't want to begin the day badly. He is good about taking me to tea or to a chophouse, places where we concentrate on our meat or our hot water and leaves. But the theater, for the last several years, has been his ruling passion, his obsession, and when he is there he is very sensitive to his own social performance, and my own—preternaturally sensitive, you might say.

I have gone with him to the Canongate just four times in the last year, including today, and each of those times he was both with me and not, present corporeally and yet diffused as a kind of turbulent energy throughout the playhouse. He shimmies like a spaniel in his seat.

And this infatuation has lately come to a head: James spent all of last summer in the playhouse, making copious but nervous love to a second-rate actress named Mrs. Cowper, known for the role of Sylvia in Farquhar's *Recruiting Officer.* Not actual love, mind you, but high-flown talk of love.

Let's be clear about that. This is 1759, and James is still almost entirely inexperienced in matters of the body.

How do I know this? James is not shy about divulging such things. Never in his life, believe me, but never less than at eighteen. He has begun to write poetry and to consort with players and secretly to publish gloomy graveyard verse in the style of Thomas Gray, but only an eighth of an inch beneath the surface he is still an anxious, quite regular churchgoing virgin. The theater is his alchemical agent.

And so by taking me today he brings me into his dearest circle. Still, why in such a rush, as I run to the Cross? James is himself often late, sometimes abominably so. And when he is, he's then tragicomically contrite for a moment, and there's an end on't. Today the play doesn't begin until six, doors don't open until five, and the early rehearsal we are privileged to attend won't begin until half past one. So we will have thirty minutes for a twelve-minute walk, in order to wait twenty minutes or so to be let through the door. I could show up at the Cross dead late, and not one lick of this, not one tittle, would be changed.

What is your *hurry* then, Johnny? It is a mystery.

JAMES IS WAITING for me, almost precisely in the spot once occupied by the octagonal monument that used to mark the Cross. It has been three years since the city magistrates pulled down and re-located the small decorative building, topped with a high stone pillar, itself topped with a magnificent fighting unicorn. It is there in my earliest memories of the High Street, that dourly clever little obstacle to traffic.

Sometime in the dim past, James told me a story about how the unicorn had helped Scottish forces crush the English at Bannockburn, before being imprisoned in stone by a wizard named Union. It was a story I loved immediately, and he told it to me regularly for a few months until, inexplicably, it began to give him dramatic, screaming nightmares and my mother barred the story from the flat.

And now the building and the pillar are no more, three years since the Cross has truly been the Cross. But James continues to insist that we meet there, out of loyalty to the unicorn—Charlie, as one of us named him some forgotten afternoon.

James is there when I arrive, miraculously, and he is alone, miraculously. There is a sort of overstuffed magnificence to him as he stands there in the space of the absent unicorn, in full sunlight, in his second-best suit. Matching coat, waistcoat, and breeches of blue corded velvet, the elephant-ear sleeves falling magnificently from his wrists, the short, tight breeches pinched precisely above his knees, lace ruffles rampant, sword hilt poking pugnaciously from the coat, hair freshly powdered and well buckled at the temples, he clearly wants to look as dressed as humanly possible in Edinburgh without quite overdressing.

But the magnificence lies not in the dressing or the powdering, but in James's own person and in the way he wears it. Sleek and dark as a stage hero, bright and winning as a spring pig, eyes black and nose just overly large, he is handsome and faintly comical. The combination is devastating in its way.

And James is the son of a Justice of the High Court in a city that worships the Law. In addition to an air of size beyond his girth, he wears an aura of importance well beyond his achievements. He cuts a figure, as my uncle Doctor John Boswell once said to me: *He cuts a very quick figure, does your brother Jemmie.*

James turns and sees me slowing to a stop beside him. He smiles absently, and I guess that he is lost in his long-running fantasy of the theater. But I am wrong.

"I miss Charlie," he says. "He was a good unicorn."

"Yes, he was that."

"He wore his horn lightly, Charlie did."

"Am I late?"

He shakes himself out of his pleasurable little melancholy, hauls up a small pretty bunch of wildflowers he has been concealing behind his hip. He smiles down at the flowers, and I can see that for James, today is a very special day indeed, more special even than I have understood. "Is not a man *always* late to the theater, Johnny, no matter how soon soever he may come?"

And then he pivots on his heel and we are off, but we are not simply walking to the Canongate. One does not merely walk with James on a bright afternoon.

No, no, no. One sallies forth.

Although his legs are moving vigorously beneath him at all times, James has a way of leaning back into the plush frame of his own body like a duke into a coach. Hands always moving, punctuating the chatter he trails in his wake. Right hand draped at his sword hilt, then cutting the air to acknowledge a bookseller my father brought off, reluctantly brought off, on a charge of piracy several years ago. Left hand diving into his coat for a silk handkerchief, then genteelly throttling off a tremendous sneeze without any help whatsoever from the right. "Ah! Rippingly perfect sneeze. Like blowing the top of a mountain away with cannon fire. A man sees the view suddenly unobstructed."

We pass a greenwife's booth, and James is struck by a mound of tea-roses. So struck that he lays hands on a bunch and after buying them presents his suddenly out-of-favor wildflowers to the middle-aged woman behind the till with a flourish. Forget that she *sells* flowers, that she is sitting in a tiny wooden box filled almost to bursting with herbs and vegetables and flowers—that this woman is in point of fact occupied from first light until dark with trying to *disencumber* herself of flowers—the truth is that the greenwife is enchanted, and we leave her still perched on her little wooden creepie, but now dimpling with pleasure.

We sally forth with tea-roses. James thrusts the bulb of his nose into the yellow profusion of the roses, sucking the scent from them hungrily.

Just at the head of New Street, we turn right, down into Playhouse Close. The alleyway is a canyon two men wide and nine stories high. Tenements and towers brood over the cobblestones. Even in broad daylight, it is always somewhere near dusk in the close. Your heels clatter louder than in the High Street, and you can feel the temperature fall just that palpable little bit.

On poles far above us, drying linen flaps like falcon wings.

At the very bottom of the canyon stands the door of the Canongate Theater. And at that door stands—slouches, lists—a middle-aged man in a leather apron. Broken vessels and capillaries stream out over his fat cheeks; white whiskers cover these tributaries like birch. But as we come to a stop, the man straightens into something like sentry-readiness, drum stomach stretching his apron warningly in our direction.

"Doors open at five, gentlemen. No admittance till then, I'm to say."

He delivers these lines with obvious relish. My guess is that he is a scenery-maker, happily filling in for the doorman today instead of hauling stage machines. In any event, James might simply inform the man that Mr. Gentleman has asked us to attend the company's dress rehearsal. But James does not. No, no, no.

"Sir," James says, resting his hand on my shoulder, "you see before you two brothers, back in their native country after a stretch of four long years. Our history must speak for us—two whose father forbid their service in the wars against the French, who sneaked away to join a Highland regiment, and who swore a blood oath to the clan leader. At last we fought in Newfoundland, and in Cuba, and our campaigns were brilliantly successful. The French and the Spaniards knew their masters. And then," he punches one gloved hand suddenly into the other, "we returned to London only to find that we were unwanted, and reviled, and hissed as Scotsmen.

"And so we've come to the theater today, sir, to revel in the performance of a good *hamely* Scottish company, to feel ourselves men again. And can any countryman blame us for coming sooner rather than later?"

The substitute doorman is taken aback, to say the least. He doesn't believe, of course, not really, but there is much here that puts belief to one side of the question. A few seconds tick by, and the old patriot seems about to strike some sort of middle ground when the door behind him bursts open, and Francis Gentleman leans way out, his bagged black hair bobbing.

"Thomas!" Gentleman shouts at the confused doorman. "Are you keeping the Boswell men, the older and the younger, on the *step*? Did I not specifically say that all persons Boswell were to be put through straight away? Stand aside, blockhead, stand aside. Let good taste pass. Gentlemen, my apologies. Excuse the ignorant prick. Come in, by all means, come in."

James gives a little answering cry of delight. For him, this is the best of all possible worlds: his name has opened the door for him, but he can tell himself his own fictions might yet have done the trick. I have no such option.

GENTLEMAN HAS HIS arm draped around James's shoulder, and, as he steers us through the dwarfish entry rooms and then through the gigantic auditorium doors and down through a sea of benches toward the pit, he is talking about everything under the sun. And although I cannot catch all of it, it is clear that he is talking a bit desperately about every thing under the sun.

Gentleman knows well enough that for James there is only one topic, Sylvia, but he threads his choice new tidbits of Sylvia in and through a jumble of other things not-Sylvia.

"Shockingly block-headed, this man Thomas," he says, directing his talk down into James's ear. "Once overturned a barrow full of nine-pound shot trying to simulate thunder for a production of *Lear,* which we may yet play this season, by the way, with myself in the lead role. Digges always nips the part for himself, but with him off to parts unknown there's a chance yet for Francis, never fear. I've always wanted to run mad across the stage, beard flying. Rend my garments, you know.

"Your Sylvia plays Cordelia, not surprisingly, and I want you to imagine, James, the transport into which the audience is thrown by the sight of her, in nothing but a wrapper of sheer green silk, weeping over her dear demented father. Kissing the old man's hand with those faultless lips."

James introduced me to Gentleman and the others of the company last summer, but only after preparing me at the flat beforehand. I could see how important it was for James that I fit in by how methodically we swotted up for that meeting.

"A likeable rogue," James had catalogued Gentleman then, "an impecunious Irish army-officer, full of agreeable nonsense. Thirty-one or thirty-two, I would say. He can play a highwayman or a clergyman with equal ease. Written some damned fine plays, and one day may succeed there. Was to buy into the management of the Canongate, but he's lost that somehow. But he does manage a bit when Digges is away. You'll love him, John. All the world loves a soldier with poetry in his soul."

This afternoon there's a wheedling edge to Gentleman's baritone. The Irish army-officer must find himself particularly impecunious this week. He sounds like a peruke-maker with too many heads to peddle.

His talk has the desired effect, however: James listens raptly to the whole stream of patter, and, by the time we enter the pit and take in the actors rehearsing on the stage, he is all but saucer-eyed in anticipation.

THE WOMAN LOOKS charmingly, no denying it. The play today is *The Careless Husband*, Old Cibber's frothy vehicle, and so rather than simple Mrs. Cowper, second-rate actress exiled from London to the provinces, she is Lady Betty Modish, a turn-of-the-century flirt and a beauty of the highest order. Brownish ringlets loose down the back, emerald gown covered over with lace and gold embroidery. Black plaster *mouche* at the cheekbone.

I have seen Mrs. Cowper several times dressed for the street, and she is an agreeable-looking woman in her late twenties. Agreeable—no angel, James's fixation notwithstanding. Her mouth is a bit big and her eyes a bit small. And she is top-heavy, to my eye. Once married illicitly to her music-master, she has somehow lost him in the workings of the world and now allows herself the freedoms of a widow. But the light of the candles, the revealing fifty-year-old fashions and the unabashed way she wears them as she turns to us—it all comes together in a very pretty picture.

She breaks off the exchange of lines to shout down to us. "Mr. Boswell! You are as good as your word. Not only in the audience, but in fact the entire audience. Well done. And you've brought me *roses!* I assume they are for me and not Mr. Dexter."

James gives a deep bow, saying nothing. As he does so, Gentleman drops me a wink, a smile hovering at his lips.

"Shall we continue?" she shouts down.

"With all my heart, Sylvia," James shouts back, voice also pitched to reach the boxes. I can tell he is half-tempted to vault onto the stage.

In another moment, the three of us are slouching on a bench, center pit, four rows back. It is James's bench, his very particular chosen bench. He says that he must be in a constant fixed location, like a star in the heavens, should Sylvia choose to direct a look or a line his way.

Scratched into this bench with a case-knife are these words: *This is the bench of James Boswell, Esq. Any man else sits here at his peril.* James, for all his outright possessiveness toward this company, could never have carved the words himself—in most things, in Edinburgh, he is still acutely aware of his social position. And so Gentleman did it for him, near the end of last summer's run, not long in fact after James confided that he planned to publish a serial review of the company's next season.

It is a cozy, half-articulated relationship they have developed over the last year and a half. James desires a thing he cannot name, which thing Gentleman then procures; for his part, Gentleman has need of things James can easily supply while remaining for the most part unaware. For James it is acceptance and access, to the theater, to Mrs. Cowper, to the closed club of players. For Gentleman, it is association, with a coming Laird, with the son of a Justice in a city where plays are still nominally against the law, where players must fake a concert and bill their own show as an odd bit thrown in free.

And it is money. It is grubby money: James has already agreed to allow Gentleman to dedicate a tricked-up version of *Oroonoko* to him later this year.

But of course their desires are partially in conflict. James wants to swim in the illusion that he is a kindred spirit, while Gentleman's needs are predicated on their essential differences. Hence the half-articulation. Hence the way they often speak to one another while each letting their glance rest somewhere else.

Such as now. James is confiding, as he searches his waistcoat for threads and stains. "The last time you played *The Careless Husband*, Gentleman, I told Sylvia that the character of Lady Betty has always made me—how did I put it?—weak in the boots. Lady Betty's beauty and her cruelty are both unmatched. She treats Lord Morelove like a tomcat, I said, to be stroked and then kicked.

"And then I looked uncomfortable, as though I had something serious to say, and admitted that it was hard for me to lose myself in the character when played by herself. Why so, she asked, more than a little miffed. Why, madam, says I, because while you come up to Lady Betty in beauty, you are *far* too kind to touch her in cruelty. And I thought that a sweet bit of flattery."

"A little slap and a little tickle," Gentleman puts in approvingly.

James gives a mock-bow in his seat, then goes on. "But she swatted it aside almost immediately, and made just to take it as an insult. We play Cibber again next week, Mr. Boswell, she said, and I want you to be present. I want you to sit in your seat, she went on, and avoid chit-chat and fooling with orange girls. I want you to pay strict attention to whether or not I reach both of Lady Betty's marks. Have I your promise, then? she demanded of me. And John, Francis, what can a man do in such a case but merely acquiesce?" He pulls back, a hand at his cravat, eyelids fluttering for effect.

"Funny you should say so, James," Gentleman says. He is sprawled over the far side of the bench, one long leg resting on the arm of the bench in front of us. "Very funny, that. Because as you know, the Canongate makes it one of its unfailing rules to forbid visits to the actors' tiring rooms."

"No one knows it better. No one suffers from it more."

"You bear up well under it. I've never seen a man return so regularly to suffer. But even you must sympathize with us a bit. Guarding the actresses, and by the way contracting for a year's wage, which no company in England will do, I can tell you, these are our only means of holding really *top* talent—a Mrs. Cowper, a West Digges, yes, even a Francis Gentleman—this far north of the Tweed.

"But something is different today. I have no idea why, but Mrs. Cowper has asked me the favor of allowing you backstage for a few moments before her performance and a few more moments after. This from her, mind you, very much from her, none of my ham-fisted meddling."

"Don't toy with me, Gentleman."

"Never! On my life, Boswell! She has a plan for the day. I am purely an instrument, a tool."

James is running over the mental permutations. "You are serious, then! Lord, it will be charming to see her before the play begins. But seeing her just after she exits is most to my taste. When the assumed character still clings to her, warm from the stage. When she's still two women at once in her own mind. That will be unbeatable. That will be *staggering*."

Gentleman examines James carefully. James does not realize it, but each time they meet, Gentleman's knowledge of him grows twice as fast as James's knowledge of Gentleman. Whatever else one might say of him, Gentleman is a quick study.

James leans over to pat Gentleman amiably on the shoulder, then suddenly swivels to me. I say very little in most situations, little compared to what I think might be said. But with James in company, I speak less than little, who knows why. Now he wants my confirmation of his triumph. "What say you to that, John? Is she not slashingly bold?"

I raise and lower my eyebrows, as though to say nothing more.

But James is waiting, and Gentleman is looking at me with some amusement, so I go on. "What do I think? I think Mrs. Cowper wants you there beforehand to prove to you and herself that she is Lady Betty, and wants you there afterward to prove to you both that she is not. To send you home without so much as a kiss."

Gentleman signals to someone downstage that he'll be there in a moment. He prepares to haul his long body upright. But before standing, he slits his eyes at me. "So you think it'll come to nothing, then, young John."

"Not nothing. James will have what he really wants, she will have what she really wants. And Cibber's creaky farce will seem full of the intrigue it normally lacks."

Gentleman claps his hands and hoots at that and begins to walk down the aisle, strides lengthening as he goes, but he turns back to point at me and call, "A deep one, your little brother, James. *Very* deep. Give me two minutes, Mr. Boswell, and then make your way backstage. The tiring rooms are yours."

James waves a hand by way of assent and then turns to me, and for a moment I think he's going to say something critical or cutting, something that will spoil the day for me. But instead he gives a gentle bridegroom's smile and says, "Look at me carefully, John. I will want you to tell me if I look at all different when I come back." He looks off toward the spikes guarding the stage. "I expect I shall."

He brings his face a bit closer to mine for effect. And for an instant I do look: I look at his dark but mild eyes, the soft chin and the lips of a *putto,* all this thrown somehow into question by the wild, fleshy exclamation point of his nose. It is a cherub's face with the mark of the goat dead center.

No wonder the world's doors either swing wide or slam shut as he approaches.

5

I AM SITTING high in a gilded box, last in a short gilded row of such boxes along the left-hand wall of the theater. Beside me sits Gentleman. Ostensibly we have come to the box to make sure that the play carries well to this distance, but neither of us is very concerned with the trickery on the stage. Just below the gold lip of the box, my breeches are open, curling away from my linen like some dull fustian peel. Gentleman's hand is lost inside that linen, the impecunious Irish fist pumping slowly up and down the length of me. I am confused by this, and I am in an ecstasy of a sort I cannot even begin to understand.

Ah, now the mystery is solved. *This* was why all the rush, then, Johnny. This was why you couldn't be late, not even a second. Not even a tittle.

So what is this thing happening, then? Is it something real, or is it an acted, an imagined thing?

Come, now—you know, Johnny, that it's both. You know that.

IT HAS HAPPENED the last two times I've come to the theater with James, and no doubt would have happened the first time had Gentleman been surer of his reception. It is a thing I am forever meaning to haul out of my memory and pore over and take apart and know, but never do somehow, a thing I've been meaning for almost a year to *do* something about.

But it is too slippery to catch, because it exists only here in the Canongate, and only in the high or the far or the dark places of the theater. It exists only with James backstage, as now, or out for a short ale with one or another of the actors. It exists only when Gentleman and I are left alone.

Which is to say it exists only when Gentleman stages it.

Both of us now have our eyes on the little lighted figures in the distance, but he is speaking to me in a low voice as he strokes, coaxing words that are hard to make out, with the exception of the word *Younger.* It is his constant joke, to call James the Older and me the Younger Boswell; but when we are like this, he drops the article and calls me just *Younger*, again and again, low enough so that it becomes almost a simple growl in his throat, indistinguishable from the word *hunger.* It seems only partially an endearment, and partially a reminder to Gentleman himself of what it is about me that excites him.

Even before I know that it is time, he bends down—bends down for all the world as though he has dropped his rehearsal schedule or needs to lace his boot—and takes me into his mouth. The timing of it is all but perfect, and he has only to draw in his cheeks softly once or twice or three times before it is done. In the very last moment, I have the volition to reach out my hands and take his head in them, my fingers sliding into the soft black waves of his hair and understanding its quality, understanding the living reality of it, and of this raw, fantastical act, for the space of a few heartbeats.

But almost immediately, I can feel him preparing to pull away, and I remove my hands from his hair. The wetness from his mouth, the infinitesimal remnant of himself that stays when he retreats, remains with me for only the better part of an instant. Then quickly it cools, becomes nothingness.

I straighten and sort my clothing. All evidence of the thing has vanished.

Gentleman straightens in his seat and fixes me with his eye once before smiling and ruffling my hair. "Imagine," he says to me then, leaning back against the gilding, "what we might find time to do if your brother actually does buy an interest in this theater?"

It's not what I expected, although in this strange new play without a name there is never any way for me to know what to expect. So I say nothing.

"Or imagine if you should someday inherit, Johnnie. Imagine that. We'd have a playhouse built special in Ayrshire. Stranger things have happened."

I nod, because he's right. Stranger things have.

We make our way downstairs, Gentleman stretching himself and talking loudly about this feature or that of the theater, inching back bit by bit into the Gentleman who is nothing more than he seems when I am with James, Francis Gentleman the impresario, the player.

As we circle back through the lobby, we pass Thomas, now sorting oranges into two piles just outside the auditorium, culling the fresh from the spoiled. He gives me a look as we pass, a knowing look, and when I glance back, he suddenly pitches me a piece of fruit.

But for whatever reason, I'm slow to pluck it from the air, and the fruit sails past me, thumping down a dark stair winding to the cellar. Gentleman doesn't break stride at the noise. I can only follow him, and as a result I have no way of knowing whether it was a ripe or a rotten thing that Thomas was trying to say.

And of course after all of this, the performance itself is something of an afterthought, an anticlimax.

EDINBURGH IS A vertical city, an encyclopedia of elevations. Living near the top of it, we have no choice but to rush down whenever we leave the flat, no choice but to climb slowly and deliberatively when we return home. I know where I am in a day by which muscles I'm in the process of exhausting.

Now James and I trace our way back up the High Street, past the Nether Bow and then the darkened Tron Church; eventually we pass the Luckenbooths, all shuttered with the exception of a dealer in sweets, a shrewd wild-haired old man who takes our measure from a distance and switches to offering ballads and kid gloves by the time we pass.

"You seem tired, Johnny," James offers as we pass the booth without so much as a word to the man. We leave him standing in his tiny wooden box, waving his cheap calfskin.

"I am," I tell him. And it is true—my anxiety and anticipation, my pleasures and enchantments and guilts and disenchantments have all combined to register as lethargy. Only a stray ripple of remembered excitement fights the feeling; my legs have no strength, but there's still a part of me that wants to run back to the Canongate. "Cibber has that effect on me. I watch him, and he makes me almost unbearably tired."

"That's because you're offended by farce," James says, chuckling to himself. "Cibber means nothing insulting by it. It is his native language."

James himself seems slightly subdued, introspective. He looks about him as he did earlier this afternoon, noting intriguing people and carriages, but conveying less of the impression that he'd like to embrace and consume them one after another. Now he seems serene, content but reflective, searching somehow.

"You've yet to tell me about your audiences backstage," I prompt.

James swings to look at me, then faces front again. He smiles, very slowly and luxuriously. "Were you right in your prediction, is what you mean. I think you were. Sylvia was quite chaste, and I do believe that was part of allowing me back after the performance, to demonstrate chastity. Score one for John today."

"I wasn't trying to score points, Jemmie."

"Ah, so you say, but I was right too." He holds a finger in the air. "I did manage to see her fresh from the stage, just as the character of Lady Betty was in the process of melting away. A *heart-stopping* spectacle. An actress is a miraculous thing, John. I've told you before that there are several men trapped inside of me, a hundred men, and to be forced to be only one would be my death. I knew today, watching Betty melt away and Sylvia gather herself up again, that I can only marry an actress. A woman equally many in number. Laugh, but that is the God's honest truth."

"I am *not* laughing. You insist that I'm laughing and scoring points. I am not. I'm rooting for you, Jemmie. Because I have a feeling you've passed a point of no return. And I would help you, now that you're helpless."

He draws in a long lungful of evening air, sorting his thoughts before speaking. Our two pairs of boots make a comforting clacking on the stones, occasionally portioning out into something that resembles the sound of a single horse being led along. Then the sounds diverge, become again the differentiated walks of two Boowollo, dragging thoir way homo.

"But, Johnny," he says after a pause, hand buffing his sword hilt absently, "there is something else. Another reason for asking me to her dressing rooms, it turns out. Something she wanted to tell me. To confess. She is a Catholic."

I have to reorder my expectations, and even then I can do nothing but repeat his words. "A Catholic."

"Yes. Devout. Very earnest about the doctrine. Very well read in it."

We begin to walk again. It takes only a moment for me to rework the day's half-joking calculations in my mind and come up with a new bottom line.

"But then she cannot be mistress at Auchinleck. Even supposing you were serious about marrying her. Even supposing father would allow it. You must give that fantasy up."

But James, of course, has come to his own new bottom line.

"Ay, give that up, or give up Auchinleck itself," he says.

I should have expected it, but I didn't, and I swing my head to see how serious he seems to be. If he were joking, he'd meet my eye and wink, but he doesn't meet my eye. He's scanning the lighted windows in the Tolbooth, and at some level this contemplation of the incarcerated he intends as a sign of the gravity of his thoughts.

"James, don't let your mind play down that road. I know you. You'll get lost and not be able to find your way back."

"Suppose it weren't play. Suppose I told you that I've read the doctrine and found much there to like. And, of course, the ceremony of the Romish Church, the pomp and the magnificence of it—truly first-rate."

"It would mean giving up a career in Parliament. You've wanted to be in Parliament since you were nine years old."

"I can live without it."

"No, you cannot. Take it from me, you cannot. I'm the one's had to lay in the bed next to you listening to you fantasize endlessly about it, listening to you make a speech on one side of a cause, and then rubbish yourself from the other side of it, back and forth, back and forth. And Auchinleck is the foundation of your entire future. You absolutely covet it, you've told me so. We've lain awake a hundred nights while you've told me all the things you plan to rip up or put down once you come to it. And it is yours by every rule and law and custom you claim to care about."

Again, he squints off into the smoke layered above the tenements, the oily, ever-present smudge that has always seemed to compromise all choices available to those beneath it. Then he turns frankly to me again. "A Catholic laird is not an impossibility, John. It's been done. There are ways to manage it."

With a start I realize that he's thinking of me, of my connivance in conveying control of the estate to him should he, in his romantic imaginings, be stripped of it. And I feel my sympathy begin suddenly to thin.

But before I can protest, he has tossed that notion away as well. "And besides, a writer doesn't *need* an estate or a career in government. A writer needs only two things. He needs to know where his heart directs him, and he needs to obey it."

"This is *rot,* James. Pure rot." I can feel myself almost getting angry now, which is absurd. This is the whim of a moment. James will want a thousand and one potential wives before he's actually wed. It's just that he's so vulnerable to exactly this sort of manipulation, by others and more dangerously by himself. "Five minutes ago you were telling me that your happiness depended on being a hundred men. Now you're killing them off twenty at a time. You'd be miserable, no title, no estate, no career in the law or anything else. A foolish little man who chose poorly. You despise men like that, you pity them."

"Alexander Pope was no foolish little man. He was a devout Catholic, and they tried to take everything from him. They forced him to live twenty miles outside London. They made a bungler like Cibber the Laureate instead. But he's still the greatest poet of the modern age. Ask any man if he pities Pope. Pope is revered."

"You are mad."

"I am a writer, sir. And I am in love."

"Twice mad."

"And *if* that is madness, then I am not afraid of it. I welcome it."

"Thrice, then."

"I *embrace* it, I tell you."

"Quadruple Bethlehem-Hospital mad, then. Stark-staring, spittle-flecked, pissing-your-own-shoebuckles Bedlam *mad.*"

We walk in silence for a few moments then, the joking suddenly turned sour. Given that my father's younger brother James took to his bed years ago, and left it only to be fitted for a strait-waistcoat, madness has never been a jest in our house. This is especially true for my father and for his son James, whose screaming nightmares about the wizard Union were only one of several shadows cast across his childhood. Only seven years ago, then twelve years old, James woke one morning to find himself without the will to leave his bed. Almost parenthetically the doctors found a delicate red rash, a nervous scurf, snaking around his thick ankles.

For the scurf and the lassitude—and in a general knock-on-wood against the specter of insanity—James spent nearly two months in a rude little inn at Moffat, drinking from the sulfur springs and being doused with buckets of hot sulfur water in an apparatus like an oversized wine cask. He had a relapse two years ago and was sent to be dunked again.

But to this day James cannot eat hardboiled eggs for the smell of the yolks.

And so suddenly, for all of these reasons, I want to take my words back, especially the part about pissing his own shoebuckles; but I tell myself that what James is proposing is social suicide, and so I leave them in play.

We cross the Lawnmarket, and after another moment skirt the Weigh-House, jutting out into the dark street. Two of the Town-guard stroll by us, hauling their axes along, beating their eight o'clock curfew again, now, at nearly nine. Caddies hauling home the early drunk, gangs of neighborhood boys at their bickers, heaving cabbage stalks at one another over chimney-tops. A covey of lawyers drifting from one oyster-cellar to another, loud and bad after a day drudging over briefs.

In and out of it all floats the shit-and-piss smell of unchambered human waste, flung out of windows back in the wynds or poured direct into gutters. The magistrates have banned this communal excretion, and their latest ban has held, more or less, during daylight hours. But evening is another story.

All of this has the feel of full-to-bursting tonight, the air of a city penned in with its own variegated excesses. Edinburgh is a lunatic, strapped down tight to a stony crag, endlessly fouling its own sheets.

And as we pass Bank Street I can see out over Market Street to the North Loch, which they've begun to drain and survey in preparation for the New Town. There is more than enough water left in the Loch for the moon to lend it a greasy shine. But that will change by autumn's end.

I can sense the city preparing to subdivide, to multiply. Like water spreading to the edge of a table, pooling, tensing against some invisible barrier until such time as that barrier is removed by the hand of God.

Suddenly James resumes the subject, but his voice is not unkind. "I'm only thinking of possibilities, John. I've not *decided* anything. It's just that I can't bear to think her forbidden me, because I was raised in the Kirk and she was not. I must be allowed to canvass the possibilities of a wife. I must. It's good of you to worry about me, it is."

Now he stops and turns on me. "But the truth is that if I know little of passion, you know nothing at all, John, nothing outside of novels. That's the hard truth of it. I have at least some experience, and that experience must be worth something. You should not pretend to know how a man driven by passion must act."

To that I can say nothing, nothing without causing the world to end.

At St. Giles Church, we take a small alleyway into Parliament Close, the vast secret square of it hidden behind the bulk of the church. At night it is always much quieter than the High Street, and we cross it nearly alone. It is like an outdoor arena, somehow, this cobbled square formed by lines of twelve-story tenements and the massive, crowned church and Goldsmith's Hall and all of the other buildings making up the walls and passageways of my early life, like something at once deeply Scottish and deeply Roman, gladiatorial.

And since Blair's Land sits spectator on the south wall of the square, it seems not merely an arena, but our home arena. Crossing it with my older brother, I am moved to vow inwardly, as he is wont to vow outwardly, that I will struggle and make a mark in the world, that I will fight and I will win and I will be remembered.

We pass goldsmith after goldsmith, the little nest of them gathered in the gloom, most of them still open late into the evening, each tending his own tiny incandescent inferno. Their lights take on a startling beauty in the deep open dusk of the Close, and suddenly their labors strike me as fine and holy, turning out plate for kings and an infinite supply of simple spoons for the dowries of common brides.

Edinburgh is a lunatic; but lunacy, of course, doesn't preclude beauty. In extremely rare cases, in fact, these qualities strengthen and flatter one another. And while it's true that Hamlet's Ophelia and the city of my birth are the only two such instances I know, then again they are each in and of themselves more than enough to make one believe.

We climb the four stories to the flat and let ourselves in. Our father is sitting before the open window in the black ladder-backed chair, with a sheaf of papers, the meat of some legal cause or other. He marks us as we enter the room, then returns to the brief.

"Where have ye two been?" he inquires.

"We have been to see a play," says James, a little loudly to my ear.

Father flicks his glance up again and manages to condense an entire Presbyterian Sunday service, with a two-hour-and-ten-minute sermon, down into two syllables.

"Lovely," he says, in his own bleak sort of poetry.

6

You need to understand that our father was not simply a man, not merely or exclusively human. In his one nondescript body were combined a hereditary Laird, a Lord of Session, and a Lord Commissioner of Justiciary, mind. He sat at the windy apex of the country's civil and criminal court systems. And when he dressed himself for Court, when he had seated the smoky, full-bottomed wig and donned the deep blue juridical robes—those billowing robes, their burgundy facings and crimson florets trailing down his breast and whispering boldly back and forth with each stride—he was a mythical figure of all but limitless power.

He could cause a tavern to be shuttered if the stink of its taps offended him as he strolled past. He could cause the very boundaries of the city itself to expand by means of certain dark rituals we could only dimly glimpse.

The one pocket of his robes overflowed with mercy, the other with destruction. He freed men from the Tolbooth, wretches who had lost all other hope. Yet he caused ropes to be knotted around the necks of other men, and those men—James and I had watched this spectacle many, many times—those men were hauled to the Gallows Stone at the end of the Grassmarket and shoved roughly from a stool, and they jerked at the end of their tethers sometimes for twenty minutes before being cut down and carted to the anatomists at the Medical College.

After these executions, James would always push his way into my bed for comfort, shivering not only at the memory of the bulging eyes, but at the realization that the killer himself slept soundly but two rooms away.

But the primal magic he worked had smudged his spirit somehow, caused my father's heart to shrink and wither and gizzen. He was capable of the odd joke here or there, and the odd loving gesture, but generally speaking he was short-tempered and disapproving, prim and pedantic and strict, and he held a grudge—for decades, if need be.

And so I think it goes without saying that, when I am sixteen and this man emerges from the oratory door set into one wall of the flat's dining room, fresh from his morning devotions, our father is, in some very effectual sense, Our Father. *Our Father of the Gizzent Heart.*

All of the flats in Blair's Land have an oratory like ours—a diminutive door off the dining room, or, in a few cases, the kitchen, that leads to a small room beneath the staircase. They were designed as prayer-cells for heads of households, although the widowed Mrs. MacKenna above us uses hers for brooms and rubbish and a place to lock her calicoe when it comes in heat. Each has a narrow slit window that allows light to filter over a chamber just large enough for a small deal table, a chair, a lamp, and a bible.

For some reason, the door of our oratory is shorter and narrower than that of others I've seen, and so when my father enters and exits he must stoop down and use the ponderous, bent-kneed steps of a giant. To me, seated at the dining room table, pecking away at Aristotle for the difficult course in Logic I'll begin in just a few weeks, there is something distinctly unsettling about the head thrust suddenly into the room, a head seemingly half the size of the door itself. I feel my stomach begin to pinch, in a way that I associate with my father's presence.

The head says, "I'm glad to've found you, John. Stay there for a moment, will you. I've some things to ask you."

He disappears back into the oratory, and emerges a moment later, again head first but this time with a fist full of documents, foolscap tied up in dirty printer's ribbon. When he's straightened up into the dining room, my father holds the fist up and says, "I'd like for you to take a look at these."

He sits down across the table from me, and separates the welter of printed material into two small ribbon-tied parcels and an even smaller book, a diminutive chipped little forty-eightmo volume, no larger than a deck of playing cards. This he puts to one side, as though it must be dealt with only eventually and in its own right.

"Now John, these are," he hesitates, frowning at the objects before him, "strange daft things, and I'd like to know what you know about them before I talk with your brother." He places a finger on the first bundle, and then looks up at me. "I want you to be honest with me, John, when I ask you these things. I've not brought you up to lie, and I'll not tolerate it. Understand me, then?"

I nod, my breath now shorter and quicker because I know that these printed bundles are not merely documents or pamphlets but evidence of some sort, and there is no way for me to deny that we have been transported somehow, unannounced, into what amounts to a courtroom.

He slips the ribbon from the first parcel and it uncurls to reveal its small secret: slugged a bit carelessly at the top are the words *A View of the Edinburgh Theater during the Summer Season, 1759.*

Although the title page lists no author, this is clearly an early proof of the pamphlet James has been working on in secret the entire summer. Some of the reviews have appeared in the *Edinburgh Chronicle,* but by collecting them and having them hawked in London as well as at home, James is making a very concerted effort to tie himself to the Canongate company in the public mind. I stare at it, his first runtish offspring.

"Do you know who wrote this sad bit of fluff?"

I can't bring my voice to lie, and so I shake my head.

"Never seen this before, Johnnie?"

"No, sir, never." This at least is true. For all of his budding exhibitionism, James has refused again and again to let me see the galley pages, which for all I can determine he hides somewhere outside the walls of the flat. At least I've never been able to find them among his things in the room we share.

I assume that my father has broken the secret somehow and found James's copy, but he immediately disabuses me of this explanation. "These pages come from a bookseller named Morley in London. He tells me he's contracted with your brother to bring out a little scandal-sheet of James's thoughts on last year's summer season."

He pokes at the pages, but carefully, prodding a stunned adder. "An ill-disguised series of puffs, is what it is. Your brother waxes rhapsodic over an actress named Mrs. Cowper. She can do no wrong, apparently. So you know nothing of this little adventure in hackery?"

I shake my head again, and then, with a temerity I find hard to understand in thinking back on it, I hear myself asking my own question. Understand, we did not question our father. But feeling the first faint pinprick of disloyalty, I ask, "Father, why not tell this Morley not to publish it?"

"That would be a large favor, Johnny. I don't like the idea of this particular pirate doing me a large favor. And the thing will surface and sink in a month."

He pushes the pamphlet proof to one side, and picks up the second roll of pages. This also looks like printer's foolscap, something else he's intercepted on its eventual way to the booksellers' stalls. But he waits before unrolling it.

"You have answered me *no* to every question I've asked, John. Don't think I've not marked it. An apprentice liar shakes his head and sweats in his chair. My next questions are far more important, and I won't brook continual shakes of the head."

"I haven't lied to you, Father. I swear I haven't."

"So you maintain. Let us start fresh, then, Johnnie."

There is another considered pause, and I can feel myself preparing to admit to something, anything, rather than answer in the negative again, when my father asks me, "Do you know a blackguard actor named Francis Gentleman?"

And the world rushes in my ears. Everything is known, I am instantly certain, all of it, as I've known since the first Gentlemanly whisper at my earlobe that it would be: the fifteen minutes Gentleman and I spent suspended in the gilded box; the twenty minutes, the first time, in a damp basement, the only time I've seen Gentleman mostly naked; the riskiest, the only nearly lighthearted encounter, the two of us in the dark behind the third of four sets of scenery shutters, the huge shutter sets being pulled apart in sequence to reveal the next backdrop, Gentleman guiding my hand, unable to contain his chortling, as we finished but a minute or two away from the final discovery.

My father knows all of this, my crashing heart tells me, and not only that but how Gentleman has been unavailable the three times this past month I've wandered to the theater on my own initiative, without James, without prior warning. How he's methodically failed to understand my fumbling attempts to tell him that I would see him oftener than I have, that I would meet him outside the walls of the theater.

My father sees not only the play with no name, but the way I am held at arm's length even by the man who taught me of its existence. He sees not only my sins, but my rejection by sinners.

"I know him," I hear myself say.

It is as though two opposing doors have been slammed in an airtight sitting room, as though the pressures inside and outside my eardrums have suddenly and violently parted ways. A veering, high-pitched tone in my ears gains subtly in volume, and I understand, without necessarily struggling against it, that I am about to faint.

But my father's mind is elsewhere. He is nodding, evidently having expected my answer. "No doubt you would, he manages the Canongate every now and again, I understand. Your brother would want to show you that he knows the great and powerful there, such as they are."

He unrolls the second set of galleys, pointing to what is clearly a dedication page of some sort. "Mr. Gentleman fancies himself a playwright, and he is to bring out an edition of *Oronooko* sometime in the next several months. His perfectly slavish dedication is to your brother, and from what I understand, James has paid handsomely for this"—he is at a loss for words—"this bit of guilt by association. Unless I'm mistaken, James could only have done so with monies given him specifically to cover the costs of his university expenses."

He looks at me, somewhat more mildly than before, expecting me to share in condemning this stunning exhibition of irresponsibility, and I realize that he knows nothing, really, about Francis Gentleman. He does not know that his second-eldest son has done things with this player that a man should do only with a woman he has made his wife, and some few other things that a man should not do even then.

And so when I lie this time, I do so with a sense of comparative relief.

"I didn't know anything about the dedication, Father."

He purses his lips, withholding judgment. And then, finally, he pushes the tiny, forty-eightmo edition to the center of the table. He erects a cage around it with his fingers, shielding the two of us and the flat from its influence. I reach for it, but he waves my hand away.

"A book of Catholic apology, Johnnie, put together in a very cunning manner by a bishop in London. The sort of thing printed and sent out into the world to drift into the hands of the young and the weak-minded, to lead them away from the Kirk and put them on the path to Rome." He opens it with one finger, to show me the title page: *The Grounds of the Old Religion,* it reads, and there is a name below, *Challoner.*

But having allowed me this glimpse, he closes the bitty book, and pushes it away from us on the table. "I am most worried about this book, John. And I will tell you frankly why. I understand that this Mrs. Cowper has connections to several Roman Catholics in the city, connections of the sort I don't stoop to understand. She has at least one botched marriage to her account, I do know. But I put all of these things together, son," he indicates the two bundles of foolscap and the book of apologetic, "and I see your brother engaged in the sort of foolery that can sink a good family in a single generation."

He fixes me with his eye. "You understand me, John."

"I do understand, sir." He wants me to know that it is not only James's own inheritance somehow at stake, but my own. I can't help but remember the night after my last performance with Gentleman, how James suggested that I might help him hold on to Auchinleck even as a Catholic, both our lives spent dodging the Treason Act so that James might indulge himself in the selection of a woman of middling beauty, the cast-off of a music-master.

The eye narrows. "And I'll not allow that. I'll cut him off and entail the estate away from him before that happens, before I die. When the flame is gone you don't leave a candle to stink in the socket. You take my meaning?"

I nod again.

"Now I shall ask you the most important question of any I have asked thus far. What do you know about this sudden taste for Catholicism your brother's acquired? Where does it come from? Who's got his elbow and leading him on this? Best you tell me now what you know."

I am angry and resentful at James for placing me in this position, here at this table, at cross-purposes to my father and my own self-interest, and this resentment is simmering inside me. I consider half-truths, hints, ways of remaining faithful to both of them. I consider confirming my father's suspicions about Mrs. Cowper, which, as I understand my father's whims and abilities, would lead almost immediately to her disappearance from Edinburgh, possibly from England as well—possibly, just barely possibly, from the world of the living itself.

And I glimpse, in a way I never quite have before, the corrupt, second-hand magic available to the weak son of a powerful wizard.

But there is never any question about where my heart lies, the real foundational timbers of my loyalty. There is never any genuine question that I will hold up my end of the deal struck when James was fifteen and I was twelve, the deal witnessed by the map of the infant city just now being scratched into the hayfields to the north.

I know I will be punished for it before I speak, and yet I look my father in the face as I do so. "James has never mentioned the Romish Church to me, Father. I know he goes to Episcopal services some Sundays, when the service at the New Kirk is finished. The Episcopal Church in Carrubber's Close. He says he likes the organ music. They're allowed to play the organ there. But I have never heard him speak of Catholicism. I swear it."

It is as good a lie as I'm capable of lying at age sixteen, a bit of truth seasoning the outright falsehood, all of it topped finally with the purely decorative sin of an oath.

My father presses his lips together again, his gestural subtotal to any series of small inner conclusions, and then he nods carefully. "I misjudged you when I said you were an apprentice liar earlier, John."

He stands with his hand on the table, and then quickly knocks his knuckles against it, putting a period to the discussion. "You are every bit the journeyman."

His steps sound the length of the trance, growing gradually faint and then I hear him gathering his court paraphernalia in the room he shares with my mother. I pretend to work with Aristotle, listening, waiting. Finally, the footsteps make their way back up the trance, and he stops beside my chair, a satchel of briefs in one hand, the white and red satin robes he wears to hear criminal cases hanging magnificently, falling just to the floor. We regard one another.

It is the current custom for Lords and advocates living near the Court of Session to parade there each day in full state, and so the freshly powdered full-bottomed wig hangs about his long jowls like the ears of a massive and disapproving spaniel. In a moment he will be gone, gone about the business of ordering the hanging of men accused of not much more than what I have just committed at his own dining room table, and I pray that he will go without saying anything more.

But it is a prayer with no real faith behind it, and he clears his throat.

"Since you are home today, with nothing pressing to do," suggests my father casually, "I wonder if you might fetch us all some water, John."

7

One morning when I was eight, I happened to be in the kitchen when the water caddie shuffled in with the first of the day's two buckets of potable water. It was an event that happened like clockwork, each day about eleven, but for some reason that morning it struck me as a brilliant adventure, this quest for water. I took it into my head to follow the water caddie out to the pump below Parliament Square, and I begged my father's servant William to ask her if I might.

So William asked this tired woman if I might go along, and she picked up the bucket of foul water he had standing by the door for her, and she smiled and said, "Ay, lad. For a bittock."

But tagging along was not enough—to *help* was what I was mad after, and William rummaged in the pantry and found the smaller water barrel he used on holidays when the caddies stayed at home. There were straps for my arms, but before handing it to me, William looked at the dust collected on the slats and told me I'd best change into my oldest clothes, and leave off my waistcoat.

When I had changed, the squat older woman and I walked down to the street, where she emptied the bucket of our foul water into the gutter. We continued along the south wall of the Square, past the goldsmiths and the dressmaker's shop, and then we descended the long Parliament Stair, what the woman called the Old Back Stair.

At the stone well, she stretched up to pull the small handle, while I steadied first her large tapered bucket, and then my own cask. But she let go the switch when the cask was little more than half full. "More than enough for you to carry, mannie," she said.

Still, the cask was heavy enough to allow me the illusion that this woman and I were caddies hauling water together, workers. People in their flats would slake their thirsts because of my work. I imagined this process repeated a thousand times around the city, buckets and casks of water rising methodically into the air, to the very tops of the tallest tenements, a rainshower in reverse, an all but invisible daily miracle.

The caddie told me that I'd make a fine soldier one day, I carried so well and so uncomplainingly. And every woman loved a soldier, she added, showing her bad teeth and the pretty smile they could manage.

As we finished the climb of seventy-six steps, each of which I counted aloud to her, someone took me by the meaty part of my arm and spun me around. With the cask strapped to my back, it threw me off balance, and I nearly fell to the cobblestones. But the hand held me, and I found my feet.

It was my father, standing beside the tenement at the head of the stairs, staring in amazement at what he had in his grip. His forehead was creased in a way that meant not simply thunder, but lightning as well.

"*What are ye doing, ye two*?" he whispered incredulously. "*What do ye think ye're doing?*" The caddie and I simply stared back, neither of us, I think, able to comprehend the crime.

Ignoring the woman altogether, my father took hold of my arm and marched me quickly toward Blair's Land, berating me in a low whisper for dressing like a caddie to perform work well beneath the dignity of a common house servant. He'd been appointed Sheriff of Wigtownshire the year before, my father, and he was greasing already for appointment to the High Court. None of these plans included having his middle child seen tipping the waste-water bucket into the gutter or jabbering with water caddies.

Needless to say, from that day to this I have never again asked to carry water to the flat, and although the water caddie and I recognize one another from time to time in the Land's staircase or on the High Street, we never speak a word. We each understand well enough that water and society both run downhill, and there is always something in her face that says making one of the two do otherwise is as much labor as she can spare.

ONE THING YOU will notice as I write this account is that my father's simplest actions often require pages of explanation. His most complex, of course, require books. No one understands this better than my father, given as he is to seeing his own actions as formal decisions, decisions that beget interpretation.

So when my father orders me to haul the day's water—to carry away the foul and return with the drinkable—it says many things to me. It says that he has already communicated this wish to William, hours before, so that William might turn away the water caddie for the day. This in turn means that my father anticipated my perjuring myself. He knew I would lie, and prepared a proper disgrace well beforehand.

It says also that William understands the disgrace, if not the reasons for it. This explains his uncomfortable look when I go back into the kitchen to ask for the same small watercask my father once stripped disgustedly off my back.

"There will be lines at the well," William says apologetically, as though the lines will be of his own making.

My father is also saying this: What stands between carrying water and having it carried is not my birth, but his continuing good will.

Having lived through this same scene once before, however, I find myself strangely unruffled by it. In fact, I know just what to do: change my clothes, and leave off my waistcoat. And I know exactly into which clothes I should change.

Stuffed into the darkest rear corner of our shared wardrobe is a sack of clothing that James calls his See-Everything Suit. It is an assemblage of old caddie's clothing he has put together from who knows where; but every once in a while when my parents are out, he will take off his modest everyday finery and put on the moleskin breeches and the rough linen shirt, wind the soiled white apron about his thick waist. He'll slip on the battered blue wool bonnet, the *shune* with the dinged buckles. And then James will vanish into the city for an afternoon. He moves around the areas where he is not known, the Lawnmarket and Cowfeeder Row and the piers, venturing sometimes as far away as Leith or Blaw-Weary.

"A man sees everything this way," he will maintain, when I can't stop myself from mocking the whole charade. "Because if your silk suit clears the way in the playhouse, it blocks your way in all of the worlds adjoining it. No man wants the son of a judge watching him dead-weight his fish in the market, or whip his horse, or parade his mistress. But dress the part and you see the naked world itself. It is magic, Johnnie."

I am laughing as quietly as I can as I pull on the various pieces of the See-Everything Suit. It looks better on me even than on James; because I am just that much taller, the pants look as though I outgrew them years ago. My wrists dangle out of the dirty sleeves, and I am just a skinnymalink, a nobody. But as far as I can figure it, there is not a single blessed thing my father can say should he see me shouldering my cask along dressed this way. Would he have me haul water in the clothes he has paid good money to have tailored for me? It is a brassy move, of course, but I have begun to feel the brass in me, as has James. We are growing up, we two.

Then I begin to laugh so hard that I actually have to sit down on my bed, because I've realized that the shoes don't fit me, not nearly, and that my own new boots would give away the whole show. And that consequently there is nothing to be done except to go in my bare feet, which is done by a great many in this city, but, needless to say, never by a Boswell.

Never, ever. It is just shy of a hanging offense in our household.

I pull the bonnet down over my head and deliberate about it. But after only another second, I think of something that is simply too tempting to be resisted. If I go barefoot, I can tell James later that not only did I wear his secret suit, but that until he himself wears it without shoes, he hasn't seen *anything*.

THE JOKE GOES cold by the time I am halfway down the Parliament Stairs, quite literally. A nirly breeze is rushing through the Closes, an early taste of what the fishermen in the autumn call the shrinking wind. A tricky wind, the kind that dies and roars at precisely the right moments to upend tables in the market, hats and skirts, and occasionally to strip a sedan chair clean away from its chairmen.

But mostly what sours the joke is what I see as I descend the long line of stone stairs: a small crowd of people, maybe twenty-five or thirty of them, grouped around the gray granite well, which looks like an eight-foot sentry-box but for the fact that it has no windows. The vessels these people have brought are spread out over the cobblestones in a long, ragged snaking line.

It is mostly women, maid-servants and caddies and fishwives, and the men are mostly boys a good deal younger than myself. The few grown men are on the oldish side, smoking pipes or seated in the windbreak where the stairs empty out into the Cowgate.

Most of the crowd stands together in small knots of talk, only their casks and buckets holding their places in line. Some turn their faces up to look as I draw down nearer, but they turn immediately away as the suit works its magic.

I can hear the pump water itself now and again, not rushing

into the bucket as it should, but pulsing slowly, weakly and then a bit stronger and then weakly again, like blood pumped through a sickish heart. I will be most of the afternoon at this, I think.

There are, however, a number of interesting things about this scene below me that I will only come to know tomorrow afternoon. Not only the surgeon, but several friends of the family will drop by to look in on me then, to see how I'm faring and to try to raise my spirits. They will bring me Spanish figs and cluck their tongues and provide me with facts I can have no way of knowing now, yet things my father knows very well and from many sources.

This year's drought is no ordinary harvest drought. The Castle reservoir, ordinarily topped off by water piped from Pentland Hills, has fallen dangerously low, low enough to cut the flow to wells down the Royal Mile by something like three-quarters. Some of the old lead piping carrying the water has also chosen this past summer to decay. Gangs of workmen are still digging it up here and there in the city, searching for the phantom drain on the system.

In the lower end of town, farmers are selling water hauled in from the country. A half-penny for each four pints, William will tell me tomorrow. It is a price he has paid more than once to avoid the crowds.

William will also tell me that it is not unusual to wait an hour or more to fill your buckets, partially because the stronger and larger often don't wait their turn, and that in this way the line itself is only a partial indication of how long one must idle there. Sentries have been posted, every now and again, in response to outbursts of violence.

Everyone in the crowd now standing and talking and smoking and shuffling to the spout knows all of these things.

But I am sixteen years old, and I have been paying attention to my studies. I've been making my first fumbling attempts to reconcile love and affection with lust and rejection. I have been oblivious. As I step onto the cobblestones, I know only that my feet are cold through, and that before I make my second trip to the well I plan to put on a pair of thick stockings and my good heavy leather boots.

When my cask is two places from the spout, a middle-aged chairman makes his way to the well. He is not a large man, an inch or two shorter than me, but he has a big pair of arms and wears an old patched Highlander's regiment coat over his apron. I will be asked many times to describe him in detail, but other than these things there isn't much. Cropped hair beneath his large slouch bonnet. He is not the first to break the line, but he is the first to do so without any pretense of fidelity to it. He does not insist that he is bringing water to a sick child, or any of the other half-hearted dodges.

He merely shoulders through to the spout as a charity school boy vacates it, muttering "Through, through," as he comes.

By now I've learned enough to stand over my cask and make it as hard as I can to pass me by. But he boxes me neatly aside with his shoulder and bends down with his bucket. When I don't move back, he looks up to fix me with a sudden, mad look.

"*Through,*" he says, with the air of saying it one last time, and it is a Highland accent. An instant passes, and then he drops his gaze again to the thin fall of water wetting his jug.

Regardless of how I am dressed, I am not used to being shoved by chairmen. And it is at that point I take another half-step forward and make as though to tap him on the shoulder. "Excuse me," I say.

THE FACT IS that I will not remember actually being struck, not tomorrow or ever after, though the bruise that surfaces on my chest will say a great deal. Never will I forget, however, my head hitting one of the granite blocks of the well, and then the fall backward to the cobblestone. The dull crashing impact at the back of my skull, and the wash of nausea.

On my back, I turn my head slightly and see bright blood puddled in the dirty cobblestone cracks beside me. I turn back because holding my head to one side is suddenly too much to manage.

Those waiting for water have pulled back into a loose ring around me. The chairman has vanished. Everyone is frozen, no one seems to be moving to help, and I feel myself pulling in slow, feathery breaths that don't refresh my lungs.

In the distance I catch sight of something beginning to drift down the Parliament Stairs, something bright red and shapeless. It moves down the staircase like a heavy ground animal, low to the earth like a badger or a sable, quick humping movements.

Just as it drops out of sight below the ring of faces, I see that it is not a beast but a man, brushing rapidly along in the scarlet cloak and black cocked cap of a goldsmith. He is a small, stout man, but not tiny; it was the cloak that made him seem hunched to the ground. There is a cane in his hand, and he works it sharply as he walks. He has a shop in the Close, no doubt, and glimpsed the commotion from the top of the Stairs. The circle about me opens, and the man kneels beside me, his face abruptly close to mine.

But I cannot meet his eyes. A black sleep is coming for me.

He begins to speak with a chairman standing behind me, asking if anyone has run yet for a surgeon, and I lose the sense of his words, resting my gaze on the gold head of his cane, which now dangles in his hand.

The red line of my blood scurries away from me, shaping angles around the cobblestones. My consciousness thins. The last thing I see is the goldsmith waving his stick at two of the caddies standing by. And then, as though he were a wizard and the stick charged with some true ancient Scots *glamour*, everything vanishes.

I AM IN a small dark room, a warm room, lying on a broad bench. Staring at a stone wall, upon which play the shadows of a small fire popping somewhere out of sight. My eyes open, close. Squinting,

I manage to hold them open, but just a slit. Daylight struggles in through the thick glass of a single window.

In a recess beneath the window stands the goldsmith. He has cast his red cloak and hat aside. He is a short, stout man, with a bit of a paunch. Beside him stands a small bench, and upon the bench are several dull gold and silver objects, an array of tools, work to be done, but the man's eyes remain on the street. And I remember hearing someone say the word *surgeon.* The goldsmith is waiting for the surgeon to arrive.

He goes then to his small fire, out of my sight, and I hear the quick gasp of a bellows. The fire leaps up, I can feel it. He means to warm me, and the heat is welcome, because my feet and my ankles are still bare and chilled through. But my head is still far too heavy to lift.

The shelves on the wall before me contain almost nothing of his trade. Goldsmiths do not like to house their stock, but work to order. Still, there are a few things, things he must lock up at the end of the night, when he has cleaned his tools and caught the day's last live embers in a stone urn. A fan of spoons in gold, a fan of spoons in silver. A cup that sits upon three delicate legs.

And on the highest shelf, in a wooden case lined with red velvet, a pair of golden pistols. Snubbed barrels, heart-shaped handles. Brilliant things. These must be his twin prizes, his single best advertisement in a country where guns are a kind of gospel.

It is an oddly hushed moment. I feel no urgency, although I understand that my blood is seeping even now into the cloth I feel knotted tightly about my head.

And I understand that the surgeon may not, in fact, be on his way. He may have stepped out for a dish of oysters, and I may die for want of his knife, my body cast away like so much refuse. The goldsmith has no idea whose child lies here on his bench, after all. As far as he knows, I am a caddie with a cloven skull, that and nothing more.

And in that strange hush, a voice is suddenly murmuring somewhere. As though the words begin abruptly in another room, and then drift closer, near enough finally to pick out and distinguish them one from another. The voice itself is low, and clearly distressed or even angry in tone.

The words roll and dip like a poem, or a ballad. *This is your father's fault,* runs the song's complaint, *and this is your brother's fault. They crush you between them. Bust you open. They bust you and they break you. And all for a bit of land. The land is all their passion. It is the only thing they love. And the only thing about this wee bit of land upon which they will ever agree is that it must never ever be allowed to fall into your two filthy hands, Johnny. Anything but that, you see. Anything but that.*

My lids weigh heavy again, but the sense of the words continues. The phrases are slow and methodical, like tableaux in a street pageant, each being dragged deliberately along in sequence. My heart has begun to thrum again in my chest. Part of me wants to answer: *But I am not crushed. The surgeon will arrive in a moment. And James was nowhere in sight. A wudden chairman did this to me.* I cannot, though. There is no volition left, anywhere in me.

But the words continue, from somewhere very near. Not the goldsmith's words, for he goes on staring fixedly out the window into the close. For a single horrible moment, I am convinced that the voice is issuing from a ghost, an angry spirit hovering in the stillness of the room.

And for the span of that instant, I am convinced that I have gone truly mad.

It is only eventually, and with great relief, that I recognize the voice as my own. It is inside me after all, and I am not mad. It is the play of my own thoughts, my own ambient outrage, and nothing more. As the murmur goes on, I listen with less concern, simply registering the cadences.

You know 'tis true, Johnny. They use you as a stick to strike one another, and now look at this, their stick is broken. Pieces, that is all, left lying heaped on the street. But you are safe now. For now you know the truth. And now you are in a fair way to make them leave you be.

My eyelids fall closed again.

When I open them, the goldsmith is seated on a creepie at my side, his face drawn worriedly to mine. He expected the surgeon well before now, and he fears, no doubt, that there will be questions and procedures to satisfy should I die here at his table. His eyes are small dark beads, with a hint of a squint, and framed by sharp, black brows.

But there is genuine kindness there as well, even I can see that. For when he sees that my eyes have managed to focus, he smiles, pats my shoulder very gently, and says something reassuring which I do not catch. And then he turns, to discern the object upon which my gaze has come to rest. In order to make small-talk, to kill time.

"Spotted my brace of show dags, have you, lad," whispers the goldsmith. The pride in his voice is unmistakable. "Lovely *speeshal* things, those particular pieces. Quite dear, though, quite dear indeed. A prince's ransom. But a wonderful history goes along with those guns, and a true history into the bargain. And they do say that a true history is the very best sort of history money can buy."

THE EVENTS OF the day had a serviceably happy ending. The surgeon, as I might have expected, turned out to be an acquaintance of my father; and within a few moments more I was carried across the Square and laid in my own bed, where I came to not long after. I was the son of a Judge again, worth hurrying through the streets, and my concussion was pronounced only mildly threatening.

When the doctor left, James came to my bedside ravenous for details, and he became so incensed listening to them that he swore he would strap on his sword and go searching the *howfs* and the oyster cellars for the caddie. He didn't, of course, because no one in the world was ever less likely to fight than my older brother. But he grew convincingly angry, and I appreciated the gesture.

And James told me, like a bedtime story, about the plans for the houses in the New Town, whose eventual kitchens would have each their own deft little taps, from which water would flow at the slightest touch.

I said nothing about what I had seen and heard in the goldsmith's shop, just before I slipped from consciousness. As best I could, I pushed those moments from my mind; the memory of them was like a dream of something forbidden, accompanied by a lingering residue of shame.

More than anything, I wanted no more doctors. I had no desire to be prodded and poked, as James had been, and floated for weeks in a washtub of sulfur water.

Though my father pressed me for details to identify the man who struck me, there was no official investigation. No account of it appeared in the *Edinburgh Magazine*. My father was clearly disturbed by my dress, my shoeless feet, and he avoided questions by hiring a caddie to search privately. Within a day or two the criminal was declared to have fled the city, most probably for the Highlands, and the incident was made to disappear.

And so, like my time with Gentleman, the truth of the water story turned out to be merely visceral, without any greater or more lasting meaning. I was not yet seventeen, but already I had begun to suspect the worst, that there was something profoundly provisional about my time on this earth, that my own life was a journal whose pages were destined to take no ink.

PART THREE

Kissing the Consecrated Earth

Saturday 30 July (continued)

When we got to Greenwich, I felt pleasure in being at the place which Mr. Johnson celebrates in his London: A Poem. *I had the poem in my pocket, and read the passage on the banks of the Thames, and literally "kissed the consecrated earth."*

Mr. Johnson said that the building at Greenwich was too magnificent for a place of charity, and too much detached to make one great whole. . . .

We walked about and then had a good dinner (which he likes very well), after which he run over the grand scale of human knowledge, advised me to select some particular branch to excel in, but to have a little of every kind.

—From *Boswell's London Journal, 1762–1763*

Greenwich, England
Saturday, the 30th of July, 1763
1:45 p.m.

* * * * * *

8

ALTHOUGH I HAVE been to Greenwich only once before, and that as recently as three days ago, putting in at the river stair before the Seamen's Hospital feels as though I have come home again. Because although the vast complex seems indisputably to be a palace—although in fact it began life as a palace—it is now merely a granite toy box for busted soldiers.

Two toy boxes, in fact: when Queen Mary, the project's first real benefactor, saw that the original massive design would obstruct the view from her own smaller residence in the distance, she had it quickly and unceremoniously broken in two. Mary was compassionate to a fault, but a view to the water was another matter entirely.

These two white palace complexes now mirror one another, each recapitulating the other's broad edifice, colonnades, and towering chapel dome in the middle distance. A broad grassy avenue—precisely the width of Mary's angle of vision—still lies open between them. One Tree Hill and the Royal Observatory rise gently behind.

But they are toy boxes all the same, a tidy location to dispose of sailors busted beyond repair, those who have somehow misplaced arms and legs and eyes, even the occasional human face entire. And those, like myself, who have misplaced something else altogether.

It is a miracle of sympathy, this Hospital, sheltering thousands of pensioners and some few of their families, indicative of a compassion every bit as extravagant as that which produced *L'Hotel Royal des Invalides,* at Paris; and it is an obscenity, indelible proof of a greedy and petulant empire.

As I say, it feels very much like home.

When the sculler nudges up against the stone steps, the waterman stretches up a thick arm to the iron gate and holds the boat snug against the landing. I unfold from beneath the wool canopy, and it is good to stretch and stand in the breeze. Along with the river smell there is a scent of cinnamon, somehow, in the air. I clear my sword from my coat and hold the waterman's eye, and for all his size and strength, it is he who breaks off the glance, with an almost involuntary bow of his head. I remember the mudlark clucking his tongue at the man, on the man's own boat, and the stout waterman doing nothing until the smaller lark was safely out of range. Only then did he seize a stone and attack.

And none of this is a surprise: I have invested more than a few hours watching the Temple stair, picking mentally through the daily scrum of watermen, selecting in advance for speed and corruption and a certain bully's timidity. The perfect waterman to ferry me along on James's perfect afternoon.

From a pocket in my waistcoat I take not merely a full shilling, but a crown, and I pitch it at him. With one hand anchoring the boat, and the other holding his oar, he can do nothing but flinch, and let it strike his chest. The coin drops into his lap, and he glares before realizing that I have quintupled his fare. The magic of cash: the glare becomes a look of disbelief, then even a wan smile.

"I have restored the pennies I took to stop your mouth, Gil Higgs," I tell him, "as well as another four shillings. A great deal of money. Easy money for little enough work, I think."

He begins to mutter his thanks, then realizes that somehow, somewhere, I've laid hold of his name.

"I will be needing return passage, and I will pay you for the day complete." I have waited until now to tell him this, quite deliberately. I point to another, smaller stair down the public walk fronting the river. "You will wait for me there, hard by that step, and be ready to row out quickly. With luck, I shall be back in an hour or two. But if night should fall, I'll expect you there still. Be ready, I say. And there will be another crown in it for you when we put in at the Temple again. A very profitable day for you, I should think."

His confusion is deepening, but he seems to know that whatever else, he had best be quit of this fare, and the strangeness that comes attached to it. His gut is telling him to push off. It is a contingency not terribly difficult to foresee: his early curiosity has dwindled into apprehension, and the sense that my day's affairs are a deep, twisty hole into which his nose should not be stuck.

Oar now racked, he has the crown cupped in his hand, suspended between returning it and bringing it to his own pocket. He sneaks a glance back toward the hanging smoke of the City.

"Well, to say truth, sir," he manages.

But before he can say more, or begin to dig in his big heels, I draw something out of my waistcoat. A book. A miniature, three inches by an inch.

I hold it out to him. "You bargain well. And I cannot have no for an answer. Let me throw a final sweetener into the pot, then."

He accepts the book, and it sits delicately in his heavy, callused hand. He prods it with a fat finger. There is nothing in the world, it seems, he was less prepared to receive: *Tom Thumb's Pretty Song Book,* with watercolor illustrations cleverly tipped-in, bound in weathered calf. An odd charming little treasure, even for a man who no doubt cannot read or write his own name.

He looks up at me. The coarse, unkempt brows knit together. He does not understand.

"Not for you, of course. For your Maggie, Higgs."

Now I truly have his attention, for the first time today. I set my hat on my head, cock it forward a touch, to the left a touch, the particular style of my regiment. Or what was, until recently, my regiment. "She has no brothers or sisters to help her beguile the hours, has she? She must spend a good part of her day very much alone. And St. Giles is certainly not the most cheerful place in which to be alone. It can be a dangerous place, I understand. But no longer. Now Maggie will always have Tom Thumb, there to look out for her when you cannot. When your wife cannot. There is not a child living can resist General Tom Thumb. To amuse her and make her feel protected, from anyone who might wish to do her harm."

Now he begins to understand.

I point to the secondary stair again, no question whatsoever in my voice. "I will expect you to wait there until I return, or near enough to that spot. Do not make me hunt for you. We may need to draw away on very short notice. And about our journey today, I will expect you to say nothing, ever, to anyone. You promised earlier to keep close as the grave. If you keep that promise then today will be the last we see of one another, Higgs. We understand one another, then."

He wishes to say something, no doubt more than one thing, but I step out of the boat and then take the steps up to the public walkway at a dogtrot. From the upper railing, I see him sitting stunned in his little green boat, scalp shining in the midday sun, still holding out the crown and the doll-sized book before him.

On another day and from another source, these would be river booty—unexpected and odd, but booty all the same. He'd have spent the rest of the afternoon slumped in a dram shop, then swaggered home with these objects to his flat in the St. Giles slum, home to his battered-looking wife and ill-nourished six-year-old.

But it is today, and they are from me, and although Gil Higgs now finds that he keenly does not want these things, he really has very little choice in the matter.

* * *

In the event, I realize, much of my design for this afternoon has come to rest on the slender backs of birds. The mudlark who brought back the tale of the Argonauts was the first. Only a quick afterthought, yet he turned out to be a bold little stroke: that particle of conversation—passing between two inveterate talkers determined to cram an entire, lovely July day with nonstop talk—that snippet would otherwise have evanesced, passed off into nothingness.

Of course, if I were in my right mind, I would have let it pass off. The world needs many things, but Johnson's thoughts on the centrality of his own labors and preoccupations are not among them.

Still, I am sentimental, and what I can capture of their day, I will keep.

And so the lark was only the first of his kind. More time and preparation by far has gone into finding and training my venerable old Greenwich canary, and from him I expect a great deal more. That is who I seek as I stroll past the Hospital's marble statue of George II, who oversees the slow stream of tired and maimed sailors as it empties off the river, year after long year.

It is a Saturday, sun-kissed, and Greenwich is a popular place for a frolic, especially the Park and the grassy slopes of One Tree Hill. The Grand Square pulses with Londoners, rich and poor, but their gowns and frocks are never quite gay enough to overcome the dull blue omnipresence of the pensioners themselves.

They are all about you in Greenwich, these superannuated sailors, no matter where on the extensive grounds you stand, slow-moving beings still got up in their naval uniforms, empty pant legs and shirtsleeves pinned up smartly, some with large chunks of skull left behind on the floors of distant oceans, reiteration after blue reiteration of the same banal, horrific theme. Some few of these, their wounds disturbingly fresh, shuffle along in an opium haze.

Every so often, though, in the palette of Greenwich color, there comes a dab of sharp mustard-yellow. Military discipline is maintained at the Hospital, everything but the lash, and the old sailors meekly obey, by and large. They couldn't be more grateful for their care, after all. But there are exceptions: the occasional instigators and malingerers, the sneak thieves and the rheumy drunks. By way of punishment, these men are forced into yellow regimentals, solid yellow from the corners of their hats to the piping of their breeches. Canaries, in the pensioners' lexicon.

The idea is to shame the man in question, as if there were not already more than enough shame in these grounded sailors to go round. The idea is to make the guilty man contagious in the eyes of his fellows, as if they were not all of them already shunned as untouchable by the world outside the Hospital. In this way, even the lowliest pensioner can pass on to a canary some portion of the abuse heaped on him by Fate. Each man spits upon a man lower still. Therapeutic, so the thinking runs, for all concerned.

But the yellow uniform has at least one unintended benefit: if one comes to Greenwich looking specifically to suborn a man, it is helpful to know at a glance which souls are the most spectacularly corrupt.

When I visited this past Wednesday, I chatted with several of the canaries I spied in the Park and along the riverfront. They are in general pathetically eager for talk, much put-upon and eager to demonstrate their innocence. Eventually, I found a man precisely to my needs.

And it is this man who rises abruptly from his bunk when I come to the end of a wide, paneled dormitory passage and knock on the wall of his cubicle. All in yellow, but with his hat apparently stripped off and tossed down upon the floor before the wardrobe, so that his white hair rides up in a fright. Face deeply lined, and eyes the troubled red of a man who has been so drunk for so many years that at best he can now be parched, but never sober. A vast tuber of a nose. He limps toward me on a long peg, stretching to the floor from mid-thigh. "One leg or no," he told me Wednesday by the river, winking slyly as we shook hands for the first time, "I am part of me a very devil, sir." Now he does not stop a pace away, but comes stumping to just within two or three inches of my face. There is about him the reek of pipe tobacco and decay. He peers up at me, and his voice is all but indistinguishable, the whisper of a well-trained conspirator: "You've brought what you promised?"

I lower my own voice to nothing: "I have, Grandfather, never fear."

He nods once vehemently, tugs at my sleeve, and draws me after him down the passage. We pass cubicle after doorless cubicle, most empty because of the sunny day, with rugs on the floors and mementoes decorating the walls, each a shipshape little still-life of unwanted retirement. Then the old man opens a door off to the left, and we pass suddenly into a dank little brick hallway, unlit, and from the sharp smell of soap and wet I can only imagine that at the end of the connector lies a washing room and some of the small army of washerwomen who provide the pensioners their two clean shirts weekly.

But the women's voices are distant and come no nearer; the old man, for his part, clearly doesn't expect them to do so. No doubt this is only one of several bolt-holes he has stumbled upon in his stretch at Greenwich.

He reaches up and pats the buttons of my coat, impatiently, like a child.

I reach inside my coat, down into the long, flat bottom pocket. He watches my hand, and then the tin flask in it, with a pathetic mixture of avidity and suspicion. I place the flask in his outstretched hands, but as he traces the smooth shiny surface, he narrows one blood-streaked eye. "Swear to me now, gentle friend," he whispers, "swear 'tis good red claret. Swear 'tis true French red you have here. None of your slag port."

With a finger under the base of the flask, I urge it to his lips. "French as the Queen's under-breeches, Grandfather."

And then he has it pressed tight to his lips, the eyes squeezed desperately shut, one gulp after another rolling down his gullet. He pulls away at four swallows, runs a hand over his mouth, then smiles dreamily and suddenly stamps his peg. No doubt it has been a year or more since he's drunk anything but the heaviest, sweetest port, or *faux* Bordeaux, cheap English wine mixed with spirits at best, boiled turnip at worst. For a man accustomed to proper French red—and my old canary was Master of Accounts on a trader plying the Channel for years before being pressed into the Navy—there are few fates worse than a steady diet of Methuen portugal. And even that he has been ordered to quit.

"Oh, Christ, but that's lovely, sir." He smacks his lips, meditatively. "And best of all, you know, it don't give you the headache. There's the magic of the French."

"And I may assume you have your notebook and pen, as we discussed?"

He pats his own pocket, before stowing the flask carefully beneath his coat. He gives me the sly wink again, something of a trademark gesture, I begin to see. "That I do. Three good short turkey quills. Nibs I've slit myself, just so, just as I like them."

He seems buoyed suddenly, sharper, more competent. The wine has quickly settled his nerves, and the promise of another flask when he is finished today must be comforting as well. Yet it is not merely the wine, present and future, that has him squaring his rickety shoulders and smoothing back his wild hair like a strolling player. It is the fact that today is palpably different from other days.

Today he is not a cripple and an outcast, but a part of something, and something just a wee bit murky as well. He believes, from a hint dropped here or there, that I am pursuing advantage in a lawsuit through extraordinary means. It has been a good long while since he has had a hand in something murky, after a lifetime of smuggling and cooking a ship's books, and I can see that he relishes the return of the thrill.

More, it is a job that requires his talents with pen and ink, his mind. He may not have penned the dictionary, but my old man can read and write quite capably, and that is more than even most able-bodied men can say. Watching him navigate the broad dormitory hall, perched a bit taller now atop his peg, I have a sense of my own good works today. Not at every moment, and not in every way, of course, but it is a comforting thought just the same.

We are standing just within sight of the landing, in the shade of the Chapel pillars, when James and Johnson come puffing up the slippery landing stairs. It is foolishness, really, to stand out in the open, next to a man dressed all in mustard-yellow, but we are far enough removed—and the crowds sizeable enough—that I take the risk. I must see what James is about to do, has planned for days to do upon lighting at Greenwich, the performance he has already proleptically described in several letters to friends.

When he and Johnson have stepped off the stair and onto the public walk, James goes one pace farther to the well-cropped grass. From his pocket he draws a crisply folded piece of paper. It is a copy of Johnson's "London," a gloomy meditation on English glory, a poem that James adores and knows by heart. He does not need that show copy, believe me. I cannot hear the words now issuing from my brother's mouth, but I know them well enough:

On Thames's banks in silent thought we stood,
Where Greenwich smiles upon the silver flood;
Struck with the seat which gave Eliza birth,
We kneel, and kiss the consecrated earth.

Then, so help me God, James actually gets down on one stout knee, and from there to his hands, among the grass and the mucky dirt. And he lowers himself still further, abases himself still further, face even with the muddy feet of passersby, and kisses the very clods of the earth themselves.

Even knowing James as I do, I would not have believed it if I had not seen it with my own eyes.

Pedestrian traffic does not stop—after all, these are many of them Londoners and used to the odd spectacle—but heads turn, up and down the walk. James finally gets to his feet with obvious glee. Johnson, somehow, looks not embarrassed but modestly approving. This wonderfully spontaneous tribute accomplished, they turn together toward the city, and their first thought—before the Observatory, before a tour of the Hospital—will be of food and drink, generous portions of both.

Altogether predictable, as I say.

And while they are packing their bellies tight again, an amanuensis will be seated neither too close nor too far from them, and he will take down the most minute details of their meal-time banter. James likes to speak of the accuracy of his journal. I intend to show him accuracy, in the representation of this day above all others.

"Go now, Grandfather. Fly to them," I urge my one-legged canary. And after he has done so, while he is making his way with admirable subtlety behind the slow-moving pair, I whistle a snatch of Dibdin's "Ballad of Greenwich." Livelier than Johnson, Dibdin, and nearer the mark:

My precious limb was lopped off—
I, when they'd eased my pain,
Thanked God I was not popped off,
And went to Sea again.

My day is meticulously ordered by the workings of other people's stomachs, and so I have a comfortable slice of time before James and Johnson will leave The Old Ship, the dank little restaurant in Fisher Alley that they have chosen. In that time, there are two places I must go, and the first is the interior of the Chapel itself. Unfortunately, it is far from empty, but the visitors are at least suitably hushed, and by sitting in the pew nearest the pulpit I am able to imagine myself more or less alone with the Lord.

Afternoon light streams in from the twin banks of windows, one atop the other, giving the impression that the Lord is in fact at home. The cinnamon smell I took in at the riverbank is here as well, somehow, as though exhaled by the candles lighting the altar.

I bow my head, and after a moment I thank Him for his most recent gifts.

I thank him for restoring my health, when the doctors at Plymouth had given it up for lost. I thank him for making me whole again, or nearly so. My eyes are shut tightly, and out of nowhere I feel the lids stinging, the hot threat of tears. But I clear my mind for a moment or two, and the sting gradually eases.

Without wishing to take up a great deal of either His time or my own, I detail once again my grudges, and the injuries these two men—one my own brother—have done me. I apologize for threatening to take a kind of violence, a kind of punishment into my own hands. And I swear to use these only as a true last resort, should the two of them persist in what has become their two-man conspiracy to deny my place in their lives.

And I couldn't mean all of this any more deeply and sincerely, I promise you: if they will but acknowledge me to one another—and that seems truly a crumb to insist upon—then I will be worthy of their acknowledgment.

I place my hand on the Book of Common Prayer, and I swear it. And the Lord knows my heart, and I feel distinctly that He approves this means of resolution.

For the Lord God knows that almost never in our two short lives has there been a moment when James and I have not struggled over this precious abstraction, this odd English thing, Samuel Johnson.

I bring the Book to my lips and press them to it tightly.

THE FIRST EDITION of Johnson's *Dictionary of the English Language* was made up of two oversized folio volumes, which our father ordered bound in discreet black calf. It was a monster, the book. For most of my young life I had to ferry the matched volumes about our Edinburgh flat cradled in both my arms, terrified that I would drop them and that a significant number of the things in the world would wink out of existence.

The title page was struck off in black and crimson, I remember, a stirring and weighty sight. The full title was one of the first short poems I ever got by heart: *A Dictionary of the English Language, In Which The Words are deduced from their Originals, And Illustrated in their Different Significations, By Examples from the best Writers, To Which Are Prefixed, A History of the Language, And An English Grammar.* Johnson's own name was stamped beneath in what looked like bright red blood.

The book was shelved, always, never lying out and to hand, as one might expect; my father held Johnson's politics in contempt, and would not give the book the satisfaction. And while James and I were free to consult the two volumes, we understood without being told that my father would be displeased if we were to seem to study them.

How displeased would he have been, had he known that for his sons it quickly became far and away the most crucial and frequently consulted book in the entire library, our common secular bible, our linguistic grimoire?

James was already determined to find his fortune in England, even as a boy, and the *Dictionary* was the earliest means of systematically refashioning himself, into a man of learning rather than of mere precocity, into an Englishman rather than an unclubbable Scot. From the age of fourteen, he and the great book were never far apart, and introducing a Scotticism into his speech became unthinkable, unless directly prodded to it by our father. Most desirable was the acquisition of purely English locutions and slang, sly native bits that might be dropped casually to me in our walks about Edinburgh.

Given that primacy, and given that it was James who nearly always dictated our games, it was inevitable that we would come to play with the *Dictionary,* to compete with the *Dictionary,* and ultimately to beat out one another's brains—if at all possible—with the *Dictionary.* More than swordsmanship, with which we were infatuated, more even than lawn bowls, proficiency in Johnsonian English became the competition *sine qua non* between us.

Between these word matches we watched for quiet moments, when the two volumes were sitting alone in the library, and then we would each shut ourselves up with them, squirreling away strange or impressive or incomprehensibly Latinate words, stocking up on Johnson's own quibbles and qualifications, so that our challenges to one another's choices might bear his stamp. The words marched in two long columns down each page, and our small fingers traced these columns reverently, up and down, stroking the book like a familiar.

Over the years, the word competition evolved and complicated, but the name was always simplicity itself: the Dictionary Game. Sets of unwritten rules crystallized, the first and most important of which was that the game only ever properly began with an insult. An English insult, of course.

We played the Dictionary Game hundreds of times, not including hundreds of fragments of games, but one afternoon I remember more sharply than any other. James was seventeen, I fourteen. I was in our shared bedroom, meandering through a volume of *Sir Charles Grandison,* not the first novel I'd read but the first I had read with my father's active consent. It was near dusk, a trace of late autumn light still floating through the window, my mother and youngest brother off on a visit somewhere, my father still hearing pleas at the Court of Session.

And James ambled in. I suspected, even at the time, that he had just been in my father's study, swotting up on the *Dictionary,* so eager was he to get up a game. Certainly he lost no time.

He came and stood over me, and then abruptly he seized the book from my hand. He read the title, nodded, and then placed it in my grip again. "Ah, Sir Charles. A nice, upstanding moral treatise. Nothing like Mr. Richardson's *Clarissa*. A horrid book, that. Full of dueling and unspeakable acts. Certainly nothing for the fainthearted."

And here he chucked me under the chin, a glint in his eye. "Certainly nothing for a weak-stomached little *nidget* like yourself."

Fighting words—or word, rather. *Nidget*: a coward, a dastard. In fact, my father had refused to allow me to read Richardson's earlier, more interesting novel, and I was still miffed about it. And of course James knew that I was still miffed about it. I tossed the thin volume onto my bed, and we were off.

"Well, it takes a coward to know a coward, James. Proof positive that you are—in point of fact—the true *nithing* here."

"Noodle, then, young puppy."

"Nincompoop."

He pursed his lips, choosing his ammunition carefully. "*Neezer*—that is, one who discharges flatulencies by the nose. And I hasten to add, that in all my circle of acquaintance, I know of none more nasally flatulent than yourself."

I hesitated, for an instant only.

"Come, come, simply declare ignorance if you must, but no delays."

"You give me no chance to speak—*nizy*, then," I shot back.

James wagged a finger. "Tut, tut, little brother. Johnson marks that as a low word, beneath you as a gentleman. Which you might know, if you weren't such a ninnyhammer."

"Far better than to be an errant *nias*, such as yourself."

His plumpish face lighted up, and he actually clapped his hands in delight. "A misuse! Indeed, a true misuse. You introduce an adjective for a noun! Tally one for James! But let us be generous. Let us set you straight if we possibly can. One cannot be *a nias*, John, though a silly fellow—such as yourself—can and will be referred to as *a nias man*. Do you see the distinction? I realize that it is a subtle one, but can you make it out at all?"

Not only was James's memory superior to my own, all our lives long, but he was a far more skillful needler. When he hit just the right tone in his teasing, my rehearsed word lists would fly utterly out of my mind. And though I believed positively that I knew more insulting words beginning with *N*, they temporarily escaped me, and I shifted letters—itself an implicit point for James.

"I apologize, sir, for the error. But surely it does not excuse such *protervity* on your own part."

"You shift letters, Johnnie. Don't think I've not marked it. A proditorious bit of strategy on your part, indeed."

"Pshaw, there was nothing proditorious about it. You grasp at straws."

His countenance was again spread over with glee. "Another clear error! You've simply reintroduced my own P-word, rather than one of your own."

I have one particular smug face, for my own part, that James cannot tolerate under any circumstances. And I presented him with it: "*Pshaw,* brother."

He saw his error, and to counter the smugness he heaped up his polysyllables, and posed a question rather than an insult. Tougher to finesse, if one were uncertain.

"*Pshaw,* indeed. I suppose it is in Johnson—barely. Bravo, my clever little princox, you have been studying your lexicons. You play an anfractuous game today, but not a poor one. With such resources, what say you to setting up as an *oneirocritick*? What say you to that, young Johnnie? To the work of an oneirocritick? Ah, I see you hesitate. You do know the *meaning* of the word, sir? It is the King's English, after all."

I couldn't bring the word to mind, if ever I knew it. And so I went round it. "Truly, you *outknave* yourself with your play today, James."

"You clearly cannot answer my term, but at least you stay within the letter at hand. A half-decent response, I suppose. When you have grown, sirrah, you may yet master this game. When you are not, as now, such a spinny little dandiprat."

I perked up my ears. I had already lost enough points to preclude winning outright, but here were some choice opportunities for needling. And I seized upon them. "Permit me to correct at least a few of your errors, brother." I cleared my throat, grandly. "*Primo,* you switched letters without realizing. *Secundo,* had you given Johnson more than a cursory inspection, you would know that *spinny,* like the majority of the words cluttering your minuscule vocabulary, Johnson cites as a barbarous term. Beneath a gentleman, as you yourself said earlier."

I was well pleased with myself, and I went breezily on to my conclusion. "I must say, sir, I find it truly risible that a young *fub* such as yourself can envision himself moving among the drawing rooms of England, when his speech so clearly marks him for the oyster cellars of Edinburgh."

Brothers show their love by combat, of course, as well as their anger and their jealousies. No fight between brothers is ever undertaken within any one clarified emotion, which is what makes the combat itself so involving, and so painful when it strays invisibly from one expression to the next. And for reasons I might have understood had I stopped to examine them, my few needles sank far deeper into James than I had intended. A rosy flush came to his neck, as it did when he was peeved, and he deliberately—maliciously, it seemed to me at the time—aimed for my own sorest spot.

"Perhaps you have it right, John, and I will remain trapped in Edinburgh my entire life—a fub, as you say. But whatever I am here, I am the *protoplast*—and that is a word you should mark well, little brother—the thing first formed by our parents as a copy to be followed afterwards. I am your original, John, and if I am a chubby Edinburgh fub, then you are destined to be nothing but an inferior copy of something nearly worthless from the start. And never forget it."

With that, he stalked out of the room.

And, as I remember, it was weeks before we played the Dictionary Game again.

9

CENTURIES BEFORE PENSIONERS limped the grounds of the Seamen's Hospital, Plantagenets and Tudors lived very well here in the old Royal Palace, Placentia, nestled within their armories and tilting yards and banqueting halls, and a warren of residences for their staffs and hangers-on. Both Henry VIII and Elizabeth were born and pampered here. But Charles II wanted something both a little newer and a little grander when he returned from exile in France, as monarchs whose fathers have been decapitated tend to do when they eventually reassume the Throne.

And so he did to the old Royal Palace complex what perhaps only a brand-new king could do: he had it demolished, in its entirety, and tipped into the Thames. Not a banqueting hall remains above ground from the days before the Stuarts. Not one timbered ceiling. Not a wall. When he began work on the Royal Hospital, Christopher Wren had the luxury of a well-scrubbed canvas.

But beneath Wren's Queen Anne block, on the eastern side of the Hospital, something survives well below ground, and that is the second spot I must run my eye over while James is feasting and nodding. Just within the entrance arches to the Queen Anne courtyard lies an ancient horse-mounting block. Without this marker, the door to the undercroft might pass unnoticed; the workmen who built the new Hospital structure above ground managed to work the existing stone entrance cleverly into the ripple and flow of their masonry. And in that tiny stone archway they fitted a newish door, of stout oak, with a newish lock.

Fortunately for me, my old man found a way to come at a newish key.

Filching this key was the only part of today's itinerary that shook his courage. He is already under a heavy sentence, as the Hospital's rules go, and he genuinely fears losing his pension altogether. I had to press him hard, and promise to pay him very well, to manage it. I have promised to return the thing to him when I have done with it, and I will do so.

When the outer door is opened, daylight falls upon three lanterns racked on the thick stone retaining wall at the top of the staircase. My canary has made sure that one of these lanterns is lit, and I lift it down. Few visitors know of the undercroft, and traffic to it is very light, but still there are enough curiosity seekers each year to warrant more than a single lantern. Johnson happens to know of this under-cellar from the days he spent living and writing in Greenwich, the years he composed in the Park and drank coffee and nosed out all the riddles of the little city. But Johnson is not the only lover of secret history, and neither is he the only one with the intention of scaring the stuffings out of a companion.

The lamplight moves with me as I drop down the first of two narrow staircases, filling the small space and illuminating the damp brick. With the Thames only a stone's throw away, James I found upon taking the Throne that the timbers of his Great Banqueting Hall were slowly moldering, and so early in his reign he caused a huge vaulted cellar to be built beneath it, stretching from his garden ponds to the Thames itself. The floor was meticulously tiled in clay. In this way the upper structures were kept dry; the ever-present smell of damp in the Banqueting Hall vanished.

And when all other evidence of James and his ancestors had

been scraped into the river like so much rubbish, this undercroft remained. That is all: an under-cellar to keep the wet at bay. One last ignoble remnant of the seat that gave Eliza birth, and, for that reason among others, Johnson has a sentimental attachment to it.

At the base of the stairs, I move out into a vestibule the size of a small wine cellar. But this is clearly meant as entrée to the undercroft-proper, which opens out through an archway to my right. I move through the arch, listening, but there is no sound.

Outside the halo of lamplight, I can sense the vastness of the larger chamber, the space broken only by thin ribs of brick vaulting that flow down into shaped stone pillars at intervals across the tile. The temperature has fallen considerably, so that the sweat at my temples and the back of my neck quickly cools. A perceptible draft moves aimlessly over the tile, as though searching for the water that gave it birth.

A trick of the lamplight renders the march of arches into the gloom infinite, but it can be no more than a few hundred feet long and a hundred feet across.

Still, it is as lightless and silent and cool as the grave, and I know that James will only barely be able to force himself to descend the steps and move out into the center of this space, even beside his imposing hero. His fear of ghosts and death and the dark is profound, and has been since he was a child.

Although Johnson has known my brother for only two months now, he knows this about him well enough, and the insistence that they visit the undercroft together this afternoon carries with it just a hint of exploratory cruelty. But this is all part of what they offer one another. For all his trepidation, James will come here, and he will indeed be afraid; he will marvel openly at Johnson's lack of fear; Johnson will comfort James; James will add that show of compassion to his accumulating mental notes of the day; and in this way they will test and strengthen their odd new complementarity. They will confirm one another in being what they each cannot help but be.

* * *

THERE IS ONE other significant advantage to employing a canary: it is possible to sit atop One Tree Hill, overlooking the town and the river, and follow the pair's progress—from the Old Ship, up through the Park's long scenic tunnel of elm and Spanish chestnut, up to the Royal Observatory—simply by tracking the mote of yellow trailing brilliantly behind. Occasionally, my old man doffs his hat and fans himself briefly, as though he finds the heat oppressive; this bit of semaphore prevents me from confusing him, at a distance, with the handful of other Hospital reprobates in mustard. I am truly impressed with him this day. He is performing flawlessly in his various roles.

At the foot of the Giant's Steps, the canary wheels slowly off and begins the labored process of climbing One Tree Hill, on one good leg, to deliver me his report.

By the time my amanuensis struggles up to me, I am seated on the wooden bench encircling the gnarled trunk that gives the Hill its name. Other than myself, the crown of the hill is deserted, though voices and laughter sift though the trees of the Park below. A small knot of deer are cropping at the edge of the woods behind me, paying me no mind. Town deer, they have been raised to fear no man.

I have my eyes closed, letting the sun bathe my face.

And so I hear the old man clear his throat without seeing him. A smile touches up the corners of my mouth, but this without opening my eyes. It is pleasant to refuse the headlong movement of the day, at least for a few moments, more pleasant than I care to think about. After all, our two quarries will be occupied for a good while with the sextants and quadrants and clocks and the *Domus Obscurata* in the Observatory's garden pavilion. I could almost doze here, almost dream.

I feel the same lethargy I felt on the sculler, the slow fingers of fugue. Finally, the old man scratches carefully at my shoulder, and then again. He has gone too far with things to have me suddenly turn whimsical on him.

"They are a strange pair, are they not," I ask him, eyes still shut. But even as I speak the words, I find myself thinking: *Devonshire junket.* The cinnamon smell in the Greenwich air today puts me in mind of Devonshire junket, covered in a whipped cream touched with rosewater. James and I ate it once, as boys, at Holyroodhouse in Edinburgh. Only once, yet it remains today our common touchstone for both an elegant and a greedy dessert.

"They are that, sir," says the canary. "The big one has his ideas, true enough."

I open my eyes, and he hands me a series of half-sheets, neatly ordered together.

"And this is the stuff of their conversation?"

"The meat of it. With as much of the words themselves as I could put down as they came running. Been a while since I was called to scratch down so much so quick. But I believe I done a neat enough job of it."

"It is the best way to come to know a man, Grandfather. To sample his conversation when he is unaware that it is being sampled. You do not hear truth, but you hear the particular range of fictions he tells his particular listener. And from this you may take your measure of them both."

He is searching my coat with his glance now, for the bulge of the second flask, no doubt. But he realizes that something is expected of him by way of response. And he rises to the occasion.

"So, belike, I have heard say," he puts in sagely, after a moment.

The Old Ship
Saturday 30 July
Just after 1 in the afternoon

Below lie the subjects they covered. The books are saved for their very words, as spoke.

First thing, they called for their lunch, fish and potatoes, bread. Sat at the table furthest to the back. And the littler one said shall we drink wine, and the bigger one said <nay, we shall drink tea now and save our two bottles for the Turk's Head this night.>

Missed something here as I was obliged to call for my own meal. It was but a minute.

The big one remarked as to how he don't like the buildings of the hospital. Not to his taste, because <too detached to make up one great whole.> And he said he thinks the whole lot too grand for a charity hospital. <What have such men to do with palaces and hunting parks and Painted Halls? They have lived aboard ship their entire lives, comfortable in their tiny bunks. One might as well transport a badger to a ballroom. Neither the badger nor the other dancers will long abide the arrangement. Here the pensioners are confronted each hour with the contrast between their battered selves and their brilliant surroundings.> Smaller lodgings in the City better.

The littler one asked, <Should not they be allotted their portion of grandeur, as they have served their King very well?>

Bigger: <A street sweeper serves his King very well also, Sir, but he lies in no palace at night. Believe me, these pensioners would find a boiled chicken and a clean suit of clothes full grand enough, no matter where they were offered.>And, said he, it makes for dependency as well. Turns pensioners almost into children. <Enfeebles those who have been rendered feeble enough by Chance.>

Littler: <True, but Sir, the Bible exhorts us to Charity. We are not to consider the effects, but to obey the exhortation.>

Bigger: Grew peevish at that, loud in his talk, and swung about in chair. <Indeed, Sir, and in Matthew it says Go ye also into the vineyard, and whatsoever is right I will give you. It matters not if a man go early or late to the vineyard, he will be rewarded, but he must go to the vineyard, Sir, for all that. Idling outside the vineyard serves no man. If a sailor has yet one good arm, then let him use it.>

Littler: <But surely if a man is rendered unable by wounds—>
Bigger: Waved hand in the air. <Now do you begin to talk nonsense, Sir.>

Here they fell to their meal, and said nothing for a good while. Bigger one ate as if starved. Didn't take pause to chew, but forked in a new bite while the old was still underway. Veins stood on his forehead as he did so.
Bigger one: <Fish is exceedingly badly dressed>
Littler: <I am just of your mind. Badly dressed, indeed.>

The undercroft is farther across than I had imagined, closer to one hundred and fifty or two hundred feet. I have a sharp moment of uncertainty, as a man might have swimming in the sea at night, when he expects to feel sand grind beneath his toes, yet does not—and then, a moment later, still does not. But it is not much farther, for all of that.

When I reach the far wall, I inspect the moist stone and find precisely what the canary has told me to expect: two short alcoves built into the wall, for wine or coal but empty today, and broom-clean. They are each deep enough for a man to take three paces into them, and I do so, leaving my lantern sitting on the clay tiles of the one farthest from the door.

Then I turn back to the darkness and retrace my steps. Once outside the alcove, and nearer the center of the floor, I turn back:

the alcove looks miraculous, glowing from some indirect source, as though it contained a particle of the Divine.

From One Tree Hill, I watched James and Johnson leave the Observatory and begin their slow saunter back down through the Park. According to James's notes, they plan to tour the undercroft next. Johnson seems to have deliberately designed this part of the tour for later in the afternoon, with evening coming on.

I have perhaps fifteen minutes, then, before the two come clamoring down the stairs behind me, and I use this time to familiarize myself with the vast space of the chamber.

There was a time when, like James, I was deathly afraid of the dark. Growing up together, we were both petrified if a sudden wind snuffed the candles in our flat. It seemed then the breath of something monstrous, something biding its time just outside the corona of light and family. And it was not uncommon for the winds curling up the Edinburgh High Street to wreak their little bit of havoc.

But somehow, in the Plymouth Hospital last year, I shed that fear completely. Now I could spend the day in this lightless chamber and fear nothing. When a man has been disturbed—so that his very sense of himself is laid jaggedly open—and then that man returns abruptly to his senses, he knows forever after that there are worse things than a room without a candle.

The undercroft's five great stone pillars, each the terminus for eight brick ribs spilling elaborately down from the ceiling, are precisely placed. The pattern is the four points of a square, with a fifth pier dropped right into the center of the figure. Otherwise the space is empty. It is so very silent that I can hear my blood course in my ears, and I rehearse the mathematics of the pillars, first walking deliberately with my arms stretched in front of me, and then, when I have my bearings, striding faster and more surely.

If I slip back all the way to the south wall, and rest there with my back against it, the glow of the distant alcove silhouettes the pillars just enough to allow me to run nearly as fast as I am able. The south wall, like the north, has its storage alcove. I remove my shoes and place them snug against the rear wall of it.

This is where I will stand, when the moment comes. As James and Johnson enter the undercroft proper, their lamplight will not reach me here. After an instant, they will mark the glow from the far wall, and they will do what insects and humans in dark places cannot help but do: they will gravitate toward it, across the long tiled floor. Another tourist party, they will imagine, or a guide of some sort. Someone, anyone, with whom they may talk, talk, talk.

When they are far enough across the floor, I will circle behind them, back up the steps, to lock the door from the inside. In my stockings alone I can move very quietly. And then, when they reach the far alcove, they will find the orphaned lantern; they will stand before it, thinking, pondering. And in that instant, I will pad forward into the light and the two parallel branches of the riverine excursion will converge and become one.

I transfer the dags from their fitted pockets beneath my arms to the long outer pockets of my coat. There, if need be, I can keep them in my hands without announcing them. Giving the pillars and brickwork now little more than a cursory thought, I walk back toward the alcove, glowing faintly in the distance. Perhaps ten minutes remain, more than enough time to advance in my reading.

They talked of the possibility of rain in the evening, even during their trip back up the Thames. The littler one seemed put out at the idea, but the bigger one bade him never mind rain should it come. Littler one: <Of course it is good for the vegetable part of the creation.> Bigger one: <Ay sir, and for the animals who eat those vegetables, and for the animals who eat those animals.>

Here they had finished their meal, and sat back with tea cups. Big one put his legs up on the counterpane of the window, as at his ease.

Then the littler began to speak of his own father. Comparing the father to his friend, after a fashion. <You and I, Sir, are very good companions, but my father and I are not so. Now what can occasion this? For you are as old a man as my father, and you are certainly as learned and as knowing.>

Bigger one seemed pleased at that, nodded head, tapped foot. <Sir, I am a man of the world. I live in the world, and I take in some measure of the colour of the world as it moves along. But your father is a judge in a remote part of the country, and all his notions are taken from the old world.>

Littler: <I cannot believe, had you been raised in Scotland, that you would have a narrow manner of thought, Sir. I will not believe that.>

Bigger: <And too, there must be a struggle between father and son, while the one aims at power and the other at independency.>

Littler said that he was afraid his father might force him to pursue a career in the Law. Did not take the exact words, but somehow he feared trickery of some kind on the father's part.

Bigger: <Do not fear. He cannot force you to be a laborious practising lawyer. That is not in his power, even a Judge of the Scottish High Court. One man may lead a horse to water, but twenty cannot make him drink.>

Littler: <I wish you was there with me, when I go down to Scotland. You keep me in mind of my own abilities, where I am too often apt to think myself powerless in contesting against him concerning my future. It is good of you, to take such charge of my education, Sir, to establish my principles. I value the chance to be in your company,

truly. It has been a dream of mine since I was a child, marveling over your Dictionary.>

Bigger: <My dear Boswell! I do love you very much.>

Here they discharged their reckoning. Bigger one cleared a path for them through the traffic in the Old Ship, swinging his stick just a bit to left and right, nudging people out of the way, like a goose girl touching up her flock. No particular mention throughout the meal of the suit at law you spoke of, unless it may possibly be with the gentleman's own father.

10

THE NOISE OF their boots on the stairs is louder than I would have imagined, as are their two voices. Most people would drop to a whisper upon entering such a place, but they continue their chatting, in the *basso forte* voices they have used all day to let the world know their business. They stop at the base of the stairs, still within the outer vestibule, letting the light of their lantern pour into the undercroft proper.

"Great heavens," I hear James say, very distinctly.

Johnson gives a low, knowing chuckle. "Heaven had little to do with it. This was the work of James the First, who would modernize his palace and desiccate his foundations."

"It is the sort of place that makes a man fear for his life, and his soul."

"Come, sir. It is a cold cellar. A man who fears a cellar full of nothing cannot properly call himself a man. And this from you, who have spent this year seeking a commission in His Majesty's Guards?"

"I know it is silly of me. I have never liked a dark place."

"Take hold of your fears, sir, and strangle them in their cradles, before they are grown. The brickwork is in the Tudor style, and well worth the look."

It is at this moment that I hear the door grind open again at the top of the stair, and what sounds like a third pair of boots descending to the first landing. And then a man calls out. The echoes of the stairway distort the voice, but I can make out that he is calling for Doctor Johnson.

Johnson answers, his voice a dull boom that fills the undercroft. "Yes, sir, I am Samuel Johnson. Who might you be, sir?" There is a short pause, as though Johnson's weak eyes were boring in on the newcomer's face in the gloom.

Then his voice booms again. "Mr. Eccles! It is good to see you, sir. I did not expect to see a familiar face today." And to James: "You will remember Mr. Eccles. Davies the bookseller brought him to the Mitre on the night of your supper there."

"I remember Mr. Eccles very well indeed, sir. We spoke together of the wild lonely prospects of Ireland."

The voices carry effortlessly in the quiet. Eccles has concealed his brogue well, but not entirely. "And of Scotland. You have an excellent memory, Mr. Boswell. How odd to see the pair of you, a moment ago, disappearing into that little door! I was passing in my carriage and thought I must have imagined you at first."

"I believe, Mr. Eccles, you are come in answer to my prayers. Mr. Johnson has insisted that I investigate the chamber beyond with him."

"There is little to investigate, sir. It is an old, empty, black hole in the ground, and I believe Mr. Johnson knows it to be so."

Johnson's tone grows just a bit stiff. "I know it to be a portion of Elizabeth's ancestral seat, and I revere it as such."

"I believe a man may revere a thing quite effectively from afar," James adds, a deliberate quaver in his tone, and the other two cannot help but laugh.

Then Eccles says, "Might I make so bold as to propose that the three of us leave this historical cellar, which has little to offer the living, and that we reconvene above ground? I find that my throat is bone-dry after my jaunt, and I should like to share a bottle with the two of you gentlemen above all things, if you haven't any plans for the next hour or so."

There is a decent pause, as the original pair consider the possibility of a third.

Johnson breaks the silence. "What say you, Mr. Boswell? We might drink one of our two bottles now, and still have another to our credit tonight, at the Turk's Head."

"You have read my mind, sir."

"Then it is settled," says Eccles.

"You have saved me, Mr. Eccles! Bless you. I shall never forget it."

"Do not encourage him in this, Eccles." There is a unmistakably stern note now in Johnson's voice. "He would make sport of it, but these irrational fears are unworthy of a man of sense and a gentleman. They mark a flaw in character. He should master them. I have a good mind to drag him back down here when we have finished our bottle."

"A point well taken, I am sure."

With that, the three of them begin the climb back up the narrow stairs, dust scraping beneath their boots. Seconds later, the door swings shut. There is a barely audible scratch as the key turns, and the tumblers fall in the lock. Then only silence, and the feel of the sourceless draft brushing my cheek.

The capillary action of disaster. And my most elaborate design is at an end.

I step out of the alcove, in my stocking feet, darkness all about me, and honestly do not know whether to laugh out loud, or to weep. For the first time today, I feel truly alone. Like a nasty game of hide and go seek, in which all of the older children simply run home once the counting has begun.

Before I realize what I have done, I've swung my fist at the stone wall with nearly all of my might, and then, before the pain of the impact can wash entirely through me, I have swung again nearly as hard. Something crackles in the bones of my knuckles.

From bright pain, the right hand sinks almost immediately into throbbing numbness, and I suck the blood from my knuckles. One of them feels splintered to my tongue, or even sunk back into the hand itself. After a long moment, I step back into my boots, but the hand is curled and lacing them is difficult.

Finally, I am forced to sit down in the dust and force my way through the process like a boy of four, lace by lace, eyelet by eyelet, all of this by touch alone.

And as I sit there, trying desperately to manipulate these simple strings, a thought comes to me, a series of thoughts really. It is as close to frightening myself with my own imaginings as I have come today.

Perhaps these events in Greenwich show more than the rushing waters of chaos and chance. Perhaps my brother is right, and he is watched and doted over, protected, preferred. Perhaps the Lord Himself put the spyglasses in James's hand this morning, so that James might see beyond his mortal abilities.

Is it possible for one man to be opposed so actively by the Lord, and never know it? And for his brother to be watched over and yet similarly unaware? And is this the same whimsically cruel Hand that directs madness to strike here in a family, and then to skip a generation, or two or three or none at all, before striking there?

My father never mentioned his own younger brother, my Uncle James. It was my mother who told my brother James and myself about his illness, on the condition that we never retail the story outside the flat. And I remember very clearly the way she hesitated and slit her eyes as she whispered the phrase *strait-waistcoat.* I had no context for the words, and I brought to mind a more or less everyday man's waistcoat. A decently tailored garment, though certainly with cunning buckles, for I understood that once in one, it was all a man could do to get himself out.

It was only as one was actually being fitted about me in the

Plymouth Hospital that I finally made the connection: this drapery of canvas and leather, with its coppery smell of sweat and hate, this loose assemblage that suddenly drew tight enough to strain my arms in their sockets—this was my uncle's particular cut of waistcoat.

And I am not proud to say that the realization threw me into a raving fit worse than anything I've ever experienced, and the doctors locked the door and let me careen around in the darkness until I'd made my peace with it.

A peace not quickly reached, however. The rough leather collar of the coat was joined to a leather crown with thickish straps; it held my head and my neck all but immobile, and more than anything it was that headgear that incited the thing inside me. Wild things will bear leashes, but never a muzzle. And so it made me twist my head back and forth, back and forth, for hours on end, blood from beneath the forehead strap finally speckling and smearing my knees. The better part of three days I wrestled.

But finally there was nothing to be done. If you look hard at an image of such a waistcoat, you'll see that restraining a man is not its only function. As much as anything else, it is designed to force a man to struggle with himself. His fight is all directed inward by the canvas. And perhaps that struggle is healthy in most cases. But not so in mine, not when all was said and done. The thing inside me wanted out every bit as much as I, and finally it was willing to bargain. And so rather than expel it or vanquish it, I treated with it.

For it had a new argument to make, in addition to the old grievances: while the doctors had told me that the strait-waistcoat would not be removed under any circumstances, another inmate across the way whispered that it was indeed possible, if a man's family came and demanded it, raised the Devil about it, and especially if a man's family had money. *And so where is your father?* the thing asked. *Where is your loving brother James? Why do they not exert themselves?*

It was an argument that became more compelling each week, for

I knew that James was merely in London, begging a commission. Father had cases to hear, but James had only his own weak case to make, and might have left off at any moment.

And so we haggled, away inside myself. I wanted to walk out of Plymouth, to all appearances cured. I wanted the thing where I could manage it somehow. I wanted to be able to go on about the business of my life. It wanted to visit James in London, to show me finally what he was, and was not. Fair enough, then.

Gil Higgs is still waiting, wrapped miserably in a cloak, nearly an hour past nightfall, when I reach the lower landing where his sculler has been tied up these last five or six hours. I imagine he has resolved to cast off twenty times today, and then rehearsed for himself twenty times over the reasons why it might be safer to wait. Rain is now threatening, and the wind has gone cold. Higgs has extended the green woolen canopy forward, to keep the coming rain off his own naked head as well as mine. We will share that little tent all the long way home, I see.

"They will slide by in a moment," I say softly when I have taken my seat. Higgs notices my bloodied knuckles, but does not reply, simply turns to watch the water.

We wait, three minutes, four, and then their oarsman moves them slowly by us, putting out into the current. Their sculler has a lantern fixed in the stern, making it easy to mark, easy to follow. I nod, and Higgs moves us out as well. His relief at pushing off toward home is all but palpable. I have returned my canary his precious key, and settled my accounts generously with him. No one may say that I have taken out my own disappointments on my good, biddable old man.

While Greenwich was the most meticulously drawn of my blueprints for the day, it is not my one and only, by a long shot. I am certainly prepared for the Turk's Head as well. But it is a longer, colder journey back up the river—a shivering cold after the day's heat—and reviewing those preparations in my mind occupies only a portion of it.

Then there is nothing left but to try to stay warm, and to watch the occasional spray of lights upon the shore, as we drift past an estate or a shipworks or a brewery. Nothing left but to tell over and over again—like a rosary worn smooth or the last few pence in an empty pocket—the moments of happiness I have been vouchsafed by the City. Of this handful, there is one remembrance I treasure above all others, to the extent that I ration my indulgence in it, for fear it will thin and go threadbare somehow. I pull it out only when the wet and the dark become insupportable.

For it is my own first London meeting with Johnson. As James will lavishly mark the 16th of May until the day he dies—the day he finally made the great man's acquaintance at the home of a bookseller—I will silently mark the 21st, my own moment of commemoration.

My own particular day in May.

PRECISELY HOW JAMES met Johnson, you well know—for it is known. James has taken no chances there. His memories of that meeting he scribbled down immediately and treasured up in his journal. My older brother has always been horrified of the light-less places in his own mind; he has always looked upon a gap in his memories as the thumbprint of mortality. And so as James sees it, the more he remembers, the more he lives, and the less he allows himself to die. But anyone who believes that his own memory lies in his own hands is worse than a fool: he is a dangerous fool. For he will begin to insist that his own version of events remain not merely his own, but become all the world's as well.

My own memory is not nearly so obliging, and I have devised no systems to compel it. Since leaving the Plymouth Hospital, I have embraced the absent places in my own mind, with mostly quite satisfactory results.

It is not unlike a progress by Hogarth, this new memory of mine: the six or eight engravings gradually tell a composite story, but one marked by unavoidable gaps in time. And yet the viewer does not experience those gaps as destructive of the narrative, but constructive, rather.

In the first panel of Hogarth's *Harlot's Progress,* for example, Moll Hackabout is fresh from the country, clean of dress, carrying a gift of a dead goose in a basket for her London relations. Of course, the London relations have forgotten her, and she is left alone at the station, where she falls prey to the Bawd. That is where Hogarth stops the action of his first panel, just as the hand of the Bawd is about to stroke the cheek of the virgin. Just before the touch that will seal her fate.

Yet by the second panel, the pox has already marked the virgin's face, and she is now more than shrewd enough to cuckold her elderly keeper.

Between those two images lie events more shocking than Hogarth could bring himself to represent, and yet those events are not lost, for they are indelible. They are understood, and palpable in logic.

IT IS MAY the 21st. I am walking down a hill, and my memory of it is sharp and bright as a straight razor because it is a hill I walk most every day now: Fish Street Hill, sloping down gently to the Bridge. I walk on the west side of the street, the better to see the Monument to the Great Fire, thrusting up two hundred feet into the black sky, over the carriages and fish-sellers passing beneath.

Why am I walking to London Bridge? Because there are days when the fish stink on the Hill—and the borrowed fish stink wafting down from Billingsgate—accumulates and seeps into my room at the Starr Inn and makes me remember that my room has no windows. And I will slowly begin to suffocate. My eyes will begin to water. The air thick with fish: dead, alive, spoiled, fresh, but fish.

And on those nights, when the sun is three hours down and the

Bridge's lamps a dull yellow phosphorescent string away over the water, I will walk out onto the Bridge simply to feel the air moving over me. Of course, that wind over the bridge brings its own stink, but at least it is air in motion. Although it smells of fish now, and smelled of fish yesterday, there is just a chance that the wind may not smell of fish tomorrow.

Sometimes I walk the length of the bridge and back again, eight or ten times in the lamplit dark, before I feel I can return to my room with no windows.

The City expanded London Bridge only recently, both above and below. Now it is wide indeed—well above forty feet—a thoroughfare in size and aspect. And like a street it has its own rights of way, and things that may or may not be done.

For instance, at regular intervals, large hooded stone alcoves rise up over the railings, and in these alcoves are nearly always men of one sort or another, watching passersby, or matching pennies, or sipping gin with an eye out for the Watch.

It is best not to walk too close to these alcoves, but if one must, it is best to avert one's eyes. Some of the alcoves contain beggars rolled in cast-off wool, some contain footpads, and some men and women looking for a place to fumble with their clothing and exchange money out of the light.

And some contain decent men seeking nothing more than a minute's peace. The paradox, of course, is that one can only know which is which by drawing close to an alcove and peering within. And then, as often as not, it is too late.

So it is best to walk as near the center of the bridge as one may without being run down by the occasional carriage crashing through the quiet and the dark.

But on this particular night in my memory, as I am walking along and as I approach the south end of the Bridge, I do look into an alcove, and I do see a man sitting quietly and alone on the stone bench that rings the interior.

Why I have looked into this alcove and no other, I cannot say. Because here is where my memories begin to find their connectivity through logic and intuition alone.

It is dark in the alcove, and this man I cannot see distinctly. But he is there, and he means me no harm.

And then, in the next instant, I am not walking south on the bridge, but north, back toward the Starr Inn, and this man is walking at my side.

How he is walking beside me is important, and here again my memory is brilliantly clear. He does not walk as near as a friend, nor beyond arm's length, as would a stranger. He walks slowly, just away off my elbow, his breath audible and deep, with a touch of a rasp, an occasional, periodic clearing of the throat. It is perfectly evident to me that we are walking by mutual agreement, and I am just a touch in the lead because the agreement is that I will take this man somewhere.

And because I then lead him across the Bridge and up Fish Street Hill, through the Starr's entranceway, between its stables, and across the smutty courtyard to my tiny room, I can only surmise that this is what I have agreed to do.

The why is unknown, but there may be many reasons for my doing what I am doing. Perhaps the man off my elbow is a countryman who has not eaten in days, a Scot denied any basic English comfort. Perhaps he is a soldier I have recognized from my regiment, a familiar face picked out in the gloom.

Suffice it to say that there are reasons, and I am confident of them as I walk. The man is no stranger, this man beside me.

Only in my room, with the door closed and the man seated before me at the flimsy table, do I realize who it is I have befriended. The wick takes flame, and the face can suddenly hold nothing back: it is Samuel Johnson.

I know it is Johnson, because I have seen engravings of his face since I was a boy. I know it is Johnson because he has been pointed out to me on the street, and once the previous week—after I found out that James had begun to socialize with the man—I trailed Johnson from a coffeehouse to his lodgings in the Temple.

It is he, and no doubt: the large, pointed, shrewd nose, the brooding lips, and dark, arching brows over eyes that look bruised with fatigue. A gargoyle's features, fleshy, piercing, mutton-fed. Eyes that have been strained over a book until they are a sad, cloudy brown.

It is he: the marks of the King's Evil, the wig worn carelessly and out of fashion. The hand occasionally trembling, the shoulders moving, as though beyond his control.

We drink a glass of wine at the table, and this seems to calm his hands. His voice begins to come deep and strong, untroubled by the tics and gutturals that punctuated his first few sentences.

The drinking itself is not what has been agreed upon, however, and we are sitting at the table still only because a question has been asked and not yet answered somehow.

But my last memory of that first meeting—the last engraving in the sequence—is this: the candle is out, sending the smell of fire curling through the room, and I have pulled off my clothes down to my linen. I am lying in my small bed, the coverlet drawn up over my chest. Near my sitting chair, I hear Johnson removing his own coat and shirt and shoes; and then the planks of the cot creak, and he is lying beside me in the dark. Without hesitation, his arms come around me, and there we lie, together. He pats my hair with a heavy hand, the way one reassures oneself that a strange dog is friendly after all, and then the big arms lock around me once more.

And that is all.

I fall to sleep in his arms, and there is none of the sudden insistent hunger of Gentleman, none of that sort of satisfaction, although I have half-suspected all along that this was the question unanswered, that this was the understanding reached somehow in the stone alcove on the Bridge.

No, Johnson lies with his arms about me, protectively so, and he and I fall eventually to sleep. Quietly, easily, contentedly. And there is nothing strange in the feeling at all.

My brother has been afraid of ghosts and spirits all his life, for instance; and to this day, if he attends a public hanging or if an acquaintance dies abruptly, he will show up at the home of a close friend and ask to share his bed. Because he cannot bear to be alone. Because he is afraid. Because there may in fact be ghosts, for all James knows. Idiosyncratic, but not so very strange for all that.

And so maybe that is all there is to it, I tell myself. Maybe Johnson and I are two men who have seen enough of London to know that more than a few of its spirits are restless, and we would have one another's company through the small hours. For although we are strangers in one way, in another I have known him well for most of my reading life.

One thing is certain: this first time is not the last time that I will meet him on the Bridge, nor the last time he will share my bed. But never will there be anything more to it than this, this warmth, this safety and this contentment.

This chastity.

PART FOUR

All Hail the Lord of Misrule

5 January 1763

I was agreeably surprised at breakfast with the arrival of my brother John in good health and spirits, although he had been for three months lately in a most terrible way. I walked with him in the Park. He talked sensibly and well.

I then went to Lady Betty's. I was rather in the low-spirited humour still. She was by herself. I talked of my schemes. I owned my unsettled views, which indeed are only so at times, as I have preserved almost an uninterrupted constancy to the Guards. She asked me to dine. I told her I now had money to support me till Friday, was not obliged by a dinner, and therefore would come. I went and had some elegant conversation with Louisa; told her all was fixed for Saturday. She sweetly acquiesced. I like her better and better every day.

—From *Boswell's London Journal, 1762–1763*

London, England
Friday, the 24th of December, 1762
9:17 A.M.

* * * * * *

11

THE WINTER SUN has been shimmering weakly behind the curtains for the last hour or so, but what brings the drowsing twenty-two-year-old James Boswell suddenly alert is the conviction that someone or something is watching him. How he knows this, he has no idea; his eyes have yet to open, and he hears nothing out of the ordinary, a bird cooing beyond the glass, Downing Street two pair of stairs below his window. But the feeling has now flowered into certainty. And there is no way around the inference that this observer must be positioned somewhere inside his own bedchamber.

From his prone perspective, peering down the length of his bed, Boswell can see his own stout shape obscured by three blankets and the bed's dull red moreen cover. Beyond that—framed by the posts of the bedstead—the door to his chamber stands inexplicably ajar. His left leg has escaped the blankets and now dangles in the chill air.

And Boswell can make out something else hovering just at the level of that leg: the white ordinary cap of his landlord's maid, Molly. For a long instant the cap does not move; then slowly it tilts, as though the wearer were bettering her angle on something strange or confusing.

Boswell remains motionless, but eventually he realizes that Molly—a somewhat prim, church-going Londoner in her early fifties—can only be squatted down on her haunches, three or four feet from his bedside, staring at his ankle.

He has a good idea what she is looking at, and, as it happens to be something he has always preferred remain unseen, Boswell yanks the leg suddenly back under the covers. Molly gives a little cry, before scuttling backward out of the room almost faster than his eye can follow. Only when she is upright and safely in the parlor does she call back through the open door: "*So sorry,* sir. But I—the door was standing open, y'see."

He closes his eyes again. "How came the door to be open then, Molly?"

"That I'm sure I don't know, sir."

Boswell suspects that he himself failed to shut the door before retiring; he was up very late the night before, composing a series of long memoranda to himself about today's events. At one point, he lay down to catch a half hour's nap and apparently slept like a stone through the night. He says nothing of this to Molly, however. Since Boswell took these rooms a month and a half ago, Mr. Terrie's maid has managed silently each morning to communicate an air of mild disapproval. But there is a delicious reversal somehow in their situations this morning, and Boswell is inclined to protract the moment.

"Molly, you may rest assured I will tell no one about this morning," Boswell pauses delicately, "your coming into my bedchamber. It shall remain just an amusing story between ourselves. Never a word to Mr. Terrie on the subject. You have my Christmas Eve morning promise, Molly."

The maid pulls the door quickly closed without so much as a parting look, and Boswell falls back to savor his favorite slice of the day. But this morning, before sinking back into the pillows, he is moved to throw back the covers and haul out the leg in question again. He takes his thick ankle in his hand and brings it up into the morning light falling through the window.

There, in the tender skin just above his heel, just below the hollow at his outer ankle-bone and just inside his Achilles' tendon, placed with remarkable precision, are the tiny black strokes, now more than seven years old. The wounds themselves healed long ago, and the dark marks have taken on a dull muted look, as his body has gradually come to terms with the ink.

In the tender hollow at the outer ankle-bone of his left leg, Boswell carries one word of two letters: NO.

IN A ROUNDABOUT way, the word inked onto Boswell's ankle is the fruit of his first nervous breakdown, ten years ago, when he was twelve. He awoke in his Edinburgh bed that morning to find that he hadn't the energy to rise—neither the physical energy nor the spiritual. He felt as though he would prefer to die, and said so. His younger brother John finally burst into tears and ran for their parents.

The doctors found a rash around both his ankles. Boswell was diagnosed with an overtaxed constitution and packed off to the spa town of Moffat to take the waters for six weeks.

Moffat proved to be a border town of 1,500 inhabitants, the size of a watch fob to an Edinburgh boy, its primary spring housed in a tiny stone hut surrounded by a great lot of rural nothing. Visitors had to walk the long dirty Well Road up into the hills, and then scramble up and down the steep banks of the Hindsgill to take the waters.

But the boy James was too enervated to scramble. He spent his first afternoon in town lying across a stiff narrow bed, head throbbing, while the Reverend John Dun, his tutor, saw to his own carefree business about town.

The dull weight in his head was enough, over the course of two days, to make James flirt with the idea of suicide. In his darkened room, he made God a series of desperate offers, to join the clergy, to eat a meatless diet, to build a showy new chapel when he should inherit his father's estate. He offered finally, on his third night there in Moffat, just before collapsing into sleep, his chastity.

And the next morning something miraculous occurred: for the first time, he felt strong enough to hike to the well, and within two days his depression had lifted and melted entirely away. The scurf vanished magically from his ankles.

His relief gave him a sunny social energy he had never known, and within a week Boswell had become the pampered favorite of the young married set in Moffat, with an open invitation to their high teas and low whist tables. Several of the men had made their new money in coal, and their wives were well dressed and bored. Boswell, with his Edinburgh manners, became their prodigy. It didn't matter that he was a child by comparison; he could make these fashionable adults laugh out loud, and occasionally nudge an angry husband back to a sulking wife. He found that he could read all of their interwoven emotions for him and for one another like a penny pamphlet.

Only later, during the ensuing years, did it dawn on him that not everyone could read these sorts of penny pamphlets, that he was somehow emotionally literate in ways that others were not. That this quality made it easy for him to step through the scrim of people's words into the actualities of their feelings. And that this in turn could make some genuine brand of intimacy available in hours, rather than years.

That he had a gift, a gift to counteract the family curse of hypochondria.

And so when the chaise finally rolled out of Moffat, the six-week cure an astounding success, he understood with perfect clarity that God had upheld His end of the bargain. Boswell returned to Parliament Square and set about upholding his own vow, but by his sixteenth birthday he was doing so with greater and greater effort.

He wrote himself increasingly long, stern letters—furious exhortations—but by almost inverse proportions the documents seemed less and less effective. And then, just as the stern notes threatened to become completely useless, he discovered a new form of writing altogether.

He was strolling down the Leith Walk in Edinburgh, killing time, in what he called his See-Everything Suit: a jumble of discarded caddy's clothing he'd put together for himself at fifteen, a disguise to allow him to go out into the city and see all of the things that fail to happen when a man of quality happens near. The Leith Walk had been of interest to him for months, with its odd shops and nearby gibbet, the Gallow Lee.

In the doorway of a tiny wonder-shop, beside a window full of stuffed squirrels and a live parrot, stood a bald bronze-skinned man, arms crossed over his chest. Boswell noticed as he passed that one of the hairy hands bore the image of a thistle. It was artfully done, the plant's stiff leaves shaded like a fine print.

The shop owner begrudged a smile and put out his hand, and it was only then that it occurred to Boswell that the ink was not *on* the hand, but *in* it.

"'Tis very old Scots, this sort o' pouncing o' the skin," the man said, tapping the thistle, "a thing from the *pechts* in the Highlands. There's folks still know the skeel, where I come frae."

Boswell had heard stories about painted men, but on faraway islands, or brought like tame animal acts through London, not keeping shop on the Leith.

"How much does it hurt?" he asked.

"Like bein' roasted alive."

"Can a man have a word, rather than a thing?"

"Have the Bible itself, ye like."

"How long will it last?"

"Till the Devil gives ye yer dixie."

It took three more shilly-shallying visits to the wonder-shop, a Wednesday afternoon and two Saturday mornings, but there was never any chance that Boswell would decide not to do this thing, now that he knew it could be done.

Of course, he worried obsessively over the details—if discovered, this was something that would shock his family and friends—and he narrowed his message, REMEMBER YOUR VOW OF CHASTITY, to the single word CHASTITY.

When it became clear that even a single word with eight letters would be far too visible for comfort, he'd sweated his entire text down into two letters, maybe six strokes of the pouncing tool. And that was how he finally found himself in the wonder-shop one morning in late September, chilly rain puddling the holes scattered over the Leith, left foot propped on a display case as the shopkeeper briefly scourged his flesh.

It hurt much more than a pinprick, and much less than being burned alive.

It was just enough pain, in fact, to allow Boswell to favor his left leg all the way back up the Edinburgh High Street home to Parliament Square. He favored the foot affectionately, carrying it home in the rain, and he would dress the wound in secret for the next two and a half weeks. Not until May 1791, on the twenty-eighth anniversary of his meeting with Samuel Johnson, when he first held a bound two-quarto set of *The Life of Johnson* in his own hands, would any fragment of his own composition manage to wedge itself closer to his heart.

And yet, set even into his very flesh, the vow had proved shockingly easy to throw over. The shopkeeper's ink bought him three years, no more.

At nineteen, he'd met an Edinburgh actress named Mrs. Cowper, a Catholic actress, and flirted with the possibility of a secret marriage. His father had somehow sensed the thing brewing, though, and abruptly sent Boswell to finish his schooling in Glasgow, a grimmer city by far, where they took their laws against the theater seriously.

It was only a matter of weeks before he reached his breaking point. On a clear night in early March, he fled to London on horseback, intent on converting to Roman Catholicism. Boswell saw mass celebrated there for the first time, and the spectacle of it brought actual tears to his eyes. It was a height of devotion such as he had never known.

But just two nights later, as though he had no true conscious control over the legs carrying him along, Boswell found himself contacting a friend of his Edinburgh friend Gentleman: one Samuel Derrick. Derrick was a would-be playwright who knew the subtler twists and turns of London after dark.

And, not incidentally, Derrick also knew where Boswell might try this thing he had worked so assiduously to avoid trying for the past seven and a half years.

That was how Boswell found himself at twenty years of age in a cold room at the Blue Periwig, Southampton Street, Strand, cradled expertly between the legs of a young girl named Sally Forrester, a sweet freckled unhurried sort whose skin was pale but whose hair and brows and nipples were all the color of rain-soaked shale.

When the frenzy was over and Boswell lay [illegible] back, Sally Forrester burrowed immediately into his side for sleep with a wife-like intimacy. He lay there with his arm around her, dumb with amazement: he hadn't thought even once of the chastity vow, from the time Derrick had squired him down the Strand to the moment he'd poured himself helplessly into this creature dozing beside him.

That was what he marveled over, when all was said and done. Not the sheer impact of female nakedness, though that was more powerful even than he had expected. No, what he came back to over and again was this newly revealed capacity of his own mind: to obtain its desires by damping and shaping awareness itself.

It frightened and impressed him simultaneously to think of it. Still, he was certain he had felt the force of the Divine in his desire for Sally. There had been something heartbreaking and holy in the spray of freckles across her chest, the shell of her ear.

And if in fact, this new sensuality was itself somehow a part of

God's design, then God had proven Himself a far more understanding and loving Father than Boswell had ever dared to hope.

Boswell had returned to Edinburgh that June with a reluctance so great it was only just distinguishable from outright refusal. With him, however, the young man brought a plan of action: to secure a commission in the King's Guards and spend the rest of his life in a red coat, as a gentleman–soldier and a Londoner, writing and romancing and defending the Capital from non-existent armies.

BOSWELL HAS PULLED on his clothes for the early part of the day—loose and easy, hair not yet tied up, breeches not yet tied down—and has rung the dining-room bell to let Molly know that he is prepared now for his tea and toast. This breakfast Molly delivers, and Boswell thanks her with a nod. The ankle remains unspoken between them.

Alone in the dining room, as he dunks crusts one after the other into his milky tea, Boswell hums to himself and completes a sort of idle self-inventory that marks his first hour of consciousness each morning. Since childhood, James Boswell has come out of sleep the way a wealthy man exits a thick crowd: patting his various pockets of memory, to see if they've been picked. This morning he has been thinking of chastity, in part because of the plans already in motion with Louisa for later this morning.

Today is a critical juncture not just in his pursuit of Louisa, but in his pursuit of a commission in the King's Guards—so critical, in fact, that he has left nothing to chance in the planning. First cup of tea finished, his hand goes instinctively to his waistcoat.

The waistcoat pocket is surprisingly deep, and Boswell's thickish fingers have to navigate familiar clutter—broken peppermints, a torn concert ticket, a snapped watch fob, itself containing a fragment of a uniform stained with what the schoolmate selling it swore was the blood of Bonnie Prince Charlie himself—before locating the first of the two memoranda he wrote for himself prior to climbing into bed last night.

He has a habit of scribbling himself quick little instructions each night, to be read the next morning; but as this is no ordinary day, the first memorandum is no quick scribble. The octavo page has been so intricately folded that it feels to his fingers like a small square of pasteboard. He hauls it up through the trifles and unfolds it. And then the note begins to speak to him:

Breakfast alone, and enjoy English jam. These twenty-four hours may well decide the three grand enterprises you set in motion weeks ago. 'Tis now time to carry them smartly to conclusion.

Enterprise the First: After breakfast, dress in Bath coat and old grey suit and stick; to Park, walk the Parade. Think seriously on what it means to soldier. Then sally to Louisa just as a free-spirited blade, but speak calmly, of poetry and the Scriptures. Above all, be warm with her, press her home. Today, today [illegible] *you blessed. Never again in the history of this world will there be another morning such as this, etc.*

Enterprise the Second: Take your dinner in Holburn, at cheesemongers, neat and quiet out of public notice. Then return home, dress in new pink suit. Use money saved on victuals to take sedan chair to Northumberland House. Savour this ride; consider that you are borne to the House of the noble Percy, for a private party of but twenty-five picked people to which you are now weekly invited. This marks you as a favourite. Be comfortable, yet genteel. Speak slowly, distinctly, best fine English only. There will be two there who can grease your commission. Push fair with both. You deserve to be a soldier, and you deserve to live in London. The Guards offer you all.

Enterprise the Third: Tomorrow you will at long last meet the great Samuel Johnson. See second note, other pocket, for particular instructions.

Boswell refolds the page, slipping the edges each cunningly inside the other, re-pockets the resulting square. He will check the memorandum six or seven times more during the day, but his satisfaction with it will never be as encompassing and profound as it is just now. Reading it gives him the sensation that someone is watching out for him, actively authoring the Boswell he has determined to be, and that—as good luck would have it—this someone is himself.

Boswell looks out at the chancy winter sky over Downing Street and feels that he is precisely, to the quarter-inch, where he should be. He heaves a contented sigh, and it feels so good that he immediately heaves another.

FIFTEEN MINUTES LATER, wearing the Bath coat and grey suit, and walking the stick he has directed himself to carry, Boswell strolls out his landlord's front door and heads up Downing to Parliament Street. There is always a delicious frisson of *recognition* associated with living out each day as he has pre-planned it, particularly in the early morning, before the day has inserted its own cumulative realities.

After a short two blocks, he hooks sharply left, and the Parade Grounds open up to the west. As always, Boswell feels a martial swelling in his heart when he looks out over the playground of the king's own Horse Guards.

Boswell paces to the very center of the large packed-earth space and stands erect. Slowly, he closes his eyes and tries his best—for a full twenty or thirty seconds—to seriously consider what it means to soldier. As he has done since childhood, Boswell imagines the violent day in 1513 when his ancestor Thomas Boswell died defending James IV at Flodden. In his imagination, the battle is always engulfed in a driving rain, cannon fire echoes, and Thomas Boswell fights thigh-deep in muck, giving no quarter, never surrendering, a cry torn from his lips, lifeless body falling finally between the enemy and his Sovereign.

Boswell opens his eyes. City life rumbles on about him.

Suddenly Boswell flexes his own stout upper body inside his coat, enjoying the answering tightness of his muscles. The winter air is bracing, and a part of him wants nothing more than to run screaming down a hillside, rain wetting his face. He wants to brandish a sword, charge an enemy, open throats, save a king.

He feels vital enough this morning to tear his stockings by flexing his calves.

12

Louisa's living situation has been thoughtfully and delicately put together, and Boswell never fails to appreciate it when he makes his now-daily visits to King Street. Her landlady, a very plump, quiet woman purported to be hard of hearing—but who has seemed in fact to hear perfectly well the several times Boswell has met her—lives up two flights of stairs. Louisa has one small room in this same flat, where she dines and reads, but takes two additional rooms up another small half-flight of stairs to the back of the building, where she sits with company and takes her rest.

Technically, the two ladies live together, protecting one another's good names; practically speaking, Louisa is a handsome, once-married, now-amicably-separated Covent Garden actress with an independent existence, as Boswell likes to sum it up.

At a little after eleven, he climbs the narrow stairs to the flat, and the maid walks him through the cramped lower floor of the flat to the private back stair. At the top of the stair stands Louisa, and Boswell stares up at her with a momentary helplessness.

She has apparently just come from an appointment, or a walk in the Park of her own: rather than the wadded morning dresses he has become accustomed to seeing, she wears a yellow satin gown, substantially hooped, and a small black cape still hanging from her hand. Never has she looked more stylish, more of the city of London, and Boswell feels a quick, disquieting flutter of self-doubt.

"Do come up, Mr. Boswell. It is good of you to stop in. You will never guess my news," she says, when he has reached the top of the stairs. "I've just come from the managers of the theater, and they talk of bringing me into the lead this coming year."

"It is too long in coming," Boswell says, kissing her hand, "should it happen today, Mrs. Lewis."

Louisa nods. "A compliment very much appreciated. I knew there was some reason I invited you to tea." Her fingers brush his arm to punctuate the joke, and the sensation stays with him when the fingers are removed.

She smiles and quickly searches his face, then his eyes, one after the other, as though for flaws. He cannot but examine her own face in return: the very dark brows framing intensely dark eyes, and the fine aquiline nose. Between the snapping eyes and the wry mouth, she gives Boswell the odd impression that she has known and been furious with him in the long-distant past, but has recently begun to exchange the anger for amusement. Her skin is fair and healthy, a girl's skin still, perhaps twenty-five at the outside. He smells roses and lemons, suspects even the darker hint of jasmine.

And the expanse of pale skin now visible above the satin bodice of her dress—here in the early dead of winter, when London has piled on all of its infinite coats and wraps—hits Boswell like a cudgel-blow.

"I am delighted to hear your news," Boswell begins, and Louisa's expression brightens at the mention of it, "and delighted to know that I am taking tea this morning with such a rapidly rising star."

She waves a hand. "Please do take it with a grain of salt, Mr. Boswell. The managers did not say anything absolutely. Still, I am glad to know they value me enough even to promise by halves."

"Of course, I am happy both for you, and for myself."

"Oh? And why so, sir?"

"As it makes me feel your intimate acquaintance, to share in it."

Louisa nods. "I hope we are intimate in that way, just to share our triumphs and our small troubles alike."

Boswell smiles but cannot avoid the memory of the previous Monday. He had come to Louisa's directly after breakfast, only to find her in a transparently bad humor: a tradesman had sent to her for a trifling back debt, and she had applied in turn to a close friend for a loan, only to be shifted. Boswell insisted on knowing the amount she needed and then, when he found to his delight that it was only two guineas, loaned her the money himself.

He'd been ecstatic at first to come in some small way to her rescue, but in the days following he has found himself wondering, replaying the situation in his mind. Was the whole scene manufactured, merely an artful way for money to change hands? To have the income of a courtesan without necessarily admitting it, even to herself?

"Our triumphs and our troubles—exactly," Boswell continues. "London has held everything for me but that since I arrived, that sense of having a place to share one's thoughts with an understanding woman. You take my meaning, I hope."

He sees that she is listening complacently, and instinctively he tries another, deeper key. "I look forward to the married state for that reason perhaps above all."

Louisa—who has been, and remains married in law—gives a small laugh and shakes her head sharply. She is suddenly animated. "You must be careful there, Mr. Boswell. You show your naïveté there, I'm afraid. Not all marriages consist of tea and genteel conversation. Or agreeable companionship."

"Surely many do."

"Surely most do not," she says without hesitation, and then tries deliberately to strike a sunnier note. "However, where marriage and good tempers chance to come together, man and woman may do very well. I think, however, that meeting just as you and I do now—as two persons, rather than as two who have had lawyers draw settlements—is the key to easiness. We know that we have license to leave one another at a moment's notice. And so we study one another's happiness."

Boswell fixes her with an eye, finds that she does not shrink from the scrutiny. "Nay, I know this must be a pose. You cannot be such an enemy of marriage."

"Not an enemy of marriage, sir," Louisa replies, "but once a victim. And so forevermore a skeptic, until such time as I may be proven wrong."

"You have never told me how you and Mr. Lewis came to—part ways."

She cocks her head at Boswell and narrows an eye. "Do we know one another well enough for that, I wonder?"

"I hope we know one another well enough for anything." With that, Boswell moves to the end of the settee closest her chair. He is within easy distance of her hand, but he restrains himself, his own folded carefully on his knee. "I have told you that my affections are engaged to you. And you have told me you are no Platonist. I have hopes—you have encouraged me to hope—that you will allow us to put aside the arbitrary rules of the public. Allow us to do so, even this morning. This morning like no other."

"Mr. Boswell, you know that I have said the thing is fraught with more trouble than it may be worth, for you as well as for myself."

"I like my pleasures fraught. The more fraught, the better."

"Do not make light."

"I have never been more in earnest."

Boswell finally gets the grudging smile he's been probing for, and he reaches out only now to take her hand. Louisa watches as he does so—the two of them watch him take it—but seems more than agreeable. And once he has her hand, Boswell holds it in both his own, clasping it, saying nothing for a moment.

Finally, he speaks. "But truly, madam, you must allow our feelings for one another to take their most intense expression. It is impossible otherwise to know the destiny of a passion such as ours. You will make me blessed, Mrs. Lewis."

"It may be known, sir."

"Or it may remain a tender secret between careful lovers."

"A thousand circumstances may be troublesome."

"Or none in the least."

There is a considered pause, as Louisa smiles softly to herself. She lifts her eyes to him, and the smile deepens, takes on what seems at first to be an outright coyness.

And then, almost as readily as he might pick up a scent entering the air, Boswell understands that it would be a serious mistake to treat the smile as encouragement. It is, in point of emerging fact, much nearer the opposite. He can see that his appeals have brought him as close to this woman beside him as he may come under his own power; the next single hint of entreaty will move her two steps away, or ten, he is suddenly certain. Not only that, but she will rebuke him—out of nowhere; harshly, perhaps—should he pursue the matter another inch.

He has a sharp intuitive sense that Louisa would like to say yes, but can only say yes to the question as put by herself, and that this all connects somehow to the deep reservoir of anger he can sense in her occasionally, when the conversation drifts over certain topics. She must be the pursuer for the last five steps out of a hundred, while he remains passive. Nothing could be clearer.

It is nearly always this way with Boswell and people. Since childhood, he has experienced the signature of their emotions with an uncanny directness, and when he cares enough to do so, he can react reflexively to these signatures, long before bringing their logic to consciousness. In this case, only an instant passes between Louisa's coy smile and Boswell's turning the conversation in a gentle but complete circle.

"I shall say not a word more, madam. I suspect I grow tiresome—"

"Not at all, sir."

"—and I would be anything with you save that, truly. But come, let us know one another better as two friends. I asked about your husband and how you came to part ways. I would be most honored to share that history with you."

Louisa straightens, and then counter-offers: "Well, it is a very personal history, even a secret. But I am touched that you desire to share it. So I will share my own deep secret, sir, in exchange for one of your own. That must be the bargain."

"Done."

"It must be a thing of which you are *properly* ashamed. You must swear it."

"As shameful as you could hope, you have my word. I swear it on my life."

She pulls her head back, considering how to begin. "You should know, then, that Mr. Lewis was an actor in a small strolling company with which I enrolled when I was sixteen, fresh from a dancing academy. He was thirty-two, a quite dashing thirty-two, and he had in mind almost from the start that we would raise a stage family together. Strolling companies are best run by men of large families, you know, as all the children may be brought in for an equal share of the day's profits. He had other schemes, of course, but this was his principal notion.

"And to trim a long story short, we were together for three years, with no sign of little tragedians whatsoever. There were other problems, more common problems, but this became the nub of his discontent."

"I see," Boswell says.

"Mr. Lewis would have an heir, and there was the end of all discussion. And if that were all of it, it might have been another thing altogether. But—here I must demand your utmost discretion, Mr. Boswell."

Boswell places a hand over his heart.

She seems satisfied, and lowers her voice just a touch. "He

more than once in the last two years of our marriage tried his luck elsewhere, so to speak. More than twice."

Boswell lowers his own. "Tried his luck, what, at having a child?"

"Or at what men do in the name of having a child. And then stormed and justified and pointed out my failings as brood-mother for his line of thespians when he was found out. You have no experience with this, Mr. Boswell, but I can tell you that when one's husband or wife finds a bed elsewhere, or simply finds another body elsewhere, it hurts."

There are clearly twin universes of misery contained in these last two words, and Louisa pauses for a few seconds after uttering them.

"Every time a bit less, of course," she continues, "but every single time, it hurts one. One's heart, and one's sense of dignity."

She fixes her eyes on a point over the settee, where the paint of the wall has bubbled slightly and cracked. Boswell tries his best to imagine a broken marriage, coming up to London with no one and with nothing, approaching the managers of the storied Covent Garden Theater with nothing save a pretty face and an anger that could be tapped at will and felt from the last rows. Louisa gathers him in with her glance, and Boswell senses this very anger now nearing the surface. "And finally he began to intimate," her voice drops to a soft whisper, "that I might try my luck elsewhere as well. In particular with the husband of one of the women he had himself been keeping with, an actor in our company. A blackguard drinking companion of his. The idea was that we might all share and share alike, I suppose."

In spite of his suspicions about where the story was headed, Boswell finds himself mildly shocked. "Surely, he could not mean that you should—well, that you might try another father? Surely he couldn't wink at such a thing."

Louisa's look is at once amused and hard. "Surely I think he could mean nothing else. He was not indirect in his phrasing. In the abstract, it was not much for him to give up in order to acquire a great deal."

At that, Boswell feels a sympathy that swells suddenly in his throat. A moment passes, and then he has the impulse to reach up suddenly and touch her cheek with the tips of his fingers. She lets him stroke her cheek this way for a moment, body just slightly tensed, eyes on his.

"I believe it would be giving up the world, Mrs. Lewis," he tells her.

Even as he says it, Boswell knows full well that it is the expected, the flattering, possibly even the fished-for response; but that is entirely secondary to the fact that he means it, at this moment in time, with every bit of the part of his heart he feels he understands.

And in a way already familiar to him at twenty-two, this flood of momentary sincerity from somewhere deep inside him bears the moment of flattery along before it, rendering it inexplicably genuine.

"Thank you, Mr. Boswell," she says, with a bob of her head. "That was indeed a pretty thing for you to say."

They sit for a moment, comfortably, like two companions in a snug winter room. Then Boswell asks, "But what is there for you to be ashamed of in all this? Madam, you are too hard. You chose to be single and honorable, rather than married and shamed, and surely the Lord would have it so. Look at the stuff of your life, Mrs. Lewis. Has He not brought you to the London stage? Has He not caused you to shine there, for all the world to see? Has He not now brought you that mark of success every woman of the stage yearns for—that final mark of Divine favor—a Boswell of her very own?" Boswell cannot help himself, and his voice rises into a thin giggle. "How much clearer could He make His approbation, truly now?"

Her laughter thrills him. He can see that he has managed to reflect her life back to her in precisely the terms she might wish, and her expression now is tinged with gratitude and fresh affection.

Suddenly she holds up a finger, wags it at him. "And now your own shame, sir, as you've solemnly promised."

Strangely enough—though he has in fact promised, and knew well that his turn was coming—Boswell has brought absolutely nothing to mind to answer this request. He sifts quickly through his life, but can think of nothing suitable, nothing disarmingly candid but essentially harmless.

Louisa is waiting, though, and so he simply says the first thing that comes into his mind, an admission that seems at first a joke, a way to buy time on the way to something more to the point. But as he says the words themselves, he suspects that he has in fact touched on one of his deeper shames, and one lurking close to consciousness for an excellent reason. "Well, to say truth, I maneuvered my younger brother John once out of something he wanted very dearly. Actually, I should say I cheated him out of it, just a few years ago. Cheated him in a game."

"Cheated is a very strong term, of course, Mr. Boswell," Louisa suggests.

But he feels the need to insist. "Cheated is the word, I'm afraid, in English at least. I cheated him blind," he repeats, chuckling in spite of the growing uneasiness he feels remembering it. "In Edinburgh, of course, we would say *swicked*."

It is when their conversation is finished—and partially because he has said not another word about it in the last half an hour, and looks to be leaving without doing so—that Louisa herself returns unprodded to the subject of an assignation. They are walking toward the door of her half-apartment when she stops and slowly takes his arm, and says with a sorry shake of her head, "Do, sir, consider what I've said about such a great step as you've proposed. It might well bring our friendship down upon our heads."

But as she says this, her hand is smoothing the sleek gray fabric of his coat, straightening his collar, finally tracing the flesh of his neck as she stands close enough to be kissed. Rather than kiss her, however, Boswell waits himself to be kissed.

"I have said that I adore you, madam. I have meant it."

"You are persistent, Mr. Boswell."

Boswell does not deny this, although he is occupied solely now with allowing her the sensation of persisting. He merely gazes at her, and she at him.

When he does not move to her, she gives just the hint of a fey smile and covers the last few inches, and kisses him. He can feel in the kiss a marked difference from their last: this she has managed, and she revels in it. He feels the warm press of her lips and then, just at the last, the sly trace of her tongue along the corner of his mouth. Her breath smells of sugar and cinnamon, as though she's just crushed a sweet in her teeth.

They remain that way, their faces hovering no more than an inch apart, when the kiss is finished. And she whispers, "If you are still of a mind, come next Sunday, let it be then. When the rest of the house has gone to church. If it is truly in my power to make you blessed, as you say, Mr. Boswell, I will do so with all my heart."

Boswell wraps his arms around her, fingers sampling the skin of her bare back, and fights the urge to crush her tightly against him. "Swear it," he whispers into her hair.

But she only kisses him again, though more fully still. "A Boswell of one's own," she murmurs against his lips, as though speaking to someone other than himself, teasing someone other than himself, "a Boswell of one's very own, indeed."

13

HAVING GOTTEN BY with cheese and apples at midday, Boswell can now—at just twenty-five minutes past seven in the evening—allow himself a delicious extravagance: a bit over a half-shilling for a sedan to carry him the handful of blocks to Northumberland House. With only 100£ from his father for the year in London, sedan rides are generally out of the question, given that he would sooner slit his own throat than be forced to write to Edinburgh begging for more.

But the memorandum in his pocket calls specifically for him to take a chair. In order to look a Lord or a Colonel dead in the eye and ask to be handed a commission that would otherwise be purchased, a man must believe he deserves that commission in the first place. He must feel his own worth, falling like lantern-light all around him.

And his last-night self knew that nothing would light Boswell's lantern tonight like being carried, every step of the way.

In the new pink suit with the gold button, then, he strolls over toward the Privy Garden Stair and begins glancing over chairs. There is no moon, and the wind off the Thames is icy, but he passes deliberately over a few battered chairs before settling on a newer sedan, glossy black, attended by two milder-looking men in clean livery.

At his signal, the men draw open both its door and its hinged top, and Boswell walks up and in, turns, and settles himself down as top and door swing shut. To Boswell's delight, there is a foot-warmer tucked beneath his bench, and he rubs the chair's padded-satin wall and feels ten years old as the chair rises into the air.

It quickly picks up speed as the bearers hit their stride—he hears one of them calling "By y'r leave there!" to clear pedestrians from the path—and now Boswell has leisure to sit back among the cushions and consider what the note asks him to consider: the privilege of being one of only twenty-five invited to the Countess's Friday night party, the chance that his commission will be secured tonight.

But somehow he finds that he cannot. Something else has been gnawing at him, beneath the surface of his elation, ever since he left Louisa's flat. It is his brother John.

Boswell has known for the last two months that his younger brother, newly a lieutenant in a Regiment of Foot, has fallen ill, ill in his mind. Although the family has not been able to piece together the exact sequence of events, Boswell's father was able to recount for Boswell the basic facts: John was on watch duty one black evening in mid-October when he began suddenly to rave, to shout at invisible men and things, and then to accuse his fellow soldiers of plotting against him when they rushed to his side.

For the last eight weeks, he has been confined to a mental hospital in Plymouth.

Although his father has reassured him several times that John is in capable hands and that he need not worry, Boswell does worry. He imagines horrific scenes, imagines his brother sprawled in a dirty cell, on filthy straw even, with Saturday thrill-seekers passing and leering in at him. Boswell knows that this isn't the case; his father has had the hospital at Plymouth inspected by an associate, and John's care there is of good quality. Still, Boswell feels—whenever he allows himself to reach for it—a deep, moldering guilt for not altering his London plan to go immediately to John's side. His father in fact offered a month ago to pay Boswell's expenses to Plymouth and back, but Boswell bristled at the assumption that his campaign for a commission might be so easily broken off, and he immediately declined.

So it comes to him now as a simple emotional equation, impossible to reduce or solve in any other way: John needs him, but he, James, has chosen to go about his business.

For some reason, since his visit earlier with Louisa, it is not the lurid vision of John at Plymouth that hovers at the edge of his mind, but a memory, something that actually happened: a game they played once, the only time that Boswell has gone beyond brotherly bickering and competition and one-upmanship, gone as far as outright deceit.

BOSWELL'S SECOND NERVOUS breakdown, at age seventeen, was in fact no nervous breakdown at all. The truth was that he'd been sitting in a stifling classroom at the University of Edinburgh, wishing for diversion, when it hit him like a thunder stroke that he didn't *need* his father to conceive of a holiday for him. His five-year-old illness had been lying there in front of him all the while, dusty but serviceable. All he had to do was fail to get out of bed again. That and lie about the reason for not getting out of bed.

So the next morning Boswell kept his bed. The surgeon brushed and scrutinized the skin at his ankles like Egyptian papyrus. And then, with even less fuss than before, arrangements were made with Dr. Hunter in Moffat, and a room reserved again on the High Street there for a six-week course.

Boswell was beside himself with delight. But suddenly there was an unexpected fly in the ointment. No sooner had the doctors convinced Lord Auchinleck that Moffat was the cure for Boswell than his little brother John conceived the idea that he would tag along as well. John cried and argued that what one brother suffered now, another brother might well suffer later. Finally

Boswell began to sense to his horror that John was making his case, inch by inch.

And so, two days before he was to leave for Moffat, Boswell casually suggested a bowling match to settle the question.

He and John had been lawn-bowling with and against one another for years, since they were children. When they were very small, they'd served as bowl-caddies for their father, fighting for the honor of lugging his stray shots back across the fresh-mown grass.

John in particular loved the game, and had gradually overcome his older brother's longstanding advantage by devoting himself single-mindedly to his play. Boswell, for his part, still played mostly because the game had become the rage among Edinburgh's lawyers and judges. When the brothers went to bowl, they were treated like princes by the advocates at the green, all of whom pleaded regularly before their father.

So between Boswell giving the actual bowling only half his mind, and John practicing mornings by himself on another green near the Tolbooth, they had wound up all but perfectly matched. Perhaps that was why the loaded set of bowls had so struck Boswell a few weeks earlier when he'd seen them in a novelty shop down the Cowgate. Half the bowls in the set were regulation; the other half were secretly weighted. Boswell bought them for two shillings, and then the bowls had sat in their wooden box at the back of his wardrobe for the past few weeks, like a brace of loaded pistols.

Once they reached the Heriot green, Boswell almost relented. It was early evening in mid-June, and the air was neither too hot nor too cold, full of the scent of the Hospital's large gardens. It was that last hour before the fading of the day, and the six-o'clock bells could be heard softly tolling from the Gray Friars Church. Everyone and everything seemed to share a lovely indolence.

But he couldn't abide the possibility that having John along in Moffat would hobble him or force him to play nanny. So he opened up the box of doctored bowls and handed John the jack. "Throw away, John," he offered.

John winked at Boswell and then kissed the closed fist holding the jack. And then he gave the tiny target ball a nice, distant toss, the sort favored by better players, those with more control. Boswell saw with a start that John had gained more skill in the last few months than he'd realized.

"You understand, James," John said, standing back from the canvas, "that if I win, I go to Moffat with you. If you win, I simply don't go to Moffat with you. I play for something, you play for nothing. Unless denying me is something to you."

It was a tough argument to refute, without laying out his actual hopes for the six weeks in the country. But Boswell answered, "I play for something too, John. I play for your agreement not to sulk, while I take the advice of my doctors."

"You're not old enough to *have* doctors, James. What you have are *father's* doctors, and even they think you're odd. So don't put on airs. You a'nt a laird yet."

It was strange, having the power to alter the game when he would, and Boswell played the first few throws tentatively. But midway through the first game of the match, almost before he was aware of the pieces falling into place, Boswell found that John had surrounded the jack with a very deftly placed trio of bowls, the last knocking out Boswell's only counter.

Of course, it was also precisely the sort of configuration the loaded bowls had been designed to rake through, and Boswell did just that, chucking two of John's bowls out of play, even blasting one all the way to the facing ditch. It was as though the world had been upended.

They played the remaining game with John in an increasing ~~nk~~. As his mood deteriorated, so did his accuracy. When they'd ~~d~~, John cursed and kicked the canvas. And then he turned ~~swell~~ an utterly hopeless look, the look that younger brothers give when the conspiracy against them is revealed to be more far-reaching even than they'd imagined.

They walked home along the Cowgate in silence, passing the very novelty store itself. This last was too much for Boswell, and he tried to salve his conscience by buying the two of them fruit-filled Bath buns, a new treat in town and one of his brother's current favorites. But John wouldn't have it. He pitched the thick bun at the gutter and trudged on in silence.

Two mornings later, as the chaise containing Boswell and his tutor rolled away from Parliament Square for Moffat, neither Boswell's father nor John was there to see him off. Only his mother and his youngest brother David waved good-bye, and Boswell couldn't help but wonder if a man had to continue throughout his life to cast family members away like ballast, in order to keep his own new self above the waves.

14

BOSWELL FINDS THAT, without thinking, he has removed the little watch fob from his coat pocket and opened it up to reveal the bit of cloth with the dark dab that might or might not be Stuart blood, might or might not be the juice of a roast beef. When he was sixteen, Boswell had paid half a crown for the fragment, and he has since alternated between considering himself gullible and blessed.

He is stroking it absently when he feels the sedan slow and dive abruptly toward the ground. In another second, the top of the chair is lifted off, and with it goes the pensive mood. Night sky and cold air flood the chair, and he almost laughs out loud at the shock, the excitement.

Boswell steps down just at the mouth of the Strand, fifteen feet from the central stone arch of Northumberland House. As always, he is infused with a childlike awe, and he feels an impulse to bow, even to kneel. But he contents himself with an actual tip of his hat to the Percy lion perched high up on the long Gothic front of Northumberland House.

Before he's reached the street entrance, a servant in elegant livery [illegible]ut of the shadows and bows. "Mr. Boswell? You are expected, [illegible]o follow me."

An upstart would have his servants challenge each guest and demand a name, Boswell gloats to himself as he falls into step a touch behind the man, *but the servant of a Percy would simply* know.

Boswell is led by turns through the inner courtyard, then into the vast vestibule of the house itself. Broad marble staircases curl gently up and away to either side, leading to the apartments themselves, but these the servant ignores and steers Boswell down a newer wing, to the Lady Northumberland's picture gallery.

If the truth were known, Boswell has surreptitiously paced off the picture gallery—at the tail end of his first visit, with the footman gone to fetch his hat and coat—and he knows it to be well over a hundred feet long. He measured it because he is in love with the Northumberland picture gallery, and has been for weeks now.

The infatuation is based only in part on the impressive amount of gilt covering the cornice and frieze, the columns framing the tall windows. More to the point is the room's stunning narrative assault: paintings are angled and positioned to catch the eye no matter where in the room one turns. Wall-sized panoramas; historical allegories; Douglas and Percy family groupings, down to and including favored Douglas and Percy pets. But finally Boswell is in love with the picture gallery because every time he enters it, it is packed to the gilded roof with Londoners more powerful nearly than he can imagine. And in his short experience of it, Boswell's luck is good in this room.

Tonight is no exception. Lady Northumberland glances up from her tea table and then actually rises to come and meet him, trailing satin and lace, leaving behind an assortment of well-heeled guests, including an earl and a slight, pasty man Boswell recognizes as a director of the East India Company.

As the countess makes her way across the room to him, Boswell forces himself to see her realistically, rather than as his patroness, rather than as the living representative of the ancient House of Percy.

The reality is this: the countess is a medium-stout married

woman of forty-six who manages to look fifty-six, with a weak chin, pudgy fingers, and kind hangdog eyes.

But her wardrobe inevitably makes up for her own lack of physical presence. The gown tonight is a masterpiece of conspicuous consumption, and Boswell appreciates it fully: cream-white satin padded with ornamented robings at her sides and thick showy satin flounces at her feet. This display is offset by a dainty cap of French lace, the hair beneath piled and only lightly powdered.

Her heavy face too has been whitened—even Boswell can see this—and her cheeks and lips expertly reddened. The powder on her face is so fine and so carefully applied that he can find the wrinkles there only by searching them out, like footpaths beneath a fall of new snow.

While she is not attractive in any conventional sense, Boswell always feels a powerful unfocused emotional rush in Lady Northumberland's presence. It is as though his mind and body have no established categories for exceptionally powerful older women and can only respond with the closest approximations: deep filial deference, alternating with a confused excitement nearly indistinguishable from sexual desire.

"Mr. Boswell," the countess says, extending her arm to him, rather than just her hand, "you favor us again. I am glad, truly. This is now three Friday evenings in a row! More than we had a right to hope from a young man upon the Town."

"I told you once, madam, that I should run about this house just like a tame spaniel." Boswell bows over the soft white thickish fingers. "It is not in the heart of a spaniel to miss a party, and a fire in the grate."

"Of course it is not. But you are no spaniel, sir, by my reckoning."

"A terrier, then, if her Ladyship pleases."

He sees the unrestrained amusement come into her face, one of [illegible]gs she seems openly to relish about his company. "Nay, a [illegible]ound, if you will insist on canine distinctions. How do your family, then, sir? All are well at home, I hope? Your father and mother and younger brothers?"

"All are very well indeed, madam."

"And your father's new house at the family estate goes forward?"

"It is nearly finished, from what I understand. My father has apparently ordered his books carried into the library."

As he says this, Lady Northumberland's tired eyes glance about the room, but they then come back to rest on Boswell. She has clearly missed his reply, but smiles good-naturedly in any event. "Well, if he is fitting up the library, that is to say a great deal. Your father would never trust the volumes there if the place were less than complete. He is a man who dotes on a book. That is fine, then, fine, fine. Even the old families such as ours, Mr. Boswell," she says, patting his arm, "must renew their settings occasionally."

This flattering comparison of their two families—combined with the thrumming consciousness that others in the room are now glancing their way—strikes Boswell nearly speechless with pride. Later tonight he will set these words down verbatim in his journal, and he silently repeats them twice, fixing them like night moths to the velvet board of his mind.

But there is no time for a suitably modest reply, because Lady Northumberland suddenly takes a half-step closer, and her voice drops an octave. He can smell her perfume, a honeyed fragrance like hyacinth.

"You will note," she tells him softly, "that the Duke of Queensberry is standing just now at the fire. As luck would have it, he was the first to arrive this evening, and I have already put him in mind of your commission. I have not been idle, sir."

Boswell takes in the duke with a controlled cock of his head, and lowers his own voice an octave. "I spoke with the duke at breakfast several weeks back. He was difficult to read, I thought. But he promised to speak with Lord Ligonier, who is Commander-in-Chief, as your Ladyship knows."

Lady Northumberland raises her eyes to Boswell's and then runs her glance over his face, his eyebrows, his ears, his lips. He watches her eyes parse his countenance. It is just this sort of on-again, off-again attention that continues Boswell in his confused and tentative gallantry.

But apparently she has only been searching his face for signs of naïveté. Her voice is amused: “This is just his way, to represent the thing as Lord Ligonier’s to give. Should he choose to accommodate you—and me—it will seem that he has done something extraordinary. Should he choose to shift you, then it is but a cruel whim of Ligonier’s. But you may trust that my Lord Queensberry has it in his power to do the thing tonight, if he would.”

“Has he, indeed.”

“Oh, this *instant,* sir, if he would.” She pats Boswell’s arm twice, raises her weak chin to search his face again, the same blunt yet idle inventory, this time taking in the cut of his new jacket as well, the showy knot at his throat. “You keep the Guards firmly fixed in your sight, whatever may be said by way of appearance in getting to it.”

Boswell cannot help but bow, this time not out of ceremony but because he feels that he genuinely *wants* to bow to her. And when he lifts his head and speaks, the feelings of gratitude and reverence make the common courtesies audibly resonant, in a way that brings her attention fully to him for a last few moments. “I am your Ladyship’s most obedient servant. You are good to me. Indeed, I set a higher value on the countenance you show me than anybody else could do, truly.”

Lady Northumberland shies a hand at him, but she is pleased.

“I know that you and my father are friends of long standing, and that many favors have passed between you over the years. And I am honored to be a part of that friendly economy, madam.” Boswell straightens his back and gives her a coy look. “But I am also vain enough to hope that some one particle of your favor may be directed he son in his own right.”

ell sees dimples appear in her heavy cheeks, and he is them. Lady Northumberland searches the top of her head tentatively with her hands, checking the seat of her lace cap before answering. "More than one particle, sir," she assures him, "more than one. Of that you may be certain."

Boswell nods. And then, more or less because he cannot resist, he follows up: "Perhaps more than two, madam?"

Yet by the time Boswell works his way through the small crowd to the fireplace, the signal has gone out for cards, and the invited have begun several distinct waves of movement toward the real amusement of the evening. Servants are steering guests to tables arranged in a loose semicircle about the fire—deeper players facing deeper players, novices deftly herded together—and breaking seals on decks.

The room takes on a new electricity: the mere scent of money has become the actual prospect of money.

There is a moment during which Boswell sees his way to a vacant seat at Queensberry's table, but he hesitates: he is under a strict promise to his friend Thomas Sheridan—who relieved him of a gambling debt in Edinburgh, to the tune of five guineas—not to gamble for as many years. Four years of the promise remain, and Boswell supposes he means to keep it. It is not the vow, exactly, that holds Boswell true to his word. Rather, he is too superstitious to sit down beside the duke, for he has the distinct sense that breaking his vow to Sheridan will knock whatever luck he has tonight straight into a cocked hat.

As luck would have it, though, Boswell is the only guest to avoid the tables. For a moment he panics, standing nearly frozen a few feet behind the countess, instinctively turning in her radius.

Then Boswell rallies, and for the next twenty or thirty minutes he convinces himself that he can actually turn the spectacle of his own virtue to advantage. Who better to defend the king than a man who does not play, a man in control of his pleasures?

But finally it is clear that those playing cards are involved in playing cards.

Boswell excuses himself to no one in particular and heads a bit miserably to the gardens for a taste of fresh air, although the night is cold, the gardens facing the river will be blasted and dead, and the air itself will taste of obscurity.

THERE, IN THE hoar-frosted gardens, Boswell faces the river and draws out his small calfskin edition of Johnson, a book he has nearly always about him. The great man's writing has always spoken to him in an oddly comforting way, from childhood. More than once during an average day, he will haul out the essays and read an appropriate passage, the way a man far more devout than himself might lean on the Bible.

Now, with just moonlight enough, ice vapor trailing from his lips, he thumbs his way to an essay he's resisted rereading to this point, although he's gone over the other essays in the volume three or four times in the last weeks. It is Johnson on sorrow, and the first time Boswell read the passage, he pulled back instinctively from its fatalism and lugubrious tone. But now, in this flat moment at the tail end of this day of his own design, he opens himself up to the voice:

> *The other passions are diseases indeed, but they necessarily direct us to their proper cure. A man at once feels the pain, and knows the medicine. . . . But for sorrow there is no remedy provided by nature; it is often occasioned by accidents irreparable, and dwells upon objects that have lost or changed their existence; it requires what it cannot hope, that the laws of the universe should be repealed; that the dead should return, or the past should be recalled.*

With this last line, Boswell is again standing on his mark at the Heriot bowling green, the trick bowl heavy in his hand. Then Boswell is moving forward once more in memory, swinging the [illegible] to the flattened sod, where it leaves his fingers and angles [illegible]way, striking his brother's careful set up like nothing so [illegible]rse.

That is the very worst of it, Boswell realizes, Johnson now forgotten, the wind off the Thames stinging his fingers in dark December 1762: had he allowed his younger brother to take the Moffat waters with him five years ago—as a precaution, if nothing else—John might not be languishing in the Plymouth Hospital tonight.

Boswell hears a distant bell away down the Strand and lifts his head. He turns and finds the gravel path again, slowly weaves the short way back through the evergreen hedge nearest Northumberland House. Just on the other side of the hedge stands a small nondescript man muffled up in a greatcoat, his face nearly hidden beneath a longish wig and an elegant, oversized, fur-lined hat. A clay pipe pokes from beneath the hat brim.

"Good evening, Mr. Boswell," the man offers as Boswell passes in the dark, and he realizes with a start that the figure is the Duke of Queensberry.

"My Lord," Boswell manages. He searches for words, finds only the weather. "You are a certainly a brave man to leave the fire. There is a bite of snowfall in the air."

The wind carries smoke back into the duke's face, and he repositions himself but mumbles contentedly around the stem, like a man who has waited for his pipe two or three hands of cards beyond his limit. "You were braver still, I see, and went halfway down to the water." He hums softly over the pipe, then speaks again, a little cunning in his voice: "If I may inquire, what book was it you took up out in the garden there?"

Without thinking, Boswell draws the volume from his pocket. "It is Johnson's *Rambler*, sir. An old favorite of mine. Excelle[illegible] the odd moment here or there."

The duke actually reaches out a hand and takes t[illegible] volume, inspects the spine, hands it back. He[illegible] the folds of the greatcoat, mumbles ag[illegible] wager with myself, then. I thoug[illegible] Richardson at best, and pe[illegible] he narrows an eye at Boswell, taking his measure, "perhaps Mrs. Haywood at the worst."

In the silence that follows, Boswell can hear the wind cracking frost in the bushes, the muffled scrape of coach wheels on the Strand. And then, almost before he is aware of it, Boswell hears himself broaching the subject of his commission directly.

"Sir, you will excuse me, I pray, for speaking to something so near my own interests, but I cannot see you without being put in mind of my great desire to serve the king in his Guards. Since we last discussed it, I have spoken at length with my Lady Northumberland, and she has confirmed me in my sense that I must hold out for nothing less than this from Fate—and from you, sir. Pray excuse my mentioning it."

The duke purses his lips about his pipe, but not—as far as Boswell can see—out of annoyance. His sense is that the duke has been expecting this subject since he left the House and first recognized Boswell standing on the lawn. The pursed lips and the drawn eyebrows, he sees, are meant to conceal what is actually a distinct form of pleasure—the pleasure of deliberating over a young man's future to the young man's face.

With an almost imperceptible shake of the head, the duke says finally. "I[...] difficult thing—I tell you this honestly, when a man i[...] It is a system of each man dipping his cup, after [...] on down a long line. This makes it a [...] sir. I tell you nothing, I am sure, [...]

[...]ns, and he has developed an [...] chooses, he can render [...] acute impressions of [...]tion—he does this a [...] he must, Boswell can focus these intuitions more actively, to the limits of his own perception and understanding. But more rarely still, when pressed to the utmost, when his own inner needs take complete possession of him, Boswell's intuitions will urge him out well beyond the calculable, beyond any recognizable social logic. With very little warning, he will hear himself begin to say things that should not, properly speaking, be said. These things will be dictated entirely by intuition, and framed in language almost before Boswell himself—his waking, calculating self—can censor or suppress them.

It is always a sensation mingling wonder and threat. When he addresses the duke again, then, it is with just this sort of blind urgency, a juggler tossing china plates in a suddenly lightless room.

"Of course it is difficult, my Lord," he hears himself begin, a bit sharply. "It is as difficult a thing as may be imagined. It is asking the world. And yet I should think your Grace's interest might do it, if any interest in London might."

"My good Boswell, such—"

"Please, let us not toy with one another, sir, but speak as two men. I ask you to allow me that favor, that dignity. You have it in your power to do this thing. That, neither one of us should deny. That is reality."

Beneath the hat, the duke's untended brows have dropped by way of warning, but Boswell continues. "My Lord, a state of suspense and hanging on is a most disagreeable thing. I have heard people talk of it, and I have read in the poets of it, but now I feel it. And I despise it, with all my soul."

"I can understand this, sir. No man enjoys it. I enjoy it even less, I assure you."

"I despise it," Boswell repeats distinctly. "It just comes to this, my Lord. If Your Grace is so generous as to make a push for me, I believe the thing may do. It is true I offer no money, but I would serve George the Third. And I would serve him in London, because under this king the arts will flourish, merit will flourish, and I feel—God forgive me for saying it of myself, sir—but I feel that I have a touch of genius in me."

The duke lets a smile play openly on his lips, then murmurs, "Genius! Oh, my dear sir, really. Are we now to speak of *genius* in this thing?" He chortles softly around his pipe stem, shifting his weight in the cold.

Boswell hesitates, then pushes stubbornly past the little mockery. "Yes, indeed I think one should speak of genius, my Lord. One might better ask why anyone speaks above a whisper of anything else."

This last remark seems to have flicked the duke on the raw, and he says nothing in return. Boswell quickly drops the little volume of Johnson he has been holding into the pocket of his coat, and bows his head. He can feel it all going wrong somehow, feel the china plates slipping past his fingertips in the dark.

But he speaks a last time in any event. "I desire to use that genius to elevate my king, and my country. And my patrons, sir. I truly believe I shall have it in my power one day to repay the favor, the great favor, I now ask. To celebrate your name in a way that will make you remember this evening—this very conversation, tonight, this moment now—with a most genuine satisfaction. But I cannot pay for that favor. I ask for your faith, my Lord."

The duke snorts, shakes his head a bit, then begins the process of tamping out his pipe and replacing it deliberately in his right coat pocket. Boswell can only take the silence as a prolonged snub, and he stands awkwardly as the man stows his pipe and then gestures formally toward the light spilling from Northumberland House.

Together they grind down the frozen gravel path in silence.

The evening is suddenly in shambles, and, as he picks his way through the ice, Boswell could almost burst out laughing at his own idiocy. Has he really just now been speaking seriously of his own genius, he wonders, staring past the trim of the duke's hat to the starless sky beyond. Has he actually just been menacing the

Duke of Queensberry with his own future prominence? It seems impossible to believe.

And then the duke stops and turns, with what seems like a hint of truculence. "And what does the Great Johnson say of genius, might I ask?"

Boswell halts himself, again looks the duke in the face. He thinks for a moment, sensing an opportunity, but his mind remains entirely blank, and he can come up with nothing. "I have no good idea, sir. But I dine with him tomorrow. With your leave I will put the question to him directly then."

The duke looks startled, then snorts again and turns away, as though his point has been proven.

IT IS SOME ten minutes later, as Boswell is retracing his listless way through the great vestibule to the entrance onto the Strand, that he hears heels tapping behind him on the marble floor. Clearly fluent in the language of these particular heels, the servant leading him pricks up his ears.

Boswell turns, and it is in fact the Countess, sweeping up behind him as quickly as her Friday-night dignity allows. She grips the satin flounces of her dress carefully in one hand, but she does not stop before him, coming instead directly to his side, and then to his ear, so that Boswell can feel her short little breaths for an oddly intimate moment.

"I have come away to tell you, Mr. Boswell, to save myself the trouble of a letter. Oh, I've tousled my cap so! But can you guess what the duke has said to me just this moment, as he passed behind my chair on his return from the garden? Can you guess, my dear sir? 'Well, madam,' said he, 'it seems as though this Boswell of yours may have merit indeed.' And then he quite patted my shoulder, as though to reassure me. Oh, is it not propitious, Mr. Boswell? Is it not as I said earlier?"

Here she grasps his arm, more tightly perhaps than might strictly be allowed, but not a great deal more. "We shall do it together, you and I, though it take the full year your father has allotted you, Mr. Boswell! Have faith, sir. We will win him to it yet."

And then—almost before he realizes it—Boswell finds himself out on the ice-hushed street, moving into the thin crowds collected in the Square without perceiving the motion of his legs and feet beneath him. He hears singing from the Golden Cross across the street, a wash of ragged voices, and he is buoyant, airborne.

This dreamy flight lasts some four slow blocks, before a small woman in a dirty yellow bonnet steps up alongside him in the dark. She matches his pace for five or six strides and then, when Boswell doesn't shy, casually takes his arm.

Boswell's mood being what it is, he pats her arm in his and walks this way for another five or six strides—smiling down at her, and she smiling back with clear dark eyes and good white teeth— before stopping finally to detach himself.

But as he does so, the woman executes a deft, practiced little figure, taking his hand at the turn and drawing it firmly alongside her own, up into the bodice of her dress, so that in a heartbeat Boswell's four cold fingers are nestled along the warm smooth side of her breast, the nipple frank against his palm. The woman presses her own hand tightly to the outside of the dress, holding this arrangement steady.

Only then does she speak, in a whisper. "Please, but my legs are frozen, sir. Just as cold as two slips of ice. They need warming, truly."

Boswell begins to draw his hand back, but the woman presses harder against the side of her bodice, holding him steady. Boswell lowers his own voice to a whisper. "Take yourself inside where it's warm. The Golden Cross is not so far away."

"You come to the Cross with me, sir, and I'll go where you will. And do what you will."

"I shall send you a coin to keep you company," Boswell says, and then in a surplus of generosity, "as well as another coin to keep that coin company. I have an early morning engagement. With a great man. It cannot be missed."

"We've time before then," the young woman argues, looking defiantly into his eyes, then tightening her hold on his hand. It is the sort of demanding approach that he likes best from such women, and on another night he would more than likely allow himself the pleasure of yielding, if only to some furtive, partial pleasure. But if he is certain of anything concerning the revolutions of the last half hour, it is that the very mention of Johnson's name has done him some sort of unquantifiable good with the Duke of Queensberry, perhaps as much as secured his commission outright.

And that conviction has already begun to expand into something more extensive and profound: he can feel Johnson's moral influence over him already beginning, feel it working in advance of their actual Christmas Day meeting, and the net effect is like a smaller, more compact iteration of his Moffat vow of chastity.

Because Boswell knows suddenly that he will deny himself this woman standing before him. He begins to suspect already that he will deny himself the consummation of his painstakingly wrought affair with Louisa as well.

When his hand is his own again, he returns it deliberately to his right coat pocket and places it on his small calfskin copy of Johnson's *Rambler* essays, and only there and then do his fingers curl protectively.

And when he leaves the woman with a three-penny piece, at last, he does so not to buy her willingness when next he runs across her, not to keep her in some sort of vague potential readiness, as he might have done last night or last week; he does so because he believes her when she says that her legs are cold, and—in the abstemious glow of his meeting tomorrow with Samuel Johnson—Boswell would actually have her go and warm them.

15

As you read this note, you sit at your breakfast table, easy in loose dressing gown, the morning of the day you are to meet the celebrated Samuel Johnson. Breakfast neat in honor, toast, rolls, and butter only. Refuse all jams, to show you may forgo any distinct pleasure at will. As you eat toast, think on true London authors: men of wit, praise, pleasure, and profit.

Yesterday you brought your first and second grand enterprises fairly to the brink: your true London love affair, and your commission. Today the last enterprise of the three: attaining the acquaintance, the general good opinion, and the correspondence of the author of the dictionary of the English tongue itself.

Let no Scotticism cross your lips; talk seldom, but that scrupulously best fine English.

Deny not your country, but hold it lightly, fondly, the way a man now astride a stallion speaks of a childhood pony.

You have committed much Johnson to memory, but while every man would have his words memorialized, no man can hear them quoted in company without affecting displeasure. Bide time; wait until alone. Then run the man's words naturally into your own, that he may appreciate depth of his impact upon your mind, soul.

Should you have opportunity, also tell him the story of how a word in his Dictionary angered father, gave birth to secret language between brothers. "You see, Sir," you may remark when the story is finished, "how your work has moulded not merely a man, but a family entire." This you may perform before the rest of the company, be they however many.

Have shoes wiped, hair powdered and dressed, sword sharpened, polished, and belted in the rakish way of a military gentleman. Better that you should enter late, as a novelty, when he has met and conversed already with the rest of the company.

Better that you should stand out clearly: a young man of family, a would-be soldier, a one-day Laird, and—above all else—a Rasselas in search of his Imlac.

Boswell finishes the morning's third reading of the Johnson memorandum just as he rounds Drury Lane, at a bit before noon, and passes quickly into Russell Street. Although his fingers are stiff with the chill, they are well-practiced, and Boswell has no need to oversee them as they return edges to intricate folds and finally cause the sheet to disappear again into his deep fob pocket. Instead, he keeps his eye on Drury Lane Theater as he turns the corner. More than once, Boswell has stood outside Davies's bookshop and watched actresses come and go at noontime. But none are about today.

Just beyond the Christmas quiet of the Rose Tavern, Boswell lets himself into Davies's. Although the shop, too, is closed, Davies prefers that his guests track their dirt over the store's planks rather than the rugs of the townhouse attached to the rear. The French door connecting the structures stands open, and Boswell can make out the play of the fire beyond and the placid movements of Davies's guests.

He pauses in the half-lit shop for a moment, among the tables and stacks of books, breathing manuscript dust. He can't help but feel that there is something fitting to his approaching Johnson through this gateway of the printed word, and he wants suddenly to slow the moment down.

In fact, Boswell is about to actually close his eyes when Davies—some fragment of his attention always on the shop—steps out of the house.

Even as booksellers go, Davies is disarming: the businessman's wig is a good ten years out of date, but scrupulously powdered and tied, over a nose too large by half, the mouth always open, talking, gossiping, laughing. "Mr. Boswell!" he cries, seeing Boswell stopped out among the shelves. "Oh, but the shop is closed, my young friend, quite closed! Come in, come in!"

Coming forward and shaking hands, Boswell confides, "I was gathering my courage, Mr. Davies, here in the quiet."

"Courage? Have you need of courage to face your friends, sir?"

"Not old friends, but new." Boswell gives a small smile. "It was Mr. Johnson who made me hesitate."

But at the mention of Johnson, Davies suddenly squeezes his eyes closed and looks pained. "I had meant to dash a note off to you. Johnson has gone to Oxford. He's sent his regrets. Too bad for all of us in the company, I'm afraid." He hesitates, and then—seeing actual, solid disappointment on Boswell's face—maneuvers hurriedly. "But there was a line in the letter, more or less to you. He has written near the end of his note, 'Tell your young man of prestigious family that I shall make his acquaintance as soon as I return to the City, and you shall bring us together, Davies.' It was nicely done for him to remember you so particularly in that way, I thought."

Boswell laughs at the praise, and follows Davies into the light and warmth of the parlor, but the news of Johnson's absence has struck him more powerfully than he would have imagined. He is not merely disappointed, but oddly hurt, he realizes.

And so—after a round of introductions and a brief, strained attempt to share the mood of the other guests—Boswell allows himself to collapse into one of Davies's deep armchairs, away from the small crush. The ivy hung at intervals about the room looks wilted to his eye.

Only belatedly does he realize that the companion chair is occupied as well.

"Looks like Davies has lost both his lions this year," the other young man remarks, surveying the room contentedly.

Davies is very much the sort of host to list off his guests to other guests, and Boswell is himself the sort to remember those lists effortlessly: the man in the other armchair is one Oliver Goldsmith, maker of translations, pamphlets, letters, and also, according to Davies, both a rising poet and a so-so novelist. Goldsmith's face is badly pockmarked and slightly popeyed, and, for a man in his early thirties who has chosen to wear his own dark hair, he has surprisingly little of it. He is bald and homely, in a pair of words, but there is a certain sleek avidity at play in his features that Boswell finds immediately intriguing.

"I'm afraid I don't take your meaning, sir."

"Old Sheridan was to come today, as was Johnson." Another sly look. "Both have clearly decided to eat their Yule doughs elsewhere."

Somewhere beneath the casual London accent, Boswell can trace the faintest suggestion of an Irish brogue, and he immediately begins to monitor his own accent more closely. "So Davies said earlier. I confess I was genuinely disappointed. I had hoped to meet Johnson today and sample the man's world-famous conversation."

"Infamous, I suppose you mean. You might as well regret missing a savage beating in a blind alleyway."

"I beg your pardon?"

Goldsmith takes a sip of his wine and considers the matter, then goes on. "That Johnson's conversation has overwhelming force, no man may doubt; but it is just the force of a cudgel, sir. He makes his point, you disagree, he shouts you deaf—*quod erat demonstrandum*. There is no true subtlety to speak of, nothing of finesse. All men agree on this as well, although not when Johnson is by," Goldsmith adds, and winks.

"You are joking, certainly."

"I'm afraid I must remain the authority on whether I was or was not joking, sir."

"But Johnson's essays and arguments have always struck me as inexpressibly subtle, as well as forcefully made."

Goldsmith sits back and lifts his eyebrows, folding his long-fingered hands over his small belly. He picks a bit of lint from his vest and seems to choose his words with special care. "Indeed. Well, neither a man's eyesight nor his taste are susceptible to argument, I suppose."

Boswell is mulling this last comment—deciding whether and how to take some vague offense—when Davies suddenly raises his voice above the drone of conversation. "May I have your attention, esteemed ladies and gentlemen!" he calls loudly, then claps his hands three times. "May I have complete silence, please!"

As individual conversations are hushed, and talk dies by turn in each corner of the parlor, Goldsmith whispers to Boswell, "Now we will all of us pay for our wine."

"How so?"

"Davies was denied his Christmas as a child in dreary Scotland, and since coming to London he has gone mad for holiday games and treats. Trust me, you shall see. We shall have the cutting of the Christmas cheese itself if we are not careful."

Standing before the small fireplace, Davies raises his glass in the sudden quiet, and silently the company does likewise. "My friends," Davies begins gravely, "we come now to a most solemn and ancient element of our Christmas day festivities. Our ancestors knew that revelry was crucial to a holiday such as this."

Davies allows laughter to percolate, then continues. "And so they created an office whereby the cheer and the hijinks of their progeny might be both stimulated and regulated down through the ages. This officer they held in greatest esteem, an esteem reflected in his most terrible and noble honorific."

"The Lord of Misrule!" the guests throw out on cue.

Davies raises a long finger in the air. "The Lord of Misrule, indeed! This Lord should be a *young* man, that his back can carry children too young to dance. He should be *merry*, that he may teach the melancholy among us to laugh. Women should burst helplessly into song when he enters a room, and he himself should have the well-turned leg of a roasted *guinea hen*."

Through peals of laughter, the guests manage another mostly coordinated response: "The Lord of Misrule!"

Goldsmith stage-whispers, into the relative silence, "Brace yourself, my friend."

But before Boswell can turn and ask what he means, Davies is going on with the ritual. "And for all of these excellent reasons, my dear, dear friends, I ask that you join me in summoning our young Scottish nobleman, our own excellent young friend Mr. James Boswell, Esquire, to his rightful Christmas duties!"

Boswell is genuinely stunned. A hot sweat breaks out at his hairline, and he looks quickly round to Goldsmith, but Goldsmith only raises a fist and joins the standing crowd in shouting again, "The Lord of Misrule!"

Davies pats the air for silence. When he has it, he asks solemnly, "Will you accept your charge, Mr. Boswell? It is an office of great moment, and we must be satisfied immediately as to your willingness and fitness to occupy it."

Everyone standing has now turned to pick him out at the far reach of the room, dropped down in the refuge of the battered armchair, and Boswell has no idea what to say or do. But then his ear picks out Goldsmith's low whisper, coaxing him along: "*Tell them it is an honor too great to be accepted. Tell them you are unworthy it.*"

"It is too great an honor, truly," Boswell repeats slowly, after a pause. "I must confess I feel utterly unworthy it."

The shouts of the crowd tell him that his answer is precisely what it should be. Davies too looks delighted, and presses him according to custom. "Only the *true* Lord of Misrule believes himself unworthy of his office. All hail the one true Lord of Misrule!"

"*I accept your charge, then, with all my heart,*" Goldsmith whispers, and Boswell dutifully repeats the words aloud.

Davies applauds with the rest, and then finishes the set piece by asking, with a long low sweep of his hand, "And please, how shall we begin the revels, O Lord? What sport would please your Lordship best?"

"*Let it be snapdragons, tell them,*" Goldsmith prompts again.

Boswell stands heavily and surveys the company, their faces held in a suspense closer to childish delight than any of them would readily admit. Already Boswell senses the last of his own disappointment over Johnson's absence lifting, dissolving in the giddy delight he feels occupying the precise center of attention.

He raises a hand in a benediction, and as with so many moments since coming to London, he lets this one stretch languorously out. The company holds its breath.

"Let it be *snapdragons,* my loyal subjects!" Boswell commands, without any clear idea whether he has directed Davies to produce a flower, or a dance, or a batch of Christmas candies. But the excitement the word produces is impressive, and Davies jogs out of the room briefly, only to return with a large blue dish in one hand and a bottle of brandy in the other. He holds both up triumphantly, and the crowd gives a little roar.

At various points about the room, guests and Davies family members snuff candles, and the room takes on an expectant gloom.

Boswell watches as his host sets the dish down on the long dining table and pours brandy carefully into it. With a flourish, Davies goes then to the fireplace and sets fire to a long stick clearly placed there for the purpose.

Finally, after carrying the flame gaily through the crowd, Davies sets the dish alight. It is an eerie blue green flame, crawling and dipping like a living thing. "The bowl is full of raisins, Mr. Boswell,"

Goldsmith offers, leaning toward him. "And the object, you see, is to snatch the plump little bits from the fire and swallow them down without burning either one's fingers or one's gullet. A secondary object is to down enough brandy to dull the pain."

Boswell is enchanted, and he watches in wonder as grown men and women line up to thrust their fingers into the fire and then gobble the raisins down, squealing and gasping all the while. There is a wild abandon in the game that mesmerizes him.

"The name derives from the German, if I'm not mistaken, *schnapps* for spirit, and *drache,* dragon. But then London speaks the tongue of the world entire, it is said."

Boswell says nothing in return, because he is thinking as he stares into the brandy flame, reconsidering his embrace of the chaste Johnsonian life. If Johnson's presence today was to mark the Lord's wish that he, Boswell, fall at once into the moral wake of the great man, then Johnson's absence might well be interpreted as the reverse: temporary dispensation to match his own sizable appetites against the banquet that is London.

"I must say that Davies knew what he was about," Goldsmith goes on. The large lips are turned up in a slight, discerning smile. "One would think you were quite pleased with your new role."

"Indeed, I begin to suspect that I am spectacularly well cast," Boswell replies, with a confidential smile of his own.

He is thinking of Louisa and her whispered promise. In a matter of days, he will lock the door to an ordinary room, turn around, and everything will have fundamentally changed: she will offer him not only every part of her body, but a leisurely taste of all of the selves with which an actress animates it.

But even before that fantasy has fully unwound itself, he remembers the girl in the smudged yellow bonnet from the night before, the girl who trapped and held his hand so desperately. His mind brings the sensation back into his right hand with wonderful clarity, and Boswell actually sneaks a look down at the fingers, flexing them once before returning them to the armrest.

Such girls move back and forth in surprisingly tight territories, usually no more than a block square, and he feels certain that if he were to walk that bight of the Strand once or twice at most this evening, she would appear and take hold of his arm again. In an instant he has made the promise to himself.

And another: once she has his arm, he will hesitate and then refuse, as he did last night, but this time only as a way of increasing the girl's level of insistence. Only as a way of stretching her desperation to its most erotic application. Only as sweet play.

The Lord of Misrule it shall be, then, Boswell thinks, and then—with a civil nod to Goldsmith—excuses himself to take his own turn snapping dragons from the flame.

IT IS JUST eleven mornings later, as Boswell hums contentedly over his toast and his day's memoranda and social calendar, that he hears boots banging up the narrow stair, well ahead of the maid. He has barely time to wipe his mouth and push back his chair before the door falls open, and in rushes a gaunt figure in a stained soldier's coat. It is his younger brother John, hat in hand, his hair and pants and boots testifying to a two-day journey on horseback.

Later that night, Boswell will reproach himself for it, but the truth is that his attention focuses first not on the tears already starting in his brother's eyes, but on a last key element of fashion: John wears his saber buckled at his side, a privilege Boswell knows has been expressly forbidden him for most of the last three months.

PART FIVE

Inside the Turk's Head

Saturday 30 July (continued)

We supped at the Turk's Head. Mr. Johnson said, "I must see thee go; I will go down with you to Harwich." This prodigious mark of his affection filled me with gratitude and vanity. I gave him an account of the family of Auchinleck, and of the Place. He said, "I must be there, and we will live in the Old Castle; and if there is no room remaining, we will build one." This was the most pleasing idea that I could possibly have: to think of seeing this great man at the venerable seat of my ancestors. I had been up all night yet was not sleepy.

—From *Boswell's London Journal, 1762–1763*

London, England
Saturday, the 30th of July, 1763
7:48 P.M.

* * * * * *

16

ONCE HE IS fairly out in the current again—having pushed off the moment my heel touched the slick Billingsgate Stair—Gil Higgs draws his big arm back and pitches something far away out into the current. It is the edition of *Tom Thumb,* no doubt, for the tiny pages flutter like a moth in the river glow. Before it can sink of its own accord, a passing smack drives the book beneath the water, and then its pretty pages are lost.

I cannot hold this little spasm of rudeness against the man. After all, Higgs has spent the day cooling his heels in Greenwich more than a touch against his will, and he is the sort to make the brassy gesture once out of reach. Still, it is worth reminding him that he is not, in fact, out of reach. Nor will be.

"Ask your Maggie, Higgs," I call to him, over the late noise of the market. "Ask your Maggie to show you her lucky charm. It will be snug in her pocket, or under her pillow, should she deny having it about her."

At that, Higgs comes partially up off his bench and shouts something unintelligible, except for the curse with which he bites it off.

But he is already shrinking in the current, and I give him no more mind. He will reach home within the hour, after one or two quick drinks. He will waste not a moment before bullying his daughter out of her lucky charm, and once he has it in his hand he will turn it over in bewilderment and realize that here again is something he does not want, yet cannot throw away.

And he will never speak of this day to another living soul. And that is all one ever really desires of a Gil Higgs, after all. Very strong back, very tight lip.

Coming up the stair into Billingsgate is always a bit like entering the Plymouth Hospital again, though without the doctors to shepherd one through the chaos. Even this late in the evening, a soft explosion of noise and smell: fishwomen staggering by under their dead, gamy loads, muttering, cursing, feet splashing along through mud ripe with the accumulated oil and scent of five hundred years; stall-keepers shouting—a genuinely threatening tone to the pleading—and then losing interest utterly the moment you've passed their little fiefdom; bare-footed guttersnipes pitching rocks and the odd stolen bit of coal at ships from the embankment, and then running madly through the crowd, knocking fish from the hands of shoppers, fish they then scoop up and smuggle down the lightless *hythe*.

I could easily have had Higgs row me to the Temple Stair, or even to Whitefriars, both a stone's throw from the Turk's Head. But James and Johnson have almost certainly landed at the Temple Stair and paused at Johnson's chambers in the Temple before proceeding to the day's final tête-à-tête.

No doubt Johnson will want to have a word with his young African servant, Francis Barber, and have an accounting of the day.

After James made it clear that he had no plans to introduce me to his famous new friend, weeks ago, I took the opportunity of putting myself in this Barber's way one morning, as he went out to shop for Johnson's supper down the Strand. And after assuring himself that I was indeed a dear friend of his master, he chatted quite readily about the great man's household. Johnson attempted once to save

Francis himself from the press-gang, though unsuccessfully. Still, he took in the young African on his return to England, and Barber cannot say enough in his praise.

Apparently there are also in the house a daft old man named Levett, who haunts the upper floors; several dusty garrets full of books; and a stone-blind woman named Miss Williams, who lives nearby and whom Johnson visits without fail before turning in for the night—visits no matter the hour, mind you.

So it goes without saying that Johnson must land at Temple Stair and stroll by his little domestic menagerie, to assure himself that all of his various charity cases are thriving. And that means that he and James are just now settling down in their private room at the Turk's Head, just now calling for their bottle and bite to eat.

And so I will have a leisurely evening stroll, up past the Custom House and down Lower Thames to Fish Street Hill, up to Cornhill, down to Cheapside and Fleet, and then on down the long slender arm of the Strand. The walk will give the two of them time to lose themselves in the fog of mutual congratulation that comes up whenever they are together. And they will have time to drink a bottle or possibly more, always a crucial consideration.

But as much as anything, I will walk up Fish Street Hill for the long, sloping view of London Bridge at night. It is a cunning thing, this massive new span over the Thames. Seeing it helps me to remember that though James would never willingly have brought me into company with his precious new literary conquest, the world often does not wait for James Boswell, Esquire to approve a meeting between two men.

Sometimes such a meeting simply happens, and no force in the Empire can either predict or prevent it.

CORNHILL IS ALL but deserted. The merchants and stock-jobbers have long since trudged home to count their guineas. I might walk down the center of the street if I pleased, so broad is the thoroughfare here and so infrequently does a coach rattle into and then out of sight. It is like a life-sized model of London, every detail faithfully reproduced, but with most of the human figures left on the shelf somewhere to avoid obscuring the workmanship. In particular, the tower of the Royal Exchange—surging fifty feet into the night sky, only to terminate in the polished brass figure of a grasshopper—seems somehow less than real, shy of actual.

Just as I pass the Exchange, a small bareheaded man drifts out from the open arches of the Jamaica walk. It becomes clear after a second or two that his slanting path will bring him directly to my side, if not actually stumbling into me, and I stop suddenly to force him to cross the street first.

Rather than do so, he stops suddenly as well, five or six feet off to my right, and cocks his head at me. He wears no shoes, and the feet are milk-white beneath his breeches.

And I find that I recognize him. It is the mudlark, the one I sent swimming after James and Johnson this morning. The one whose vulgarity would have cost him an eye, had Gil Higgs half the ferocity to which he pretends.

The pattering rain has thoroughly matted down the brown hair, but he is smiling as he stands there. Of course he is a man who spends more time swimming than walking, and so the wet wouldn't disturb him. And yet there is something uncanny in the smile.

"Out walking in this rain, are we?" he asks suddenly. The smile gives way to a look of exaggerated curiosity, as though the question is also somehow a joke at my expense. There is no salutation, no bow of the head, no *sir* to render the question any less provoking.

There is also no overt threat in his posture. He is a smallish man, but I remember the muscles in his arms and back. And a knife or a razor can always do what muscle cannot. Far too much effort has gone into this evening to allow it to be sidetracked, however, even a bit.

Watching his face, I put a hand inside my coat pocket, and find the dag there.

He takes in the movement, but shows no real fear. Only the same mock-surprise. He goes on then: "Might wager Old Greenwich was a bit of a disappointment, day like today. Didn't get in all the sights you'd planned, have to imagine."

"That's none of your affair," I say quietly.

He considers that, then throws back more nonsense: "'Tisn't my affair? Well, isn't *that* a shame, then? Hoardin' it all up for yourself, this affair here?"

The challenging smile breaks over his face again, and suddenly it dawns on me: this young man, maybe two or three years older than myself, is himself well down the road of insanity. Now that I've placed it, I recognize the behavior from Plymouth and remember it well, for nothing could be more striking. The complete and utter disregard for rank and custom, the sly winks that say everything is a plot and everyone a plotter.

And I feel myself relax a bit. Here is no cutpurse, no threat. Here is a relatively well-functioning lunatic, a man whose mind fastens on the banal, the meaningless, and forces it to signify. I have dealt with his sort before.

"'Twasn't what you were hoping, Greenwich?" he repeats.

"Actually, if you must know, it was not."

"Shame, shame. Still, more than one way to skin a cat," he adds, then takes another step toward me.

"You are out of luck, my friend," I say, "for we are blocks away from the water, and I haven't any further errands suited to a mudlark, at least not this evening."

He stares at me for a moment. For the first time the smile wavers, and something else shows through, something far less sunny. He squints an eye. "There's some along the river who don't take well to bein' called *mud* larks, y'understand. If you take my meaning—*sir*."

I could swear that there is offense in his tone, as though he were the gentleman and I the shoeless and hatless wretch who has stumbled up out of the rain, speaking in riddles.

"And what do those who take offense prefer to be called?"

"River lark's got a sweeter sound to it. Much sweeter, most people think."

I tip my hat. "I shall remember it. And now you will do me the favor of getting on about your business." Both he and I continue to ignore my odd posture, right arm held across my chest, hand still thrust into the inner coat pocket there, dag still curled against the palm of my hand.

He looks at me and then takes a step or two closer. Again, the mark of the truly mad: an instinct for survival so faint that they will cut off their own toes to see if it is possible to walk without them. He certainly must know from my red coat that I can defend myself.

Yet finally his gaze does come to rest on the hand I have thrust in my pocket. And he stops with still a foot or two between us. Then he shakes his head, almost chuckling to himself, even muttering a word or two under his breath. Finally, in a bid for sarcasm, he answers me as properly as he is able, which suggests more than a bit of schooling at some point in his drifting: "Well, *perhaps* you will do me the very *grand* favor of telling me, sir, just what exactly *is* my business this night, *sir?*"

He is looking at me with such intensity, head cocked again to one side, that finally I can do nothing but laugh myself. The earnestness, mingled with the absurdity of his milk-white feet jutting from his flannel breeches, it is all too much. This is the effect of the Thames running in and out a man's ears for the better part of a lifetime.

"You try a man's patience," the lark continues, and he seems utterly serious.

Which is about all I can stomach of his insolence. "Off with you," I tell him. Suddenly I stomp my boot on the cobbles, and he flinches, actually bringing a hand up to shield himself, taking a quick step back.

And then, as the mad are wont to do, he becomes suddenly

solicitous, as though the heavens were about to come crashing down upon him, and only my advice could save him. He is all but wringing his hands now.

"I should go about my business, then?" he asks plaintively. "Find my place and stick to it?"

"Always good advice," I answer, resuming my unhurried movement back up Cornhill, "for a young man who would avoid the gallows."

THE WEATHER HAS turned genuinely vicious by the time I finish the deliberate stroll up the Strand. The wind and the rain now have real bite; although it is late July, one can feel winter teething. Every fourth merchant seems to have shirked his duty to light the street; every fourth cobblestone seems to sink under my shoe, driving up needles of muddy water. But the wet stockings and shoes are nothing, less than nothing.

Within the half hour, I will know precisely what James and Johnson have to say *to* me, and what they have to say to one another *of* me.

And these are the only things that matter.

St. Mary's is entirely dark, not a lamp to be seen inside the looming mass. From the iron fence surrounding the churchyard, one would think it was Somerset House across the way that claimed to be the holy place, the sanctuary for seekers: light pours from the central arch and forms a brilliant semicircular pool there in the street. You could almost dip it with your cupped hands.

And I suppose the Turk's Head Coffee-House—last in the row of dull brick buildings adjoining the Somerset arch—could be a tiny, subsidiary refuge, for it too sheds light and the voices of men audibly pleased with their situations. The house's white window frames glow as though newly painted, and from where I stand I can see nearly all of the common room through them, certainly all of the space that could conceal my brother and his now more-or-less tame bear.

To be expected: they are lounging by now in their private room on the second floor, oblivious to all else.

Still, a thick knot of men stands before the fireplace, and I watch them through the window for just a moment to make sure they are all who and what they seem to be, mere idlers and hogs of the fire. Finally, as the woman of the house pushes her bulk through them to tend the coffee pot, they break up and turn and show me their faces and then re-form, never ceasing their empty conversations. They are none of them worth my consideration.

And so when I enter, I look at no one and I speak with no one. A few patrons perk up when the bell atop the door sounds, but seeing only a vague young man of twenty or so, unattractively soaked through, they quickly go back to their coffee and tea and port. I pause only to brush the water from my sleeves and to strip off my hat, and then I walk directly though the place, heels knocking on the planks, as though I have an errand to complete. And of course I do.

Before an instant has passed, I am walking down the dim hallway to the Turk's Head kitchen, and I would bet a hundred pounds that not one man in the common room could bring my face to mind tomorrow, should he be asked. I have always been less noticeable than my father and brother, but since leaving Plymouth I find I am all but invisible. Light passes through every part of me but the red coat.

Invisible to everyone, that is, but the lady of the house. She is setting down a congealed platter of Welsh rarebits when she catches sight of me, and she all but drops the silver in her haste to come to my side. A boy of eight or nine sweeping beans from the floor looks up at me standing in the doorway, curiously, but the woman pushes his head down to his task as she passes.

She comes up to me, wiping meaty hands on a soiled apron, eyebrows raised knowingly, and a smile playing about her lips. This woman—whose dark glossy hair and sad green eyes were no doubt fetching when she was a slip of twelve—is another of Johnson's charity cases, of course. He frequents her house and brings all of his acquaintance here because she is a good, civil woman, in his estimation, and needs the custom. He is determined to lift her house single-handedly into profitability.

And for that—because Johnson has offered her his very public attention and concern—I wanted very much to dislike the widow, Mrs. Parry. I was certain she took his aid for granted. But having come twice in the last week to discuss the details of tonight's festivities with her, I have seen that no creature could be more fawningly grateful, more utterly in awe of the great man. There is more than a little of the pleading spaniel about her, a fat, mooning, greedy spaniel.

And that has allowed me not merely to dislike her, but to go most of the remaining distance to hating her.

"They are here, sir," she stage-whispers, "settled in above, just as you wished. They called for their favorite room almost to the second when you said they would." Her eyes are actually crinkling with pleasure, which is understandable. As coffeehouses go, this one is well aired, but yet it is a dull life of boiling grounds and scavenging coppers. Not tonight, though.

Because tonight I have offered her the chance to plan a surprise birthday party.

It isn't the sort of party she might plan herself, and there are a few aspects of it that she would have otherwise, but in the main she is delighted to be my co-conspirator.

I show my own teeth and raise my own eyebrows. "That is most excellent news, Mrs. Parry. One hates to have a party spoilt. And you've reserved the other two rooms, as we discussed?"

She is nodding before I've finished my sentence, so eager is she to demonstrate compliance. "Everything up the stairs is your own, sir, all the three rooms together. I've never understood why the gentlemen prefer the room to the back rather than the room over the street, which has a lovely lookout over the Strand. But I suppose it's the carriage wheels and the dust. I've placed the roast hen and the other things in the empty room, as you wished, and I'll be taking the gentlemen their meal directly.

"And I've just ten minutes ago taken them the bottle of port. Their first bottle was standing just half empty on the table, just as you wished, sir. They were surprised to see the second, for they hadn't rung, but says I, it comes from an *admirer* of Mr. Johnson's, and he did look so very pleased. Most evenings the gentleman drink just the one bottle of port, and then maybe a pint more if they've a mind to set to it. Mr. Johnson looked as if he might send it away," the mooning green eyes widened, as though Johnson's displeasure were the worst of all possible worlds, "but when he knew it was a *gift,* from a man who admires all his books and wonderful writings, well, sir. You could see he looked so very pleased."

A thought occurs to me looking down at her, the plump face shining with sweat. "Have you read Mr. Johnson's work, Mrs. Parry? Any of his wonderful writings?"

She actually drops her head. "No, sir. I haven't, to speak truth. Oh, I am terrible, sir." Her thoughts move slowly enough from one side of her mind to the other, before reaching her lips, that one can almost track their shambling progress beneath the brunette coils. "I can read, though, as could my husband, and I will read the Good Book of a morning. And my husband would read his Bunyan, whilst he lived."

"Do you not know, then, for what particular book it is that Johnson is renowned above all others?"

A pause. "No, sir."

"Truly? You've never once heard it mentioned?"

The eyes are wide now. But she shakes her head.

I cannot keep the disbelief out of my voice. "It is the *Dictionary,* Mrs. Parry."

She gasps, but says not a word, and I cannot help but laugh in disbelief. "Mrs. Parry, it is the dictionary of your *language.* He is the first man to accurately draw a map of the English language entire. No explorer of China or the African coast has ever or will ever do more. That you and I may understand one another so perfectly is in no small part a tribute to the work of the man sipping port in that little chamber upstairs."

I can tell that my words will elicit a long, stumbling apology—for her careless reading, for her faulty education, for who and what she is—and it is something I can certainly do without. And so I move things along. "But let us talk literature another day. You will remember, madam, that we will have guests this evening, a goodly number, though I cannot say at the moment precisely how many." A significant pause then, my eye directly on hers. "And as I indicated when last we spoke, some of those guests will be women, and some of those may be women with whom Mr. Johnson would not wish publicly to be associated. We understand one another, madam."

As I say, she does not like this particular aspect of the surprise party—has not since I mentioned it in passing last week—but for all her protestations of moral rectitude, Mrs. Parry understands that in addition to paying her well last week, I will pay a good deal more this evening, and Johnson will pay well over the long term.

And no doubt these women of ill repute would not be the first in her private rooms, if we were in fact to entertain any this evening.

In any event, she nods, lips a little tight. So much for the decency that Johnson lauds in her. But then, if she has been lowered in my eyes, Johnson has been lowered in hers. We are all in good company, then.

"Excellent. To review, as you serve the gentlemen their meal, I shall come up the stairs behind you and slip into the empty room beside their own. Once you've satisfied them and they have no further commands, you will exit, leaving the key with me, and I will lock the oak door to the stair as you go down. My guests will be coming up the back stair, which you showed me and which seems entirely private and suited to the purpose.

"Should we need anything more than the food and drink already upon the table, I will come downstairs personally to request it. Otherwise, we are to be left strictly to ourselves. No prying eyes or peeping toms. Mr. Johnson will be highly displeased if his very uncharacteristic night of revelry becomes the subject of public sport."

She is shaking her head, eyes on the floor. "Never, sir. Not in my house. I've told my other waiter, and young Michael, that they mustn't venture up the stair. Private party, I've told 'em both. Private is private, I've told 'em."

I put my hand on her shoulder, and I can feel the heat of the big body beneath it, like the lathered flank of a Shire workhorse. "But think, Mrs. Parry," I go on, in the most soothing voice I can manage, "do think how grateful Mr. Johnson will be when I tell him tonight, on our walk home, the clever way you managed the details of the affair with me. Nothing so moves a man as an attention paid upon his birthday. You shall have his heart forever."

She is pleased enough to forget the nymphs up the back stair, and a genuinely lovely rose blush steals over her features. "We do try our best here, sir. And thank you for your kindness to him. God love you for it, sir, truly."

She reaches out very hesitantly, to touch my sleeve, which I allow.

"Not at all, Mrs. Parry. After all, a man is fifty but once."

Which is true, with the notable exception of Samuel Johnson, who actually turned fifty just shy of four years ago, but who—in the mind of Mrs. Parry, and the Lord God willing—will turn that momentous corner once again tonight.

As I am closing the door to the stair behind her, Mrs. Parry spins unexpectedly about and looks up at me, in order to exchange one last secret wink, and it is all I can manage to wink back at her. But then she is gone, her big hams and feet working the flaking staircase like a concertina as she goes.

I turn the key in the lock and place it in my vest pocket. And in the sudden quiet I can hear them, talking. Or, rather, it is Johnson I can hear, the insistent bass vibrations of the voice working their way through the thin walls.

Wrapping my fist about the door's knob, I give it a silent experimental pull. I have already tested it earlier in the week, when I inspected the upstairs rooms with Mrs. Parry, but there is no shame in reassuring oneself. It is a good door, this, solid oak, newly fitted up. A man might batter his way through it with the proper tools, but it is thick enough to defeat even the largest and most determined shoulder.

Treading lightly, I turn and make my way along the narrow passage. It is decently lit by a single lamp midway down. A threadbare green carpet snakes down the heart of the passage, tacked pragmatically to the floor, and I can move all but noiselessly.

Not that I worry overly much about noise. For all James and his guest know, the other chambers on this floor will be occupied with other drinkers, as are they ordinarily. They have no idea that I've taken possession of the rooms surrounding them, of the entire floor. It is a surprise party, after all.

Before me lie four doors. First on my right, the door to my own empty chamber; then on my left, a smaller, colder room for which I have no use this evening; and then, finally, the room containing James and Johnson, their bottles of port, their fire, their beefsteaks, the culmination of their lovely day's excursion together.

And away beyond their chamber—directly opposite me—the door leading to the house's back staircase. This door gives me not nearly the satisfaction of the first: it is a paneled door, thinner, and rattles a bit in its frame. Still, it has a lock, and I have the key, and once I've used it I retrace my steps down the passage with decent confidence.

My own chamber is prepared as specified: the meal sits cooling upon the board, a bottle of wine stands open, a second unopened but at the ready, and a pretty range of glasses has been laid out for my guests. A tidy fire plays in the grate.

It would be an admirable little welcome for guests, if any were expected; but even so, here are all my needs of the next half hour very adequately met. I have not eaten for hours, and only the Lord knows how long it will be before I have the chance again. So I must sup. And of course the curiosity to hear their conversation as I do so is overwhelming. Fortunately, no amanuensis is necessary here—I have had the table placed near the wall connecting this chamber to James's. And as I sit down to my meal, I can hear their voices clearly enough to follow their conversation.

James is speaking of our family—bragging of it, that is to say, and of the family seat at Auchinleck, the newly built house and the Old. His voice is a bit higher in pitch and lower in volume than Johnson's, and so I merely manage to follow the drift. But I have heard him speak at length many times of those he invariably refers to as our "venerable ancestors," and I would guess that he has been speaking now for the better part of half an hour on the subject.

But when Johnson's voice booms, I hear every word.

"I must be there, sir," Johnson insists, "and we will live in the Old Castle; and if there is no room remaining, why then we will build one." And then the two of them go about the business of planning the inconceivable: a trip together to Scotland, which Johnson claims to detest, and particularly the family's Auchinleck estate, which James claims to love.

It is a thing I could not have imagined. As I listen, I can feel the anger suddenly stirring its limbs inside me again. It makes my breath come short and the blood suddenly charge in my veins.

I have an impulse to pick up the chair next to me and dash it against the wall, to throw the two of them into a panic, to let them know their words have immediate consequences.

Still, it won't do to approach the most delicate part of the evening in a rage. Too much planning has gone into the day, and too much may still be gained.

I take off my coat and force myself instead to begin eating the meal laid out for me, tearing into the chicken and wolfing it silently down, but without a trace of satisfaction as I do so. The meat seems to drop into my stomach and away from me somehow, without ever lessening or reaching the hunger. Of the wine I drink little, a sip here or there, nothing to dull the senses or the reflexes.

And I cannot help but brood and simmer. It is not enough that they would claim the Town as their own and publicly deny me any share in its more exquisite pleasures. It is not enough that the two of them have thrown me only private scraps of friendship, never acknowledging me in the light of day to one another, or to their host of powerful friends. Not enough that of the entire city of London, they have left me the run of a single room beside a damp, stinking stable.

Now they are laying plans to work the same neat trick at Auchinleck, my own home. To make me a stranger there as well.

I listen to Johnson's voice filling the room next door, and I cannot help but wonder: Can there be two Samuel Johnsons, in fact, stalking the streets, haunting the coffeehouses? Two rough citizens, twins for all the world, yet one so ferocious and unreachable, the other so very present and kind and near?

WE MET FIRST on London Bridge, yes, but after that he knew where to find me, and that he might find me, when he would.

Up Fish Street Hill, through the disheveled courtyard of the Starr Inn, and past the stable he would come, every week or so, late at night, once he had laid his own domestic menagerie to sleep, salved his conscience with a visit to the blind Mrs. Williams—then would Johnson come and knock softly.

And I would open the door to him, for reasons not so different from those motivating my brother: Johnson and I were also necessary to one another. We were also two fractions who had somehow stumbled onto the secret of the whole number, though another number entirely, of course.

He needed to come at night, when his presence would pass unremarked; he needed secrecy. And I needed him any which way I might have him, if only to feel as though secrets might exist for the purpose of including as well as excluding me.

Always we drank a glass of wine or two at my small table, and never was the wine the reason for his presence. Always we lay and fell together to sleep, and never was there more or less to it than a deep, abiding togetherness. A sense that sleep might come now because trouble could not.

And yet that is not the entire truth. There was something more.

Some nights I would wake in the smallest hours to find him no longer beside me, candlelight falling from the table across the room. His heavy body eclipsing the candle before him, he would be stretched across the table top, head cradled on his left arm, sleeves open and dangling, his right hand moving slowly but tirelessly back and forth across the page. I would lie there and watch him as he watched the pen twitching in his own hand, puzzled over it himself like a mouse he'd surprised foraging in the dark.

I padded over to him one night and stood just behind him in my bare feet.

What are you writing, I asked, as softly as I could.

He started at the sound of my voice, then sat upright, turning to face me in his seat. He had no wig, and his hair was shorn very close to the scalp. Here and there were scars visible beneath the short fringe. A faint rumble sounded in his throat as he stretched, and righted himself, and considered the question. He looked exhausted.

It is a fable, he answered finally. *A silly, small thing.*

What is it called?

It is called nothing. I shan't name it until I am certain it will survive its birth.

Read it to me, please, I asked.

But he shook his head without hesitation. *It is far from complete. It is a nothing, nothing more than a trifle now.*

Then I shall keep watch for it in the bookseller's stall, and buy it as soon as ever it appears.

He cocked his head at me, finally gave an exhausted little laugh. *You will never find it, then. This will never appear under my name. I intend another pen name entirely, for even a trifle may tell on one.*

Tell it to me, then, I demanded. *At least tell me some stray bit of it.*

He seemed to consider the possibility, a finger outstretched to brush the final words he'd written, to test the ink there. He turned the finger over to reveal a small letter *e* inked with perfect legibility across the pad.

It seemed to decide him, somehow, and he told me the story in its entirety.

It is the story of a girl named Floretta, Johnson began. *Floretta rescues a goldfinch from certain death, only to discover that the tiny bird is in reality a pisky queen, Lady Lilinet. This queen has wondrous magical powers. And she offers Floretta the use of two fountains, one sweet, to grant her wishes, and the other bitter, to rescind them when they prove unwise.*

For what does she wish? I asked.

What you might imagine. For beauty, for love, for gold, even wit and imagination. Each is a curse, and each time Floretta must then drink the bitter water of the second fountain, to return her life to a semblance of its original form. Finally she asks the first fountain for eternal life. And that too is a curse, worse than the rest. She grows old, peevish and diseased in her body, and she lives in terrible fear of senility, of imbecility. But she cannot die.

Johnson had his eyes down on the paper, and it was clear to me that he had now gone far beyond what he'd managed to commit to the page. He was describing the thing as it existed in his mind alone, or rather the ache of it in his own breast.

What does she do then?

Again he looked dully down at the paper before him. *She does all that she can do. Floretta drinks of the second fountain and asks that her immortality be taken from her. An act that renders her mortal once again. The pisky stands over her as the life ebbs from her body.*

I waited, but there was no more. With the candle obscured behind him, his expression was hidden from view.

Is there no more to the story? I asked finally.

Only this, he said, and then slowly brought his lips to mine. Again, it was not like Gentleman's kiss, not devouring, but warm, and human, and quick with life.

And when he had kissed me, Johnson drew back, his face again striped with shadow. I could see his lips move, but not his eyes. *Lilinet kisses Floretta and then watches over her as she passes into death. Thus ends the tale,* he said.

Something in his voice made my heart stumble.

That is the end of your fable? I asked finally. *Is there no way for Floretta to be wakened, no charm to heal her? Even from the sovereign of these magic beings? It cannot be so.*

He shook his head, then folded the page carefully. *No, she must die. And once dead, she must remain so.*

But you are the writer, I protested. *You have only to wish it to make it so.*

There was silence as he considered the accusation, and suddenly I could hear noise from the stable, horses being roused. Daylight was not far off.

You have heard not a word I have said, have you, John Boswell? he asked after a moment, then touched his fingers briefly to his tongue and pinched the candle out between them.

* * *

AT MY DIRECTION, Mrs. Parry has left a basin of warm water, a pat of soap, a nail brush, and a small clean towel on a table beside the fireplace. There is also a hank of lemon, which I crush over the water before dipping my fingers. I let them soak in the warmth for a moment, and then begin to use the brush on my palms, the backs of my hands, the knuckles, then the nails. When I've finished, I dry them on the towel and hang it on a nail above the fire to dry.

No doubt Mrs. Parry thinks me a fastidious host. But the truth is that the dags are short, snub-nosed weapons, the handles just half the span of my hand, and the gold of them polished to a sheen. Excellent in their way, but a poor sort of weapon to manipulate with greased hands.

Now, as I pull them out of my coat and lay them on the table before me, my clean fingers adhere nicely to the gold. The guns were cleaned themselves this morning, before first light, and loaded carefully. My only regret about these weapons is that I will never be able to show them to James Bruce, the overseer at the Auchinleck estate. Bruce was the man who taught me the finer, and then the finest, points of marksmanship.

Summers at the estate—when my brother James was off chasing actresses in Edinburgh, and my father locked up in his study—Bruce would teach me to swallow my breath, slit an eye, and hit a hummingbird sipping from a bud at twenty-five paces.

The only thing James Bruce loved more than his pointers and his newly planted trees were his guns. And he liked to say that in the most important ways, the guns were no different than the dogs. *They want nothing more than to please, you see,* he would say, burnishing a piece with his thumb, *but a man mustn't forget that they are animals, finally, and they've a muckle mouth full of teeth.*

And I remember the teeth, as I re-prime and check the loading of each piece. Hammers uncocked, quiescent, the dags lie together now on the table, giving back the firelight in a deep ruddy glow. I check my coat pocket as well for my little *cartouche* box. Inside it lies an additional charge, a clever paper packet containing both powder and ball. The charges that came with these pistols were exceptionally well manufactured, the bullets themselves deftly wound up in a little twist at the end, to allow the user to bite them off cleanly and quickly should the need arise.

And beyond their unusual quality, these packets held another distinct charm: the lead balls at the tip of each had been dipped in gold as well. They gleam like tiny suns. The goldsmith who made these pieces was an artist, rather than a craftsman, and apparently he could not abide the thought of unpainted lead marring his twin golden dreams.

But then these dags were meant to down a king and a king's consort. Or so the story goes.

Four charges came in the cartouche when I purchased the guns, and I can't run my eye over the two loaded weapons and the spare packet remaining without recalling the fourth, missing, golden bullet.

By now it must lie in the fob pocket of Gil Higgs, his index finger stroking it worriedly even now. Or perhaps it lies in a box hoarded away somewhere out of the reach of his drab wife. But it is safe, that much is sure. It can only be a treasure for Higgs, this strange gold-dusted sphere, though not the sort one cares to haul out and wonder over. Rather it is the sort of treasure that must be saved, but must also be regretted.

But I am confident that even if Higgs manages to hide the evidence for the rest of his days, he will never forget the moment when his Maggie opened her filthy little white hand to reveal the gilt secret.

Nor will he ever forget the little story she told: how a man in a red coat had given it her one day, in the street, and told her she might have another whenever her father said the word.

In the cheap mirror over the fire, I wipe my face with a damp napkin, untie and then retie my longish hair. There is a small scar running into the dark brow over my left eye, a tiny white hash mark there, the companion to a larger mark under the hair at the back of my head. Both are mementos of the fight at the water kiosk in Edinburgh years ago, and both, in that indirect way, gifts of my brother. I wet my finger and smooth the dark hair of the brow over the hairless notch, as I do when I would be presentable.

Thus satisfied, I put on my coat and return the pistols to their facing pockets beneath my arms. Then I seat my hat, cocking it forward a touch, to the left a touch. If ever a man should remember his military training and dignity, it is now.

Only then do I leave the room, walk directly down the short span of hallway, and rap twice quickly, loudly on the door to their chamber. There is a marked silence, and a pause: clearly this is no Mrs. Parry begging entrance.

And then, before either can answer, I simply open the door and walk in.

17

I HAVE SAID that this new memory of mine functions, when it will, like a Hogarth progress, giving up only a linked series of static remembrances, these punctuated by blackness, nothingness. And it is a genuinely puzzling thing, to realize that one's mind contains something like an editor who—for reasons of his own—has taken suddenly to holding back bits of the past. It is an effect I chose not discuss with my Plymouth doctors, as I had in mind being discharged, and that as quickly as possible.

And it did not seem such a cross to bear, really. Still, if I dwell on it, it is unsettling and even frightening.

For it implies that one is simply a tool in the hands of a larger, more capacious version of oneself—a self with a more methodical understanding of events. And this overmastering self acts under a certain logic, or set of principles, which it will under no circumstances explain.

All of which leaves only one of two working hypotheses: that the disappearance of memory is designed to protect me, or to protect this hidden editor himself. Either I contain a powerful ally, that is, or something that cares nothing at all for me.

Still, as my mother is wont to remind both James and me, God is good and balances what He must take with what He is prepared to give. It is no less so with me. If I have lost reliability of recall, I have gained an intensity of perception that I cannot remember from earlier in my life. It is as though the present, passing, ephemeral moment is also a piece of art I may study somehow at my leisure.

And that is precisely what happens as I enter their room. The scene is spread out before me, and I experience it perhaps more profoundly than any other in my short life. The moment lingers even as it runs.

Like the empty room I have just quitted, the one I am entering is composed of dark paneled walls and faded though clean plank flooring. The fireplace here is significantly more elaborate, with an impressive mahogany mantel, but no fire burns within it. No doubt Johnson is easily overheated in the summer months, even with a cold rain raking the window. And their room seems if anything a bit warmer than my own. Their endless talk generates its own heat, apparently.

A tall, lacquered clock stretches nearly to the ceiling, and as my gaze sweeps across it I note that it is just fifteen minutes to nine.

Other than the clock, the only furniture is a massive oak table pushed into the corner of the room nearest the fireplace. And as I turn my attention there, I begin to see why James and Johnson prefer this back room to the room over the street.

It may well be, as Mrs. Parry says, that they don't fancy dust and the sound of the occasional fish-crier, but clearly there is something more: built cunningly into the walls of that same far corner of the room is a cushioned semicircular bench, just large enough for two large men to lounge comfortably. With the heavy table drawn up snug, Mrs. Parry at his call, and the fireplace no more than a poker's distance away, Johnson must see this wall-bench as the spindle around which the very London universe turns.

It is an intimate spot, placing his listener within very easy reach, and I suppose it is not just any companion Johnson would usher into it.

Seated there now are Johnson and James, perhaps all of two feet between them. James still wears the violet suit, his newest and current favorite, a measure of the importance he attaches to today's excursion. He looks about to burst his matching violet buttons, so smug and well-fed does he seem. Johnson is characteristically in brown, coat, pants, and waistcoat.

And I am struck again: my twenty-two-year-old brother has known this man—this gruff, unapproachable literary lion—all of two months, and they are different in almost every conceivable way. Yet they club together like old school chums.

They have pushed themselves a bit more upright at my knock, but it is clear still from their posture that they have spent the last hour slouched against the wainscoting, arms thrown out along the rail, stomachs tight with good beef, making credible headway through the second bottle I've had them sent, generally luxuriating in the sense of a day well handled. Now there is this insistent knock, though, and they have been moved momentarily out of their indolence.

But not completely. Even now they project the air of men determined to deal with this disruption quickly and return to their talk of books and their new fantasies of travel.

That is, until I have taken a step or two into the room and James registers my face. His response is something of a gestural explosion: he sits bolt upright, and the placid, well-fed expression collapses; the eyes go wide, the mouth drops open, and he brings a hand out and up suddenly, as if to point, or wave, or shield himself. And then the hand simply drops back uselessly to the wine-stained cloth.

But he is not finished, at that. In his shock, James tries to rise, to take control of the situation, but the pitch of the bench and the bulk of the table before him make it difficult, and finally he can only squirm awkwardly in his seat. So much for the social mastery my brother claims to have cultivated this past year.

Had I no idea how desperately he has tried this year in London to prevent my penetrating his new circle, I might be disappointed to see him look so very distressed, so entirely unable to counterfeit pleasant surprise.

But I know it very well, of course.

Still, it is no pleasant thing to experience, this mixture of open alarm and anxiety on the face of one so recently a playmate and confidant. One so recently a true brother.

I have prepared a greeting, in the same way that I have prepared all else today, but there is no need, for James's shock drives him to speak first. His manners have left him entirely. He simply blurts the words: "Good Lord! John, you are in London again. There must be—"

Again James pushes off the cushion with his hand, as though he would rise to his feet, but again settles back down. And then his eyes come to rest knowingly on mine, as though he has discerned the truth suddenly. "Is it Father, John? Has something happened to Father? Tell me quickly. Is there some illness at home?"

I come to a stop at the far side of their table, and I cannot help but laugh out loud at the question. It is so like James to construe the world according to his own deepest desires.

"Father is very well, as always," I tell him. But I cannot resist another chuckle and an old dig: "Calm yourself, Jemmie. You are not yet a Laird, I'm afraid."

The laughter and the old farcing seem to relieve him. He settles back a bit against the wainscoting, and a sheepish smile touches his lips. Only then does James remember his manners, and he turns with some alacrity to his companion.

"Please, sir, do excuse my lack of civility. And permit me to introduce my younger brother, John Boswell. John is—well, he was recently in London, for several weeks, and returned then to Edinburgh. On business of his regiment." With that deft little euphemism, James swings back to me, takes a breath and forces a full smile. That I am to second this empty little summary is amply clear.

"And now apparently he is back again," James finishes.

"Apparently so," I say.

"And this, John," he informs me then, hand cocked nonchalantly to his left, "is the celebrated Mr. Samuel Johnson."

It is true that James has spent a vast amount of effort concealing his London conquests from me. But it is also true that now, with no choice but to acknowledge his prize of prizes, he does so with barely restrained glee.

And with good reason, I must admit: it is our Dictionary Game taken to the highest imaginable level. He has taken possession not merely of the book, but of the Lexicographer himself. As far as he knows, James has won the game for all time.

I pull off my hat. And only then do I allow myself to do what I have wanted to do since entering the room: I pause and make a full bow before Johnson, the lowest the circumstances will permit, and the most sincere of which I am capable, bringing my hand even to my heart.

As I do so, I can feel the emotion rushing to my face, and I determine to down it, to let neither of them see my need written there. Yet I am reluctant to straighten and look into the man's face, for then there will be no returning to the world that Was. The most pressing question will be answered: either he will own my friendship, my companionship—own my *self,* cracked and patched as it is—or he will not.

When I do straighten, it is to find Johnson looking me over slowly, the unkempt brows knitting in concentration. His glance has all the appearance of genuine benevolent curiosity, as though he is in fact looking over the brother of a good friend for the very first time.

He meets my glance just once, but holds my gaze longer than one might engage a stranger's eye. I'm certain I can see him inside that glance, the Samuel Johnson I know. And I almost sense that he is saying something with the directness of this look, conveying a message, even pleading with me somehow.

But then he smiles, and it is a prepared little smirk.

And he says to me, "I am very pleased to make your acquaintance, sir."

There I have my answer, or one of them. The world that Is: he will not acknowledge me, at least not of his own accord.

For the first time in my experience of Johnson, he reminds me of a man in every aspect his inferior—of Gentleman, that is. Gentleman had the actor's ability to disappear completely into a version of himself that had never whispered in my ear, never held me, never seen me as anything other than the painfully shy, tagalong brother of a wealthy patron. Gentleman's face, his eyes, could utterly disavow what he had done with great eagerness just moments before.

He could give you the impression that he was altogether innocent and uncomprehending, that your memory was the stuff of dreams. That you were insane.

Effortlessly, Gentleman could do this. Later, he would apologize and cajole and explain the need for secrecy. An actor lives by the public's favor, he would plead. And then he would do it all over again. And for weeks the betrayal would ache like a needle broken off in my heart.

Now, here, Johnson waits for me to complete the pleasantries, looking down his long gargoyle's nose, the smirk still in place.

And I find that I can only smile myself. After all, I am not unprepared, this night at least. I have much to fall back upon. And so I do something I never quite managed with Gentleman: I push a bit.

"Have we never met before, then, Mr. Johnson?" I ask.

"I have never had the pleasure, sir. It is a deficiency well remedied, however." The second bottle of wine has loosened his tongue a bit, heightened his gallantry.

"You are kind, indeed. But I have the most distinct recollection of a meeting. And that not too far in the distant past. I might swear it was recently, in fact. And certainly somewhere in London."

"I cannot imagine why."

"How strange. It seems so very clear to me, this impression."

Johnson hesitates. "You have the advantage of me then, I am afraid. I remember no such meeting." A button is missing from his waistcoat, allowing his stomach to force his shirt unflatteringly out into the light.

Sensing a slight shimmy in the conversation, James moves to right it. "No doubt you are remembering an engraving of Mr. Johnson's face, John, seen in a bookseller's window. I believe," he says to Johnson, voice taking on just the slightest sheen of flattery, "that such engravings of your countenance are common enough in the City these days, sir."

The great man nods complacently, and James smiles to see the compliment push home. And I smile as well, before pressing my thumbnail again against the exposed conversational nerve.

"I have seen such engravings, certainly," I say, and I hold his eye. I cannot keep a very faint chill out of my tone. "None a proper likeness, of course. But on my *life,* I believe we have met before. Perhaps we have eaten beside one another in a chophouse."

"I am sure we have not."

"Or passed one another on a bridge. Nothing remains so firmly fixed in a man's mind as a face glanced in a flash of lamplight, especially out over the water."

Johnson's smirk has disappeared all but entirely now, slowly replaced by a stony indifference. He glances once, but significantly, at James before putting a period to the subject. Suddenly his phrases are punctuated by sharp throat-clearing noises, like little barks. This is how he directs conversation, then, by showing his displeasure openly and easily.

"I cannot speak for whether I have been seen, sir. But certainly I must be allowed to be the sole and the only judge of what I myself have *seen.* I have never seen you before this moment, and I am not accustomed to having my assertions on such matters challenged. It is an odd point to insist upon. The important fact, I believe, is that we see one another *now,* and that your brother's introduction secures my good will. Let us speak no more nonsense about engravings and bridges, sir."

Predictably enough, James—whose senses have been carefully attuned for the sound of ruffled feathers all day—matches Johnson's tone.

"Indeed, let us turn to more practical questions, John. You have come a long journey, if you've come from home, and you have found us here dining agreeably, of all the coffee houses in London. But how is it that you have stumbled upon us, and why? You say it is not Father, but why then are you come? What is the matter? Pray let us have it."

There is a small backless bench resting beneath the near side of the table, and without asking I draw it out, set myself down upon it. "Oh, you are not so very difficult to trace, the two of you. You cut quite a figure about town. I have had much intelligence of your doings, I assure you."

Like the reference to his engraved image, this remark improves Johnson's mood, so much so that he shares the implicit compliment with James. "I have told you, have I not, Boswell," he says, "that the sight of an old dog laboring to keep pace with a young one would quickly become a jest. We are a sad pair."

"We are well matched for all of that, sir. I labor to keep pace in conversation, and so it is all one."

There is a nail jutting from the wall, just within reach, and I hang my hat upon it.

James watches the action, and it seems only then to dawn on him that I am making myself more or less to home.

But before he can ask his questions again, I answer them. "From your landlord, James, I learned that you planned to spend the day with Mr. Johnson, and that you would be rowing to Greenwich."

Here James blushes, his boasting revealed.

"And from your servant Francis Barber, Mr. Johnson, I learned that you were returned from Greenwich, and headed here to sup. As I say, neither of you would be a difficult animal to track singly. Together, you must give up concealment altogether."

More self-satisfied chuckling, before James leans forward, as if to clear away a last, annoying cobweb of mystery. "All right, then, I confess it. I *am* proud of a day's jaunt with Mr. Johnson, and may have hinted as much to Mr. Terrie. But why is it that you have come, John? What is the matter, then?"

I can only look at him, my brother. For even now, staring back at me, he has no idea. That I might have tracked them across the City simply in order to be *with* them, to be one of the party, he cannot imagine. Or perhaps he does imagine it, but wishes to pretend it cannot be so.

And so I tell him, plainly.

"Nothing is the matter, James. I have come to spend the *evening* with you. And with Mr. Johnson, if you will both have me. Is there such mystery there? Must I spell it out so very plainly? I have gone a long day's journey myself today, and I would have a glass with you. With you both, if I may."

But I can see immediately that the words find no purchase. Again Johnson and James exchange a look, and I see very clearly to the end of the next five minutes. Even to my own ear, my voice sounds pleading and schoolboyish rather than easy and sociable.

"It is wonderful to see you, of course, John," James begins earnestly, "but you find us only just now beginning what we have put off and put off all afternoon. Mr. Johnson has been so good as to agree to consult with me on the course of my education, before I sail for Utrecht. Tonight is perhaps our last opportunity. And as you know better than anyone else, attempting to educate me would consume the whole of any man's attention."

James has never been able to bear inflicting genuine pain or disappointment, for all his love of needling, and he throws out something quickly by way of consolation. His eyes are pleading with me.

"Come to me in the morning, when you have rested, and let us breakfast together. Then we will take a turn together in the Park and plot a fitting celebration of your return. And perhaps," here he shoots an inquiring glance at Johnson for approval, "the three of us may find another quiet evening before I leave to dine together in a more leisurely way."

Johnson gives a perfunctory half-nod, but no other sign that he approves the throwing of this bone. He has drawn back on the bench, drawn his arms up across his chest, and seems simply to be waiting out the tail end of this conversation.

And I try again, in a lighter vein, wagging my finger, but with less of a sense that anything is to be gained. "Ah, it is not right of you, James, to monopolize the conversation of a man such as Mr. Johnson. Truly it is not. I too have spent my youth reading and marveling over the *Dictionary*, after all. And I too smuggled in the *Rambler* when I was supposed to be studying my Latin."

My voice breaks up into nervous laughter. "And I am famished after my journey, famished this instant, not tomorrow morning. It is not a great deal to ask, I shouldn't think, to sit and listen and call for a bite to eat. Not a great deal to ask of an older brother, when a younger comes up to Town. And a soldier at that! Come now, don't be hard. Pour me a bumper, and I will pour you the next."

My insistence has left James at a visible loss about how to proceed. Above all, he does not want the little standoff to escalate into something unpleasant. That would tear the fine tissue of his day's excursion beyond repair. And yet sharing the day with me is nearly as unthinkable.

But of course there is no need for him to find a solution. His mentor and protector has sensed that James has been placed in a box, an uncomfortable one, and so suddenly Johnson flares to life.

He leans as far forward as the heavy table will allow, the big arms unwound and suddenly alive with irritation. The tiny barking tics of a few moments ago are lost in the low, sustained roar.

"See here, sir, I have lost patience with you," he says, all but glaring at me. "I have lost patience, and I tell you so openly. You have come where you are not invited, after wheedling information to which you were not entitled. You have rapped on our door, interrupting our conversation, and then marched into the room without waiting for the courtesy of an invitation.

"It is not enough that I assert, as a man does a thousand times a day, that we are strangers. You would have us previously acquainted, and *insist* upon it, put me to the odd task of disavowing it. I find it impossible to believe that he who raised your elder brother with such a notable sufficiency of manners can be responsible for your own questionable upbringing as well."

The blood is rushing to my face now, and there is no disguising it. James looks openly horrified, not for my sake of course but for his own. His body language could not be more clear: he has turned his back on me almost entirely, in a bid to calm his new friend.

Yet Johnson is not finished, not nearly so. He goes on, pointing his finger directly at me. "And now your brother welcomes you, but merely suggests a more appropriate moment to celebrate your return. He offers you his attention at breakfast, and in other ways. Attentions not every heir of every house in the Kingdom would offer a younger sibling. And *again*, you defy his civilities and make it clear that you will obtrude yourself until such time as you are asked directly to leave. If that is the only currency you will accept, then consider yourself paid.

"It is shockingly poor behavior, I tell you, shockingly poor. And being a brother—indeed, being a soldier—excuses none of it, but renders it in fact all the *more* inexcusable. We have much to discuss, sir, and little enough time in which to do so. That said, we will thank you to leave us to it."

Johnson finishes the rebuke out of breath, and his chest heaves a bit with the effort. His lips are tightly shut; the air whistles in his flaring nostrils. He is shaking his head slowly, back and forth. And then he sees something on the table that puzzles him, and he squints down at it.

It is my fist, resting on the tablecloth. And in my fist is one of the dags.

Johnson can only stare at it, confused perhaps by the dull sheen of gold.

And as he does so, I cock the piece audibly with my thumb. I swivel the muzzle so that it faces directly into the white hole produced by the missing button on Johnson's waistcoat. It feels good to point the weapon directly at him, directly at his large body. And it has a remarkable effect on the volume of the conversation, as well.

"John," James manages, testing rather than breaking the silence.

I say nothing, and Johnson—drawn up stiffly against the wall bench, fists balled, face a gathering thunderhead—remains mute as well.

Only then does the depth of James's enchantment become clear: rather than address me, and the gun in my hand, and the present threat to his own safety, he can think only of clearing his name with Johnson. "Sir, my brother is not well, has not been well. It has been a difficult few months. I should have told you before now. John has been hospitalized. His history of—"

I shift my gaze, but not the piece in my hand. "It is *our* history, James. We are a half-mad race, we Boswells. Do not deny it. I'm sure Mr. Johnson would prefer the truth of the matter, rather than fairy tales."

Johnson speaks then, nearly sputtering with rage. Still, the voice is low, and respectful of the weapon finally. "You have no idea *what* I would prefer, sir. You have no idea how civilized men *behave*. I will thank you never to speak in my name."

I look at him, and let my own voice come up. "And I will thank you to remember which of us can snuff out the other like a candle flame, sir." I pause a moment to let the threat settle in the warm air. There are only two reasons to draw a weapon—one is to kill outright, and the other is to manage behavior. In the second case, it is best to clarify the sort of behavior you seek as quickly as possible, better for all concerned.

"I've come to have a conversation with you both, a conversation I have found difficult to start in any other way. And I intend to manage this conversation very carefully, and believe me when I say that I will sooner see one or both of you dead than see it go unfinished. Honest answers are all that I ask, and such answers are the only door out of this room for the two of you. I'm afraid you must take me at my word. But I am yet a man of my word: if you deal honestly, no harm will come to either you."

James has always been on the heavy side, prone to sweating through his vests under the best of circumstances. Now his face all but shines in the light. This moment is precisely what he's feared since I came up to London in January—that I will shame him, harm him, blast his prospects. He has felt all of this and more, no doubt, but kept his fears to himself. But the three of us shall keep our secrets no more.

"I begin with Mr. Johnson. Do you know the particular word for the object I hold now in my hand, Mr. Johnson?"

Johnson's lips remain tight. He will not play, apparently.

"It is a word that appears in your own dictionary, sir. Come now."

James very slowly begins to lean forward, as though to speak with me, and for the first time I move the piece in his direction. "Do not interrupt, James. Surely Mr. Johnson can answer a simple question about the book for which he is so widely acclaimed. Can you not recall the word, sir?"

"It is a *pistol*," Johnson says finally. He cannot tell whether to humor me, and hope to talk the gun from my hand, or to thunder at me and demand it. And so his answers to my questions are at once careful, withering, and quiet.

"A brilliant response, Mr. Johnson. Your famed perspicacity is on full display. Yes, it is a pistol. Cocked and loaded, at that. But come, sir, what *sort* of pistol? Any man will call it a pistol, but only a writer of dictionaries would know its more specific name. Perform your function for us, if you will. If you can."

"John! You cannot talk to Mr. Johnson in that way," James hisses softly, unable to stop himself.

But Johnson answers in any event. "I am no expert on firearms."

"Indeed, and yet your dictionary contains all of the various terminology. Where came all of this recorded knowledge if you did not originally possess it yourself? I do seem to recall a story that your clerks—the men who actually wrote the book out in longhand—were Scots, were they not? Perhaps it is they who should be given credit for the work. Perhaps the authorship was more joint than is commonly understood. I hope you take note of this development, James."

Johnson does not take the bait, drawing short, shallow breaths. "I do not *know*, I tell you. Make of that ignorance what you will."

"It is a *dag*, sir. A word that appears prominently in your dictionary. Do you know the derivation at least?"

Johnson's face expresses happiness and joy only with great difficulty; it is designed for outrage, and anger. It is a troll's face. Now it is doing what it does best: the eyebrows slant down like two great dark slashes, the jaw juts out, and the wild networks of capillaries in his cheeks are aflame with color. His passion begins to get the better of his reason, clearly.

He begins, in a word, to become comfortable with the situation, comfortable enough to begin to assert his anger, and that must be quickly stamped out.

Suddenly, I lift the pistol into the air, my arm tightly outstretched, bringing the muzzle as close to his heart as I am able.

Not close enough to be swatted by one of the man's big hands, but close enough so that he may actually peer down into the open mouth of the thing and see a world lacking its Samuel Johnson.

Johnson speaks, but very softly and carefully. "You will not fire. There are twenty men below stairs who will take you the instant you do."

I continue to sight down the length of my arm, and out over the snub nose of the dag, and my own voice is comparably careful. "This is a very quiet piece, actually. And Mrs. Parry has been told to expect the tumult of a birthday party. With crackers and everything festive. She has assured me that our celebration will remain quite private."

James cannot restrain himself. "John! For the love of *God.* If that piece misfires, you may kill him before you know it. You may *kill* him."

"Be silent, James. One of us has spent a great deal of time learning to use firearms, and that one of us is not you. This pistol will fire precisely where and when I wish it to fire." I close an eye, slowly. And I allow myself to imagine what it might feel like to fire the piece. I allow my finger to test the very slight play in the trigger.

I realize that I could do this. I could pull the trigger, in fact. A part of me wants to do it, even now, before the man has finished his trial.

And the moment I know that fact about myself, the two men opposite know it about me. The effect is magical, instantaneous: Johnson shrinks back down into himself visibly, bows his head, brings his temper immediately back under cover. There is a story told in London of Johnson threatening to thrash a little mimic who planned to mock him from the stage, one Samuel Foote. Johnson apparently showed up with a cudgel and sat in the front row, glaring throughout the performance. And he frightened the man out of his bit of comedy.

But Johnson has no cudgel now, and it is he who faces the threat. And he is predictably malleable. Something glistens in the very corners of his bloodshot eyes, tears of frustration perhaps.

"Do you know the derivation, then?"

"Derivation? Of what?"

"Derivation of the term *dag*. You know it, or you do not."

"It is a corruption of the word *dagger*."

"Country of origin?"

He clears his throat, eyes on mine. The tone, finally, is deadly dry. "I believe it is from the French."

I lower the pistol and rest the hand holding it again on the table. "Just so. A corruption of the French word. And your definition runs thusly, '*A handgun or pistol, so called from serving the purposes of a dagger, being carried secretly and doing mischief suddenly*.' It is one of your better entries, I must say. Evocative, yet crisp and admirably to the point."

"Thank you," Johnson says after a pause, and then allows himself a small, ironic smile. And I find myself smiling back.

It is the first bit of decent acting he has managed. He would take me off my guard, perhaps move the conversation onto lighter topics, our shared love of words, possibly allow James to soothe me with some talk of our parents or our childhood.

But, despite the smile, Johnson's eyes remain watchful and livid behind it all.

James too has picked up on Johnson's attempt to lighten the mood, and he makes his own timid gambit. "John, please listen. Mr. Johnson does not know you as I do, and he has no way of knowing your sense of humor. But I think he begins to see, as do I, that you cannot be serious. You cannot be, John. You are paying me back for not welcoming you properly to London." He reaches for the bottle I had Mrs. Parry bring them. "Let us do so now. And we will continue your conversation wherever it leads. You have my word as a gentleman. But you must put up your weapon, John. You must."

"I must do nothing of the kind. It is all very much by the book, by definition: I have carried this dag here secretly, and I will do mischief suddenly if my questions are not answered. You say we have never met, Mr. Johnson."

Johnson meets my eye, remains silent.

"I say we have. I say we have met often in the last handful of weeks. Do you still deny it? Will you put me to the task of telling my brother how and where we have met?"

Now Johnson's expression falters, much as James's did earlier, guilt and disbelief chasing by turns across his face. He seems horrified, hunted. He can no longer tell himself that our secret will remain so. He knows now that I will have it out in the light, no matter what may come of it, no matter whom it may injure.

"You are genuinely mad," he whispers, sneaking a glance at James, only to find that James is anxiously watching him now, rather than me.

James clearly senses something beyond his grasp, and his head is cocked slightly, in bafflement.

"We met on London Bridge, Mr. Johnson. Some six weeks ago. You remember it as well as I. And you came to my room that evening, and you remember that as well. And James at least will know it all, if not the rest of the world."

Johnson is shaking, physically, with rage or fear it is impossible to tell. But his hand comes down on the table hard. "You lie—I have no idea why, but this is a desperate, unaccountable lie."

"It is you who lie, sir, and you will admit it. It may be that I can produce witnesses, but there is no need for that this evening. You will admit it, or you will die right there as you sit, atop your plush little bench, square in the middle of your own favorite back room in this benighted, godforsaken little coffeehouse. This is where the much-celebrated life of Samuel Johnson will end. Here and now."

There is humming silence again. That is when it becomes clear that Johnson would rather risk death than own me to my brother. For he turns slowly to James, and says in a low voice, though more than loud enough for us all to hear, "He has but one shot, Boswell. There are two of us, after all."

And I see James begin to work those dearer calculations in his own mind.

Only then do I draw out the second dag.

And the sight of it is more than James can bear. Actual tears start in his eyes, and he breaks suddenly into something like confession.

His voice is thick, but anguished, honestly so. "Johnny, I am so *very* sorry for what I have done to you. God knows that I am. I have regretted a thousand times the argument we had this past winter, because you were *right,* I was intent on hiding my life, my friends, my new acquaintances from you. I was unutterably selfish. London was new to me, and I feared that any false move might cause it to be snatched away from me. But that is no excuse. It was unlike a brother. And I am sorry for it, deeply, deeply sorry for it, and you must believe me."

My brother at least will spill his secrets, confess his sins to his god—half of what I want from this evening. And that is something. So I usher James along in his revelations, and in his self-condemnation, bit by bitter little bit.

"And so you kept me in the back rooms, and the bakeries, and the unfashionable chophouses. And you never once hinted that you were leaving me to wait upon the great and the mighty, did you?"

"It was wrong. I have admitted it. I have asked your forgiveness."

"And when you were laid up with the case of clap you had courted so long, you told me you were being denied to all visitors, including me. When the truth is that Garrick visited you, and Eglinton, and all the fashionable world. You made it an absolute standing policy to lie to me."

"I did, Johnny. I am not proud of it, as I told you in March." He turns to Johnson, unable to meet the man's gaze. "John found my journal, and saw that I had told him, told him a series of untruths in order to—"

"Told him *lies,* James, in order to keep your routs and masquerades and actors and countesses all to yourself, like a greedy evil little boy with a strawberry tart who must sicken himself rather than break off a piece for another who is starving."

James now has tears wetting his face. His hair, which he had so cleverly dressed this morning, has gotten the better of its ties and hangs wildly about his face. He is broken, clearly. The pretensions of social poise and maturity are all in tatters.

But there is a difference in his instinctive priorities now, even in his presence across the table from me. There is a distinct change, and I can feel it now.

He is pleading directly with me, the brother he has known and mostly loved since childhood, rather than with Johnson, who can be nothing by comparison, nothing but James's own narcissistic ambition given human form.

It is no act: James would not lose his life, but he would not lose me either. And I realize that that is something I came here to reclaim tonight as well.

"Jemmy," I say to him. And then I tip up the muzzle of the piece in my left hand, to show him that his life is safe with me, as always.

"You have done nothing that cannot be undone, James," I reassure him. "For I forgive you."

I can feel some of the anger subside within me even as I say the words, and I cannot help but remember a conversation we had long ago, about his Catholic actress in Edinburgh, when he wanted my connivance in a plot against everything he was raised to hold dear. I hear myself saying now what I said then: "I would help you, now that you are helpless, Jemmy."

And the entire massive oak table between us rises up suddenly into the air, impossibly, looming.

Plates and wine bottles and glasses shower over me, crash behind me. Silverware flashes by my face.

And then the table itself comes rushing at me, before the edge of it strikes my rib cage, and the weight of it topples over onto me, knocking me bodily to the floor.

I smell the stench of powder, and my ears are ringing.

The gun in my right hand is suddenly scalding hot. It slips from my fingers as I fall, clatters across the floor and strikes the wall. I can see it, gleaming in the low light.

But the world has gone truly mad, for the table—which must weigh twenty stone or more—continues to hover over me for an instant and does not complete its fall.

Rather, amid what I realize are James's terrified shouts, one corner of it rises somehow again, so that the whole pivots heavily on one corner alone. And the free edge of it then comes down like a blade, hard enough to snap my forearm.

I snatch the arm back, and the wood batters only plank flooring.

Then it rises again, the table edge, like a thing with a mind and a hunger of its own. The massive table spins slowly in the air, seeking me.

Johnson has hold of the other end, I realize too late, and I hear him straining with the effort to maneuver the thing, to crush me with it. His breathing is deep and frantic.

Again, the sharp edge comes down. But the table is too heavy finally, and it slips from his grasp, striking the floor hard just beside my shoulder.

Then, with a low cry, he simply drives the now cockeyed table forward with all of his strength, battering me once against the wall with the heavy leading leg of it.

It is my ribs that take the worst of it, again, and the pain lights up the entire right half of my body, an incandescent pain, like burning phosphorus.

I scream, only to hear the table slowly dragged back across the planks for another driving blow. But the second dag is somehow still in my hand. And in an instant Johnson and James have both seen it. And they have seen as well that with the table drawn away, I have only to raise my arm to have them in my line of fire again.

Which ends our conversation. In a rushing, almost tumbling movement, Johnson turns and bolts, following James through the open door out to the corridor.

Out and into what amounts to a long locked room. For I have the keys to the exits in my vest pocket.

But although I have only a moment to set things right again, I have the presence of mind to snatch the still-hot pistol from the floor and thrust it into my outer coat pocket. Midway I stop for an instant to stare at the thing: a small black halo now marks the gold barrel, as though the heat of the last shot has come half-way to bubbling the metal there. And I can hear the goldsmith again, as he turned the things teasingly in his long-fingered hands, telling me that these were designed for use by King George's own trained assassin, a man who would need no second shot.

Heaving with my legs, I force enough space between the table and the wall to stand upright, but as I do so there is a stab of pain across the lower half of my chest. A cracked rib or two, at the least.

I hear them drumming on the heavy oak door to the front stair, then boots crashing against it. And then, because there is no other choice, footsteps come pounding back down the long hallway to the rear exit.

I come around the end of the table and make as quickly as I can for the corridor. But Johnson has fallen against the lighter door, and bashed his way through it apparently, for the only thing I see when I reach the hall is a single flash of violet, disappearing without a trace into the black of the rear stairwell. Then they are gone.

And even as I pursue them down into what looks like nothing so much as a vast black hole in the ground—the broken door listing uselessly to one side—I am kicking myself for underestimating the man's strength. For no one knows it better than I.

HE WOULD LEAVE in the morning before the sun was up. He would pat my hair, carefully, and then leave me, stooping to avoid the low plaster roof above the bed. From the mat, I would watch him haul on his trousers, his large white shirt, the stockings, and the stolid shoes with their dull, conservative buckles.

Only once did I ask if I might follow him out into the City again, follow him to where he needed to go. Before the light, before we might be seen.

And he looked at me, lying there, and pursed his lips thoughtfully, and said I might.

Fish Street Hill was slick with the last night's rain, bringing up the smell of fish but mixed with the cleaner hint of open ocean. The Monument was only barely visible against the sky, brooding there in the dark, tinged with purple. Down we went, to the Bridge, and then together down the ranks of slick, unlit steps beneath, and then out among the little docks and clusters of moored vessels and warehouses making up the north bank.

Dark ships large and small splashed softly out in the current, like living things, like dolphins, eyes yellow with candlelight.

At last we reached a small dock not unlike the others, but this one he knew well, and he crouched down and placed his shoes and his stockings in a small wooden trap fixed beneath it. Then, in the first glimmer of morning, he stripped off his coat and his shirt and these he folded carefully and placed them also in the box, out of sight and up out of the current.

God be with ye, John, he said to me, and began to walk out into the water, the muscled, articulate arms spreading to embrace the Thames.

He fell slowly forward, taking the water on his deep chest, thick fingers paddling. And then the muscles ceased to play and began to work, effortlessly. He stroked at the water, three, four, five times very quickly, hands knifing through it. The power there was striking. And when he had nearly reached the shipping lane, the big shorn head came up once, for a last long breath, then plunged beneath the surface. A kick of his bare feet, and he was gone. Somewhere out in the deep current, moving swiftly.

A thing of the river.

PART SIX

At Present a Genius

Wednesday 9 February

How easily and cleverly do I write just now! I am really pleased with myself; words come skipping to me like lambs upon Moffat Hill; and I turn my periods smoothly and imperceptibly like a skillful wheelwright turning tops in a turning-loom. There's fancy! There's simile! In short, I am at present a genius: in that does my opulence consist, and not in base metal.

My brother drank tea with me and took a cordial farewell, being to set out for Scotland the next day. We parted on excellent terms. He is as fond of being at home as I am of ranging freely at a distance. My friend Erskine came and supped with me. I am excellently lodged. I get anything dressed vastly well. We had a very good evening of it.

—From *Boswell's London Journal, 1762–1763*

London, England
Wednesday, the 12th of January, 1763
10:30 P.M.

* * * * * *

18

IF THERE IS any satisfaction more profound than strolling into a respectable inn just off Fleet Street with a Covent Garden actress on one's arm, a false name on one's lips, and a sack half full of almond macaroons dangling from one's fingers, then James Boswell has never experienced it. Never has he come close, in fact.

He and Louisa had prepared their roles well, of course—complete with hackney coach and luggage and the macaroons to simulate a married couple fresh from the road—but still the reaction of the people at the Black Lion exceeded Boswell's expectations. And their earnest use of his pseudonym, given that it actually belonged to Boswell's favorite Edinburgh leading man, sent shivers of delight through him, each and every time.

In this happy blur of falsehoods, the travelers were ushered into the parlor and then up to the room reserved for them. And when Louisa coyly refused to undress in front of him, Boswell had tromped down the stairs and gravely desired the girl to go back up and see to Mrs. Digges.

Now, as he waits for Louisa to be unlaced and unhooked, brushed, powdered, and scented, Boswell stands in the little courtyard behind the inn, holding a candle. The night is very dark, and it is bitterly cold, but then that is the point of standing in the courtyard in the first place: Boswell's notion is that the more miserable he makes himself while he waits, the more pleasurable will be the transition to Louisa's arms.

And the plan is working perfectly. He has come down without his greatcoat, and feels himself being quickly chilled to the bone. Even in the closed courtyard, there is a wind, and the candle flame darts entrancingly back and forth inside the glass flute, holding Boswell's eye.

Finally, to make himself more miserable still, Boswell touches a few of the mental keys that he ordinarily takes great care to avoid: the faint possibility that he may be pacing a battlefield this time next year, stepping over bodies pouring blood; his infant child Charles, somewhere in Edinburgh, five weeks old, more or less fatherless and as yet unaware of it; and finally his brother John, whose appearance in London a week ago had first filled Boswell with pleasant surprise, then given way almost immediately to a train of niggling worries.

John had looked healthy enough, and he sounded remarkably like himself, Boswell thought. There was nothing of the inmate in his demeanor, nothing out of the ordinary in his talk. Other than his obvious relief at being released from Plymouth, John seemed very much John: a tall, inward, occasionally moody young man of nineteen, though now in a red coat and with more than a hint of the military in his bearing.

Still, Boswell could not get over the fact that his brother had spent nearly the last two months in an asylum.

Boswell had always been fascinated with hypochondria, if not outright madness, but here now was that fascination brought directly home to him, visited on his own younger brother. It was shocking, like watching lightning play away in the distance and then having it suddenly strike an inch away from one's boot.

It seemed undeniably ominous, especially given that their uncle

John Boswell's mind had degenerated so spectacularly in the middle years of his life. And there was the strange dissymmetry at work, as well: while John had been confined to Plymouth, Boswell had himself been turned loose finally in London, had shouldered his way into more than a few of the highest social circles the metropolis had to offer.

But now that John was free and had made his way up to Town, Boswell couldn't help but feel that his own fresh new London self was likely to be impacted, changed or qualified or even harmed somehow, and in a way beyond his control. It made him anxious, and it soured his stomach, almost from the moment John surprised him at breakfast. His mind was a tangle of questions.

And so he had invited John for breakfast the next day as well.

That was January 6, Twelfth-day, and, rather than breakfast in his flat, Boswell proposed a walk through the City, the sort of thing they used to do together as boys in Edinburgh. John readily agreed, but drew the line at Boswell's second idea—celebrating the English holiday by eating a penny Twelfth-cake at every shop where they could get one, up the length of Piccadilly and then back down the other side.

But he followed gamely along as Boswell set about stuffing himself.

It gave their conversation a pleasant on-again, off-again rhythm, in fact. Boswell would spy yet another tiny bakery tucked into a run of shopfronts, and they would stand together at the window, tricked out with a wren in a gilded cage or a shiny brass lantern. Each time, Boswell would duck inside and pop out again in a moment, with a penny cake sugared over but little bigger than a snuffbox.

"Twelfth Day!" Boswell would cry, holding the next miniature cake aloft. Only then would he devour it. But between stops and cakes, Boswell watched his brother. And after a while of this, he saw that John watched him in return, which moved Boswell to come to the heart of the matter.

"You have told me the facts, Johnny. But you haven't told me how it *felt*," Boswell began again, as they waded into the crowd outside St. James's Church. "You have yet to describe the way it *seemed* to you. That is what I would know."

Although John was taller and wearing a soldier's coat, the crowd tended not to part for him, and so Boswell was moving them through, holding his stick chest-high. He turned to catch John's answer, only to find his brother making a sour face.

"Of all the things I worried about in Plymouth," John said above the noise, "the worst was that I might in fact be released."

Boswell stopped and turned to him. "You were frightened of being released from the hospital?"

"Indeed. For once outside, I could only expect to be badgered to death by you about how it felt to be inside."

"John, I am serious. It is no joking matter, truly it is not."

"I can assure you I need no one to remind me of that."

Boswell steered them into the street and around a surly-looking group of chairmen, holding the wall. "I was worried about you," he continued, in a lower voice, "and you know me well enough to know that I am worried about myself as well, Johnny. I admit it. It is a family worry. I have been hoping you would share something of what you learned with me. At least a bit of it."

John could hold out no longer. He sighed by way of surrender, measuring Boswell with his glance. The glance stretched out though, and Boswell could sense a trace of something like distaste or disappointment in it. "You would know how it feels to be *mad*, is that it, Jemmie? Is that what you want from me, then?"

Boswell hesitated over the blunt language, then simply nodded.

"Well, then, let me answer once, and let that be an end of it."

"Of course, Johnny."

They moved forward again, and John thrust his hands into his pockets, twisting them there. He waited for a woman and her two small daughters to pass, and then began. "To be honest, I don't remember it, not clearly. That you must believe. Those days are murky in my memory. As though someone had attempted to rub out a charcoal impression, if you take my meaning. Dark and blurry. I remember being angry. That I can tell you. Very angry. Angry enough to scream and beat my head against a wall."

"Angry enough to harm your fellow soldiers?"

"Angry enough to *want* to harm them, want to batter them into rubble if they stood in my way," John answered, and a little laugh escaped him, but it was at odds with the redness of his eyes, the anxious way he scanned the crowd. His face was thinner, and longer somehow, than Boswell remembered.

"It is not a feeling one revisits with any pleasure, believe me," John finished.

And though he knew he was pushing, prying, Boswell could not help but ask what he wanted to know in yet another way. But he softened it by patting John's arm.

"You remember the anger, but not what you thought at the moment? Father said you—" Here Boswell paused, tactfully, tapped his stick along the stones. "At least it was reported to him that you raved at your fellow soldiers, accused them of things. Accused them of some conspiracy against you. Have you no memory of what you were thinking then, what caused the rage?"

John stood there in the street, and Boswell could tell that he was earnestly searching his memory. Not because he wanted to answer Boswell's question, necessarily, but because he would know the contents of his own mind, and finally did not.

"Each time I feel that I might remember more clearly," John managed, "the recollection steals around a corner. I see only its coattails as it disappears. Enough to be certain I have lost something, but never enough to be certain what it is I have lost." He hesitated a moment. "It is as though the memories themselves know which way I will turn my eye, and they wait until the very last second. And then they flee."

"As though they are taunting you," Boswell could not help but add.

"Very much so," said John.

That was all that either could say for the moment, because just then Piccadilly opened on the right into Baker's Pass, and Boswell spied three neat little bakeries standing next to one another down the side street, all perfectly in a row. And although his Twelfth Day vow had originally extended only to both sides of Piccadilly proper, it simply wasn't in Boswell's heart to deny England one more small smidgen of devotion.

BOSWELL STANDS IN the courtyard behind the Black Lion, now cold through to the marrow. If not miserable, he is at least stiff and shivering and thoughtful as he retraces his steps back through the yard and up into the house.

In reconsidering it, he can't help but be disturbed by two aspects of his Twelfth Day walk with John. He pushed his brother too hard, Boswell sees now, let his own fears take precedence over any concern for John's comfort. It was badly done. But also there is the matter of the walk itself. Rather than begin in St. James's Park and then take in the Strand and Fleet Street—Boswell's own unfailing daily walk—he took John to the Green Park and walked him afterward up Piccadilly.

He told himself at the time that the holiday displays along Piccadilly would outdo the Strand, but the real purpose now seems inescapable: to shepherd John away from Boswell's particular favorite route and the people they might meet along it. There is something in the realization that makes Boswell think less of himself as a brother.

The ground floor of the Black Lion is alive with lamplight, wonderfully warm. Boswell feels his spirits rise with the temperature. As he nears the stair, the chambermaid passes, head bowed, but he can make out the words, "Mr. Digges, sir," and again the sheer ludic pleasure of this evening comes home to him.

At the top of the stair, Boswell stops and draws a folded paper square from his waistcoat. Beneath the chandelier, he carefully untucks its interlocking edges. Even as Boswell's memoranda go, this one is tiny, secretive, and it blossoms into a message little larger than a daffodil. The voice is, as always, his own:

You go now to enjoy a woman you suspect you love, a handsome actress seen and desired by thousands of men. Yet it is you she has chosen. You are in full glow of health, youth. A more voluptuous night you may never experience. Remember each detail, and to-morrow walk out for air as she dresses, make notes. The last month of your journal builds the story of this intrigue. Tonight you satisfy Louisa and yourself; tomorrow you satisfy readers. One of whom will be yourself, years from now, in your comfortable Auchinleck retirement. That Boswell will envy you this night. Yet he will thank you, for committing all to paper. Keep best faith with him.

Boswell moves forward again, reworking and pocketing the square as he does so. His nose picks up the very lightest trace of perfume as he nears the chamber door—so very faint, in fact, that the scent may be generated entirely by his own imagination. But either way, it smells delicious.

He considers knocking, then realizes that he is well within his fictional rights to simply walk into the room.

But for the banked coals in the fireplace and a single candle, flickering at the bedside table, the room is dark. And he was not mistaken about the perfume: the scent lingers in the air, not Louisa's everyday choice, but something sharper, slightly more acrid. A bowl of negus, wine rich with fruit, sits beside the candle, as he ordered.

Louisa lies motionless beneath the coverlet. Only her dark hair, her slim hand, and a bit of her profile are visible. He sees the rise and fall of her breathing and the suggestion of a smile on her face, but she is silent. Boswell too says nothing, pausing to remove his coat and then his waistcoat, hanging each in turn on a chair near the window.

His shoes he unlaces and pulls off, then his shirt and breeches and stockings, and still Louisa says nothing. Finally, he comes to the bed wearing only his linen, and sits down upon it. Louisa's eyes remain closed, but the dimple in her cheek is unmistakable.

Boswell leans down to the shell of her ear. "Mrs. Digges," he whispers, "I must have a word with you. The table you set tonight was deficient, shockingly so. The melted butter was oiled," Boswell presses his lips softly to her lobe, goes on, "and with the meat upon the sideboard I am old friends, I'm afraid, having rejected it yesterday."

The dimple deepens, and then finally Louisa cannot help but smile outright. Her eyes remain closed, however. "Please, Mr. Boswell, we must drop the pretense. It is a wicked thing of us, to tell such lies."

Boswell leans to the ear and whispers again, a bit more loudly. "I will not have my authority questioned, Mrs. Digges."

"Do stop. You are terrible. You positively delight in the subterfuge, I believe."

"You could not be more correct. What man or woman does not delight in it? The subterfuge is like the sugar on a Twelfth Day cake. Without it you have a dull mass of flour and grease. But I will bargain." Here Boswell moves his lips down from Louisa's ear, to the perfumed hollow between her neck and jaw. "Within this room, we will cease to be Mr. and Mrs. Digges."

"I am glad you begin to behave."

"If you will agree to act the Queen in *Hamlet,* while I play the Prince."

Her eyes are still closed, but the dimple disappears. "Now you are simply wicked, sir. We must agree to be ourselves, plain and undisguised."

Boswell ceases nuzzling. "You are right. A mother and son would not do. Quite right. But suppose I play Claudius to your Gertrude."

"Mr. Boswell, please. You go from bad to worse. Claudius is a murderer."

Boswell purses his lips, considers it. "What say you to Polonius, then?"

Louisa buries her face in the pillow, her hands squeezing it tight, and he is uncertain for an instant whether he has pressed too hard, even in jest. But she is laughing, chortling, Boswell can make out after another second.

Louisa sits up suddenly and brings her arms and bare shoulders out from beneath the blanket, tucking the material snugly back around her breasts. As always, the dusting of freckles across her chest catches his heart. She settles back against the pillows, holding the blanket in place, holding his eye. "Here is the bargain, then, if we must bargain. You may speak any line from Hamlet, and I will give you back the speech that follows. One set of lines, and that is *all.* You must agree, hand on heart, that you will be satisfied with that and no more."

Boswell is impressed. "I may prompt you with any line, by any character? And you will give me the next speech? In the entire play? You have a prodigious memory."

"It is my profession, after all. And I work at it."

Boswell is almost beside himself with delight, and he takes her hand, brings it to his lips. He can prompt her to speak any set of lines he thinks will best fill out the journal entry he will write tomorrow; and tomorrow he can record the fact that she actually did so in good conscience. It is writing his life as though it were fiction.

The possibilities are all but endless. But Boswell is nothing if not amply prepared. He settles on the last two lines of one of several speeches he has spent part of yesterday and this morning memorizing.

It is Hamlet, because for all of his other joking suggestions Boswell has never for an instant intended to play anyone other than the Prince of Denmark.

"Those that are married already," he begins, watching her face for signs of recognition, "all but one, shall live, the rest shall keep as they are. To a nunn'ry, go."

Louisa closes her eyes for a moment, and when she opens them again, she fixes her gaze on Boswell's face. She looks deeply into his eyes, face impassive. They watch one another for five full seconds, then ten. Only slowly does her expression sadden, and for an instant he thinks she has simply failed to remember the answering speech.

But the eyes seem gradually to gather the candlelight, and he realizes with a start that the shimmer there is the first hint of tears. Louisa continues to look at him with open, authentic hurt, as though she has somehow seen beyond the walls of the Black Lion, seen him for the worst that he is capable of doing, the very worst that he is capable of being.

"O what a noble mind is here o'erthrown," she begins softly, a catch in the voice, and Boswell must remind himself several times as the speech continues that she is not in fact speaking to him, at least not directly.

19

IT IS NEARLY one the next afternoon before Boswell and Louisa leave the Black Lion and step into a hackney coach Mr. Hayward has himself personally fetched. It is a later start than what they had planned, but having promised his select readers an extraordinarily voluptuous night, Boswell has hardly been in any mood to see it finished prematurely.

Only well after three in the morning—when the extent of the voluptuousness could no longer be in any doubt—was he content to sleep.

And this morning too he has given Louisa a good hour to rise and dress, during which time Boswell patrolled languorously up and down Fleet Street, finally ducking into the Somerset Coffee-House, where he called for a dish of chocolate and wrote up a pleasingly thick little packet of notes for himself.

Those notes are now in Boswell's breast pocket, and as Mr. Hayward closes the coach door behind them, Boswell relishes the feel of them there, almost as much as he savors the presence of Louisa on the seat beside him. She is bundled once again in her gown, her boots, green coat, sable cap, feather muff. Only her pretty face is visible, the pale cheeks and red lips, but when he catches her eye, Louisa gives a sly smile, and then turns to look out the window again.

They are headed for Soho Square, where she has errands to run and where no one she knows will see her alight from the coach. As the coach clatters past the Temple, Boswell catches a quick glimpse of the door to Samuel Johnson's Inner Temple apartments. In spite of his promise to bring Boswell and Johnson together, Dilly has said nothing about the possibility since Christmas Day, almost two weeks ago, and Boswell is suddenly mildly disappointed all over again.

Yet, if he *had* met Johnson on Christmas Day, Boswell has no doubt that he would now be celibate and dedicated to a virtuous Johnsonian existence. The events of last night would never have occurred. There would be no delicious ache in his muscles. The notes in his pocket would not exist.

And these considerations lead him back to a place his thoughts have taken him more than once before: the suspicion that God himself is ordering Boswell's year in London, that He has delayed Johnson's influence for a reason, quite possibly because He too could not resist seeing the Louisa story brought to its sweet, natural conclusion.

As they reach Holborn Street, Louisa puts the feather muff aside and reaches over to take Boswell's right hand firmly in both of hers. "Mr. Boswell," she begins, "I have but one favor to ask of you before we part."

"You may ask anything of me. I can deny you nothing now, you must know."

She smiles again, presses his hand, but her expression is no longer playful. In spite of fresh powder, he can read the long night in her face, in the tiny lines here or there, the very slight puffiness beneath her eyes.

She hesitates, then brings it abruptly out. "Whenever you may cease to regard me, or to care for me, pray don't use me ill, nor treat me coldly."

"Madam, come, let us not talk of such a thing!"

"Please, for that I could not abide. Truly I could not. That sort of calculated coldness designed only to bring on a separation, it is inhuman. Just inform me by a letter or any other way that it is over. Be kind in that way. That is the only favor I ask."

Boswell feels his heart go out to her, instantly and unreservedly. He cannot resist taking her in his arms for a moment, whispering to her, consoling her. "Madam, have you forgotten last night so soon? How intimate we have become? Indeed, we cannot answer for our affections. No man or woman can do so. But you may always depend on my behaving with *civility*. You must trust me for that, if for nothing else."

With that, they roll into the Square, and the coach driver pulls up short, leans down to rap softly on the side of the carriage. Louisa comes quickly out of Boswell's arms, begins to gather herself to alight, but before she can say or do anything more, he suddenly hugs her tightly again, so tightly that she can only laugh in delighted surprise.

"I suspect I love you, Mrs. Digges," he whispers as they come apart.

And Louisa strokes his cheek and then kisses him quickly and matter-of-factly on the lips, as though she understands very well that he has just confessed far less than he might otherwise have done.

BOSWELL WATCHES LOUISA go until her fashionable green-and-sable outline is lost irretrievably in the Soho crowd. And then he watches just another moment more, to see the world press on without her, and to test his own response to her vanishing. When the coachman finally calls down for directions, Boswell gives him Louisa's own address on King Street, and the hackney lurches into motion again.

By the time they've navigated the Square, Boswell's sense of direction has been upended, any trace of Louisa's path erased. And although he misses her already, a small, reasonable voice inside says that tomorrow will be soon enough.

For the last several years, Boswell has had the romantic but unshakable idea that he will know his soul mate because she, and she alone, will discover the tiny letters inked at the hollow of his ankle. There is a children's-fairytale quality to the idea, of course, but that is precisely why he clings to it.

Still, the fact that Louisa is apparently not his soul mate causes Boswell's spirits to rise in any event. Finding a soul mate, like meeting Samuel Johnson, could easily ruin everything were it to happen a month or a year too soon, after all.

When the coach reaches King Street, Boswell tells the driver to wait, then goes to the door of Louisa's flat. There he asks for Louisa, and expresses some visible surprise when told that she is not at home. That accomplished, Boswell returns to the coach and for lack of any better idea gives his own Downing Street address. The night with Louisa has left him with the tingling feeling that he can cajole the city into giving him whatever he desires.

But after a quick moment, he can think of no good way to advance his two other Grand Enterprises, for Dilly will take his own sweet time producing Johnson, and Boswell is not to breakfast with the Duke of Queensberry until the following week, to discuss his commission. Then he has a wonderful idea.

Drury Lane Theater is only another block or so back through the Market, and if he cannot call on Johnson, to whom he has never been introduced, he can certainly call on Garrick, to whom he has, at least technically. Of course the chances of catching the great man in the theater and unoccupied are slim indeed, and slimmer still that he will consent to see a young man with no appointment whom he does not remember.

But the truth is that Boswell could not give a fig for the odds this afternoon, and he has the carriage brought immediately around.

IN THE SAME way that Johnson has always been an icon of morality and Englishness for Boswell, David Garrick—the Kingdom's most celebrated actor—has always signified culture and manliness and style. Boswell actually met Garrick very briefly two years ago, on his mad first excursion to London to convert to Roman Catholicism.

Since coming back up to London two months ago, though, Boswell has tried several times to cultivate the acquaintance by calling for the great actor at his house, but his cards have all gone unanswered. The thought of simply dropping by the theater itself has never seemed a possibility before now.

Having conspicuously dismissed the coach just outside the theater's Russell Street entrance, Boswell breezes through the stone arch and up into the foyer. He knows that the theater's offices are somewhere up off the gallery stairs to the left, but on a whim Boswell simply stops the first person he encounters, a middle-aged man with the look of a bookkeeper, and asks him to tell Mr. Garrick that Mr. Boswell would be delighted to speak with him, if he has a moment free. The man seems startled, but then simply nods and disappears. And when Boswell hears footsteps less than a moment later, he turns around fully expecting to see the bookkeeper once again, shaking his head and offering to take a message.

Instead it is Garrick himself, hand thrust out and his gravelly bass overwhelming the small foyer. "Mr. Boswell, what a genuinely delightful surprise! I was speaking of you just the other day with Mr. Sheridan, who says you have got a prologue for his wife's comedy that shows great promise. He said you were come up to Town, but I said he must be mistaken. You could not be in London without giving us the pleasure of your company at tea, I said. But Sheridan seemed quite sure, and here you are after all."

It is more than Boswell can well answer at once. As Garrick pumps his hand, he manages, "Indeed, I have called once or twice for you, sir, and left a card—"

"A *card.* Ah, there's the trouble," Garrick says, beaming. He is burly, but surprisingly short for an actor, Boswell remembers now. His suit—matching coat, breeches, and waistcoat of red corded velvet—is fashionably out of fashion, and it immediately makes

Boswell think less of his own figured vest. The face is dark by London standards, almost swarthy, the shadow of his beard clearly visible although Boswell would be willing to wager that Garrick was neatly shaved just this morning. "My wife has been known to order the day's cards cast to the four winds, if she feels our home is in danger of becoming a branch of Drury Lane. But in my defense, I must report that I bowed to you some weeks back in the House of Lords, but you did not observe me. My feelings were quite hurt, I assure you."

"Indeed! I am sorry for it. Of course, had I known—"

"Had you known, I could not have taxed you with it, and I should have had no defense for missing your calling card not once, but twice. And we should have no end of recrimination. I consider us well off. Have you seen the paintings of Mr. Zoffany in the Piazzas? Ah, these you must see, although, truth to tell, they are most of them of me."

And they are, of course: Garrick as Macbeth, Garrick as Lord Chalkstone, Garrick in a host of roles, as well as a series of sketches showing multiple Garrick prototypes, in a range of different attitudes.

Boswell is absolutely enchanted: it is like the Northumberland Picture Gallery, but with every other one of the paintings modeled after oneself. He looks over at Garrick, who is himself busy looking his various likenesses over, and speaks the first words that come to his mind. "Mr. Garrick, I would dearly love to know your secret."

"What secret is that, pray?"

"*This,* sir. All of *this* about us," Boswell says, waving a hand at the theater and the gallery, laughing.

Garrick looks back at the wall and nods once before steering Boswell away. "My secret? There is no secret. But shall I invent one for you?" He walks a moment in thought, then lowers his voice to a stage whisper. "As much as possible, strive to be someone other than yourself. Not as a whim, but as a deliberate mode of life." Garrick waits a beat, then adds, "I have found it a useful pursuit."

Boswell searches the man's face to see whether, and precisely how much, he is being kidded. "But suppose, in doing so, a man should lose himself altogether, never to find himself—his real self, that is—ever again?"

"You say such a man is lost. I say he is free. Indisputably free."

By the time they reach the foyer again, Boswell has sketched his plan for the Guards, which is to say his plan to remain in London, as well as his father's standing opposition. But Sheridan has backed him to the hilt.

"To be sure," Garrick maintains, "it is a most genteel thing, and I think, sir, you *ought* to be a soldier. As well as whatever suits your genius. The law requires a sad deal of plodding."

With a start, Boswell realizes that the man has moved him back precisely into the spot where they shook hands fifteen minutes previously, down to the direction each is facing and the approximate amount of space between them. He has the distinct sense now that Garrick, while still physically present, has already begun removing his attention elsewhere. It is as though the large spirit is emptying gradually out of the small stout body, a few particles at a time, and regathering itself somewhere in the theater, or in the city, or in the world at large.

But at the very last he manages to capture Boswell's heart forever.

"Sir," Garrick says, taking his hand in parting, and looking him sternly in the eye, "you will be a very great man. I have an aptitude for knowing these things, you understand. And when you are so, remember the year 1763. I want to contribute my part toward saving you. You must therefore fix a day when I shall have the pleasure of treating you with tea. We must plan this campaign at much greater length, that is certain."

It is all Boswell can do to name the same day a week hence.

"Done! And then, Mr. Boswell," Garrick says, turning on his heel and calling the last words brightly over his shoulder, "the cups shall dance and the saucers skip!"

* * *

Boswell is so exceedingly delighted when he walks out into the thin sunlight again that it is all he can do to restrain himself from hailing another hackney coach. It is a good long walk in the cold back to Downing Street, but he comes quickly to his senses: the fact is that he's already pledged himself to skip several meals in order to cover the cost of the room at the Black Lion last night, as well as the coach to it and from it.

Still, the walk is colder even than he expected, and by the time Whitehall dwindles into Parliament Street, he has given up replaying the Garrick incident and is concentrating entirely on covering distance and warming his fingers. So bent is he on reaching his lodgings that Boswell nearly brushes past his brother John idling on the corner of Downing Street before he recognizes him.

Although John is bent forward looking into an apothecary's window, finger brushing against the glass, there is no mistaking the head and ears rising up out of the drab brown surtout. He takes John gently by the shoulder, startling him still.

"Johnny!" Boswell says, more genuine concern creeping into his voice than he suspects John will bear. "Had we arranged to meet today? Am I late again? I *am* sorry if so. You look frozen solid."

John chafes his hands together, and Boswell sees he has no gloves. It suddenly strikes him that John's entire appearance today has something slightly haphazard to it, from his hat, which he has jammed down over his forehead, to his breeches and stockings, which are spattered with street dirt, as though he dressed in the dark and began walking before the sun was up. There is something wild in his appearance that is more than the sum of its various details.

But John smiles easily. "No, Jemmie, we had no plan. You can be sure that if we had, I wouldn't have waited so long for you as I've done. But I thought I might drop by and entice you away from your writing. Your landlord said you might be back soon."

"But has not Mr. Terrie offered you a warm place to sit indoors? Or offered to let you into my rooms? I will speak to him if he has not. I will *berate* him, in fact."

John jams his fists into the pockets of his overcoat, and Boswell can see that sitting under the eye of Mr. Terrie for twenty minutes or a half an hour would be torture, and worse than torture should Mr. Terrie decide to make conversation.

He stops John before he can answer: "We shall take it out of Mr. Terrie's hands entirely by having a set of keys made for you. And I shall tell Mr. Terrie that he must accept your presence as he would my own. What say you to that?"

John's face brightens, but as it does Boswell's own heart is suddenly freighted with guilt. He has shown his brother so little of the City, has offered so little of himself, and his meditations of last night come back to him.

It could hardly be helped, Boswell thinks, given John's surprise arrival just at the point where Boswell's plans were moving into their most demanding phases. Yet the fact remains that he has seen John almost not at all, and when he has, Boswell has generally reduced their hours together to a line or two in his journal, as though shielding even its pages from the sudden fact of John's presence. He strikes a bargain instantly with himself that he will make this day John's most memorable yet in London, and his heart buoys up immediately.

But when the evening is through—after an admirably silly performance of Brome's *Jovial Crew,* after John has said good night and trudged off toward his own anonymous rooms—Boswell finds himself bent over his journal, rereading the entry for the day that he has just penned.

I dined nowhere, but drank tea at Love's, and at night went to Covent Garden gallery and saw The Jovial Crew. My frame still thrilled with pleasure, and my want of so much rest last night gave me an agreeable languor. The songs revived in my mind many gay ideas, and recalled in the most lively colors to my imagination the time when I was first in London, when all was new to me, when I felt the warm glow of youthful feeling and was full of curiosity and wonder. I then had at times a degree of ecstasy of feeling that the experience which I have since had has in some measure cooled and abated. But then my ignorance at that time is infinitely excelled by the knowledge and moderation and government of myself which I have now acquired. After the play I came home, eat a Bath cake and a sweet orange, and went comfortably to bed.

The writing is passable, Boswell allows, but one thing about the entry is inescapable, even in his fatigue: John is nowhere to be seen.

It is Boswell's last thought before snuffing his candle, that he has methodically created two lives, one that John may share, and one closed and hidden away from his brother. He has made of his life a series of nested boxes, and allowed John access only to the outermost, the plainest and shabbiest—the least Boswell, in short, of all the boxes.

Still, as he lies in the dark, winter keening quietly outside the window, Boswell tells himself that it simply isn't to be helped. For the moment, it is all he can do to wedge the door to London society open far enough to force his own shoulder inside.

Later, John may follow with far less trouble, and he should be content with that prospect. Boswell even allows himself a bit of manufactured annoyance with his brother's unspoken demands. *For when all is said and done,* he thinks just as sleep begins to move over him, *I am eldest.*

WITHIN A WEEK, as though his fleeting thought has closed a pending enchantment of some sort, Boswell's life is in ruins.

Every noble prospect before him has been overthrown, completely and methodically smashed; and what is worse, it couldn't be any clearer that completely and methodically smashed is what God Himself now fully intends Boswell's various plans to be. For each of Boswell's three Grand Enterprises the Lord has carefully matched with a stunning disappointment, one per day for three days running.

It began Tuesday, the 18th of January. Boswell was invited to the Sheridans', to speak with Mrs. Sheridan about the prologue he had written for her new comedy. Although he would detest himself for it later that evening, Boswell literally sang in the street as he went, so ecstatic was he with the idea of hearing his lines spoken in Drury Lane on opening night. And having heard Garrick praise them only days before, Boswell could only congratulate himself on the prospect of hearing that all was settled.

But before Boswell had taken more than a sip or two of his tea, Thomas Sheridan leaned over to tap him on the knee, a bit roughly. The man's long, pale face hovered uncomfortably close, the faint bite of brandy there on his breath. "Why, sir, don't you ask about your prologue?" Sheridan prompted.

"Indeed, sir, I am too indifferent," Boswell replied with a smile, after an awkward moment's pause.

Sheridan put on a sober look, but deep in the eyes was a twinkle of malice. "Well, but prepare your utmost philosophy."

Boswell felt his stomach tilt. "How so?"

"It is weighed in the balances and found light."

"What, it is not good?"

"Indeed," Sheridan replied, shooting a glance at his wife, "I think it is very bad."

The next hour was one long pedantic nightmare: Sheridan pointing out supposed flaws in Boswell's lines, one by one, and shouting him down whenever Boswell made bold to defend them. Yet the connection was too valuable to throw away in an argument, and Boswell managed to smile and take it.

He slept very poorly and awoke the next morning, Wednesday

the 19th, to the odd sensation of heat in his groin, an intense heat at that: reaching down, he found his left testicle had swollen in the night to the size of a ripe plum.

Boswell sat up suddenly in his bed, the bedclothes scattered about him, and he could feel a cold sweat break at his hairline, then work its way quickly over his entire body. He clung to the faint hope that perhaps he had simply strained himself somehow during his various rendezvous with Louisa over the last several days.

But as the afternoon wore on, even that scant hope dwindled. He tried his best to make light—"Too, too plain was Signor Gonorrhea," he quipped in his journal—but a weight bore down on his chest, and having spent Tuesday night despising Sheridan, he lay awake deep into Wednesday night hating Louisa, and then himself.

By the next morning, Thursday the 20th—when Molly walked into his dining room during breakfast with an elaborately sealed letter—Boswell knew enough to let the letter lie a moment. There was an Old Testament quality to his days suddenly, and he had the eerie sense that he could hope for nothing but retribution in the post.

However there was no escaping it, finally.

And indeed, the letter was from the Duke of Queensberry, with whom Boswell had an appointment in several hours, an appointment to which he had looked forward for weeks. Clearly the note was meant to pre-empt the meeting: the duke repeated his high regard and his desire to help, but made it sufficiently clear that a commission in the Guards was a fantasy and no more.

The rest of that Thursday passed in a treacherous haze. Boswell felt nauseous and weak as he moved about the icy streets, boots sliding between the cobbles, clutching his coat about him to fight the chills, and conducting the anxious self-examinations that hypochondriacs have no choice but to conduct.

Other than his rejection by the duke, he could later remember only two scenes from that very long day when he sat down to record it that evening. His friend Douglas, a surgeon of some reputation, had confirmed that Boswell's was a very strong infection indeed and might take months to cure.

And then, in a fit of righteous anger, Boswell had gone straight to Louisa's flat and broken with her, as directly and indignantly and hurtfully as he was able.

She had seemed quite genuinely surprised at first, had Louisa. She'd sworn her innocence, sworn the infection could not have come from her, sworn she loved him and could never hurt him so. Boswell answered her arguments, but in truth he was taken aback by the force of her insistence.

Still, she is an actress, after all, Boswell told himself harshly, *and most likely a consummate dissembling whore.*

He swore in his own turn that he had been with no other woman for the last two months. And his own surgeon had told him that the woman who had given him the infection could not have been ignorant of it. "Madam," Boswell finished stiffly, "I wish much to believe you. But I own I cannot upon this occasion believe a miracle."

"Sir," she said, reaching for his hand, but not before Boswell was able to snatch it back, "I cannot say more to you. But you will leave me in the *greatest* misery. I shall lose your esteem. I shall be hurt in the opinion of everybody, and in my circumstances."

He left her actually in tears, still begging leave to inquire after his health. "Madam," Boswell had archly replied, his hand on the doorknob, "I fancy that will be needless for some weeks."

And while he was proud of the line for most of his walk back to Downing Street, and thought it would look savage and fine in his account of the breakup, by the time he reached his flat Boswell thought worse of himself for it, all the more for insisting that there had been absolutely no women other than she, which was not strictly true. There had been the girl in the yellow bonnet, of course, though Boswell had been scrupulously careful there and had done nothing more than toy with her a bit, in this way or that, and so had run no risk, to his way of thinking.

Still, his own small inconsistency nagged at him and sapped his vengeance.

And the following morning, when it couldn't be avoided for another moment, Boswell entered purgatory itself: he was to remain in his rooms, stay warm, eat little, and what little he did eat was to be plain and easily digestible, toast and tea and weak veal broth and the like. Douglas would drop by his medicines—chalky acidic masses slathered with what tasted like spoiled honey—and bleed him in case of swelling.

Company was allowed, if kept to a reasonable minimum, and Boswell clung to it as a lifeline. Seeing from his window a chariot stop at his door did more to cleanse his blood than anything Douglas could prescribe.

After a miserable day or two, his afternoons were tolerably full: Lord Eglinton came to see him, and the Scottish Lord Advocate, as well as his friends Erskine and Dempster.

John too visited him, faithfully, but mornings only. Boswell had told him, with more than a grain of truth, that by afternoon he was exhausted, and it would be best to meet over breakfast, when Boswell was fresh. John was good enough to respect his wishes, and came bearing newspapers and oranges.

But Boswell had no illusions; he knew very well that he was keeping John at arm's length from the rest of his company, but he could no longer bring himself to care. He was sick, and struggling to hold his own life and fortunes together. John was stout and healthy, and must look after himself.

All in all, Boswell has been a model patient for the better part of the last two weeks. But tonight, February 3, marks the opening of Mrs. Sheridan's new comedy, *The Discovery,* the very play from which his prologue was so brutally snipped. For some perverse reason, he cannot bear the thought of missing the first performance. Something in him rebels at the idea of passing this particular night at home, ill, diseased, forgotten.

At three, Boswell quickly swallows an apple tart, then wraps himself well up in two pairs of thick stockings, two thick shirts, and his greatcoat. He has Molly call him a sedan chair, and, once snugly inside, his spirits suddenly rise higher than they have in weeks. He feels fragile, but pleasantly so, like a rare piece of china being transported to a demanding buyer.

The play is dull, and Boswell savors every moment of it.

It is only a few hours amusement, but more than enough to send Boswell home in a pleasant whirl. He comes back through the dark streets, the sedan chair bumping along from one pool of lamplight to another, and for the first time in weeks he recaptures the sense of destiny London has always stirred in him. And he is inspired: he will use his convalescence to write a full-scale comedy of his own.

He comes up the central stair quietly, to avoid disturbing the Terrie family below. Something is odd, though, he sees immediately: although he left his room dark, now candle or lamplight glows in the crack beneath his parlor door.

Boswell stops just at the top of the stair and listens. He can hear nothing.

At the door itself he hesitates, although the rooms are his own. Only then does he remember giving John a set of keys some weeks before. But it is only when he actually opens the unlocked door and sees his brother seated at his dining table—two stacks of manuscript pages neatly ranged before him—that Boswell remembers leaving his journal lying out when he left for the theater earlier in the day. It is his general practice to lock the loose pages in a teak chest beneath his bed, but every so often he does not, if he is careless or in a hurry. Such as this afternoon.

"Hello, Johnny," Boswell says softly, and he expects that John will give a guilty start. It is not the first time in their lives that they have stood in these respective positions, his younger brother surprised in possession of something not entirely his own, and Boswell allows himself a wry smile.

The smile is wasted on John, who does not look up.

"I am glad to see that you have taken me at my word and made yourself quite at home," Boswell continues, coming into the room. There is a whiff of irony in the words, but nothing challenging; the truth is that Boswell has had a wonderful evening, the first in weeks, and at the moment he is inclined to generosity and mildness in all things.

And too he takes an overweening pride in his journal, although it is full of what the world may never see. In fact, rather than upbraid John for opening it, Boswell finds himself actually moving about the room a bit more quietly than usual, as any man does when it is his own writing being read.

Only when John has finished the sheet in his hand and placed it in the proper stack does he look up, and Boswell is startled to find his face distorted with what looks like anger. He seems almost too incensed for words.

"It is a fine life you lead, James," John begins, voice quivering, tapping a hand quickly on the stack of pages before him, "finer even than I had imagined."

"You must be joking," Boswell responds, carefully. "You know I see almost no one these days, but keep to my bed."

"*Almost* no one is precisely right. But the afternoons do seem lively enough, what with the small parade of lords and ladies and who knows who coming to pay their respects. I would swear that you said you were far too fatigued by afternoon for visits then, but clearly your medicines are having the desired effect."

"I'm not sure I understand what it is you would imply."

"Oh, I'm quite certain that you do."

"John," Boswell allows himself a heavy sigh, "you make a molehill into a mountain, truly. Once or twice have I had a noteworthy guest. And frankly I have been delighted when it has happened. It is deadly dull in these rooms, day after day."

Boswell has made a conscious decision to ignore the belligerence in John's voice, and now he begins unbuckling his sword and hanging up his hat as though nothing were out of the ordinary.

John throws himself back in his chair, arms cinched across his chest, openly glaring. "Perhaps I exaggerate your company today. But what I truly admire is your life before you were—" John spits out the words "—before you were clapped and then ordered to bed. You breakfast with Garrick. You frequent Court. You aspire to meet Samuel Johnson, even to form a *correspondence* there. And who knew that the Countess Northumberland holds a lavish private party each Friday evening for a handpicked few, and a grand rout every few weeks for all the world? It fairly boggles the mind."

"There is nothing mind-boggling in it. I have a commission to secure, and I have been setting about it."

"And it is *actors* and *authors* and heiresses that will secure it for you, is it? Please, don't treat me like a child, James. You have had your nose in every London gathering of more than four people since you arrived. And such gatherings! Where the commissions are ripe for the picking, and one has one's choice of geniuses and patrons and beauties. It must be a very fine thing indeed. You are certainly to be envied, James."

Boswell draws out a chair at the other end of the table, and for lack of anything better to do he takes a sweet orange from a bowl before him, begins peeling it as slowly and carefully as he is able. "John, you misunderstand. You know that before you return home you will most certainly be invited to—"

"Of course, I understand, Jemmie. There is no need to explain. Plymouth didn't disturb my understanding to that extent, although what can the mad brother know of the extent of his own disturbance?"

"Now you deliberately find insult where there is none. You are having a fine time playing the martyr." Boswell pops a piece of the orange in his mouth, but it is tasteless, and his own voice sounds haughty in his ears.

"Everything makes so much *sense* now that I have read these pages. The world fairly falls into place. It makes perfect sense, for instance, that a dear friend of our father, like the Countess Northumberland, would limit her invitations to only one of his sons."

"John, you may take offense all around, but clearly none was meant."

"After all, she scrapes by on such a modest income that she has no choice but to choose between us. Her economy is truly to be admired."

Boswell continues placing orange segments in his mouth, but his chewing and swallowing is purely mechanical, for the show of normalcy; the tension and the day's exertion have combined to make him almost light-headed, and his forehead is damp. He realizes he is hours past the time to take his medicine. He wants suddenly to hold up his hands in a truce, the way they did when they were young, when one of them was genuinely hurt by a bit of wrestling.

But John is in no mood to relent, and it is in self-defense, Boswell tells himself, that he for the first time offers a jab in return. "You may be indignant, John, but the truth is that the Lady Northumberland is no doubt entirely unaware that you have come up to Town. You are simply not in her thoughts, I'm sorry to say. And the same is true for Lord Eglinton. *That* is the reason you have not been invited, John. It is no mystery."

John looks at him in genuinely stunned surprise. Only too late does Boswell realize the error in what he has said, and he would quickly correct it, but before he can do so John has pushed the table violently from him and jumped to his feet.

"*Unaware?* Of course she is unaware, Jemmie! She is unaware of my presence because you have *kept* her so. You have kept everyone so! You have all but kept me unaware of myself, by introducing me nowhere, and making sure to take me only where no one is to be found, and it is because you are selfish through and through, and because you are ashamed of me. I am sick to death of it, this evil sort of betrayal.

"And it is all here, the very *precision* with which you have done it. Nothing could be clearer from reading through this—" John bats savagely at the taller of the manuscript piles, and some of it spills onto the cloth, and from there to the floor—"this sickening bath of self-love and—and selfish, foolish social climbing."

John looks at him, and for a moment Boswell thinks that somehow this last charge has caused the fire to go out of him. John's voice is lower, when it comes, but it is clearer and colder for the change. "Why did you not come to me at Plymouth? Why did you not come to me when you heard that I was kept there?"

The questions go through Boswell like a lancet, and he can say nothing, face flushed, sweat suddenly cold at his collar.

"I hate you, Jemmie," John says. "You've become just the selfish, mean, grasping, cold-hearted little bastard you once swore to me you'd never be, never let Father make you be. But it turns out it had nothing to do with him at all. It is you alone. You and the streaky little pier glass you have in place of a heart."

Boswell is struck dumb.

"I hate you, Jemmie," John goes on distinctly, his eyes now shining with tears, "and I wish you dead in the ground this moment. Dead in the ground, and your mouth stuffed with wet clay."

It is not the first time a mention of hate has passed between them in anger; they are brothers, after all. But never has one or the other of them used the word with such bitter application. And then John takes the pages of the journal, both the read and the unread, and pitches the stacks across the table into Boswell's face, so that they actually strike him before he can put up his hands.

By the time the pages have fluttered to the floor, John is gone.

Only later, on his hands and knees, gathering the scattered pages and shuffling them laboriously back into order, does Boswell notice something queer: tiny burn holes distributed at seemingly random intervals throughout the manuscript, each about the size of a petticoat button, as though the pages had been held deliberately over the candle, just close enough to singe the paper without igniting the whole.

Boswell sits marveling over the pages, and suddenly the randomness gives way to pattern: John has used the candle flame to remove his own name from the journal, as well as the phrase *my brother.* The near-mechanical precision of the destruction is remarkable. In each instance, a hole large enough to swallow a brother, no larger or smaller.

A WEEK LATER, John stops by unexpectedly just before teatime, to apologize and to take his leave, before setting out for Scotland the next morning. It is awkward at first—Boswell is feeling low and feverish, and they had parted so strangely the previous week—but by the time they have finished their tea, he cannot look over at his younger brother without the threat of tears. John too seems deeply affected by the farewell, and grateful to be reconciled. Neither mentions the riddled manuscript, and Boswell feels certain that neither of them ever will.

It is not until John has stood up from the table, and taken his hat in his hand, that Boswell remembers the spare set of keys. He realizes immediately that there is no way to mention it, though, without moving the conversation back to its initial awkward moments, without reinforcing a separation between them. And John will be back above the Tweed in two days time.

So Boswell makes a conscious decision to say nothing. Instead he tries to think of the keys as a parting gift of sorts, two small iron tokens of his affection, something palpable of London that he has given freely and without reserve.

* * *

With John gone, Boswell is again free to concentrate exclusively on himself, his own health, his own heart, his own dented dreams. By the 28th of February, he has kept the house five complete weeks, taken every foul pill prescribed him, and has been completely cleared by Douglas, his surgeon. His first few chilly walks in the Park are tinged with novelty, and he delights in the feel of his weak legs carrying him about the Ring.

With genuine spring in London, the unstoppable confidence Boswell brought with him the previous November returns. And although it takes an additional ten weeks, eventually this restored charm makes its effects felt where they have been longest resisted. On the sixteenth of May, nearly five months after the disappointments of Christmas, Davies belatedly proves as good as his word.

Boswell is standing by Davies's fireplace in the back parlor, having finished his second cup of tea, Mrs. Davies just gone to see about some business in her kitchen, when the bookseller steps up and touches his shoulder. Boswell turns to see that beneath the drab businessman's wig, Davies's face is suffused with expectation and mock solemnity.

He says nothing, merely holds Boswell's eye.

"What is it?" Boswell asks finally. "What's happened?"

Davies points discreetly to the glass door leading to the bookseller's shop. "Look, my Lord, it comes," he whispers, and Boswell recognizes the line from Shakespeare: Horatio alerting Hamlet to the presence of his father's ghost.

Boswell turns, and through the panes of the door catches his first full glimpse of Samuel Johnson. In that first passing instant he is disappointed; his eye, trained from birth in the nuances of dress and the corresponding nuances of station, registers the shabby clothing on the big frame, the greased look to the wig. It is impossible not to notice that the lace hanging from the man's cuffs is dun and limp with age.

Still, the figure is larger even than he expected, shoulders wide as a door frame, and the movements it makes are odd and brusque and unpredictable.

As Davies goes to him and makes to shake his hand, Johnson catches the movement from the corner of his eye and rears back slightly, bringing his weak vision to bear as best he can, before smiling thinly. He hulks over Davies somehow, although the bookseller is himself of more than average height; the large hand not engaged in greeting his host curls instead into a fist, which bobs slowly in the air, altogether of its own accord.

Eventually Davies says something, Johnson lowers his head to hear, and then swivels to pick out Boswell by the fireplace, standing stupidly, empty teacup in hand. Johnson squints across the distance, an unintentional scowl printed over his fleshy face.

And that is when Boswell's early disappointment suddenly leaves him, to be replaced by a powerful feeling very much its opposite: the feeling that here is another order of being entirely, something preternatural, greater even than he has allowed himself to imagine, almost biblical in intensity.

I drank tea at Davies's in Russell Street, and about seven came in the great Mr. Samuel Johnson, whom I have so long wished to see. Mr. Davies introduced me to him. As I knew his mortal antipathy at the Scotch, I cried to Davies, "Don't tell him where I come from." However, he said, "From Scotland." "Mr. Johnson," said I, "indeed I come from Scotland, but I cannot help it." "Sir," replied he, "that, I find, is what a very great many of your countrymen cannot help." Mr. Johnson is a man of a most dreadful appearance. He is a very big man, is troubled with sore eyes, the palsy, and the king's evil. He is very slovenly in his dress and speaks with a most uncouth voice. Yet his great knowledge and strength of expression command vast respect and render him very excellent company. He has great humour and is a worthy man. But his dogmatical roughness of manners is disagreeable. I shall mark what I remember of his conversation.

Late that night, Boswell finishes penning the entry with the distinct sense that his life has changed unalterably. Already in his mind is the idea of marking down Johnson's conversation over time, of visiting Johnson's rooms to secure more of it. Already he has an inkling that the list of quotes he has managed to smuggle home to his diary will need to be set in a more fully rendered scene some day. Still, Boswell is proud of the entry for May 16, and he takes care to write out a clean copy before turning in for the night. And because he has reason to be newly infatuated with his journal, he is especially careful in putting it away: he ties a neat bow with the twine he uses to bind it, locks up the tea chest he uses to store it, and places the key under the fruit dish, as is his habit.

The next day is a blur of social engagements, and at each one Boswell casually retails his fresh recollections of Johnson. He is delighted to find that when speaking of Johnson, he acquires some of the man's authority, even with the most exalted listener. The effect is intoxicating, and he experiments with it until he can find no more drawing rooms to haunt. Only well past midnight does Boswell round the corner of Downing Street, there to find an agreeable young girl loitering in the dark, as though she were waiting for James Boswell and James Boswell alone.

Alice Gibbs is her name, it turns out. She is new to the trade this month, with an incongruously brilliant smile, and in seconds they have come to terms.

Even as Boswell is squiring her to a snug alcove nearer the Park, stroking her hip, he is marveling at his own recklessness. It is passing strange: even as he pulls up her skirt and petticoats, he is reviewing all of his weeks of resolutions; as she swears that she is safe, he is telling himself that she lies, yet pressing his lips to the nape of her neck; and through it all, he is warning himself to draw back, even as he wraps his arms tightly about her narrow waist and thrusts into her again and again, like a mongrel, in the dark open air of a street less than a block from his own doorstep.

Within moments, it is over, and Boswell drifts back to his rooms on a curling wave of genuine panic. As soon as he has locked the door behind him, he goes immediately to the tea chest, thinking to read Johnson's words again, by way of penance.

There in the chest are his manuscript pages, but he has the distinct sense that something is wrong somehow. For the twine securing them has been quickly knotted, rather than done up in a careful bow. And the stacking of the pages hasn't the precision Boswell ordinarily insists upon before locking them away. Tiny details, but enough to send him first to the fruit plate, to find the key exactly where he left it, and then to his landlord, to ask about visitors. Mr. Terrie remembers none, however, and Boswell returns to his rooms convinced not only that his mind is playing tricks, but tricks that he deserves to have played.

It is as though the sordid act on the street has changed not merely his memory of the Johnson entry, but the manuscript itself. As though following Johnson's path will produce one sort of reality, and straying from it another sort of physical life altogether. The disordered feel to his manuscript is a sign and a warning.

But even there, in the deepest reaches of his self-loathing, Boswell finally manages to take heart: signs, after all, are never vouchsafed to the unforgiven.

PART SEVEN

Last, Least Bastard World

Saturday 16 July

He advised me to keep a journal of my life, fair and undisguised. He said it would be a very good exercise, and would yield me infinite satisfaction when the ideas were faded from my remembrance. I told him that I had done so ever since I left Scotland. He said he was very happy that I pursued so good a plan. And now, O my journal! Art thou not highly dignified? Shalt thou not flourish tenfold? No former solicitations or censures could tempt me to lay thee aside; and now is there any argument which can outweight the sanction of Mr. Samuel Johnson? He said indeed that I should keep it private, and that I might surely have a friend who would burn it in case of my death. For my own part, I have at present such an affection for this my journal that it shocks me to think of burning it. I rather encourage the idea of having it carefully laid up among the archives of Auchinleck. However, I cannot judge fairly of it now. Some years hence I may. I told Mr. Johnson that I put down all sorts of little incidents in it. "Sir," said he, "there is nothing too little for so little a creature as man. It is by studying little things that we attain the great knowledge of having as little misery and as much happiness as possible."

—From *Boswell's London Journal, 1762–1763*

London, England
Saturday, the 30th of July, 1763
9:24 P.M.

* * * * * *

20

THE REAR STAIRWELL is black, but for a spill of lamplight where the door has been battered away above, and a wash of moonlight where the door to the street now stands open to the wind below. The two flights of steps between are lightless, though, and I take them two, three, then four at a time, vaulting out into the nothingness, the railing clutched in my burnt right hand, the second dag snug in my left.

I have no fear at all of falling, somehow; it is as though the world is illuminated by instinct. Very thinly illuminated, but illuminated still.

Beyond instinct, there is the animal sort of cunning, and that tells me a good deal as well. A soldier really only ever learns two things, and they are obedience and cunning, which is to say, the hunting of men little different from himself. And while the officers of my regiment found me deficient in the former, the latter came easily. Once I had got beyond my shyness, in fact, cunning seemed to come back to me, like a language learned and loved and lost in childhood.

Cunning says that James and Johnson are not lying in wait for me at the bottom of the stair, or just outside the rear door. Of that I am all but certain, for James is a coward, and Johnson is a poor man who has spent the bulk of his life leveraging himself into sudden parity with London's wealthy and powerful. He is a genuine literary celebrity now, and no man guards his life as blindly as the newly celebrated. The two of them will run as far and as fast as their fat legs will take them.

Still, they are not far ahead of me, maybc a stone's throw, for all their head start. Under normal circumstances, that lead would allow them to circle to the front of the building and run for the Catherine Street watch stand. Or they might reach the soldiers at the gate of Somerset House, or even, if they both were to scream at the top of their lungs, rouse those billeted in the Savoy Barracks.

But circumstances are not, of course, normal. I have spent a good part of the last several weeks making sure of that fact.

There was a Lieutenant Garraway in my regiment, himself a second son of a nobleman, and perhaps for that reason of a philosophical turn of mind. And it was his habit to speak of each major contingency in war as creating a world separate and distinct from our own. *A bastard world* was his phrase for a military situation upended by the worst imaginable turn of events.

But even a bastard world, Garraway believed, could be redeemed by forethought. The best officer imagined the most potential worlds. It was as simple as that.

It took very little of imagination to suppose that if James and his hero were to escape the locked box in which I'd placed them, the rear door was the likeliest possibility. And so in fact this bastard world—the one in which my bootheels strike the ground floor of the stairwell and send a jolt of pain across my left side—has received the bulk of my attention.

So much so that when I have run out into the light rain and jogged quickly around the row of darkened Somerset coach houses, I know almost precisely what I will see: three men standing at the unlit far end of the estate's stable yard, barely visible, almost huddled up together against the north wall of the Old Somerset friary.

Other than these three, there is no one in sight, for the weather is more early March than late July, and although there are likely a hundred servants and guards within a stone's throw of where I stand, they are none of them fools, and each prefers his fire and his bottle.

The air is cold, but not fresh. One could almost choke on the smell of wet stable, drenched horses, and slovenly stalls.

The three men stand confidentially close to one another, water dripping from them, as though sharing a secret. And of course they do: the man with his back to me has his hand held down low at his hip—casually enough to escape notice should a coachman glance over on his way across the upper part of the yard—and the hand holds a pistol.

His pistol is not in a league with my own dags, but it is a serviceable piece. Having purchased it this past week, having cleaned and oiled and loaded it, I know it to be reliable enough. Johnson and Boswell stand before the man in the frozen, slump-shouldered attitudes of the genuinely terrified; only their eyes are wide and alive, and as I slow and come up on them, James suddenly opens his mouth to call out my name.

His instinct is still to call to me for help, even now.

But James stops short when I bring out my own dag, and hold my finger to my lips. Very quietly, I whisper to the two of them: "I'm afraid we must insist that you remain silent. Make a sound, and you die."

Again, as in the Turk's Head, James's eyes seem suddenly to be swimming with tears, though whether it is rain washing his face is impossible to say.

Johnson does not move or speak, but his hulking form seems to strain almost visibly against motionlessness, as though a turn of the head or the swing of a pistol tip will release him from a spell, and he will suddenly bellow and surge at me. His rage is there in his eyes, though he holds them half-closed. The gaze is unflinching, and it sweeps back and forth between my face and the face of the man who took the two of them up halfway through their dramatic escape. It could not be clearer that Johnson is watching for an opportunity, but more than that he is studying our features, committing us to memory. Again, he is a celebrity, this man. He is already preparing—when this ordeal is finished and the world bends its knee once again—to have us crushed by the bailiffs and the courts and his powerful friends into a very fine powder indeed.

His instinct is still to assume that any loss of his own power is momentary, even now.

But Johnson is checked in his attempt to memorize the man's features, as they are carefully and discreetly covered. A black cloth shields his face, his nose, even his smallish ears from sight, and a slouch hat disguises his head, the glossy seal-brown hair. Only his eyes and his dark brows are visible.

Again, I cannot help but be reassured by my own handiwork. The only thing I have left to chance in the case of this man is his own courage, his own heart.

The eyes above the cloth reveal the struggle, without a doubt. This third man looks over at me, and his expression is impressed with the enormity of what he has done, painfully impressed. He has waylaid two gentlemen, using a pistol and a mask, and even though he has not picked a penny from their pockets, and will not, he could very easily hang for his actions of the last ten minutes. And he well knows it. He kept his glance stony until I arrived, but now that I've come, his pretense has all but collapsed. Beneath the mask, his breathing sounds thin and rapid; above it, the eyes hold a pleading look, as though he would have me somehow take back what I have had him do.

It is the mudlark, of course. Or riverlark, I should better say.

If I am surprised to find him here, pistol in hand, to find him my confederate, it is only for a brief instant, because a part of me has known all along that this was the case, that our two earlier meetings today were no accident. That our existences have become somehow intermingled over the last weeks or months.

That wave of knowledge now reaches the forefront of my awareness with hardly a ripple.

This effect too I've become familiar with since Plymouth: a moment when two parallel sets of memories can no longer be held in mutual exclusion, for whatever reason, and the thing inside me must let go a part of its hold. And once it does so, the recollections then come washing together. In a moment's time it is all but impossible to say how or even why they were ever distinct.

I understand now that if James and Johnson and I had finished our business in the Turk's Head—if we had none of us come running down the back staircase—the mudlark would have remained more or less a random London figure to me, a stranger.

But that realization seems unimportant, hardly worth considering. I am here now, and the mudlark has performed his function well.

And I am glad to see him, not simply because he helped to form one side of a larger invisible box into which James and Johnson managed to escape, but because he is himself and I think well of him. I haven't time to reassure him at length, and so I do so as quickly and efficiently as I am able, with a clap on the shoulder.

It has the proper effect. He seems to take heart, and the stony look comes back over his face.

Almost as if he cannot help himself, James moves a half-step toward me, a soft moan strangled in his throat. The words remain at a whisper, though, for, as I have said, my brother is a coward. "Johnny, for the love of *God,* tell me why you're doing this. Please, Johnny."

Before I can speak, the lark takes a step forward himself and jabs James in the sternum with the barrel of his pistol, hard enough to drive him backward. The metal thunks audibly against the bone.

"You'll shut your filthy fucking mouth," the lark hisses, and I'm surprised for an instant at the heat in his voice, the authentic anger.

But then I have spent several weeks constructing for him a long, detailed, painful fiction involving James Boswell and the Great Dictionary Johnson.

In this fiction, I am brother to a luckless young maid come up to town from Edinburgh, one Peggy Doig. Here she was tempted, and fell into the habit of meeting the two gentlemen nights at the Turk's Head. They shared her between them like a one-shilling whore. By them she was ruined, got with child, and later savagely beaten when she let it be known. And now—most ominously of all—she has vanished without a word, and I have questions that must be answered.

It is a fiction, yes, but built out of the dirty flotsam of truth. And while the lark's anger is based on that convenient fiction, it is not misplaced ultimately, not really. He knows these are bad men, and bad men they are.

"You're lucky you haven't had your throat slit for you already, wi' what you've done," the lark spits once more at James, and then he lapses back into silence.

James has his hand over the injured spot at his breastbone, more than a bit of the whipped dog in his manner. But now Johnson offers to speak. He too keeps his voice low, as instructed. His manner has changed substantially: two men with guns are an entirely different proposition than one. Here there is no oak table with which to beat us. And so he is determined now to find his way out of this madness through compliance and persuasion.

"You must stop a moment and consider, John," Johnson says, and it is odd, hearing my Christian name fall from his lips, "before it is too late. You are no highwayman, though you make use of them." Here Johnson flicks his gaze down at the lark, making it clear that the man is an inferior species altogether. "You have prospects even now. This is beneath you. You have yet to commit any capital crime. You have yet to rob, or kill. And much is forgiven upon repentance, especially in one who has suffered as you have suffered."

He is speaking gingerly of my time in the Plymouth Hospital, of course, but the mudlark seems to take it as a confession of all the worst he has been told.

It is a good reminder, however, that I must separate the lark out from the discussion as soon as possible. And we have been too long out in the open, whatever the weather.

I answer Johnson politely, and quietly. "I suggest you take your own advice, Mr. Johnson. You have also yet to commit any capital crime, though you have much to repent."

I bring up the dag and, as before, I let them know what will be expected of them. "Now we will walk slowly together, the four of us, down toward the river, and we will do so in this fashion: James in front; you, Mr. Johnson, a pace behind him; and we two will walk a few paces off to the right. The high wall surrounding the Somerset estate will be to your left almost the entire way, and I will ask you to walk as near to it as you may, just in its shadow. Remember, not a sound. Ignore any passersby. We will shoot only if we are forced to do so. And you have still my word. Answer my questions honestly, and you will sleep in your own beds tonight."

And then we are moving, in an uneasy little knot, down to the water: James, then the lark off in the gloom to his right, followed by Johnson, and I bringing up the rear.

Somerset Water-Gate, the lane bordering the Somerset estate to the west, ends in a public stair at the waterline of the Thames. And much is made of the fact that the Crown has opened the estate's river gardens to the public during daylight hours, as well. But the truth is that the Water-Gate itself is no gift to the rabble. It is less a cobbled lane, and more a drainage sluice on a massive scale, running from the Strand directly down through the estate's large stables and coachyard and dingy garbage sheds.

That Londoners use the thoroughfare and the steps to the river is incidental, for the point has always been to move the waste of Somerset residents away from the delicate noses of Somerset residents.

And so when our small party moves awkwardly down the Water-Gate in the drizzling rain, hugging the estate's long dark brick wall, we are just four more random nasty urban bits running down to the river, and from there to the sea.

With one exception: rather than continuing down into the water itself, the lark urges James to the right, down to the damp walk that fronts the river, and we all execute the turn, not smartly but well enough.

The going is slower now, as Johnson and James must watch their feet as well as our guns. Other than the damp shuffling sound of our boots, only Johnson's labored breathing marks our passage. He is a large man, and strong, but not used to the ongoing demands of an evening such as this. And that is fine. The less strength he has when we reach our destination, the better. I will not underestimate him again.

In the moonlight, one can just barely make out a series of tiny wooden docks, stretching out into the deeper dark to our left, raking the water like long, thin fingers. Each dock is surrounded by a broad fan of tiny craft, skiffs and fish-smacks, and all of these are empty, deserted due to the weather.

Only once, as we move over rotting wooden slats and treacherous Thames mud, do we pass another living soul: it is a fisherman, and his son, most likely, working beneath a cheap canopy on their flat-bottomed boat. So silently are they sewing at their lines that I am not aware of them until suddenly one of them tosses a bit of garbage out into the water, and it splashes into the river only a few feet off to James's left.

They glance at us idly as we pass, this grizzled older man and his son, a boy of fifteen or sixteen. Even in the dark, they know we are somehow of a higher quality than themselves; even in the dark, they leave us to our business, because nothing good can come of interrupting us.

And I have chosen well with the lark. As we come up on the pair of them, without any signal from me and without hesitation he presses closer to James, leaning in prohibitively, and I can only imagine he has brushed the tip of his pistol against my brother's shoulder, or perhaps his side, and then the moment where either of our guests might call for help is past.

James's face is a study in misery. Occasionally he glances up from his trudging, the mud sucking at his shoes, up and away from the river, out in the direction of the Strand only five or six blocks to the north. Garrick's townhouse waits quietly just up Cecil Street, if James could only find his way free to run the short length of it. But he cannot, and I've taken extra pains to impress upon him that he cannot, because I grew up with James and understand that if he is to be told no, he must be told no firmly or not at all.

At one point, Johnson, whose sight is poor and who has been lumbering along as best he can in the dark, spins unexpectedly about to face me. It is obvious that he does not mean to confront me, for his hands come up immediately in a gesture of supplication. But there is in his manner a strange combination of exasperation and surrender, and he hisses at me, there in the dark by the water: "You wish me to admit that we have met before and have spent time together. I will *do* so! I will admit it. I should have done so before now. I will give you what you demand. But you must *stop* this madness while there is time, John."

James and the lark have stopped in front of us. For all of Johnson's frustration, and in spite of his admission, his whisper remains low enough to all but escape James's hearing. He still believes he can extricate himself from this situation without admitting all, openly.

I take one step back and fully extend my arm, bringing the pistol up even with his face, and Johnson gives a snort of frustration. He turns, but before taking another step, he suddenly claps his hand to his head and tears off his unpowdered little wig, which is now soaked through with the rain, and pitches it out into the Thames. And then he trudges on again as before.

It is a small moment of defiance—to be expected in a man of his temperament—but of course it is also a clue thrown out to whoever may follow behind us, whatever authorities may eventually come to his aid. The man is nothing if not wily.

But it is nothing to worry over, not really. By first light all will be decided, all City business concluded.

Only when we pass within sight of the darkened hulk of the German Church, and then over the base of the Savoy Stairs, do I hold my breath. A small crowd at the bottom of the Stairs would be difficult, if not impossible to navigate.

But although I can hear men shouting somewhere away up the Stairs toward the Savoy, there is no one about at the waterline. The pattering rain has sent each London creature to his own little den.

And then I can relax a bit. For on our right suddenly rises a small tower of lumber, stacked in pallets some fifteen, twenty feet high. And that tower is followed by another even higher, and another, and another. We have reached the Beauford Timber Yard, though the lark says it is known on the river as Dirty Lane, for the alley that bounds it to the west.

Whatever the name, the stench of river muck and rot and fish gives way to the oddly pleasing scent of freshly cut wood. It is a country smell somehow. Even in the rain, it smells like a place where a man might build a house out of sight of his neighbors, rather than packed in together as they are all here in London, like vermin gathered just above a flood.

Soon we have our charges moving through what amounts to a very narrow passage, bounded on the one side by the lapping Thames and hard on the other by a massive wall of timber ready for shipping.

At the front of our line, the lark pushes James sharply to the right, and the two of them suddenly vanish.

Then, with Johnson stepping slowly and carefully in front of me, we accomplish the same trick: squeezing between two pallet walls into a small alley that opens up quickly into a makeshift courtyard. All around us are squared-off stacks of timber and pallets, walls of them reaching up fifteen feet here, twenty feet there.

Up and to the right, a sawpit yawns, the wood dust heaped up in great piles. This open interior is like a makeshift amphitheater, with the moon barely visible in the darkling sky.

Wood scraps and chips are scattered everywhere, some of them jagged, and again the going is difficult; Johnson stumbles once and seems to hurt his leg. But he curses softly and moves on. A barely audible skittering noise seems to travel with us as we move deeper: wharf rats, giving us a comfortable berth, though not fleeing, for they are bold enough. They know that even in daylight they have very little to fear from men limited to the aisles between the stacks.

It is the watchman's area, his tiny riverside fiefdom, and ahead on the right, nearly indistinguishable from the lumber towering over it, is the watchman's own shanty. Through the shanty's one narrow slit of a window, a lantern glows faintly.

No watchman comes out to challenge us, however, because he has been paid decently well to be elsewhere. It mattered not at all that he and the lark have been more than once at odds over lumber and chips filched from the yard. For a half crown, the watchman was more than willing to take the lark at his word, that it was only the shanty itself that was wanted, and privacy.

When we come up to the small door, I break the silence, my voice very low. "Inside are two chairs against the back wall. You will enter one by one and seat yourselves in those chairs. Rest your hands, palms up, in your laps. When you have done so, I will enter, and not before. I will mark you through the window here."

The lark motions James inside, then roughly pushes my brother's head down below the crossbeam as James ducks to enter. Johnson turns and casts one look back at me, and in the darkness his bulging eyes look white and wild. The lark allows Johnson to duck his own head, because even a man with a gun would hesitate to do it for him. And then they are both inside, and I see through the window slit that they have taken their chairs, grudgingly turned their palms up.

With the lark watching the two of them through the open doorway, I take the moment to reload the pistol fired in the Turk's Head. There is no moon to speak of, and only a hint of lantern-light reaches my hands as I begin, but it is no matter. I have handled guns all my life, and handled these dags more than enough to do so blind. I tear open the paper packet with my teeth, half-cock the piece with my thumb, and prime it.

I glance up to see the lark watching me work, and I jerk my head toward the shack, giving him a look. A bit sullenly, he goes back to his task.

I close the frizzen and pour the rest of the powder into the barrel. Press the ball and the paper wrapper down into the barrel, and ram the charge very carefully home with a thin rod set cunningly into the dag's underside. Again, I can't help but be taken with the things: even the bitty ramrod has been cast in gold.

Not thirty seconds have passed. "That's done it, then," I whisper to the lark.

And then something unexpected happens.

The lark looks at me and, although he is clearly still overwhelmed, he asks to come inside, to stay with me, and I see that he is in earnest. "Makes no sense handlin' 'em yourself," he whispers, almost pleading. "I'm in to the ears now as it is. Let me come along, help you get it done. Whatever it is."

"You have done enough," I tell him.

"Let me stay outside here and keep an eye. They give you the slip before. You needed me back there."

"Your part is finished."

"You needed me," he repeats stubbornly. "Just to keep an eye out."

I say nothing, but I look at him, his brows like rain-soaked slate, and he can see enough to know that I will not change my mind. He shakes his head, the black cloth covering his look of disgust, and then stares off toward the water. He has no idea what I have planned, exactly, but it's clear that he's more frightened of leaving us and loping off home than he is of whatever may happen in the watchman's shack.

He makes one last attempt, holding my eye.

"It's to be like that, is it?" he asks, a hint of heat in his voice, as if somehow I've betrayed him, am betraying him even now.

When I say nothing, he bends down into the low door to give James and Johnson a last savage look, and then the hand with the pistol vanishes into his long coat pocket and he is gone without another word, vanished through the tall black divide in the towering walls of lumber. Gone back to the river, where sky is inevitably up, and water inevitably down, the current fixed and trustworthy, more or less.

I take a dag in each of my hands, and remind myself that I have only two shots left, no matter what may happen. And on the heels of that reminder, a thought pops into my head out of nowhere, a strange thought, of the sort that comes to me every now and again. It is a thought about Mrs. Parry, of all people.

I realize now that while I took great pains to force Gil Higgs to remain silent, I made no attempt to do so with Mrs. Parry. On the contrary, I met with her several times, more than enough for her to recognize me and identify me after the fact if things at the Turk's Head were to go very poorly.

It dawns on me now that the third golden bullet—the extra bullet now lodged in the wall or the ceiling of her rearmost upstairs room—was for her.

That was how she was to be kept silent. Her life was to be ended.

And I was to end it myself. Or at least my finger was to have pulled the trigger. Had Johnson not forced me to fire accidentally, that plan would have moved forward and the evidence of it would have been held out of my awareness. It would have been just another secret kept by what is inside of me. It is only the fact that the number of bullets no longer matches the number of targets that leaves a thread hanging somehow, visible and telling. And that thread I have just pulled.

But this revelation refuses to settle in my mind, refuses to take on the air of normalcy, for it is more than I can believe. Mrs. Parry is guilty of nothing, guilty of nothing but gluttony and ugliness and a fawning submission. She is a fat spaniel without the capacity for sin. And yet the thing inside of me would have put a bullet in her head without a thought, without even a memory to anchor the act in time.

And for the first time in a long time, I am more than just afraid: I feel a bodily, yearning ache to be rid of it. If I could take a scalpel to my chest and slice it out somehow, I would do it gladly. But I cannot, and I know I cannot. There is no way to be rid of it—that was all I learned of any consequence at Plymouth.

It will have its angry way, here and there, now and again. And the best I can manage is to keep it focused as strictly as possible on the application of justice.

WHICH IS HOW I find myself seated, once again, in a straight chair opposite Johnson and James. It might almost be thirty minutes ago, at the Turk's Head, but for a few small alterations. This watch stand is a low-ceilinged structure barely large enough to house the three of us, fashioned quickly, no doubt, out of the least salable odds and ends the yard had to offer. The small lamp stands on an upturned box to our left, throwing our thin shadows against the facing wall. And that is all, in the way of furnishings.

Johnson has no table to toss. There is no clientele downstairs, a hallo away, because here there is neither downstairs nor anyone within shouting distance. Johnson and James might call to their hearts' delight, and no one—even if anyone were to hear them—would be able to place the sounds. We are seated at the center of what amounts to a vast timber labyrinth, and it would take someone standing at the very entrance to the watchman's courtyard to understand that the noise they hear is coming from the heart of the stacks of lumber themselves.

Johnson's wig is at the bottom of the Thames, of course, and his ill-shorn head looks particularly large and jowly without it. His eyes are doubly underscored: they sit in their piggy folds of skin, and those folds sit themselves in pronounced black bags, so exhausted does he look, from the wine, the long day, the unexpected tumult.

His skin was flushed earlier to a ruddy red, with the heat and the confrontation in the coffeehouse; but it has cooled, apparently. If anything, Johnson's face is now pallid, all but drained of blood.

The rusty suit looks like a dead skin about to be sloughed off. He has lost another button from his shirt, so that now, in addition to the gap exposing his large belly, his neck is open to the dingy linen beneath. Wet through with the rain is the good lexicographer, and spattered everywhere with dirt.

Likewise, James's snowy stockings are soiled, and his violet suit has darkened over with the wet. In his haste to leave the Turk's Head, he has left his sword behind, the only piece of his wardrobe that might have been any use to him. This tells you all you need to know about my brother's highly publicized desire for a commission in His Majesty's Guard: he ran higgledy-piggledy down a back staircase and left his sword dangling on a nail behind him.

James's hair has long ago escaped its silken tie, and it straggles mostly to one side of his face, where he has deposited it with an unthinking swipe of his hand. While the events of the last hour or so have added ten years to Johnson's looks, James seems more and more a boy every moment, stripped of his London manners and well out of his depth.

I have my dags in my hands, and my two hands resting lightly on my two knees.

And so we begin.

"Gentlemen, I must remind you that we were in the midst of a conversation." The way they watch my mouth form words is deeply satisfying. I have their most perfect attention. "I had pledged to leave you in peace once you had answered my questions truthfully. And I made it clear that you would not leave if you failed to do so. You see now that I was very much in earnest."

Johnson responds by immediately taking his hands off his lap and crossing his arms over his chest. Like casting his wig into the Thames, this refusal to leave his hands where I may see them is carefully calibrated resistance: little enough, so as to live through this ordeal, yet just enough to live with himself afterward.

And so a quick reminder about the guns themselves is probably in order. I brandish them just a bit, letting their showy barrels catch the light. "We spoke earlier of the linguistic history of these dags. But you might be interested to know their physical provenance. If we may believe the goldsmith in Parliament Close, these were poured at the command of King George II himself, and meant to equip an assassin. This assassin had orders to kill Bonnie Prince Charlie and his accomplice, Flora Macdonald. It was Flora Macdonald, you will remember, who had dressed the Prince as a waiting maid and spirited him away from the King's men on the Island of Skye."

I buff the dag in my right hand against the damp material of my breeches and bring it to bear once more. "In spite of himself, King George had a deep respect for his nemesis and the Stuart line. And so he caused the guns to be poured of almost solid gold. Even the bullets were dusted with the metal. Death fit for royalty. I think it a very thoughtful compromise, actually."

When I have finished this history, Johnson and James exchange a look, and it is a significant glance, mixing confusion and alarm and mutual resolve. One would think they had known one another all their lives, for the communication they seem to manage in a glance.

"Put your questions," Johnson barks, then purses his lips, breathing loudly through his nose. He stares at me for a moment, breathing, simmering, utterly unamused by the goldsmith's tale. "Put your questions. Allow us to answer them. Put your questions and end this nightmare."

"I fully intend to do so, sir."

He purses his thick lips again, wind whistling through the big nostrils, then brings himself to go on. His body is motionless, but his expression itself is an attack of sorts. The softer look he had at first in the Turk's Head, the familiar look that begged me to keep his secret, is entirely gone. He hates me for exposing him. Nothing could be clearer. But the truth will out, and he has no one to thank but himself.

He is still going on. "Put your questions, and then keep your word and allow us each to go about our business. You insist upon honesty. It is an insult that you should stress it so. We are men of honor. This is your own eldest brother, your own *flesh,* for God's sake. He has shown you nothing but *affection.* A more open and plain-dealing man I have never met."

I cannot resist a smile at that. "Plain-dealing, you say. But then you should know, of course, having spent several full weeks in his company."

"Your sarcasm does not change my assessment of his character, I can assure you, sir." There is open contempt in Johnson's look now. He has all but curled his lip. "Quite the contrary, in fact. Quite the contrary. If your brother fails to reach your standards, that seems to me excellent reason to believe that he well exceeds my own."

The anger struggles in my chest, but I put it down. He is baiting me, nothing more. He and James must still believe that the lark is keeping watch outside the door somewhere, a useful misperception.

"I find your parallel intriguing, Mr. Johnson. You would draw a clear distinction between us, with James cast as the plain-dealer. James, why not tell Mr. Johnson where you took your constitutional this morning, before walking over to the Temple? And where you stopped off after that? It seems a year ago, but your memories on this point are surely more vivid than my own."

James says nothing, head hung like a dog.

"James had several meetings this morning before keeping his rendezvous with you, Mr. Johnson. He was a very busy plain-dealer indeed. There was the meeting in St. James's Park, first, with several women of exemplary moral character who happened to be up and taking the air just before dawn. And then there was an even more touching scene with the mother of his natural son Charles. I assume James has mentioned Peggy Doig and the child he had named for the Stuart martyr. No? In any event, James wished to be certain that little Peggy was quite recovered from the hazards of childbirth, and so apparently he examined her quite thoroughly—"

James can contain himself no longer. "You said you had *forgiven* me, Johnnie! Why must you—why must you *torture* me, and attempt to tear me down as—"

"I *have* forgiven you, James. Truly, I have. But Mr. Johnson must know enough to be able to forgive you in his own turn. And so another question, James, and this one I will have answered, not avoided. What have you this moment in your right waistcoat pocket, brother?"

James looks startled, even amidst the startling elements of the moment. He flicks his glance over at Johnson.

But the question itself sits poorly with Johnson. He leans forward, scowling down the impossibly long troll's nose, even waving a thick hand at me. "Put your questions, damn you! You have threatened our lives—you *continue* to threaten us, and you may wound us either through your malice or your incompetence—and we have said we will answer and have done with you, sir. But do not insult us with *absurdities.* Do not trifle with things in pockets, or else you may go to the Devil, pistols or no. I assume you have, even in your gross obvious madness, some *grievance,* something that we can address—"

I bring the dags into the air, and he stops speaking. As always, the effect on their two postures is striking. They cannot look directly at the barrel, but must avert their eyes slightly. They have seen these guns fire once tonight, of course. They know they are loaded. They know the guns are altogether real.

"I will decide what is absurd, Mr. Johnson. My purpose tonight is to expose each of us for what we truly are. James was good enough to begin that process at the Turk's Head. I insist now that he continue it. What have you in your waistcoat, Jemmie?"

"A memorandum," James admits. He dips a finger into the pocket, touching the thing absently, but makes no move to draw it out.

"Bring it out."

He does so, but with great reluctance. And now we have Johnson's attention, his curiosity engaged, without a doubt. He watches the tiny folded square come into the light as if it were a living creature. He is a writer, after all, and here is writing for him to read. Johnson is struggling so visibly for mastery of the situation, and now it has moved suddenly and unexpectedly into his own realm of expertise. He cannot wish it otherwise.

"Open it," I say.

"John, you know it is nothing, some scribbled notes for myself. Nothing more."

"I know nothing of the sort. I know that you spent upwards of an hour on this little note, in all likelihood. And I know it has a great deal more to say about you than you have to say for yourself. Open it."

The thing springs open in James's hand, and it is clear immediately that it contains more than a few scribbles. It is long and detailed. I have seen James construct these memoranda for himself over the years, and it was a good bet that today, of all days, he would come armed with comprehensive self-direction.

"Read it," I tell him.

"John," James pleads.

"It is a man's private correspondence," Johnson puts in, but weakly. Again, he would know what is on this page as well as I.

"Mr. Johnson," James says to him, "the note was meant only as a way of making the greatest use of the time you are good enough to spend with me."

"Read it, James. I will not tell you again to do so."

And in a faltering, deliberately mechanical voice, James reads.

"*Today is the day,*" he begins, "*to which you have long looked forward, your riverine excursion to Greenwich with Mr. Samuel Johnson. It will be the most glorious of all your year in London. You are to be congratulated for bringing it about. The weather promises fine, and you are to have his company for the entire day. You must make the most of these hours; let them mark you the way ink seeps into the page as the pen scratches along. Above all, mark his language exactly, that you may frame his remarks justly in your journal tomorrow evening. Steal a stray moment here or there, as you may, to jot down notes of particular remarks. Do not let him observe you doing so. It may inhibit his talk. He may think you rude.*"

Here James pauses, and his eyes seem to skip down the page.

"Leave nothing out, Jemmie. I will read it myself when you are done."

James looks up at me, and again he is merely my older brother, and a part of me feels for him. He has spent a year, nearly enough, preparing the ground for this relationship, and now he is being made to display the dirty tools he used cultivate it.

"*Johnson is a man of learning, and moral precept, and conversation. He is a didactic being, with a need to instruct, and you attach yourself to him insofar as you agree to be instructed. Make this clear. He has promised to direct your education, and you may hold him to this directly. He can only be flattered at your persistence there.*"

Again, James breaks off. "That is—that is the tenor of it. Notes on how to conduct myself. Nothing of which to be proud, perhaps." His glance goes again to Johnson. "But nothing of which to be ashamed."

Johnson, however, is staring at me. His attitude has grown almost visibly more contemptuous. His voice drips disdain. "Your brother has found a means to regulate his conduct, by means of notation. Am I to be shocked?"

Johnson throws up his hands, then barks, "I *applaud* him for it, I tell you. Perhaps he has been less than moral in his conduct; he would not be the last young dog of whom it might be said. But your second example outweighs your first. Your brother has found a means to regulate his conduct. He cares to do so, to *perfect* himself. You sit here, however, guilty of kidnapping and threatening murder, and lying, everything that is base—and I tell you, sir, you had been better off with a note or two in your *own* pocket. It might have saved you a trip to the madhouse, for all we know."

I know James well enough to know that this is not all. His memoranda, for a day like today, always run deeper. "Come, there is more. Continue to the end, James."

James's eyes are threatening to well up again, with embarrassment now as much as anything else. But the fight has gone out of him almost entirely, and he continues to the end this time. He keeps his eyes on his own words.

"Do not be afraid to flatter him. Flattery may be made a very fine thing. When you come to Greenwich, have a copy of his London in your pocket, and when you reach the line about 'kissing the consecrated earth,' actually do so. Mind no one passing by. Show him that you risk scorn on his behalf. He will be delighted, though he may protest. Study his happiness constantly. And show him how his words shaped your boyhood. Tell him the story of the secret language. Secure his correspondence, above all. Your commission has failed to make your fortune; but here is another way to rise. Here is another king whom you may serve."

When he has finished, James thrusts the note out to me, but I wave it away with the dag in my left hand. He doesn't bother to restore its more intricate folds, but creases it once carelessly down the middle and slides it into his outer coat pocket, its secrets now spent. He does not look at either of us now.

"Well done, Jemmie," I tell him.

"You may go straight to the Devil, John," he snaps, but that is all.

I turn to Johnson, and I smile again. For the smile seems to pierce the big man's thick hide like nothing else. "Here is your plain-dealing young Scot, Mr. Johnson. He has planned to meet you for months, if not years. He has hounded his acquaintances for an introduction. He has written your lines, and his own."

"He would meet an author by whom he has been inspired," Johnson counters petulantly. "If that is a crime, every man of any learning would wear chains."

"Then, when once he has got your ear, this plain-dealer, he walks about with little scripts in his pocket, scripts full of flattery and greasy little courtier's tricks."

"If all courtiers were genuinely moved to kiss the earth at Greenwich, I tell you I should be better pleased with the state of the Court."

I cannot help but raise my own voice. "There was nothing *genuine* in the *case.* That is the very point. It was written out the night before, like an actor crying on cue. It was deeply planned. There is nothing heartfelt here. It is all rank ambition. He thinks you particularly susceptible to flattery, and he exhorts himself to lay it on even thicker than a young man like himself might ordinarily risk."

"He was taking *vows,* sir." Johnson's eyes are flashing, the cords of his neck now stretched taut. He looks as though he might spit across the four feet that separate us. "Vows of which you would know *nothing.* To be humble, before the Monarchy, before a mentor. To accept learning and instruction. To serve in *humility,* sir. You see weakness of character, but this is a man who would serve before he attempts to command."

"And you are to be his new king, this note tells us. That is grand indeed, for a boy come up from Lichfield."

At the mention of his boyhood village, Johnson leans forward, looking down the crooked nose. He drops his voice almost to a whisper, a taunt. "And what of it, sir? If we are not to have a Stuart on the throne, but merely choose a likely man among several? Your brother would serve a king of learning. Why should it be a crime for him to say so? Why should that merit taunting from the likes of you?"

Even knowing what I know about Johnson, and James, the response feels like something just this side of blasphemy. But before I can answer, James suddenly comes to life. He sits up straighter in his chair, and I can see that our discussion has set off some train of thought in his mind, something that has nudged him out of his fatalism. It is almost as though he has a plan of some sort.

He begins to speak, but his voice catches on tears or regret, and he must clear his throat first. "I mentioned in my note the story of the secret language John and I shared when we were boys," James goes on. He is addressing Johnson, but with his eye on me. It is amusing to see, as he begins his storytelling, the way he also begins to put himself back together, one small fragment at a time: he straightens the set of his waistcoat, brushes a bit of dust thoughtlessly from his knee. Narration begins to set him right again. James continues. "When we were boys, our father bought a copy of your dictionary, Mr. Johnson. And for a while it was displayed prominently in his library, and he was wont to check it every so often, for usage. We were amazed, as boys, that it had cost ten shillings."

But in the midst of this opening, Johnson turns savagely on him, bullying him into silence. "You begin to rave as well as your brother, Boswell! This is no time for reminiscences. Remain silent, sir, and let him come *out* with it, and have it over."

James pulls back as if stung. But I clarify the situation again. "You are the one who would do well to remain silent, Mr.

Johnson. I will decide when we have sufficiently canvassed the matters at hand."

"I have understood your threats, sir!"

"And you, sir, have already confessed to part of what you were earlier concealing. That is a confession I would have my brother hear from your own lips."

Johnson glares, but the mention of his earlier confession silences him.

"But first I should like to hear James finish his story. It would be a shame if his artful memorandum should have no effect on the reality our conversation. And I suggest you listen carefully, if you would learn why we three are sitting here, as we are. If you would know something about the Boswells."

I tip up the dag in my right hand. The fluctuations in the lamplight give the pistols a curious appearance. The play of light makes them seem almost molten, liquid gold, and occasionally the effect catches my eye.

James would sooner slit his own throat than displease his hero, and he steals a glance over at Johnson. But then, with the air of one who believes his story will secure its own pardon, James steels himself to continue with it.

"Our father would consult the dictionary every so often, as I've said. But then one afternoon, having been informed of something by a man at court, he came home and went straight to the library and searched the book for a single word."

Johnson waits, anger still suffusing his countenance. When he does not inquire, James moves the story forward himself. "That word was *oats.*"

"My father was livid," I cannot help but add.

"I will never forget your definition," James goes on, his voice sounding a bit stronger now. "It ran, *A grain which in England is generally given to horses, but which in Scotland supports the people.* And while I know you meant it as a jest, one in good nature, my father took it as an intentional insult. He knew that you had no love for Scotland; that was well known even in Edinburgh. He brooded on the supposed slight all through our dinner, and when we had finished, he walked into the library and tore the page from the book. No fire was burning, or he would certainly have burned it. Instead he crumpled it and threw it on the scrap heap."

Johnson sits blackly with this for a moment, then snorts, adding only, "And this man is a High Judge in your country. Taking his pique out on an inanimate object."

I have no idea why James has chosen to tell this story, but it is one I like well enough, and always have. At some level, James has steered the conversation here to involve me, to make me nostalgic for the days when we conspired together against my father.

But even understanding the purpose behind his introducing it, I cannot help but add little bits to the story. "And there James found it, and stole away with it back to our room. Where we smoothed it out, and pressed it flat beneath a stack of books. And over the next several days, we studied that definition."

James takes over almost immediately, as he has done all our lives. "We studied the entire *page,* in fact. It was a page of writing our father had forbidden. The words on it were stricken from the language, in effect. But we were beginning, then, to see that our father did not control the world, not entirely. And so we made a copy of the page—"

"*I* made a copy of the page," I correct him, "for the simple reason that James would not share the sacred original."

James looks over at me, and then nods, or bows his head rather. "That is true. I would not share it. It was my own page of Johnson's dictionary, and it was my prized possession. But I allowed John to copy it. And we made a game of it. The idea was that twice each day, we had to use one of the forbidden words in a sentence while speaking to Father, and we had to do so when the other of us was present. Given that all of the words began with the letter *O,* it was no simple trick."

Outside the shack, perhaps as far away as the Savoy Stair, there is the sound of shouting, voices raising an alarm. We all sit frozen for a moment, suddenly painfully aware of the guns in my hand again, and then the noise dies away.

After another instant, the silence of the timber-yard re-establishes itself. I wait an instant longer, by way of insurance, and then continue the story myself. "Of course, one can only use good Johnsonian vocabulary for so long before it becomes . . . noticeable, shall we say. A word like *oberration* will begin to stand out in conversation at the breakfast table. And so finally my father recognized the pattern, and had the truth out of James."

James has his eyes down on the dag in my left hand, seems in fact to have his gaze focused on the very mouth of the snubbed barrel, the blackness there, as though it were a magic lantern showing the Edinburgh flat and my father's rage.

"He found the page of the dictionary I had saved, and he made me confess that John had copied it out as well," says James.

"In other words, James implicated me to save himself. No hero, even then."

"This time the scrapheap was insufficient. He burned both copies, and stood watching until they were both ashes. And he did not spare the rod that day." James looks up and into my eyes, and although I know he has his own skin in mind, I cannot help but feel the kinship there. "We were both soundly beaten for playing that game."

"My father," I say, turning now directly to Johnson, "wished to impress upon us the way that the English shape the world to their own advantage, using any tool that may come to hand."

Maintaining an impotent rage seems finally to have become too much for Johnson. He has slumped back in his chair, and there is as much injury as anger in his air. His breathing, always labored, now seems to be occupying more of his attention, and there is an audible rattle when he inhales; his back too seems to be troubling him, and he works a shoulder to ease a muscle pinching there.

"Had your father truly felt that way," Johnson counters, "he would have cast out the book in its entirety. But he understood it to be indeed a tool, and one of superior English workmanship. One he could not do without. Yet he would posture before his sons."

It is at moments such as this when I feel that killing him would be merited. He reveals so very smug a view of the universe, in which England naturally occupies the center, and the English tongue the center of that center, with Samuel Johnson the center-most pin anchoring the English language entire.

I cannot keep the sarcasm from my tone. "Yes, quite. Your book has had its effect, Mr. Johnson, and you must take responsibility for us, James and myself. We have been shaped by your grammar and syntax, even in the provinces. Your vocabulary has made up our world even as far away as Scotland. We have grown up accenting our words as you would have it done. We are your handiwork, for good or for ill."

Johnson is silent a relatively long time, lips again pursed, air whistling through the cavernous nostrils. But when he speaks, the words are uncharacteristically plain and simple. "You are none of my handiwork. And you are not of your father's making either. He was narrow in his view, and heavy-handed, but clearly he sought to instill respect. And you have none, John Boswell, none for your father, none for your brother, none for your country, none for your self. You are a sadly deluded young man. You have surrendered your reason to gratify your own sickly sense of self."

"Mr. Johnson," James nearly takes Johnson's sleeve, then thinks better of it, "my brother needs rest, and the care of his doctors. But in his heart, he is as decent a man as I have ever known. You must believe that, sir. John is no criminal, no matter what tonight may seem to say of him."

I ignore James, and repeat Johnson's barb. "I am deluded, then, am I?"

Johnson sits up, brings his shoulders forward. His eyebrows are thick, and they do not trace a straight line over his eyes but rather slant up at an angle. It gives him an air of perpetual suspicion and doubt and even distaste, an air that now perfectly matches the look on the rest of his face. He has had enough of this night, enough of me.

"Yes, very obviously so." He looks around the shack, at his own chair, the lamp, the door. "You have made it painfully obvious, and yet you remain willfully blind of the fact. You have some invented grievance, and you would keep us captive indefinitely while you relive it again and again in the warped world of your own mind.

"I have *done* with you, sir. You are no better than a wounded animal that must be dealt with on its own terms. I defy you. Do you understand me? Must I spell it out for you? I defy your games and your threats and dirty things in pockets."

He is very near a breaking point of some sort, and I bring both guns to face him. I don't worry as much about a sudden movement from James; he will remain as passive as he is humanly able. But managing Johnson is a minute-to-minute affair, even when one is holding the weapons.

"Let us speak then about delusions, but let us begin with your own, Mr. Johnson. For James has revealed himself all but entirely. Let us turn to you."

He meets my eye, lowers his jaw a bit. Beneath the thick lids, his eyes are large and protrude just enough to render them unusual, fish-like. I stare into one until he blinks it, then responds finally. "I have no delusions, sir."

"As you wish. You said at the Turk's Head that you and I had never met. You tried your best to bully me out of maintaining that we had."

His head is bowed a bit now.

"And yet on our walk over here you *admitted* your own falsehood to me, your own attempt to deceive. You admitted not only that you had concealed the truth, but that you were wrong to do so. And I would put it to you this way: that it is *you* who are deluded, *you* who remain alienated from your very deepest self. Because the fact is that you and I have shared—"

Something about the last phrase, or the impassioned way I say it, has both of them staring directly at me, as though I have spoken in another language entirely.

But I push on with it. "You and I have shared a very great affection. And it has been the saving of my life, sir. And I am not ashamed of it. In fact, I have gone to nearly unimaginable lengths to prove it to be genuine, because I will no longer have it denied or rendered invisible."

James is now examining Johnson with outright perplexity. And for his own part, Johnson's face is a wash of emotions, anger and outrage and something I can only interpret as regret, even shame.

"Did you not say so on our way over here? Sir, did you not *admit* it to me?"

And then Johnson can remain silent no longer. "Yes! I did say so," he blurts out, hands slicing at the air, his heavy body rocking in his chair with frustration. "I said so in the way that a man on the rack confesses to heresy! Because you left me no other *choice,* but would have it so! I was trying to end this horrific nightmare. That is *all.* I thought, for a moment, that hearing me say those words might put an *end* to all of this. And in a moment of weakness I went along with your damnable lie."

"Do not attempt to deny the truth now, now that someone else may hear. Can you not see, James, what this man would be at?"

Dags or no, Johnson's voice has risen beyond a bark almost to a shout. "I do deny it! I deny every particle of your twisted and deluded view of the world. We have *never* met, not once before this evening! You have clearly read my books, and perhaps in some mad way you have construed that—"

"Oh, do not flatter yourself so, Sir. Other than your dictionary, your books are mildly amusing at best. And at worst they are soporific. They will none of them conjure a world. No, you have already admitted our connection, sir, and I *hold* you to that admission. It is the one moment this evening you have managed to face yourself in the mirror, actually face yourself."

Here I gather in James with my glance, for in some way this has all been staged for his benefit. He is the intended audience, and has been all along, the lone representative of all the rest of the world, as well as the go-between to the rest of my family. He is the one who must hear what must be said.

"And I will tell James the rest that you will not admit. That you and I met on London Bridge, when you called me to an alcove there. That you came back to my rooms and eventually shared my lodgings, shared my bed. Yes, shared my bed, chastely, as *companions*, as two who cared for one another, *loved* one another. That you wrote there, sometimes in the middle of the night. That we—"

Johnson is out of his chair now, up on his big legs. James has him by one arm, trying vainly to pull him back to his chair. Johnson isn't closing the distance between us, not yet, but he has lost all other rational consideration. He is sputtering with rage. Still, the words find their way out. "You are more than a mere liar or a damnable thief," he manages, "you are true evil, and, worse, evil with the appearance of decent family and breeding. You have—you have *fattened* somewhere in the dark on your own poisonous envy, and you slither into London like the Devil himself, to destroy us, to pervert our understandings of one another, of our very *selves.* You will not be satisfied until we too are mad, or mouldering in a grave."

"He is ill, Mr. Johnson!" James pleads.

I stay stock-still in my chair while Johnson raves.

"You say you will allow us to leave when I have capitulated, agreed to the twisted version of the world your fantasy has produced. But you *lie.* I tell you that you lie through your teeth. For that would never be enough. *Never!* It is not the past you would control, but the present and the future. You would displace your brother in my affections, and nothing less will satisfy you. If you are not stopped this night, he will have your knife in his back by morning."

I cannot hold my tongue any more. "It is *you* who would manipulate—"

"Silence!" Johnson thunders.

And then in the sudden quiet, he yells again just as loudly: "Silence, I say!"

He could not raise his voice any louder. We have been talking in whispers and low voices for an hour, but this is a genuine bellow, one that must reach the boats moving far out on the darkness of the Thames.

"You have surrendered your purchase on reality *entirely*," Johnson goes on. The blood is up in his face again, and his cheeks are brick-red. "And your greatest delusion is that I would favor you with a single particle of my affection! That I would bring my pen and ink to whatever stinking hole in the earth you have managed to scratch out and line with leaves and twigs and bits of string, and call your rooms! That I would *work* there, and solicit your opinion! There is an excellent reason you have found yourself in the madhouse, sir, and it is this: you have become a monster. A mad—" Johnson loses his words again in his rage, but then drives on: "—smutty shriveled *thing*, and no one will associate with you by choice. That is the truth of it."

James half-stands himself. His voice is sharper, harder now. "Mr. Johnson, please! He is *ill*. He is not himself, and cannot be held accountable for his actions. You must remember that. You must find the self-control that he cannot."

Johnson turns on him, and James actually averts his face from the direct blast of the man's anger. "Hold your tongue as well, Boswell! He will know what he is, I tell you! He will know what he is!" Johnson wheels back, and takes a heavy step toward me, daring me almost. His arms are held out at his sides, and he is a great physical presence in the small space. He comes forward swaying very slightly, like a bear nearly too heavy to move on its hind legs.

"*That* is why you have been locked away, John Boswell, because you would *force* yourself on a society that has made the decision to dispose of you. And dispose of you we must, because you corrupt what you touch. *Love* you, sir? *Love* you? I could sooner love a maggot curling in my porridge. You would match wits with me? You would attempt to convince your brother that it is I who deals in lies and delusions and trickery?"

He takes another half-step. He realizes that he is skirting the line where I must defend myself, but he is determined to push me, to push his way out of this situation entirely if he can.

"For the love of God, look no further than your own two hands! Look at the objects in your two hands. Do you not find it at all strange that a young man such as yourself, busted from the Army, with no claim to inheritance, without work and apparently without a father's allowance, should be in possession of two pistols cast in solid gold? Even *plated* in gold? Truly, how could you come by such weapons?"

Of the thousand different ways James or Johnson might have taken the conversation, this I could not have predicted. He might have settled as easily on my boots, and how I came by them. I cannot fathom his meaning for a moment.

But then I have it: he means to imply that I have stolen them. And that therefore I am no better than a common criminal, no agent of justice, but a petty thief.

And while I don't owe him an answer, I cannot help myself. "I told you I had them from a goldsmith in Parliament Close. They cost nearly every guinea I had. And every guinea I could secure from my father. Money that was meant to last out this year."

Johnson has balled his white hands into fists, each as big as a cannonball. He is still standing in front of me, nearly over me, and I am tallying each move of his muscles.

He points his finger at me, his long fat finger, points it directly in my face.

"You are deluded, I tell you. Can you not see that? Your weapons are precisely the sort a man such as yourself would be expected to carry. Two hunks of cheap metal. You might buy both for ten pounds, and have the case thrown into the bargain."

He thrusts his finger down toward my hand now, his entire arm shaking as he does so. "Your brother will say nothing because he would not rouse you from your sleepwalking. He is afraid you might be injured somehow in the waking. That is because your brother knows what it *is* to love, sir. That is because your brother is twice the man you will ever be. Not because he is eldest. Not because he stands to inherit, but because he *deserves* to inherit. That is why he cannot bring himself to tell you."

I will not look down, for it is a trick, no more. I remember purchasing the guns at the goldsmith's shop in Edinburgh, haggling over price. In the last months, I have sat for hours in my rooms, cleaning and polishing them, fitting them for the purpose I had in mind.

A trick, and a child's trick, at that. Johnson is just close enough to rush me if I shift my attention, and he has fooled me once tonight already.

But in the end, it is not really a matter of choice. His taunting has pulled a thread now hanging loose in my mind, and finally I steal a glance down at the dags in my fists. Only to find them gone.

And in their place, two plain pistols of scratched gun-metal black. Guns without decoration, carving or style. Leaden, mere things. They give back none of the lamplight.

I hear Johnson give a short bark of triumph.

And that is something the thing inside of me will not bear, and it takes what it wants. My right arm snaps up, perfectly level with Johnson's big chest, and before I can complete a single thought, it has pulled the trigger.

But Johnson is no longer standing before me.

He is careening away, just as the hammer falls, and in the muzzle flash I see that it is James who has slammed him aside at the last instant, James whose improbably rushing body now occupies the space before the gun's barrel. James who will die. He has saved his King, after all.

None of this matters, however, because the gun does not fire.

It explodes in my hand instead.

AND THEN I am lying on the floor of the shanty, looking up at the ceiling. James and Johnson are gone away, and there is a horrible ringing silence. I cannot feel my right hand, but my chest is on fire. Sulfur smoke hangs still in the air. I manage to bring up my left hand, then to swipe the tips of my fingers lightly over the flames in my chest. And they come away vivid bloody red.

But the cause and the effect of it escape me. I cannot seem to piece together what has happened, for some reason. My mind is dull. It is as though, rather than some shard of the pistol exploding into my chest, my heart itself has exploded out of it.

SOMEONE IS TOUCHING my face, carefully cradling my head. I open my eyes. It is the lark, down on his knees next to me. The black cloth he was wearing is gone, and his eyes are bright with tears. His dusty skin is pale in the lamplight. He never left, even when I insisted upon it, but waited and kept watch somewhere out in the dark timber-yard, in the wet and the miserable cold, all this time.

He brings his face close to mine, looking into my eyes, and then he presses his lips quickly to mine. And suddenly I know why he could not bring himself to leave.

"I tried to tell you," he is saying, berating me softly, for he believes me dead or too near death to matter. "Tried to hammer it into your bony skull. But you wouldn't have me stay, couldn't have us seen together even by those two. Not by the great and powerful, even knowing what they are and what they've done to you. Stubborn, hard-hearted, stuck-up bastard, you are. Can never be troubled to listen, not for a minute. 'Tis always done your way, isn't it?"

He runs a fingernail along my cheek, traces the curl of my ear. "I was welcome at night, and come daylight what was I then? Bit of trash bobbing out in the flood. Wouldn't notice me on the street. Pretend we was strangers. But you needed me, and I told you all along. All along."

He taps me on the forehead with his neat fingernail, for all the world as though he means to remind me, for the next time round. "You needed me all the way from dawn to dark, too, and that's the truth of it."

And I remember it all now, this man and how I know him, and it has indeed been the saving of my life. I remember again the alcove on London Bridge, and in it, there in the gloom, sits this young man, offering no harm of any sort, hesitant himself even to say hello.

The lark was not the only man I met in those first weeks walking London Bridge, but he was the last, that I know now. He was the last because he turned out to be what I needed, what I had been looking for on the Bridge all along.

In the weeks since, he has come to me nights straight from the water, come padding up Fish Street Hill, smelling faintly of salt, his legs and feet cold as river ice. More than once have I chafed the life back into those feet, those legs. We have talked late into the night.

And it has not been chaste, not even the first night we met out over the water. Mostly it has not because I haven't ever wanted it to be so.

But that hunger has been no failing. Just the reverse. As I glimpse it now—as an entire set of memories washing in all at once—it seems almost another sort of fidelity entirely, a chastity shared by two rather than endured by one.

I can see all of this now because the thing inside me is dead. For all of the things I have never known about it, will never know about it, I have known every minute of the last several years that it was *there.* Even in Plymouth, as I was telling my doctors I was come back to myself again, I knew it was there, in me. I could always feel it, listening.

And now I know it is not. It is dead by its own hand.

All of this I would tell the lark, but I cannot. Dragging breath through the flames in my chest is all that I can manage. And then there is the sound of men tramping heavily up the river's edge toward the timber-yard, and he presses his thin lips once tightly to my forehead, and I hear his boots scuffing across the floor of the shanty. And he is gone. Back to the flood, forever this time.

Leaving me alone. In this last, least bastard world.

Coda

21

James and Johnson ran together as far as the Somerset Water-Gate before James could bring himself to run no farther. They had run past the Savoy Stairs, past the German Church, because as far as they knew an armed accomplice was still at large, and he had shadowed them and prevented their escape once before. And so Johnson's plan was to reach the Somerset Estate, run up the lawn to the main house itself, and secure a party of guards there. Then they would all return in force, hunt up the other gunman and render me such help as they were able.

But finally James found that he could not leave me for dead. And Johnson, for his part, found that he could not bring himself to let James return alone.

And so they reached a hurried compromise: in Dutchy Lane, just at hand, lived a surgeon with whom Johnson had some passing acquaintance, a man named Watkins, and they ran directly to his home, to find the doctor sitting at whist with two other gentlemen. Within moments, all five were pounding down the river way to the timber-yard.

They found me unconscious, blood staining the floor about me, and Watkins at first gave me over for dead. But whatever his fingers felt as he searched the wound in my chest gave him hope enough to have me carried on a pallet to a rooming house just three doors down from his own.

It was there that he removed the dag's shorn firing pin from my chest; there that I would remain for the next several weeks, never entirely out of danger, never fully conscious. And it was there that James was to weave one of his most successful fictions, in which he and his younger brother and Doctor Johnson had all three been accosted by a masked footpad and taken to the timber-yard, there to be robbed and murdered. In this version of the story, I struggled with the masked man, the man's cheap weapon exploded, and he was able to flee the scene, never to be heard from again.

Certainly Doctor Watkins had no reason to disbelieve this tale, nor the elderly woman hired to nurse me. And it may be that the glamour of it even secured me more solicitous care than I might otherwise have received.

What is worth noting, however, is that Johnson himself was never to contradict this story, not then and never after. Perhaps at first he thought I was all but certain to die, and therefore it mattered little how the events themselves were represented. And as I gained strength, James made it clear that he planned to transfer me back to Plymouth when I could be moved.

But more importantly, the night at the Turk's Head had fundamentally changed Johnson's relationship with my brother. While it had always been curiously strong, particularly for an acquaintance of seven weeks' duration, now it was granite.

Would they have been so joined without my efforts to wedge them apart?

No one can say, and I have ever after been more than diligent in my efforts to avoid considering the ironies.

But one thing is certain: Johnson had seen that James was willing to die for him, finally, and no man can see such a thing and remain unmoved. Wherever they two might find themselves in the world, divided even by countries or whole continents, they were now emotionally inseparable, and that for life.

And they would look out for one another, legalities be damned, ethics be damned. Only two weeks earlier, Johnson had counseled James to keep a daily journal "fair and undisguised," and James had admitted that he had been doing so since coming up to London. Johnson lavished praise on him for being so far advanced in such a project.

"And now, O my journal," James wrote that night in celebration, "are thou not highly dignified? Shalt thou not flourish tenfold? No former solicitations or censures could tempt me to lay thee aside."

But disguise was now precisely what Johnson recommended. He persuaded James to trace back through the pages of his journal and systematically blot out anything that might contradict the story they were both now engaged in telling. Doubts about my sanity were to be erased. What few footprints I had left in James's book were to be swept unceremoniously away.

And further, Johnson insisted that James write up the events of July 30 from beginning to end, as he had originally planned, but in a calm narrative vein, recounting their trip down the silver Thames and a quiet evening together at the Turk's Head, with no mention of their being interrupted, no mention of threats or accusations or violence or bloodshed.

No mention, in a word, of me.

Anyone reading the entry in my brother's journal today can only come away with the impression of a lovely afternoon at Greenwich, followed by talk of books in a little coffeehouse down the Strand, talk that stretched agreeably into the late hours. An exquisitely English day, in short.

And this is what Johnson seems to have had in mind. That in the pages of his journal, James might cast a spell restoring his new King to all his former glory, and a quiet, decent English splendor to the world itself.

It was a fair compromise, I have come to suppose: my life, my freedom, in exchange for having my name stricken from the only record of the Boswells that will probably ever be kept.

There was a time when such a prospect would have enraged me; it was, after all, a much less systematic revisionism that had so angered me originally. But by the time I left Plymouth several years later, in 1766, I found it impossible to understand how a series of scratchings in a book, or the lack of such scratchings, could once have wounded me so deeply. I wanted nothing more than retirement, at that point, nothing more than to leave the company of those afflicted by disorders I no longer shared.

Nothing more than simple quiet.

My brother sensed this about me, I believe. For all of his selfish use of the talent, he had always the power to look into men's hearts and read what was written there. He sensed that while I remained exhausted in my emotions and my thoughts, and always physically somewhat weak, I was mad no longer. Some years later, doctors at the hospital in Newcastle would second this opinion.

And so James conceived and executed the single most charitable act he would ever accomplish, either as Laird or as a literary celebrity in his own right: James took me from the hospital at Plymouth, where I might well have spent the rest of my days, and he opened his own home to me at Auchinleck.

He opened the circle of his growing family as well: his wife Margaret, his sons Sandy and Jamie, and his two pleasant girls, Veronica and Effie. I was there when little Davie died only days after his birth; both Margaret and James cried on my shoulder that night.

Still, I was never treated entirely as an uncle, and I never sought such closeness. My place in the circle was more like that of a lodger of whom the family has grown fond: never forgotten at the table or at holidays, but watched half-consciously, as even the most welcome guests in a home are watched.

By tacit agreement, James and I never again spoke of Samuel Johnson, and he never offered to show me his journal or any of the other works he was ever to compose about the man. Another fair compromise.

In the summer of 1774—when Johnson finally made the trip to Scotland that he and James had first discussed that night long ago at the Turk's Head—I remained in the country while James met his mentor in Edinburgh. When their travel plans called for them to visit my father at Auchinleck, I removed myself by roundabout route to the city.

After they had gone on to the Hebrides, Margaret and the children and I followed their progress across a map hung for the purpose on the wall of James's study.

When Johnson died in 1784, James put the entire family in bombazine and crepe, but it was understood that I would dress as always. Again, these arrangements seemed to me not provocation, but the enduring rhythm of our lives, a way for all to go on.

When James came finally to inherit, I too moved back into the New House in Ayrshire that my father had built with so much pomp. There it was that Margaret died in the summer of 1789, while James was away on legal affairs in London. Along with the overseer, I began the preparations for her funeral and helped to manage the house until James and the boys could reach Auchinleck.

And when James himself passed away six years later, again in London, and Sandy had inherited, he came to me one morning and asked for help in putting his father's library into some sort of order. I think in a way he meant to ease the awkwardness of the situation, his stepping into the role of Laird while his once-mad uncle watched from the sidelines. Sandy had his father's easy grasp of humanity, and it was like him to consider my feelings.

But the task itself was very real: James was notoriously chaotic in his affairs and in his scholarship, and the room off the library at Auchinleck where he wrote was hopelessly disordered. Sandy knew nothing of what had transpired thirty or more years before with Dr. Johnson, and so he made no stipulations of any sort, but charged me with sorting and categorizing all that I found.

What I found, of course, was the single largest collection of

Johnson artifacts the world will ever know. Thousands of letters, journal entries, engravings, sketches, books, pamphlets by, to, about, and concerning Samuel Johnson. For one who had been all but forbidden to speak or read about the man for the bulk of his adult life, it was an almost overpowering experience.

In Plymouth I had become convinced that the memories of Johnson and me together in London were entirely false, and that they were in fact a warning sign from a mind teetering disastrously close to the brink. We had never been close, I came to realize; we had never met, in fact. I had confused the lark and Johnson, somehow, for reasons I will never entirely understand. And I always held it as a first principle thereafter that allowing myself to wander down those roads again would represent the most dangerous sort of self-indulgence.

But everyone was dead now, I told myself, everyone who had played even the smallest part in those events, both real and imagined. Everyone was dead and buried in the cold forgiving earth, with the exception of myself.

And so I began to read.

For some weeks I simply read every day, careless of any attempt to make meaning or order of what I read. My eyes would begin to strain, and I would realize that the sun had gone down. It had been a long while since I had so given myself to the experience of words on a page, to the sheer enchantment there.

I lingered over *The Life of Johnson* for a solid two weeks, morning to night, prowling through the notes, hauling the fat volumes with me throughout the house, reading as I took my porridge in the morning and my negus at night. James had spoken of the work in my presence a thousand times—his masterpiece and a book he loved like his own offspring—without ever once offering me a copy.

And now I could read it, at my leisure.

I am not ashamed to tell you that I cried over that exquisite book, more than once. For my brother was a genius, and what he could read in other men's hearts, the welter of emotion that he found there, he could also commit to paper, in a way that always eluded Johnson himself.

But eventually I commenced the task of separating all of the various manuscripts chronologically, beginning with work actually by Johnson. And it was only then that I came across an oddity.

Among James's books was a volume by a Miss Williams, the same blind woman Johnson visited each evening, no matter how late, before himself retiring. It seems the woman had some literary pretensions of her own. An attached note in James's hand explained that Johnson not only helped Miss Williams edit and sell the collection—*Miscellanies in Prose and Verse, by Anna Williams*—he had helped to fill it out with a small piece or two of his own. The publication date of the volume was 1766.

One of the several pieces Johnson contributed was a strange, bittersweet tale called "The Fountains."

It is the story of a girl named Florette, who rescues a trapped songbird, only to find that the bird is in actuality a pisky queen. And the queen, Lady Lilinet, offers her two magic fountains by way of reward, one sweet and one bitter. The first will grant her any wish; the second has the power to call that same wish back when it proves tragically unwise. Of course, each of Florette's several wishes comes true, but in ways Florette could neither have predicted nor desired. Finally the very process of wishing itself seems to drain the life from her.

And in the end she dies with a last kiss from the pisky queen.

It was undeniably the very story I once woke to find Johnson writing late one night in 1763, at the small table in my room at the Starr Inn, on the top of Fish Street Hill, in the shadow of London Bridge.

A memory of Johnson and me together that I have assumed to be false for the last three decades.

And yet, if Miss Williams's little volume did not appear until three years after the night at the Turk's Head Inn—three years after I was forbidden Johnson's works—there would seem to be no way for me to have known the odd little story in the first place, other than from the mouth of the author, who had in fact not yet committed the thing to paper.

It is a neat little paradox, in short.

Still, the nagging questions to which it gives rise might once have staggered me, for it seems at least narrowly possible that Johnson was indeed one of the men I met on London Bridge, though not the last and perhaps not the most important; that his anger and his indignation were in part the most desperate sort of pretense; that what he felt for me, what we felt for one another, did manage to find expression in some fragment of his life's work after all.

It is possible, that is to say, that even after leaving Plymouth for the last time, I may have spent the bulk of my life continuing to mistake truth for madness, and madness for truth.

These possibilities are a great deal to contemplate here in seclusion at Auchinleck, in my bed at night, or on the very long country walks I have come to favor, the twelve miles out to the post office in Ayr, for example, and the twelve miles back again. They are a great deal to put right in one's mind.

Because there is also the countervailing possibility: that the simple act of coming into contact with Johnson's papers again, after all these many years, has again disordered my reason as I have always feared it would.

But these considerations cannot consume me. Not at this point in my life. Not with a new century just on the verge of wiping clean the sins of the old.

Books sustain me, as well. For there on James's shelves stand countless works of biography—his own, Johnson's *Lives of the Poets,* and many more. It was always his greatest enjoyment, and one I have come to myself late in life but with great passion. In addition to James's own version of Johnson's life, I have read Mrs.

Thrale's, and that of Sir John Hawkins. These three books I feel as though I could never read thoroughly enough. They cannot help but contradict one another, of course, and yet they are all three captivating in their own ways.

For each of their versions of the man is as true as any other, no matter which volume weighs or sells the most. They are each but stories, tales. Each an imaginative sketch from a different vista.

Even James's journal, his biography of himself, betrays staggering contradictions as one reads from day to day, let alone year to year.

And in that way, biography has provided me with a comfort in my later years of the sort I was never able to discover in the Bible my mother gave me as a boy. Not the lie of fixed character that any biography tells in its own right, but the truth of multiplicity that they tell when taken together.

There are many Samuel Johnsons, that is to say. And it matters little which one considers first or last, I have decided. One of these men loved my brother, and one of these men loved me, and the memory of each is sacred in its own regard.

John Boswell, Esq.
Auchinleck Estate
Ayrshire
February 1798